About the Author

New York Times #1 bestselling author Jennifer L. Armentrout lives in Martinsburg, West Virginia. Not all the rumours you've heard about her state are true. When she's not hard at work writing, she spends her time reading, working out, watching really bad zombie movies, pretending to write, and hanging out with her husband and her Jack Russell, Loki. Her dream of becoming an author started in algebra class, where she spent most of her time writing short stories . . . which explains her dismal grades in math. Jennifer writes young adult paranormal fiction, science fiction, fantasy, and contemporary romance. She also writes adult and new adult romance under the name J. Lynn. Visit her online at www.jenniferarmentrout.com.

JENNIFER L. ARMENTROUT

Sentinel

HODDER

First published in the United States of America in 2013
by Spencer Hill Press

First published in Great Britain in eBook in 2013
by Hodder & Stoughton
An Hachette UK company

First published in paperback in 2014

1

A CIP catalogue record for this title is available from the British Library

Paperback ISBN 978 1 444 79802 9
eBook ISBN 978 1 444 78147 2

Typeset by Hewer Text UK Ltd, Edinburgh
Printed and bound by Clays Ltd, St Ives plc

Hodder & Stoughton policy is to use papers that are natural, renewable
and recyclable products and made from wood grown in sustainable
forests. The logging and manufacturing processes are expected to
conform to the environmental regulations of the country of origin.

Hodder & Stoughton Ltd
338 Euston Road
London NW1 3BH

www.hodder.co.uk

"Some people say when life gives you lemons, you make lemonade. But when life gives you one seriously ticked off god gunning for your ass, you prepare for war and you hope for paradise."
—Alex (Alexandria) Andros

Pronunciation Guide for *Sentinel*

Aether:	EE-ther
Agapi mou:	ah-GAH-pee moo
Akasha:	ah-KAH-sha
Apollyon:	ah-POL-ee-on
απόλυτη εξουσία:	ah-POL-ee-tee EX-shoo-shee-ya
αήττητο:	EYE-tee-toe
Daimon:	DEE-mun
Deimos:	DEE-mohs
Δύναμη:	TZEE-nah-mee
Hematoi:	HEM-a-toy
Ixion:	ICKS-zee-ahn
Phobos:	FOE-bohs
Θάρρος:	THA-roesh

I

Feeling came back in my feet first, and then my legs. A pins-
and-needles tingling rushed over my skin, causing my fingers to
spasm. The sweetness of the nectar still coated the inside of my
throat. My body ached as if I'd just completed a triathlon and
come in dead last.

Or like I'd had my ass kicked and gotten patched up by a god.
Either/or . . .

Movement beside me brought the whole side of my body
closer to a hard warmth, and I thought I heard my name called,
but it sounded like it was on the other side of the world from me.

I was moving at the speed of a three-legged turtle, so it took
a while to blink my eyes open, and even then it was just a thin
crack. When my eyes adjusted to the dim lighting, I recognized
the buttercup-colored walls and all the titanium trim of the
dorm rooms at the University in South Dakota, the same room
Aiden and I had done a whole lot of not sleeping in right before
Dominic had brought us news of Deity Island survivors. Things
. . . things were different then; it already felt like years ago.

A terrible heaviness settled like a stone in my chest, pressing
all the way down to my spine. Dominic was now dead. So were
the Dean of the University and his Guards. It had been a trick
played out by Ares, who'd been masquerading as Instructor
Romvi. Our enemy had been among us the entire time. My
dislike of that man had been epic before I'd discovered who he
really was, but now? Every fiber of my Apollyon being loathed
him. But my hatred of Romvi/Ares/Asshat wasn't important. So

many people were dead, and Ares knew where I was. What was stopping him from coming back for round two? And what was stopping him from killing more people?

I heard my name once more, and now it seemed louder and closer. Turning to the sound, I willed my eyes to open. When had my eyes closed again? I was like a newborn kitten or something. Daimons across the nation shuddered in fear. Gods, I was lame.

"Alex."

My heart skipped a whole beat, and then sped up in recognition. Ah, I knew that voice. My heart and my soul *knew* that voice.

"Alex, open your eyes. Come on, baby, open those eyes."

I really wanted to, because for him I'd do anything. Fight a horde of half-blood daimons? There. Tangle with ticked-off furies? Sign me up. Break a dozen or so rules for one forbidden kiss? Done. Open my eyes? Apparently that was asking too much.

A warm, strong hand curved along my cheek; the touch was so different than my mother's, but equally powerful and heartbreakingly tender. My breath caught in my throat.

His thumb traced the curve of my jaw in such a lovingly familiar way that I wanted to weep. I should weep, actually, because I couldn't fathom what he'd gone through when Ares and I had been locked in that room. Come to think of it, I should've cried when I saw my mom. I'd felt the tears, but they hadn't fallen.

"It's okay," he said in a voice gruff with exhaustion and emotion. "Apollo said it could take some time. I'll wait for however long it takes. I'll wait forever, if I have to."

Those words pulled my heart all over the place, twisting it into mushy knots. I didn't want to make him wait for another second, let alone forever. I wanted—no, *needed*—to see him. To tell him that I was okay, because I *was* okay, wasn't I? All right, maybe I didn't fall into the "okay" category, but I wanted to relieve the harsh edge of stress in his voice. I wanted to make him better because I couldn't make my mom better, and I knew I couldn't make myself better.

There was a part of me that felt vastly empty.

Dead.

That was it. I *felt* dead inside.

Frustration coursed like acid in my blood. My fingers fisted in the soft sheets as I dragged in a deep breath. He stilled beside me, like he held his breath and waited, then let out a ragged exhale.

My heart plummeted.

Gods, all I needed to do was open my eyes, not walk a tightrope.

That frustration quickly flipped to anger—a soul-deep kind of rage that tasted of hot bitterness. My heart rate picked up, and that's when I realized *it* was there—the cord. It had been absent in Olympus, but it was back. I hadn't felt it at first because I'd only been acknowledging the ache in my muscles and bones, but the cord connecting me and the First buzzed like a million yellow jackets, steadily increasing until I swore I could see it in my mind, an amber-colored cord tangling with a blue one.

Seth?

His reply didn't come in the form of thoughts or feelings, but a rush of energy so pure it was like being zapped by lightning. Strength poured into me, a torrential downpour of vitality encasing every nerve ending. Every distinct sound in the room was magnified. My own breathing, more steady now, and the deep and slow inhales of the man beside me. Doors opened and shut in the hallway outside the room, and there were voices, muted but distinct. My skin came alive. Glyphs bled through, swirling across my body in response.

I didn't understand it, but I knew Seth was lending me his power, like he had in the Catskills when I'd fought the furies for the first time. He'd claimed no knowledge of what had happened, chalking it up to adrenaline, but Seth had . . . he had lied about a lot of things.

But now he was helping me. It didn't make sense, since I was much easier to deal with in this state, but I wasn't going to look a gift horse too closely in the mouth right at the moment.

My eyes flew open.

And I saw him.

Aiden was on his side, facing me. His hand still cupped my cheek, his thumb smoothing along my skin, and I could feel the marks of the Apollyon gliding toward his touch. His eyes were closed, but I knew he was awake. Thick, sooty ashes fanned the tips of his broad cheekbones. His dark brown hair was a mess. Waves tumbled over his forehead, brushing the graceful arches of his brows.

An ugly, purplish bruise marred his left eye, and I wondered if he could even open it. There was another violent mark, an astonishing mixture of reds, shadowing the strong line of his jaw. His lips were parted, neck and shoulders tensed.

Without warning, I was thrown back to the very first time I'd seen him.

The Covenant in North Carolina no longer stood, but it felt like I was there again, standing in the training room used for novices. I'd been practicing with Cal and Caleb. I'd done something incredibly moronic, which was nothing new, and the three of us had been laughing. I'd turned and had seen Aiden by the doors. At that time, I didn't think he really saw us. He was a pure-blood, and they didn't show any interest in halfs, so I had assumed he was just dazing. Even then, I'd been captivated by him. To me, he'd honestly been the most alluring male I'd even seen—a face that could be both hard and beautiful. And those eyes, flashing between heather gray and quicksilver, had been permanently etched into my memories from that moment on. That curiosity had been inflamed when he'd shown up in

Atlanta, saving me from some really annoying and talkative daimons three years later.

Our love had never been easy.

As a pure-blood, he was untouchable to me even though I was the Apollyon, and even now he risked everything to be with me. He was my strength when I needed him to be, my friend when I needed someone to talk me down, my equal in a world where by law I would always be less than him, and honest to gods, he was the love of my life.

And he would wait forever for me, just as I would wait forever and a day for him.

Except forever will probably end up being fairly short, whispered an insidious voice, and it was right. Even if I managed to get past all the obstacles between me and Seth, and transfer his power to me, there was no doubt in my mind that, even as a God Killer, I was going to have problems fighting Ares. And if, by some miracle, I survived that, there was a really good chance the other gods would kill me.

So why even bother?

Aiden and I could run away together, live as long as we could and *be happy*. He'd do it if I asked. I knew he would. We could hide until we couldn't hide anymore, but we'd be together, and we'd be alive. And for a little while, there'd be no more pain and no more death to deal with.

A huge part of me, especially that dark, cold place that had been born when Ares held me down, agreed wholeheartedly with that plan. *Run away*. Nothing seemed smarter or simpler to do.

But I couldn't, because there was too much that had to be done. People relied on me, and the world would descend into absolute chaos if Ares wasn't stopped.

I held onto that needle-thin thread of duty with my life and spoke. "Hey."

His lashes fluttered opened, revealing silvery eyes that never failed to make the muscles in my stomach tighten and my heart do a little pitter-patter.

Our gazes met.

Aiden jerked up, his face paling by several degrees, making the bruises along his jaw and left eye stand out in stark contrast.

Fear exploded in my stomach, which was kind of strange since terror typically wasn't my first reaction to sudden movements, but I scrambled against the headboard. My breath stalled out as my body protested the sudden movement.

"What?" I croaked. "What's wrong?"

Aiden stared at me with wide eyes. Color hadn't returned to his face. He was as pale as a daimon, and while disbelief shattered his gaze, pain churned in them.

He reached out but stopped short of touching me. "Your eyes . . ."

"What?" My heart beat so quickly I was sure it would jump out of my chest and do a little jig on the bed between us. "I opened them. I heard you asking me to."

Aiden winced. "Alex . . ."

Now I was really starting to freak out. Why was he reacting this way? Had Ares rearranged my face so badly that my eyes were on my chin or something?

He glanced toward the door and then back to me, his face going stoic, but he could never hide his feelings from me. I could read everything in his eyes. There was so much pain in them that it broke my heart, but I didn't understand why.

"What are you feeling?" he asked.

Uh, what was I *not* feeling? "I'm . . . I'm going to go with confusion. Aiden, tell me. What's going on?"

He stared at me so long I started to feel a wee bit self-conscious. Several seconds passed, and then I really became convinced that my eyes *were* on my chin, but then it made sense. Panic unfurled in the pit of my stomach and spread like a virus.

Springing from the bed, I hit the floor. Hot slices of pain

ricocheted up my still-healing bones. I stumbled to the side, catching myself on the wall.

In a heartbeat, Aiden was off the bed and beside me. "Alex, are you—"

"I'm okay." I bit back a moan.

Aiden reached out, but I pushed away from the wall before he could touch me. Each step hurt like Tartarus. Sweat dotted my forehead, and my legs shook with the effort to make it to the bathroom that joined the two suites together.

"I have to see," I gasped out.

"Maybe you should sit down," he suggested, close behind.

I couldn't. I knew what Aiden was thinking. I was connected with Seth, and maybe he even thought this was a trick of some sort and was waiting for me to break free and pull out Deacon's ribcage, but Seth was quiet on the other end of the cord.

Reaching around me, Aiden pushed the bathroom door open, and I all but fell inside. Light flooded the small but efficient washroom when he found the switch on the wall. My reflection formed in the mirror.

I gasped.

This couldn't be me.

No way.

Uh-uh, it wasn't, and I refused to believe it, but the damn reflection remained the same. I had changed. Dramatically. The pressure in my chest returned and doubled as I gripped the edge of the sink.

My hair hung an inch or two past my shoulders now, the edges ragged and uneven from the dagger Ares had used. I picked up a strand, wincing as I discovered it was a good deal shorter than the rest. Did the rest of my hair hang in Hades' war room now?

My skin was pale, as if I'd been sick for months and hadn't seen the sun. But it wasn't even that. Hell, it wasn't even the fact that, yes, my eyes were amber-colored. Identical to Seth's in clarity and shininess, they were like two topaz gemstones. And they were glowing, like you could see me in the dark kind of creepy glowing, and I got why that set Aiden on edge. Great, I had glowing, honeycomb eyes. Big freaking deal.

It was *my face* I couldn't get over.

I was as shallow as any other eighteen-year-old girl, so yeah, this . . . this was major.

Across my cheekbones and nose, faint pink lines crisscrossed over my skin. My forehead was the same. A web-like network of scars covered my face. Only one side of my jaw, where Aiden had been touching me earlier, had escaped the . . . well, the deformity.

Dazed by what I was seeing, I slowly lifted my arm and ran my fingers across my cheek, confirming what I suspected. The lines were slightly raised, like stitching. Apollo and his son had healed me. The nectar was still doing its mojo in my system, but I knew these scars were proof of just how badly I'd needed the gods' help to heal.

Like anything else, there always had to be an exchange.

When anything was gained, something had to be sacrificed. No one needed to tell me. I knew these scars would never fade.

"Oh, my gods . . ." I swayed.

"Alex, you should sit down." He reached for me again.

"Don't," I snapped, holding a hand up between us. My eyes widened. My hand was also covered with scars. I wasn't even sure what I was saying "don't" to, but my mouth kept moving. "Just don't."

Aiden pulled back, but he didn't leave. Leaning against the threshold of the door, he folded his muscular arms across his broad chest. His jaw set in a hard line.

The pressure moved into my throat, swelling like a balloon and then exploding like a late summer's day thunderstorm. "What are you waiting for? Me to go all Evil Alex on you again?" I swung forward, losing my balance. "That I'm going to use—"

Aiden shot forward, catching me before I cracked my head against the wall. "Dammit Alex, you need to be careful and *sit down*."

I wrenched free, stumbled back a step, and plopped down on the closed toilet. Air punched out of me. Dear gods, it felt like my tailbone had been cracked. I sat there on the toilet, my butt feeling like someone had literally kicked me in it. Aiden stared at me with warring levels of hope and distrust in the eyes I loved so much. I felt about seven kinds of dejected.

Aiden stepped forward, crouching down so that we were at the same eye level. "You don't want to kill me?"

Most of the rage seeped out of me. Nothing like hearing the man I love ask a question like that to really take the wind out of my sails. "No," I whispered.

There was a sharp intake of breath. "You don't want what he wants?"

"No." My gaze dropped to where his hands rested between his knees. Good gods, the knuckles were bruised and the skin was torn open, as if he'd punched a . . . then I got it. Aiden and Marcus had been banging on the titanium doors of the dean's office with their fists.

My heart ached as I watched those battered hands open, close, and then open again. "I don't even feel him. I mean, the cord's there, so I know he's somewhere, but I don't feel him. He's quiet."

His hands unclenched, and even though I wasn't looking at him, I could tell that most of the tension had left him. He believed me for the most part, and I couldn't hold the residual suspicion against him.

"Gods, Alex, when I saw your eyes, I just . . . They glowed like that when you escaped the basement and . . ."

When I had almost killed him.

If I lifted my lashes, we'd be face to face, but I couldn't bring myself to do it. He shifted closer. "I'm sorry. I should—"

"It's okay." I was so tired. Not the physical kind. Oddly enough, it was more of a ... spirit-weary sort. "I understand. You had every reason to think that. I don't know why my eyes are glowing. Seth's there, but he's not trying to influence me."

"Yet" hung unspoken between us.

"And he's not talking," I added, keeping the fact that Seth had lent me some of his own juice out of the conversation.

I shifted my gaze back to my own hands and the scars that marred them. They hadn't been like that in Olympus, or at least I hadn't noticed.

"It doesn't matter," he said. "It's you, and that's all that I care about—all that matters."

I wanted to believe him. I really did, but the horror in his face when he'd seen my eyes haunted me. I knew Aiden had hated them from the moment they appeared after I'd Awakened, and I couldn't blame him. These eyes would always remind him of Seth and everything I'd said and done back then, especially when they glowed like yellow light bulbs.

"Alex." His much larger hands covered mine. There was a long stretch of silence. "How are you feeling?"

I shrugged a shoulder, then winced. "Okay."

His hands circled my wrists, and I suddenly was on the verge of tears but didn't know why. All I wanted to do was curl up in a ball, right there, on the bathroom floor.

"I've never been more scared in my life than when you forced me and Marcus out of the room."

"Me, too." I swallowed hard. I don't know what made me do it, but I pulled my hands free and slipped them between my knees. "How is Marcus?"

"He's hanging in there, but he's going to be relieved once he learns you're awake." Aiden leaned in, his breath warm against my cheek. Every instinct insisted that I lift my chin a fraction of an inch to meet his lips, but I couldn't move.

There was another pause, and the words he spoke next were

heavy. "I know why you made sure Marcus and I were out of that room when Ares attacked. It was incredibly brave, and so like you."

My fingers dug into my stiff denim jeans. Gods, were they the ones I'd worn during the fight? Patches of dark dried blood covered the legs like paint. Squeezing my eyes shut, I was sickened to find that the images of what has caused the stains lingered.

Aiden took a deep breath. "But if you ever do anything like that again, I will strangle you. Lovingly, of course."

I almost cracked a smile at the same thing I'd thought about him not too long ago, but the smile never made it to the surface.

He wasn't done. "We promised each other we'd face this stuff together."

"Ares would've killed you," I said, and it was the truth. Ares would've killed him and Marcus if they had stayed in that room, and he would've relished doing so.

"But I would've protected you," Aiden countered. "I would've done every godsdamn thing there was to save you from having to go through what you went through in there. When I came into the room and saw you . . ." He broke off, cursing under his breath.

"You would've died trying to protect me. Don't you get that? I had to do it. I couldn't live with myself if you or Marcus died—"

"And do you think either of us can live with ourselves knowing what that bastard did to you?" Anger snapped through his voice. So did frustration. "Look at me."

At a loss of how else to explain the obvious to him, I shook my head.

"Godsdammit, Alex, look at me!"

Startled, my head jerked up and my eyes met his. They were a furious shade of gunmetal gray, and they were so *open*. Raw pain flowed from them, and I wanted to look away from that, to take the coward's way out.

"My heart stopped when that damn door closed on me. I could hear you two fighting. I could hear him taunting you, and I could hear him *breaking* your bones. And there wasn't a damn thing I could do about it." He placed his hands on the sides of my legs. Tension rippled through the muscles in his arms. "You never should've faced something like that alone."

"But you would've died."

"And because I love you, I am willing to die to save you from that. Don't you dare take that decision away from me again."

My mouth opened, but there were no words. So much was going on inside my head and chest. What he said had split my heart wide open and then stitched the wound closed. But what would I have left if he'd died? I would've been beyond heartbroken, and I couldn't even bear to think about his death without hurting. If I had to do it over again, I would make the same decision because I loved him. So how dare he expect me to do anything less?

I knew I needed to say those words to him, but they . . . they just couldn't get past the ball in my chest or pop the lid on the pressure inside me. I shivered, numb and chilled to the core.

Aiden went to grasp my shoulders, but he stopped, his fingers curling around air. "You have my heart, and you also have my strength. Make no mistake, I am willing to die for you, but you have to trust that I don't want to leave your side. Ares wouldn't have taken me out easily, because I would've fought to stay alive and be there for you."

I heard him, and I felt what he said, but all I saw were the Guards that Ares hadn't even touched. Dominic, whom he'd snapped in two with the twist of his hand. The Dean he'd tossed out the window with a wave of his arm. All the wanting and needing in the world wouldn't have saved their lives.

He let out a ragged breath when silence filled the bathroom. "Say something, Alex."

"I . . . understand."

He stared at me, dumbfounded.

The numbness had seeped into my muscles. "I want to take a shower. I need to get out of these clothes, and I need to bathe."

Aiden blinked, and then his gaze dropped. Some of the color brought back by anger drained as if he'd just realized I was in the same blood-splattered clothing I'd worn when I faced Ares. "Alex . . ."

"Please," I whispered.

He didn't move for the longest time, and then he nodded. Rising fluidly, he stopped halfway and pressed his lips to my forehead. My heart thumped heavily, but then I realized his lips were touching those scars and I winced.

Aiden pulled back immediately. Concern etched into his striking face. "Do they—did I hurt you?"

"No. Yes. I mean, it's tender." Truth was, it hadn't hurt at all. Not like the rest of my body did. At first, it had actually felt nice. "I just need to shower."

He hesitated, and for a moment I thought he wasn't going to leave, but then he nodded again. "I'll get something for you to wear when you're finished."

"Thank you," I said as the door closed behind him.

I stood slowly, feeling like I was ninety as my joints popped and my muscles stretched. Stripping off the soiled clothing took an indecent amount of time, and as I turned the water on and steam filled the bathroom, I stepped in. Hot water doused me from head to toe, pricking my raw skin.

The water coursed through my hair and down my body, filling the tub with red and circling the drain like a grotesque raspberry swirl. I washed my hair twice, going through the mind-numbing mechanics until I was satisfied when I didn't see a hint of pink in the bottom of the tub.

Only then, as I turned off the water and felt the spray lessen until it dripped down the plastic walls, did I look down at my body. From my toes to my collarbone, with only a few places where there were no bones to break, I was covered in the thin lacing of pink scars.

Good gods . . . I'd never seen anything like this before. I looked like one of those patchwork dolls.

I stepped out of the shower, legs shaking as I twisted to the side. My back was much worse. The coloring was darker along my spine, where many of the vertebrae had been smashed. Had all these bones broken the surface, or had the injuries burst blood vessels? There had been too much pain when it'd happened for me to tell.

Apollyon or not, I couldn't believe I'd survived this. None of it seemed real.

The numbness in my chest spread like a weed. Maybe I was struck stupid by what I saw, because I had known it was my body that looked like this, but the knowledge had only sunk through a layer or two.

A strange mark on my back, near my hip, caught my attention. Colored like a pale pink rose, it didn't follow the typical pattern of the rest of the scars.

Swiping the mist off the mirror, I twisted to get a better look at the mark on my lower back. My mouth dropped open. Holy Hades holding hockey sticks, it was the shape and distinct form of a *hand*.

"What the hell?"

"Alex?" Aiden's voice came from the bedroom. "Are you okay in there?"

Heart pounding, I grabbed a towel off the rack and wrapped it around me. That was the last thing I wanted Aiden to see. Opening the door, I forced what I hoped was a reassuring expression. "Yeah, I'm fine."

The look on his face said he didn't believe me, but then his gaze dropped. It wasn't the towel that had caught his attention or the fact that so much flesh was exposed. Deep down, I knew why he stared and why his lips thinned. I knew that, when he saw me, it wasn't my body that held him immobile.

It was the patchwork of web-like scars that now covered almost every inch of me, and it was the first time he was really getting to see them in all their glory.

Embarrassment flooded my cheeks with heat. There'd been scars before—daimon tags and, of course, the stab wound—but never like this. It was ugly, really ugly. No way around that.

His gaze flicked up, meeting mine, and I couldn't stand to see the emotion churning in his silver eyes or go through another conversation like before.

Hurrying across the room, I grabbed the fresh set of clothing he'd set on the bed and stumbled around, nearly falling into the bathroom. "I'll be right out."

"Alex—"

I shut the door on whatever he was going to say, which would be something ridiculously supportive and typical Aiden, but I knew better.

It wasn't okay. This body sure as hell wasn't beautiful anymore, and I wasn't stupid enough to believe that.

Tears clogged my throat as I ripped the towel away and threw it to the floor. It was stupid to get upset about this, because it surely didn't make the Top Ten List of Messed-Up Problems right now, but damn, it burned like a fire in my chest.

Once dressed, I stared at the door. The tears never fell, but the invading numbness spread, leaving behind the worst of emotions: anger and pain.

And fear and anxiety.

2

Who knew glowing eyes could set an entire room full of people on edge? Everyone, even my uncle, couldn't stop staring. Or maybe it was my face that held them morbidly fascinated. From a distance, the scars weren't so noticeable, but after Aiden assured the group that I wasn't psychotic, everyone got all up close and personal.

The hugs were ... uh, awkward.

Even Deacon's embrace was stilted, and crap was serious if he wasn't cracking jokes or messing around. I didn't know if it was because they were worried about my injuries or because they feared I was going to Apollyon-out on them and snap their necks when they least expected it. I wished Lea were here. She would've just come out and said what everyone was really thinking without having qualms about it.

But Lea wasn't going to stride into the room. Lea was dead, and the sharp pang that accompanied that thought hadn't lessened one bit.

We were in the common room near the main academic campus building. It was almost identical to the one I'd found Caleb in the day I returned to Deity Island, except this one was outfitted with nicer furniture and a much bigger TV.

Olivia's caramel-hued cheeks were a shade paler than normal as she stepped back from me, her curly hair pulled back in a tight ponytail on top of her head. "How are you feeling?"

"I'm okay." It was my standard answer, changed out with "all right" and "fine."

Her gaze met mine and quickly flitted away. "We've all been so worried. I'm glad that you're . . . okay."

I didn't know what to say to that.

Laadan was a lot more tactful, but while she'd always remained a picture of cool collectiveness, the linen pants she wore looked like she'd slept in them and strands of raven-colored hair had escaped her twist. She met my stare and somehow managed to keep the sympathy in her expression to a minimum.

Aiden stayed close to my side, either as my own personal bodyguard or just wisely within tackling distance. He was unusually quiet while everyone settled into chairs or took spots against the wall. Unable to stand still, and figuring I needed to work the ache out of my legs, I paced, and Aiden never strayed more than a step or two away from me.

I asked the first question that popped into my head. "How long has it been since Ares was here?"

"Almost three days," answered Marcus, and he made talking look painful. Half his face was a swollen array of blues and purples.

From the sofa, Diana, one of the Head Ministers from the Catskills and my uncle's potential kissy-kiss interest, followed my movements with wary eyes. "Apollo removed you immediately afterward. You were gone for maybe an hour, and you've been . . . asleep since then."

I glanced at Aiden. My stay in Olympus had felt much longer than that, but time worked differently there, like in the Underworld. Minutes here were hours, if not days, there. "Has Ares returned?"

Aiden shook his head. "No. Apollo threw up wards to keep him out."

"Why didn't he do that before?" I asked.

"Apollo didn't know it was Ares until it was too late," Aiden answered patiently. "And I believe he assumed the University was safe."

"Yeah, and we all know what assumptions do." I passed by the TV again, vaguely aware that it was on a news station. "I thought the talisman was supposed to prevent the gods from discovering where . . ." I reached for the necklace and found that it was gone.

"Ares must've taken it," Aiden said, a muscle spasming along his jaw. "The only thing that we can come up with is that those Guards and Sentinels on the highway had made some sort of contact with Ares, Lucian, or Seth, and they put two and two together."

"Or someone is working with him." No one in the room looked like they wanted to believe it. "Ares said he has many friends."

Marcus's eyes followed me warily. "That is something we've taken into consideration, but . . ."

"But how would we know who it is?"

He said nothing, because what could he say? Anyone could be a traitor, but believe it or not, we had bigger problems at the moment.

I took a deep breath and kept my eyes trained on the minuscule space between Deacon and Luke on the couch. "There's a good chance Seth knows where I am."

No one in the room made a sound. Not even the guys in the back of the common area. There were twenty or so Guards and Sentinels from the University. I recognized a few from the group that had been led by Dominic, the ones who had met us at the walls when we arrived here. I truly hoped there were more where they came from.

"Besides the fact that Ares had to have told Seth where I was, I . . . I let the shields drop when I was fighting Ares." Shameful heat flooded my cheeks as I now stared at a tiny tear in the rug.

"We figured Seth would be aware of your location by now," Marcus said quietly. "I'm not an expert when it comes to the whole Apollyon connection, but Seth was able to feel what you were experiencing before you Awakened. That's how we were able to find you in Gatlinburg when you . . . when you . . ."

When I'd left to find my mom when she'd become a daimon. I could feel several eyes on me, especially a pair of silver ones. "Yeah."

"Does that mean he felt exactly what you were feeling when you fought Ares?" Aiden asked, and his voice was deceptively even. That was also known as the calm before the apocalyptic storm.

"Do you really want the answer to that?"

"Yes."

Glancing at him, I wished I hadn't. Aiden looked like he already knew the answer and was ready to murder someone, and that someone was Seth. I started pacing again. "Yes."

Aiden swore loudly. His brother jumped to his feet and went to his side, saying something too low and quick for me to make out. Aiden's hands clenched at his sides, drawing my attention to his busted knuckles.

I wanted to go to him, but I felt rooted to the floor, near where Olivia sat on a black chaise lounge. I willed my legs to move toward him, but nothing happened. Frustration and uncertainty poured into me, overriding the numbness, and my anger skyrocketed.

My gaze locked with Aiden's, and a godsawful sensation lit up my chest. I yearned to run to him, but a cold primal fear, a need to run *away* from him, was equally powerful.

"Alex," Olivia whispered.

I looked at her and saw her eyes widened with anxiety. Actually, *everyone* was staring at me with the same expression. What the . . . ? My gaze dropped.

Oh—my feet *weren't* on the floor.

My heart tumbled over. Closing my eyes, I forced myself back down. Relief crashed into me when my sneakers hit the carpet. "Sorry," I said, putting some distance between me and those in the room. "I didn't mean to do that. I'm honestly not even sure how that happened."

"It's okay," Laadan reassured with a small smile.

With wide eyes, Deacon remained by Aiden's side. "If your head starts spinning . . ."

"Shut up, Deacon," Aiden growled.

He made a face but remained quiet, and I really felt like a freak.

I remembered what it felt like when the shields came down between Seth and me. So much fury had burned through the connection. Seth had been epically pissed, but I wasn't sure if it was because of what Ares had been doing or if it was something more than that. The connection had fed him everything: all the pain and the hopelessness I'd felt when Ares had gotten the upper hand. And when I'd wanted to die instead of facing another second of soul-shattering pain, Seth had gotten a taste of that bitter, rotten emotion.

How could he have been okay with that? Did the means really justify the end for him? I'd experienced way too much at Ares' hands to hope that Seth had changed. It seemed more believable that his anger was associated with me not submitting to Ares more than anything else.

Another random thought formed. The prophesy of Grandma Piperi, oracle extraordinaire, came back like a cold sore. *You will kill the ones you love.*

Part of me did love Seth—pre-jackass, of course. He was a part of me. We were yin and yin, and Seth had been there for me for a lot. I'd never forget that, but I was no longer so blinded by how he used to be that I couldn't see what needed to be done. If I couldn't get the power of the God Killer to transfer to me, I *would* kill him.

Or go down trying.

But that prophecy didn't mean just my loved ones would die by *my* hand. Kain, a half-blood Guard who'd helped Aiden train me, had been turned by my mom in an attempt to reach me and died by Seth's hand. Caleb had been murdered by a daimon because I'd been so emo over Aiden and we'd snuck out to get food and drinks, even knowing that there could be daimons on campus. And my mom had been turned into a daimon—her true death—because of me. Then I *had* killed her. Even though I couldn't claim to love Lea, I'd respected her a great deal toward the end, and her death was also linked to me.

And more people I loved would die.

I crossed my arms, ignoring the way my bones cracked from the movement. "The University isn't safe with me here."

Aiden whirled toward me, his eyes narrowing into thin slits, but before he could speak, Marcus stepped in. "There is no other place safer, Alexandria. At least here, we have Sentinels and—"

"Sentinels and Guards are nothing if Ares finds a way in. And let's say he doesn't—we still have Seth to worry about."

"We can't leave here." Luke leaned forward, dropping his arms onto his knees. "Not until we've rallied the troops and you've fully recovered—"

"I'm fine!" My voice cracked on the last word, a humiliating lie detector.

Luke raised a brow.

"Whatever," I said. "I need to leave."

"You. Are. Not. Leaving."

Everyone in the room turned to Aiden, including me. His words hung in the air, and challenge seeped out every pore. "I have to," I said.

"No." Stalking forward, his powerful muscles rippled under the black shirt he wore. The black shirt of a Sentinel, and gods, he was a Sentinel through and through at that moment. "We already had this discussion. All of us know the risks, Alex."

Challenge accepted. "But that was before Ares went all god badass on us."

His eyes turned a furious shade of silver as he stared down at me. "Nothing has changed."

"Everything has changed!"

"The technicalities have, maybe, but nothing else."

I stared at him, dumbfounded. "It was one thing when we thought it was Hephaestus or Hermes, but it's *Ares*. In case you don't remember, he's the mother-fu—"

"I know who he is," Aiden gritted out.

"Children," Marcus admonished.

We shot him mutual death glares.

Marcus ignored it. "Aiden is right, Alex."

Of course he took Aiden's side.

"We all know what we're getting into." He gestured at his battered face. "Trust me, we all know, and like we said before, we are in this together."

"What about them?" I totally remembered when everyone had stood up and announced that they had my back. And one of them was dead now. I gestured at the back of the room. "What about every person at the University—the students, and all the people who came here for the safety it once offered? Are they willing to take that risk?"

A Sentinel next to the young one who'd been with Dominic the day we'd arrived here stepped forward and said, "If I may speak?"

Aiden sent him a look that a wiser person would've run from.

Apparently this Sentinel wasn't used to running. Then again, none of them were.

"What is your name?" Diana asked.

"Valerian," he answered, and I pegged him to be in his late twenties. A half-blood, of course.

"Like the root?" Deacon asked.

Luke rolled his eyes.

The man nodded. "Most people call me Val."

"What do you have to say, Val?" Diana spoke again.

"Everyone here has been affected by what is happening. I can't name one person who hasn't lost a friend or a loved one. Not to mention we lost our Dean and our friends when Ares attacked. I can't speak for everyone, but you will find that the vast majority of those who reside here are willing to do just about anything to see an end to this."

Then they all were idiots.

I shook my head as I turned around. None of the Sentinels or Guards here could stand against Seth, let alone gods knew what else Ares could throw our way.

Aiden caught hold of my arm in a firm but gentle grasp, as if, even in his anger, he was aware that my body was still healing. "Stop being so stubborn, Alex."

"You're the one who's being pigheaded," I shot back, and I tried to pull free, but Aiden held on, a warning flaring in his eyes. "I'm trying to protect them."

"I know." His voice lost a fraction of its edge. "And that's the only reason I'm not throwing you over my shoulder and locking you in a room somewhere."

My eyes narrowed. "I'd like to see you try."

"Is that a challenge?" he asked.

Someone in the back of the common area cleared his throat. "So I'm assuming these two have some sort of past?"

Deacon choked on his laugh as he plopped down on the sofa. "That would be an affirmative."

Aiden's gaze slid to his brother, and he took a long, nice, deep breath.

"Wow." Deacon elbowed Luke. "This would be awkward if it weren't so entertaining. It's like watching our parents—"

"Shut up, Deacon," both Aiden and I snapped at the same time.

"See!" Deacon grinned. "They're like peas and carrots."

Luke turned to him slowly. "Did you just quote *Forrest Gump*?"

He shrugged. "Maybe I did."

And just like that, some of the tension seeped out of Aiden . . . and me, too. He let go of my arm but was like Velcro on my hip. "Sometimes I worry for you, Deacon," he said, his lips curving up on one side.

"I ain't who you should be worrying about." Deacon jerked his chin at me. "Little Miss 'I Gotta Be A Martyr' over there is the one you should be concerned with."

I made a face, but everyone in the room, even the bulk of Sentinels in the back, stared back at me with determined expressions. There would be no convincing them otherwise. I knew I wouldn't be leaving here alone, and I really didn't want to. Honestly, the thought of facing Ares or even Seth alone scared the bejebus out of me.

And I would need an army—a really big one. Hopefully, the Sentinel who'd spoken up was right that the vast majority of people here wanted to make a stand, because we were going to need them.

Letting out a long breath, I looked up at Aiden. "Okay."

"Okay, what?" he prompted.

He was so going to make me say it. "I will stay here."

"And?"

Dear gods . . . "And I accept everyone's help and whatever."

"Good." He bent down, swiftly kissing me on the cheek. "You finally see the light."

I flushed and then really turned beet red when half of the room—half bloods so unaccustomed to seeing a pure and a half together—stared at us open-mouthed. Even though they'd suspected there was something between us, seeing the proof had to be shocking.

In the lull of conversation, I caught a bit of what was on the news. A full-scale war had broken out in the Middle East. Entire towns had been leveled. One of the sides had access to nuclear weapons and was threatening to use them. The U.N. was calling for global intervention, and the U.S. and U.K. were sending thousands of troops overseas.

I had a real bad feeling about this.

"It's Ares," Solos said, speaking for the first time since this whole meeting of the minds began.

I turned toward him and was reminded that my scars were nothing compared to the jagged mark covering his handsome face. "Do we know for sure?"

Marcus nodded. "His presence in the mortal realm causes discord, especially when he's not masking what he is."

"And we saw something very in-ter-resting on the tellie yesterday," Deacon added.

"Yep," Luke chimed in. "One of the commanders of the attacking army was sporting a very fashionable armband with a Greek shield on it. I have no idea what Ares hopes to gain by starting a war."

It seemed obvious to me. "He just . . . loves war. He feeds on it like the gods used to feed on mortals' beliefs in them. And if there's a huge war that splits a bulk of the world, he can swoop in and subjugate mankind."

"Very true," Diana said softly. "Ares' love for war and discord is well-known. He grows stronger in times of great strife."

"That's exactly what we need." Aiden folded his arms. "Ares growing stronger."

Moving a few steps over, I leaned against an air hockey table. It was hard seeing one and not thinking of Caleb. "Ares wants to rule. He thinks it's time for the gods to reclaim the mortal realm as their own, and I wouldn't be surprised if there are other gods supporting him." Namely Hermes, but other than Marcus and Aiden, they didn't know Hermes had helped Seth contact me.

There was a round of artistic uses of four letter words from those in the back, ones that would've brought a smile to my face at one point in the past.

"Well, at least we know what Ares wants. He's looking for a war," Aiden said, addressing the room like the leader he was and I so obviously hadn't quite learned to be. "And we're going to give him one."

3

As a group, we decided we would hold a meeting the day after tomorrow for anyone on campus who wished to join what Deacon had named the "Army of Awesomeness". Diana and Marcus, who apparently had jointly taken over the day-to-day operation of the campus after the dean's death, picked the Council's coliseum as the location of the meeting. All twelve of the University's council members, plus a handful from other locations, were on campus, and Diana swore they would have no problems with us making use of what was considered one of the most sacred buildings on campus.

I had a hard time believing it.

But the day before that wouldn't be about recruitment for the A.O.A. or battle strategies. That day would be the day the dead were given their rightful burial.

After the meeting had ended, I quickly skedaddled out of the common area and headed outside, needing the fresh air. The oxygen in my lungs felt stale, my brain full of holes. Once the anger had faded, all that was left were the dull ache of my healing body and the odd numbness in my core.

Night had begun to fall, and although it was the middle of May, cool air brushed my cheeks and made me grateful for the long-sleeved shirt Aiden had dug up.

I strode past the main building and looked up, sucking in a gulp of air when I got a good look at the top floor. The window facing the courtyard had been boarded up. My gaze fell to the marble pathway below. It was cracked.

Shuddering, I hurried around the wrought-iron face separating the courtyard from the walkways. Like the one that had been on Deity Island, flowers and trees from all around the globe blossomed here, despite the climate. The clean scent of roses and the sweeter scent of peonies mixed with the heavier scents of grapes and olive trees.

Stopping near the entrance, I stared up at a marble replica of Zeus. With his curly hair and beard, he looked more like a mountain man than the all-powerful god he was.

Couldn't he have stepped in at some point, put the smackdown on Ares, and ended all of this? Surely Zeus could find a way to get around Seth and take out Lucian. But even if Zeus did, that still left Seth for him to deal with . . . and me.

Further into the courtyard, a statue of Apollo glowed, lit by a small lamp at its base. His face was turned toward the sky.

"Where are you?" I asked.

Once Apollo had blown his cover as Leon, he wasn't able to stay in the mortal realm for long periods of time without weakening. I wondered if it was the same for Ares, and if so, did he hang out in Olympus with the other gods or did he have a hidey hole somewhere?

Turning from the statue, I started back down the path, because it wasn't like the hunk of rock was going to answer any of my questions. Passing several smaller buildings that looked like miniature Greek temples, I skirted the Council building. Busts of the Olympian twelve were carved into the four sides of the building, which closely resembled an ancient temple. Like always, a measure of dread knotted in my stomach as I hurried past.

Council buildings had never held good memories for me.

Beyond the Council building, I looked back. Dorms rose into the sky behind the main academic buildings. The University really was its own city, but other than the patrolling Guards, I hadn't seen a student yet.

It was probably a good thing they were keeping the students in their rooms. The last thing anyone needed was a bunch of pures running amuck, feeding off hysteria.

Gods, I sounded like an old fart.

I *felt* like an old fart.

Coming to the end of the pathway, the marble walls in front of me rose into the night. Spotlights situated every few feet atop the walls cast light throughout the campus. In the shadows of the twenty-foot monstrosity surrounding the University, Guards and Sentinels were stationed where sections of the wall had taken some damage.

I sat down on a bench and stretched my legs out, working the healing muscles and tissue as I watched the men. Even from where I sat, I could tell that they were all half-bloods. Every damn one of them, and I couldn't help but think of my father. I'd given up hope that he was here because Laadan would've found him by now. He could still be at the New York Covenant in the Catskills. He could be anywhere, or he could be dead.

Rubbing my hands down my face, I told myself not to think that, but man, I was so rocking a Negative Nancy vibe like there was no tomorrow. Or maybe I was just being a Realistic Rachel? How could he have survived? How could Ares not know that my father had been at the Catskills? Surely he would use my father against me if he could.

And what would he have chosen for his life if he'd had a choice to be something other than a Sentinel, Guard, or servant? What would any of these men out by the walls have chosen? Did any of them ever think about that?

I had, at one point in my life, when I'd been living among mortals, way before I knew what I was or had even heard that stupid prophecy. I'd wanted to work at a zoo. Not the biggest aspiration for one to have in life, but I loved animals and because all creatures could be controlled by compulsion—therefore pure-blooded daimons—I'd never had a pet. The few times I'd visited a zoo, the workers had always seemed to enjoy their jobs, and I wanted that. I wanted to be happy with what I was doing with my life. I used to think becoming a Sentinel would fulfill that need.

Funny thing was, when I'd been living among mortals, all I'd really wanted was to be back at the Covenant among my own kind. Now I wasn't so sure I wanted to be a Sentinel if I survived this.

Glancing down, I put my hands on my stomach, like a pregnant woman did. The cord buzzed along, a constant open connection. I closed my eyes and focused, like I had the night before I went toe-to-toe with Ares. Gods knew I probably looked as much an idiot now as I did then.

Seth?

There was no answer—nothing on the other side. Like the cord went out into space and just ended.

Footsteps crunched over the gravel, and I didn't need to look behind me to know who it was.

Aiden had been following me the whole time.

The footsteps stopped behind the bench.

"I'm not going to run off," I said, and I wasn't planning to.

There was a pause. "I know."

A few seconds later, he came around the bench and sat beside me, his hands resting on his thighs. Neither of us spoke for what felt like forever. He was the one to break the silence first.

"I'm sorry for yelling at you back there."

I choked on a laugh as I slid him a glance. "No, you're not."

One side of his lips tipped up, but it wasn't a real smile that showed off those dimples. I hadn't seen one of those since I'd woken up this afternoon. "Okay," he conceded. "I'm not sorry for what I said, but I am sorry for raising my voice."

"It's okay."

"I wish you'd stop saying that."

I stood a little too fast, and my knees backhanded me in the form of sharp bursts of pain. "But it *is* okay."

My back was to him, but I could *feel* the frown in his voice. "Everything is not okay, Alex. I'm pretty sure the world is coming down around us. It's all right for things not to be okay."

I placed one foot in front of the other as if walking a balance beam, but my equilibrium hadn't caught up with the healing, and after three steps I could've easily passed as a drunk.

"It doesn't mean you're weak if you admit that things are pretty screwed up right now," he continued.

I stood still. "This isn't a very motivating speech."

Aiden laughed dryly. "It's not meant to be. More like a dose of reality."

"I think I've had enough doses of that recently."

He let out a heavy sigh. "You don't have to be okay with what happened to you, Alex. No one expects that. I sure as hell don't."

Turning around slowly, I opened my mouth to tell him that was the last thing I wanted to talk about, but that wasn't what came out. "If I'm not okay with that, then what am I supposed to be?"

His eyes met mine. "Angry."

Oh, there was a whole lot of that.

"You can be upset—scared—and you can rage that it wasn't fair, because it *wasn't*. A lot of this stuff hasn't been fair for you, but especially this. Nothing about it was right, and you've got to let yourself experience those emotions."

"I am." Kind of. Strange thing was that I felt all of those things, but it wasn't enough. Like a cap on a bottle unscrewed just enough to let a little bit of air in.

A sad look crossed his face as he shook his head. "You're not. And you've got to let it out, Alex, or it will rot you from the inside."

My chest rose sharply. I was already rotten on the inside. "I'm trying."

"I know." Aiden leaned forward, his eyes never leaving mine. "I'm sorry I doubted you this morning."

"Aiden—"

He raised a hand. "Hear me out, okay? The last thing you needed when you woke up after something like that was to have me react that way. I know that didn't help."

It wasn't the choir-singing, romantic reunion I imagined, but I also understood. "My eyes . . ."

"That's not a good enough reason for how I acted."

"It's not that big of a deal, Aiden, but I forgive you."

Aiden stared at me a moment longer and then sat back. His gaze drifted over my face and then to the sheared locks. I wanted to hide. "Come here," he said gently.

The coldness seeped into my chest, and I stayed in place, but the words burst out of me as if my mouth had been hijacked by inner Alex. "I look like Frankenstein."

"You're beautiful."

"I look like Frankenstein with a beauty-school-dropout haircut."

Our eyes locked again. "You've never been more beautiful to me than you are right now."

"You need your eyes checked."

He smiled a little. "And you need your head examined."

I bit down on my lip.

"Come here," he said again, raising his hand.

This time, I didn't think about the numbness and the coldness in my chest. I pushed past them and forced my legs forward. In three uneven steps, my fingers curled around his.

Aiden tugged me into his lap, fitting me against his chest so I could hear his heart thunder in his chest. His arms swept around me, holding me in place. A breath shuddered through him, and gods, I loved it when he held me like this.

His lips brushed my forehead. "*Agapi mou.*"

I smiled against his chest, and in the dark, I could almost

pretend that everything was normal. And in that moment, I needed that. I really did.

Just as the sun began to crest the horizon, thousands of students, hundreds of staff members, and those who had sought refuge converged on the cemetery that rested beyond the dorms, nestled against the fortress-like wall surrounding the back of the Covenant.

The cemetery was a lot like the one on Deity Island. Statues of the gods oversaw the massive mausoleums and graves, and hyacinths bloomed year-round. To me, those flowers had always served as a twisted reminder of what could happen if you were favored by a god.

I wondered if there'd be a flower named after me one day. *Alexandrias* had a nice ring to it. Hopefully they would be beautiful, like a dense spike of vibrant red flowers, and not look like something you'd find growing up from a crack in the pavement.

In death, a half and a pure were treated as equals, and like my mom had once said, it was the only time the two races would rest side by side. But things were still segregated amongst the living, even when there was no greater time than now for halfs and pures to come together as one.

Pures took center stage, situated in front of the funeral pyres. It didn't seem to matter that only one of the linen-wrapped bodies had belonged to a pure, and the other three bodies belonged to halfs. Ritual and law decreed that pures got first-row seating, and so they did. Behind the pure-blooded Council members, students, pure Guards and Sentinels, and civilians, stood the half-bloods. I knew they could barely see the pyres or hear the memorial speech being given by Diana and another Head Minister.

Our group stood off to the left of the masses, there but separate. We had followed the somber procession through the campus just before dawn, and the eight of us had moved as a collective group to the side, as if we all agreed without words that we would be a part of this but would not separate into the class structure.

One would think most of the eyes would be faced forward at a funeral, but they weren't. A lot of people stared at our group, namely Aiden and me. Some of the stares were openly hostile. Others looked disgusted. Those looks came from the pures. The halfs just seemed shocked and awed.

Aiden's hand tightened around mine.

I glanced up at him, and he gave me a faint smile. There was no way he didn't know half the congregation was staring at us, but he held onto my hand. I think he knew I needed that connection.

It was funny how things were so different. Before everything had happened, whenever Seth was around large groups of halfs, he got stared at in wonder.

I got stared at because I was holding hands with a pure-blood. How messed up was that?

Looking over the crowd, I caught the eye of a pure-blooded student. Pures looked just like halfs, but all of us had this gods-given, wonky ability of sensing the difference between the two. He stared at us like he wanted to rip my hand out of Aiden's and then take a day's worth of time to explain why we shouldn't be holding hands.

My eyes narrowed on him as I raised my free hand and scratched the bridge of my nose . . . with my middle finger.

The pure's head whipped forward. Back in the day, I probably would've been beaten for that, but I was the Apollyon, so I doubted he'd go tattle. And honestly, there were much bigger problems than a half and a pure being naughty.

Tightening my grip on Aiden's hand, I forced my gaze to the pyres. The words spoken were in ancient Greek, and for one of the first times in my life, it didn't translate into "wha-wha-wha." I understood the language, and the words were powerful and moving, prayers and accolades truly fit for those who'd died by Ares' hand, but there was something missing. Not that Diana or the other minister was doing anything wrong. I didn't understand it at first, but then I got it.

What was missing . . . it was *inside* me.

The words spoken meant something, and I felt the somber pall hanging over the campus. As the torches were placed along the foot of the pyres, I even thought about Lea and how she deserved this kind of burial, not a hastily dug grave out in the middle of nowhere. My chest ached for her and all those who were being mourned.

I mourned.

But while I felt these things, I really didn't *feel* them. The sharp pang of grief, a feeling I'd become well familiar with over the past year, was numbed. When the orangey flames licked into the air and covered the bodies like blankets, I didn't turn away like I always did. The finality of it was muted. There was this ball of coldness deep in my chest, sharp shards of ice in my veins, and every so often fear, spiked like the flames.

Fear and pain were things I did feel—they were real, and tangible enough that I could taste them. Everything else was dulled, like I was disconnected and detached from the rest of the human scale of emotions, and I didn't understand why.

Realizing this caused that very fear to skyrocket, bringing along a nice little dose of anxiety, and it figured that, since fear and apprehension were like two peas in a messed-up pod, it made sense that if I felt one, I'd feel the other.

My heart was pounding like a jackhammer and my palms were sweaty by the time the funeral was over and the sun was directly overhead. The crowd started to move back toward the campus. There'd be a feast in the memory of those who were lost, and most of group was attending it. Marcus had left to join Diana. Solos was chatting it up with Val, and Luke and Deacon were walking ahead with Olivia.

Air sawed in and out of my lungs at an alarming rate, and I only became aware of how slowly we were walking because there was a good distance between us and the crowd ahead.

The cord was spazzing out. Maybe it was reaction to my anxiety levels or something, but sights and sounds were amplified. The calls of the birds were shrill. Leaves rustled like a thousand papers crinkling. The sun was too bright, conversation from the mass of people too loud. Gods, the pressure came out of nowhere, clamping down on my chest—holy crap, it was hard to breathe—like someone had put vise grips on me. A sharp, hot tingle swept up my spine and spread along my head.

There was something definitely wrong with me, and it wasn't of the panic attack variety. Running through my head on repeat was one thought: why couldn't I really *feel* anything other than this? Where was the grief? Why did my chest feel empty and cold unless I was angry or scared? But last night, when I'd been in Aiden's arms, the numbness hadn't felt so bad, like the lid had been unscrewed just a bit more. And I was normally a pretty emotional person. In any given day, I experienced a hundred different things like I was trying ice cream flavors.

This wasn't right or normal, and it terrified me.

I stopped suddenly, and so did Aiden. Holding onto my hand, he looked over his shoulder at me. "Alex?"

My chest hurt. "I can't feel anything."

Facing me fully, he cocked his head to the side, brows lowered. "What do you mean?"

I placed my free hand on my chest. "I can't feel anything *in* here."

Aiden started to let go of my hand, but I held on for dear life. "What's happening?"

"I don't know." I took a shallow breath. "I can't feel anything except—except fear and pain. Everything else feels muted. I can't cry—I didn't even cry when I saw my mom."

Shock flickered across his striking face. "You saw your mom?"

"See!" Panic dug in with rotten claws. "I didn't even tell you about that, and I tell you everything. I haven't even *thought* about it, not really. I'm like meh. Everything is meh."

Concern replaced the surprise as he shifted closer. "Do you think it's Seth?"

I shook my head so fast the choppy hair smacked my cheeks. "He's not talking to me."

"But that doesn't mean it's not him," he reasoned, and anger flashed among the concern.

"It doesn't make sense. What does he have to gain from doing this? Then again, does it have to make sense?" I pulled free then, tugging the hair back from my face. "What if I'm broken? What if this is how I'm always going to feel? What—"

"Whoa. Slow down, Alex." Aiden cupped my cheeks. "You're not broken. You're not going to always feel this way. You've been through some crazy stuff. It's going to take time for you to process everything. Take a deep breath. Come on, just a deep breath. Inhale, and let it out slowly."

I gripped his wrists, barely able to get my fingers around them, and did what he said. "Okay. I'm breathing."

"Good." The silver hue of his eyes was my entire world. "Keep breathing with me."

I kept breathing, but I also started moving. I don't know why I did what I did next. Maybe it was because if I didn't really feel this, I was screwed six ways from Sunday. Rising up on the tips of my toes, I kissed Aiden.

Yeah, totally not appropriate after-funeral behavior.

But I kissed him.

I needed to feel something other than numbness, pain, and anger, if only for a little bit. And when Aiden kissed me, I'd always felt so many emotions I was dizzy from them.

Aiden lifted his head slightly. "Did you feel that?"

"Yes," I breathed, shivering as our lips brushed.

His lips curved into a one-sided smile. "I was kind of hoping you'd say you didn't so I'd have a really good excuse to kiss you again."

My fingers dug into his arms. "You don't need an excuse."

And I didn't have to wait long. His lips were on mine again, an incredibly gentle sweep that sent another tremble through me. It was slow and soft, kicking my heart rate up. The tingling in the back of my neck resided and returned, spreading across my belly and lower, but it was a different sensation. I *felt* Aiden—I *felt* love in his arms, and I didn't want to lose that feeling.

Desperate to keep the numbness and colder, darker feelings at bay, I pressed against him, practically stepping on his shoes. He was so much taller than me, but we made it work. Well, Aiden did. The arm around my waist tightened, and I was lifted onto the tips of my toes. He supported most of my weight as I reached a hand up, threading my fingers through the hair resting against the nape of his neck. Heat swept through my veins; it felt like it had when Seth lent me his energy. Like I was opening my eyes again and coming alive. Glyphs rushed to the surface and spread across my skin.

So all I needed to do was kiss Aiden to feel something real and good?

Sign me up for that.

But in the back of my mind, I knew that wasn't normal, or right, or half a dozen other things. I ignored that annoying voice because, seriously, that voice wasn't helping right now. I deepened the kiss, parting his lips and sweeping my tongue inside his mouth. A deep, sexy sound rose up from his chest, and his other hand wrapped around the back of my head.

"Alex." There was a soft warning in his voice.

"What?"

His head tilted to the side, causing his nose to brush mine. "You don't know what you're doing."

I almost laughed. "I know exactly what I'm doing."

"Gods . . ." Aiden cradled my cheek as he shifted my hips closer to his. My stomach dipped in such a pleasant way. "You've been through a lot. You're still healing and—"

"And what?"

"I'm not perfect. I only have so much control." His eyes were like heated quicksilver. "And if you keep kissing me like that, we won't even make it somewhere private."

Oh, me likie the sound of that. "And there's something wrong with that?"

"No. Yes." He pressed his forehead to mine, and the once-wonderful dipping motion suddenly twisted. "You've been—"

"I'm okay. I'm better than okay when I'm like this with you." A desperate edge rose to my voice as I clutched his arm. "I need this. I need *you*, Aiden. Please don't—"

Aiden's mouth crashed into mine. Whatever I had said was like finding the map to a treasure. Bam. Right there. His kiss swept me up into a place where I wasn't thinking. There was no Ares. No looming battle to plan for. No Seth. No pain or fear. All I felt was warmth and love and *Aiden*.

All I felt was him.

We made it into the closest building—the training center. Aiden opened the first door he found unlocked. A supply closet. It would work.

Our gazes locked. His were like liquid pools of silver, and his chest rose sharply. "We need to talk about what you told me," he said.

"I know."

"But not right now."

A breath caught in my throat.

In one powerful lunge, he was on me. Our mouths came together as he backed me up. My hip bumped into a cart. Folded white towels toppled to the floor. There was an ache in my bones, but a deeper one drove me to ignore the pain. "When you were in that room, I thought . . ." He kissed me again as his hands dropped to my hips. They trembled. "I thought I'd never have this with you again. Gods, Alex, I . . ."

I brought out mouths together, silencing both our fears. Aiden's fingers were tight on my waist as he lifted me up, placing me on the now-cleared cart. My heart skipped a beat as his lips trailed across my forehead and my cheek. There was a lot we should be doing, but at the moment, nothing seemed more important than this.

We kissed like it was the last time we'd have the luxury of drinking each other in. My breath caught again. Coldness seeped into me like a chilly, rainy day. My insides numbed. The moment that thought formed, I realized how true it was. There was no promise of tomorrow or the next hour. Ares could find a way in. Seth could show up. Aiden could—

"Hey, where'd you go?" Aiden asked softly, holding my cheeks with the tips of his fingers.

When I didn't answer, he brushed his lips over mine, coaxing them open with infinite patience. He pulled me back into the moment, away from the coldness building in my chest.

He gently tilted my head back. "Stay with me. Okay? Stay with me."

I curled brittle-feeling fingers into the front of his shirt, grounding myself in the feel of him. His lips touched mine, pushing away the invading numbness. He tilted his head, deepening the kiss and—

A shrill, eardrum-bursting alarm went off from somewhere within the campus, starting as a low hum that increased, causing Aiden and me to jerk apart.

Sliding off the cart, I glanced up at the flashing red light above the doors. I recognized the sound, knew what it meant. My muscles tensed as my wide eyes met Aiden's.

There was a security breach, and just like at the Covenant in the Catskills, I knew this wasn't a false alarm.

We were under attack.

4

Aiden flipped from sex god to warrior god in about two seconds flat while I just sort of stood there, rooted to the floor like one of the many statues outside. My lips still tingled in a pleasant sort of way, but the ball of ice was back in my chest, spreading like a winter storm.

He spun toward me, dipping his head and kissing me quickly. "We'll have to pick this back up later."

Then he started for the door.

I forced myself to follow him out of the supply closet and down the empty hall. Sirens continued to scream, and the whole time all I could think was that Ares was back and trying to get past whatever wards Apollo had thrown down. It couldn't be Seth, because I didn't feel him.

My steps were slow, but Aiden's were long, purposeful strides. He was ready to face whatever waited outside. I wasn't. In my chest, my heart was throwing itself against my ribs, and my palms were sweating again. The rush of nervous energy made me feel sick. An image of the shattered aquarium and the vibrant-colored fish flopping on the floor filled my head, followed by the sound of Ares' cold, taunting laugh.

I can't do this again.

Air punched from my lungs in an unsteady rush as Aiden pushed open the heavy double doors. I had to do this. Battle was what I'd prepared for, and as a Sentinel, we could be walking into a fight at any given moment. That was why two Covenant daggers were attached to Aiden's legs, hanging from his black tactical pants. The same were secured to my thighs, their weight so familiar that I'd forgotten them.

A Sentinel never left home without them.

Reaching down, I curved my fingers along their slender handles. This is what I'd trained for. Well, kind of. I'd trained to face daimons, not a cray cray God of War.

I have to do this.

Outside, we headed toward the front of the campus. Several Guards had taken up defensive stances outside the coliseum-style building that held the common rooms and cafeterias. Most of the campus would be in there right now for the feast, but as we rounded the building, pure-blooded students were being ushered inside, their faces pale and fearful.

I wondered if I had the same look on my face. If so, I bet that wasn't very reassuring to them.

"What's going on?" Aiden asked one of the Guards.

The half-blood shook his head. "Something's going down at the wall. We've been ordered to get all the pures into one safe area."

"It can't be what they said," another Guard said, eyes wide as he gripped the handle of his Glock, his attention being pulled toward a group of pures who appeared from the side of the building. "Hey! You all need to get inside. Now!"

"What did they say?" I asked, happy to hear my voice didn't crack, but there was no answer. The Guards were distracted with the lagging group of pures. "Never mind, then," I muttered.

Before I could start forward, though, Aiden turned to me, putting his hands on my shoulders. "You should stay back."

"Huh?" It was the only thing I could come up with.

Determination flashed in his gunmetal gray eyes. "Alex, you're not completely healed, and we have no idea what the hell is happening up there."

A big, really irresponsible part of me wanted to say "okay" and skip into the building to join the frightened masses, but no matter how scared I was, I would not fall apart. "I'm fine, Aiden. I—"

"You are a lot of things, Alex. Strong. Brave. Beautiful. Incredibly sexy," he said with a quick grin. "But you are *not* fine. You and I both know that."

Okay. He had a point. "You're right, but you don't understand. I can't hide. If I do . . ." I took a deep breath and decided to be honest for once. Go me. "If I don't go out to that wall and face whatever's there, I never will. You get that? And I can't let myself do that. I have to . . . I have to get over this."

And that was true. So much was riding on me. I needed to face Seth and transfer the power of the God Killer from him to me, and that was going to require a major throwdown between us. Then I'd have to face Ares. I couldn't wimp out because I got my ass handed to me. I needed to pick myself up and get going. I'd done it before.

But this time is different, whispered that annoying voice that sounded so much like me.

I ignored the voice. "I have to do this or . . ." Or I would hide again.

Aiden looked away, drawing in a deep breath. His shoulders tensed, and I knew he was going to argue with total Aiden logic. He let out the breath. "Okay. But stick close to me. If it gets out of hand, and if I think you can't handle it, I'm throwing you over my shoulder. Do you understand?"

Color me surprised—and a little annoyed—about the high-handed statement, but I got that it was coming from a good place, and the sirens weren't shutting up anytime soon. I nodded.

"Deal?"

I sighed. "Deal."

"Then let's do this."

Picking up my pace, I forced my tired muscles to work as we jogged down the pathway. As we got closer, we were joined by several more Sentinels, and I could already see a couple dozen near the wall.

The sirens eased off, but the thick, unnatural tension hanging in the air like heavy clouds told me that whatever had happened hadn't ended. Scanning the grounds, I felt my stomach dip. To our left, a small group of Guards and Sentinels crouched, circling something. I recognized Luke, Olivia, and Solos, and I wasn't surprised to see them in the thick of things. They didn't hesitate. Even though Luke and Olivia hadn't technically graduated, they were Sentinels.

I, on the other hand, was a poser in black.

Solos straightened, tucking back a strand of shoulder-length brown hair that had escaped his low ponytail. He turned at the sound of Aiden's voice, and the jagged scar stood out against his abnormally pale cheeks.

I didn't hear what he was saying. My gaze was fixed on what the other Sentinels were staring at.

A body was on the ground, totally unrecognizable. Male? Female? No clue. It had been a Sentinel, that much I could tell from the tattered remains of the black uniform. The skin and clothing looked like they had been *pecked* away until only thin slices of flesh and muscle remained. Even the eyelids and eyeballs were removed.

My stomach turned. "Good gods . . ."

Olivia rose, smoothing her hands along her thighs. That's when I saw the other Sentinel on the ground, knees bent and hands clenching over her stomach. Blood streamed across them. Deep, vengeful cuts tore through her cheeks. Her left eye was a bloody mess. Moaning softly, she was trying to stay still as another woman wrapped white gauze around her face, covering her destroyed eye.

"They were out doing rounds, down by the burnt-out cars. They're saying they came out of nowhere," Olivia told me in a hushed voice. "She almost got taken out by them pulling him back to the gate."

I tore my gaze from the body. "*What* came out of nowhere?"

Olivia opened her mouth, but the eeriest high-pitched squawk I'd ever heard cut her off. It was a constant crescendo of harsh screeching.

Several shots boomed and my chin jerked up. Beyond the wall, a dark cloud zoomed across the horizon, heading straight for us. Except it wasn't a cloud.

I took a step back, my hands going to the daggers.

The cloud arced up and shattered into hundreds of mother-freaking crows.

My jaw dropped open. "Holy crows . . ."

"There's a couple of eagles mixed in there," Luke commented.

"And a few hawks," Aiden added.

I rolled my eyes. "Okay. Holy birds of prey! Is that better?"

"Much," Aiden murmured.

The birds blanketed the sky, so thick they eclipsed the sun for a moment. I'd never seen anything like it. They swirled overhead, a dark, ever-expanding funnel. They changed course suddenly, flying down toward us like little, winged torpedoes with sharp claws and beaks. I thought of the flayed body and almost hurled.

"They're possessed!" shouted a Guard. Dirt streaked his white uniform.

I wanted to thank the guy for the obvious. I wasn't an animal specialist, but I knew birds didn't go psychotic for no reason, which meant there had to be daimons nearby . . . either them or a god. A god could influence our feathered friends. But my smartass response died on my tongue when the birds from hell swooped.

They were on us in seconds.

Dipping down, Olivia shrieked as she batted one away. "Ah! Birds! Why did it have to be birds?"

I smacked one before it got its gross little claws in my already jacked-up hair. How in the hell were we supposed to fight a swarm of birds? Talons grazed the back of my hands, and the pain was sharp and quick.

Solos spun around, his arm arcing gracefully. A dagger flew across the space, tip over handle, and embedded deep into the back of an eagle that had attached to a Guard's shoulder.

Well, that was one way—a little time-consuming, but effective. However, I had a better idea. Waving my arms like a deranged crossing guard, I darted toward Aiden. He'd grabbed a hawk off a fallen Sentinel. Tiny red scratches bled on his cheeks.

"Fire!" I yelled. "Light the sky up!"

Luke was swinging at the sky with his blades like a cracked-out chef. "Olivia and I will cover you two!"

Sheathing the daggers, Aiden raised his hands, brows lowered in concentration and the line of his jaw tightened. Sparks flew from his fingers, and a second later, his hands were on fire. I reached over, wrapping my hands around his wrist. I took a deep breath, ignoring the wings that came awfully close to my cheek and the willies the feeling gave me.

Closing my eyes, I used the air element and pictured the flames moving up in a steady stream and then spreading like a ceiling of fire. Aiden could get the fire into the sky, but not as quickly and at the magnitude he could with my help.

"That's it," Aiden said, his skin hot under my fingers.

I opened my eyes. For a moment, I was awed. Using the elements was still new to me. Fire, a vibrant shade of blood-red, pulsed over Aiden's hand and exploded outward in a massive ball. Wind blew my hair back from my face as the inferno licked into the air, rolling toward the wall and back to the campus, consuming the birds in its path. The blaze wasn't natural, but a product of the aether that Aiden carried inside him. It ate the crows up, leaving nothing but a fine sprinkling of dust behind.

When most of the birds were destroyed and only a few were

left to dive-bomb us, Aiden closed his hands into fists and I let go of his wrists. Only then did I see the faintly glowing glyphs on my hands. No one but Seth could see them, but they still made me feel a little weird when they came out to say hello.

"That was so *Resident Evil,*" said Luke, his eyes wide. "Awesome."

I cracked a grin, a little breathless. "It was kind of Alice awesome, wasn't it?"

Luke started to nod but stilled when a Guard flew past us, arms flailing as he tried to get one of the remaining birds off his back. He frowned. "I'll never look at a bird the same way again."

Shooting him a look, Aiden stepped forward, snatching what I guessed was a hawk off the back of the yelping Guard. The hawk twisted in his grasp, and I got a good look at its face. The thing's eyes were all black—no pupils or irises, just like a daimon's.

I turned away from the sickening crack that followed. Once the animals were that far under the control of a daimon or god, there was just no undoing it.

Several Sentinels staggered to their feet, battered and cut, but no one had gotten it as bad as the two who'd been by the burnt-out cars on the access road and were most likely blindsided by the birds.

A shiver snaked its way down my spine, and my hands automatically went to the daggers on my thighs. Tiny hairs rose on my body. All around me, halfs and pures reacted to the peculiar tension seeping into our skin. My glyphs swirled, changing patterns and forming new ones.

"They're coming!" yelled a Guard near the top of the wall. His white robes flapped like wings in the wind.

I was kind of expecting a griffon to come out of nowhere, but that's not what slammed into the iron gate with enough force that it rattled the massive structure and split open the skin of the assailant.

It was a daimon.

Face as white as the Guards' robes and veins as thick as black snakes, the daimon backed up and charged the gate again.

Wiping blood off her hand, Olivia shook her head. "What is it doing?"

"Other than rearranging its face?" I flinched as it slammed the gate once more. "Maybe it's really hungry."

Daimons were pure-bloods that had become addicted to the aether in the blood of pures, and only within the last year we'd learned they could also turn halfs. They were what originated the whole vampire myth without the hotness. It started eons ago—something Dionysus had done, most likely when he'd been bored.

Most of our problems stemmed from the gods' boredom.

Another daimon joined in, then another, and another. Each time they whacked into the gate, I flinched. Their exposed flesh was mangled and bloody.

Solos was at the gate, able to pick off two of them by shoving daggers through the gaps. Daimons were highly allergic to titanium. It cut through their flesh as though it were water. They burst into shimmering blue clouds, one after another, but more joined in, bouncing off the gate. My gaze went to the sides. The hinges were weakening.

I moved, seeing dozens and dozens of daimons behind the ones at the gate. Aiden summoned fire, catching several of them ablaze, but they kept coming at the gate until the fire consumed them.

This was *so* not good.

But a frightening realization occurred. When I'd been all Team Seth after I'd Awakened, I'd learned he and Lucian were working with daimons, feeding the monsters pures who weren't siding with them. The daimons could be here because of Ares, or they could be here because Seth was coming. Either way, it was unlikely that this many would just show up in the middle of nowhere, like it had been during the Council meeting in the Catskills.

"We have to do something." Luke unhooked his daggers, eyes narrowing as he turned to me. "Can you do your Apollyon thing? Like you did with the automatons?"

Figuring I should do the same as Luke, I unsheathed my daggers. My hands shook, and I hoped no one noticed. "I can't promise I won't take the gate out in the process. Maybe if I could get outside, slip up behind them."

"Not happening." Aiden stalked forward. "They'd be on you in seconds."

With all the aether in my veins, it would be like ringing the dinner bell, but if I did get out there, I could do something. I could end this before it got out of hand. My mouth stayed closed, though, which was so unlike me that I wasn't sure I *was* me anymore. A week ago, I would've been scaling those damn walls.

Sentinels don't show fear.

All I knew right then was fear.

More slammed into the gate, causing the center to bulge dangerously.

"Open the gate!" shouted Aiden, grabbing a shoulder of a Guard. "If they break the gate, then we will have an open wound to protect."

"That's insane!" argued the Guard. "If they get past us—"

"They won't get past us. Have half of us form a line several yards back," Aiden ordered. "The rest of us will stay here."

Luke shook his head and muttered, "That would be the oh-shit line."

Beside him, Olivia snorted. Her fingers opened and closed around the handles of the daggers. "You know, this isn't too bad."

"It's not?" I asked.

She shook her head. "This could've happened during the funerals."

The gate rattled like dry, angry bones once more, and then the Guard sprang into action, shouting orders. Letting the daimons in sounded crazy, but Aiden was right. Even if we stopped this attack, we would be vulnerable with a giant hole where the gate should've been.

Half the Sentinels and all the Guards moved back, forming the oh-shit line. Olivia and Luke remained by the gate, ready for battle. I forced my lungs to inflate as two Sentinels volunteered for the near-suicidal mission of opening the gate.

Aiden stalked to my side, lowering his head and speaking low enough for only me to hear. "This is about to get crazy. I know you don't want to hear this, but you should go back to the common area. Find your uncle and—"

"I can do this," I said, and then repeated it in my head about five times. "And you guys need my help. I can do my Apollyon mojo without worrying about the gate."

His eyes turned into a dark, tumultuous gray. "Alex, I really—"

"Too late," I interrupted as the Sentinels threw open the gates.

Aiden whirled, and before I could take another breath, the daimons were inside the gate, swallowing the two Sentinels in a massive wave. He cursed and glanced back at me. I didn't need him distracted. Daimons couldn't kill me, but they could kill him.

"I'm okay." I tightened my grasp on the blades. "Go do your thing."

He appeared to want to protest more, but there really was no time. Dipping down at the last possible second, he caught a daimon in the stomach with his shoulder. The force of the blow flipped the daimon over onto his back. Aiden spun, thrusting the dagger deep into the daimon's chest. Within seconds, it was nothing more than a shimmery pile of dust. Aiden whirled, shoulders taut and mouth pressed into a slash of a line. He took out another daimon and then another. If Leon/Apollo had been here, they would have been keeping count.

I turned at the sound of pounding feet. A daimon was gunning for me, eyes as black as midnight oil and skin leeched of color. My muscles tensed the way they did in the seconds before engaging in battle, but it was different this time. They locked up completely. My mouth dried. My heart went straight into cardiac territory. It was like when I'd seen my mom in that alley back on the island. I was immobile.

You can't fight. You can't do this anymore. You're broken.

My internal voice was *such* a shit-stirrer. I was frozen. Around me, the sounds of metal clattering and grunts of those fighting amplified until it was all I heard.

The daimon drew to a halt, sniffing the air, and then its mouth dropped open, revealing a row of shark-like teeth. It howled.

My mind . . . something was wrong with it. I knew it was a daimon before me, and I knew I didn't even have to use my daggers. I could use fire or wind. I could tap into akasha, the fifth and final power that only the gods and the Apollyon could wield, but I didn't see the daimon. In its place, I saw one pissed off, seven-foot god. I saw Ares.

My breath burst from me in short pants. I took a step back, swallowing down the rise of bile. "No."

The daimon slammed into me, knocking me flat onto my back. The daggers flew from my hands, skidding along the dry dirt, kicking up plumes of dust.

"I gave you the easy way out," Ares said, digging his fingers into my shoulders. "But you chose this, and everyone you love will die because of it."

Someone shouted my name, and the image of Ares blurred around the edges. Ropey black veins bled through in his cheeks. Jagged teeth appeared behind a cruel mouth. A powerful shudder worked its way down my body, and the glyphs on my skin started to go crazy, like there was a god . . .

A flash of white light blinded me, and then the daimon exploded into a cloud of blue dust. A silver arrow plopped down on my chest.

"What the . . . ?" I picked it up, squeaking as it stung my fingers.

"I'll be needing that," came a soft, musical voice I'd heard only once before. The arrow was plucked from my fingers. "Thank you!"

I looked up and discovered why my glyphs were doing a cracked-out version of the electric slide on my skin.

Decked out in her bubble-gum-pink camo, she stood above me, silver bow propped against a shapely hip. Her red hair was pulled up in a ponytail, but the long, curly mass fell to her waist. Static crackled from her all-white eyes. "Are you trying to get a tan?"

Sort of stupefied by her appearance, I pushed myself to my feet.

"What are you doing here? Is Apollo—?"

"My brother is currently getting chained to some rock by our father because of Ares." She loaded another arrow. "Zeus is mighty upset, and of course is blaming Apollo for the mess. Like how was he supposed to know what Ares was up to?" She let go of the arrow, and it zinged past my head. A fleshy grunt told me she had hit her mark. "It's not our fault Ares got hit with the crazy stick about a hundred times."

Another arrow flew from her nimble fingers. This time it blew past my head, and I was pretty sure I was centimeters from having my ear pierced.

"And you need to buck up, buttercup," she said, her full lips tipping up into a megawatt smile. "Loverboy is about to be taken down for the count."

"What the—?" Her words sank through, and I spun around. My heart dropped.

Aiden was surrounded, two daimons at his back and two at

his front. No other Sentinels were around. The daimons were going straight to the pures because they, like Artemis and me, were chock-full of aether. This was good for the halfs, since it gave them the advantage. But not Aiden. Blood trickled from the side of his throat. A female daimon in front of him had blood on her pink, chapped lips.

He'd been tagged.

Aiden had been tagged.

Oh, that flipped my bitch switch from meh to pure "I'm going to cut a bitch" rage.

Whatever funk had invaded my system was overshadowed by my fear *for* him. Forgetting Artemis and her sudden, unexpected, and really bizarre appearance, I launched forward. My muscles and body knew what to do. Brain clicked off. Instinct kicked in. Finally.

I came up behind the two daimons and slammed my dagger into one of them. The other sensed my aethery goodness and whirled on me.

It screeched. "Apollyon—"

"Shut up," I said, dipping down as it swung on me. I sprung up, kicking and swiping the legs out from underneath him. "I know I smell good. I'm sure I taste good, too."

Thrusting the dagger down, I took the daimon out, and then popped up. Slipping under Aiden's arm, I went straight for the female with *his* blood on *her* ugly face. Flipping the blade back, I swung my arm, catching the female daimon in the jaw. Her head smacked back, and the pleasure I felt would worry therapists across the nation.

"Damn," Aiden said under his breath, and then took down the other daimon.

The female daimon charged me, practically impaling herself on my dagger. Blue dust blew into my face. "Gross."

Artemis was making short work of the daimons and looking disgustingly beautiful doing so. With her cheeks slightly flushed and her lower lip sucked between her teeth, she darted around, popping the daimons off one after another. And once the Sentinels began to realize that a god was in the mix, everyone pretty much stopped what they were doing.

The legion of daimons wasn't going to kill us. Nope. Artemis was here.

She sprang onto a tree trunk, spinning like a ballet dancer. Sun glinted off her silver bow. Three arrows flew from her bow, zipping between Sentinels and smacking into daimons.

Holy Hades' butt crack . . .

I did not want to piss Artemis off.

Within a minute, over a dozen daimons were nothing but shimmery blue piles of dust, and Artemis hadn't even broken a sweat. Not a strand of hair was out of place. Slipping the bow into the harness strapped across her back, she winked at Solos before blinking out and reappearing like right in my face.

"Good gods," I gasped, taking a step back. "Was that necessary?"

She cocked her head to the side. "Ares is playing dirty. These," she waved her around, "are from him. He led them here, and more will come. The First is on the move."

"Seth?" Aiden swiped his hand over his neck. "He's coming here?"

Artemis' creepy god eyes shot all kinds of static when she looked at him. A fine shimmer surrounded her, like she'd been dipped in glitter, and then the camo get-up disappeared.

My eyes widened.

A true goddess stood before us, dressed in white, nearly transparent linen that hugged her curves and revealed more skin than a thong. A silver band covered her upper arm. A moon hung from it, shining as if it had been dipped in light.

Her lips curled in a smooth, seductive smile. "Hey there, how about you ditch the little Apollyon over there and get with—"

"Hey." I folded my arms, trying to keep my own eyes on her face. "Aren't you supposed to be a *virgin* goddess?"

A soft, tinkling laugh came from her. "Honey, have you ever heard of kiss and don't tell?"

"Have you ever heard of a bra?" I demanded. "Because I can see your . . . you know. *Everything*."

Aiden cleared his throat as he averted his gaze, brows raised. Artemis laughed again as she turned her attention to me. "I will aid you when I can, as will the others, until Apollo can return to your side. We cannot allow Ares to continue. You must transfer the power of the First to you."

How she went from hitting on my boyfriend to all serious war-death-blah talk was beyond me. "It's at the top of my to-do list, along with—*hey!*" I leaned back from her suddenly outstretched hand. Her fingers grazed my cheek. "Stop it!" I jumped back as she went to touch me again. "Man, you gods are so weird."

Artemis wrinkled her nose at me. "There is something wrong with you."

"Uh . . ." That didn't seem very polite. I glanced at Aiden. He was staring at Artemis, but not in the way every other guy except Luke was staring at her. Correction. Even Luke was checking her out. "Care to explain?" I asked.

Her eyes narrowed, and then her hand snaked out again. I forced myself to stand still and let her feel me up, because seriously, she didn't appear like she was going to stop until she did. She cupped my cheek and placed her other hand below my breasts, between my ribs.

"Um . . ." I was really starting to feel a bit wigged out. "I really hope this has a point, because half the guys are staring at us like they're hoping we're going to make out."

Aiden coughed.

The goddess's lashes swept up. "There's something inside you."

"Well, I do have organs and . . ." I trailed off, remembering how Apollo's son had said the same thing. Concern swelled. "Like something that doesn't belong there?"

"I don't know." She removed her hands—thank the gods. "You should do something with your hair."

And then she blinked out of existence. Really gone this time, because the marks of the Apollyon calmed down. I reached up, self-consciously patting the jagged ends of my hair as I glanced at Aiden. He stared at me, looking like someone had punched him in the gonads. He opened his mouth to say something, and then he pivoted on his heel.

Having no idea what that was about, I took in the carnage of battle. Blood pooled over sparse grass and bodies littered the ground, some dying and others already dead. There would be more funerals. I saw that my friends still stood. Somehow, the relief of not facing another day without any of them was just a drop in the bucket of suckage.

Fighting was a desire and need that had been bred into me, as it was into all halfs who didn't go into servitude. Except somewhere between when Poseidon destroyed the Covenant on Deity Island and I woke up after Apollo returned me from Olympus, fighting had lost its appeal.

An entire life of this?

I thought about when I told Aiden I wasn't sure I wanted do this anymore, but that was back before Ares. Everything was different now.

My gaze found Aiden.

He was kneeling beside a fallen Sentinel, one who couldn't be much older than me. The wind picked up strands of Aiden's hair, tossing them off his forehead. He looked up, his somber gaze meeting mine, and I thought I saw the same weariness in his stare.

We both were so . . . so over this.

5

Long after the sun had set and the campus was calmed as much as it could be after a nearly disastrous attack, I fell into bed. Freshly showered, I'd stolen a pair of sweats and a T-shirt from Aiden.

I was exhausted but antsy. I knew I should sleep, because I would wake up to the big day to recruit for the A.O.A., but I stared at the ceiling, wiggling my feet until Aiden slipped in, tugging a shirt over his head.

My eyes dropped to those finely designed stomach muscles. Did it make me a bad person that, despite all the terrible stuff happening, I was staring at those indents on either side of his hips?

Aiden let the shirt fall, covering up all that gloriousness as he came to the bed. He bent down, placing his hands beside my head. His lips pressed against mine, and warmth flooded me, like it had before the Hitchcock movie came to life.

The way Aiden kissed me, well, it never ceased to affect me. Every time was like the first time. Butterflies buzzed in my belly the second our lips touched. My chest always fluttered, and I could never get used to the fact that he was kissing me. That we were together in spite of the laws forbidding it and everything that stood in our way, including each other. When he lifted his head, I let out a little sigh, and he kissed the corner of my lips.

Stretching out on his side, he leaned over my stomach, putting his weight on his elbow. "You should be asleep."

"I know."

"But you're not."

"Neither are you."

One side of his lips tipped up. "How are you feeling?"

"Okay." I reached down, my fingers brushing just below the tag he'd received. The skin there would always be a few shades paler than his natural tone. The bite had been so close to his jugular. Although he was a pure-blood, the bite could've taken him out of commission for a while, or even killed him. "What about you?"

He wrapped his hand around mine, pulling it away from his neck. He pressed a kiss to my palm. "I'm okay."

I tried not to let it show, but fear spiked in me. "You've never been tagged before."

"There's a first for everything." He lowered my hand, but kept holding it. "It's really not that bad."

I disagreed. "I want to kill that daimon all over again."

Aiden smiled then. A real one, showing off those deep dimples. It seemed like it had been so long since I'd seen him smile like that. "It was kind of hot how you popped out of nowhere and owned her."

"I need a shirt that says, 'I owned her.'"

"I can do that for you, but I like seeing you in my clothes."

A flush crept across my cheeks. "I probably should've asked."

"You never need to ask." He squeezed my hand gently. "Are you hungry?"

I groaned. "No. Gods, no. My stomach feels like it's going to burst from all you made me eat earlier."

He didn't say anything to that and closed his eyes. Thick lashes fanned his cheekbones, and I got a little lost staring at him. A year ago, I never thought we'd be where we were now. A year ago, I never thought I would've frozen in the middle of a fight either.

Aiden's eyes had opened, and he was staring back at me. "What's going on inside your head?"

Sometimes his ability to read me was frightening. "I hesitated out there."

"It happens, *agapi mou*."

The endearment almost broke me. "Not to Sentinels," I whispered, staring over his shoulder. "I completely froze, Aiden. I couldn't move. I didn't want . . ."

"What?" he prodded when I didn't continue.

I wet my lips and said quietly, "I didn't want to be out there."

"Who would?"

Pulling my hand free, I shifted my gaze to him. "You don't understand. I didn't want to be there. I didn't want to fight. I wanted to be anywhere but where I was, and when I saw that daimon, I thought I saw—" I cut myself off. I couldn't admit that I thought I saw Ares. He would think I was insane. "I just locked up. What if I do that again and more people get hurt or killed?"

"Alex, you're not responsible for those who died today." He shifted so that his face was right over mine. "Don't put that kind of crap on yourself. It's not right."

But it IS right, whispered that voice. "People expect me to fight and kick ass. You can't tell me the people out there didn't expect me to take out those daimons. And if Artemis hadn't shown—"

"You would've snapped out of it. Just like you did," Aiden said, cupping my cheek and forcing my gaze to his. "You're being too hard on yourself. What you've been through is going to affect you, and you're not giving yourself any time to deal with what *just* happened. You're not okay, Alex, but you're not broken and you're not damaged."

My breath shuddered from me. "Then what am I?"

"You're someone who is incredibly strong and brave, and who has been through way too much. Too many people expect too much from you. And it's not because you're weak. You're eighteen, Alex. Even if you were twenty-eight, all this crap would be too much." His fingers trailed down my cheek, the path slightly uneven from the raised scars. "You're the Apollyon, but you're only one person. And you're not alone. You have me. You have Luke, Olivia, and your uncle. You have Solos, and you have my brother, although he's a little crazy." A small, quick grin appeared on his lips. "And tomorrow, you'll have a whole army. You're not alone in any of this. You'll never be alone."

I blinked back the wetness gathering in my eyes. "I think you spend your spare time studying a book full of the right things to say."

He chuckled softly, and then his lips brushed mine in a quick kiss. "Nah. I just love you, Alex."

Raising my hands, I placed them on his smooth cheeks. The tiny scratches from the birds had healed over already, leaving behind faint marks. "I think I'd go crazy without you."

He kissed my cheek and then stretched out beside me, snaking an arm around my waist. In the quiet moments that followed, I didn't feel numbness or fear. I was content, warm, and I felt a little like my old self. Tomorrow was going to be a big day, and who knew what was waiting for us beyond that. I didn't want to think about any of that. Not right now.

I rolled onto my side and stretched up, bringing our lips together. The kisses started off slow, nothing like this morning when they'd almost had a fevered pitch to them, but then they deepened and my heart kicked up, thumping in my chest. His hand curled around my hip, tugging my body to his. Pressed together, a shiver danced down my back as his fingers slipped under my shirt, skimming the bare skin of my waist. My hand moved across his chest, and I wished I had some kind of Apollyon power that made clothing disappear. That would've been really handy right about now.

He eased me onto my back and slid a leg between mine. His tongue swept in, scattering my thoughts and pulling me in. A delicious tension built in my lower stomach, and when his body shifted against mine, I gasped. My reaction was immediate, rocking against him.

Aiden shuddered as he lifted his head. Those eyes were heated silver. "We need to press pause for a second."

I knew I couldn't have heard him correctly, because he moved his leg in a way that had me trembling, then kissed me again, nipping at my lower lip.

"Seriously, we need to talk for a second," he said, his voice thick.

A small grin pulled at my lips. "Then stop kissing me."

"That's an excellent idea." He pressed his lips to the sensitive spot under my ear. "Yet so incredibly hard." But then he did sit up, cross-legged beside me. "I want to talk to you about something."

The way he said that made my stomach dip. And he was rocking the "Aiden is being serious" face. "Okay. About what?"

"About what Artemis said to you out there today."

"About my hair?"

He shot me a bland look. "No. When she said there was something inside you."

"Oh. That? Weird, right? Apollo's son—Hippo-whatever—said the same thing when I was in Olympus." I sighed, trying not to be too freaked out by it. "I have no idea what they're talking about."

"You don't?" Surprise flooded his voice.

"No." I frowned. "Do you?"

Aiden opened his mouth and closed it. Several seconds passed, and then he thrust his hand through his hair, scratching his head. "Think about it, Alex."

Crossing my ankles, I gave a lopsided shrug. "Enlighten me, wise one."

"You're really going to make me say it?" He swore under his breath as his hand fell to his lap. "Of course you are. Don't you think there could be a possibility that whatever Artemis felt, or saw or whatever, means you're . . . pregnant?"

I stared at him. "*What?*"

His dark brows lowered. "Pregnant."

"No." I coughed out a laugh and rolled my eyes. "No way."

Aiden looked at me like I was half-stupid.

"What?" I made a face. "There's no way it could be that, because that just isn't possible. I would, like, know if that was it, and I would totally be . . ." Wow. I sounded kind of stupid, because it really could be *that*. I'd had my shots, but I honestly couldn't really say when the last one was, and who knew if they were really a hundred percent effective, or if they even worked on Apollyons, and when *was* my last period? And . . .

Oh my gods in Olympus . . .

I sat up, nearly knocking Aiden off the bed. My eyes were wide. "Pregnant? Bun in the oven? A little Alex or Aiden running amuck? Okay. A little you would be so adorable, but preggers? Oh gods, have I told you how much I hate the word 'preggers?' Like, is 'pregnant' such a long word that you have to shorten it? I feel the same way about 'hubby.' Seriously? Hubby and preggers are the stupidest—"

"Alex, whoa." He chuckled. "Slow down. Take a breath."

I tried to take a breath, but I couldn't get it around the word *pregnant*. It formed a ball of "holy crap" in my throat. "It can't be that, can it?"

His chest rose, and then he nodded. "It could be, Alex."

Whoa, I was blown away by the prospect. Pregnant? Me? I wanted to laugh, but if I did, I was pretty sure I wouldn't stop, and it wouldn't be the cute kind of laughter. It would be the hysterical, crazy-as-balls kind of laughter.

"That . . ." I let out a stuttered breath as I glanced down. I was half-tempted to pull up my shirt and start pressing on my stomach. I didn't, though, because that would cause me to have an absolute nervous breakdown.

"That changes everything."

I lifted my gaze, meeting Aiden's. His eyes were a bright silver, and my heart skipped a beat. When they were that color, Aiden was feeling something strong, something good, but I didn't know what to think. Pregnant with Aiden's baby? I could *not* be a mother. Seriously. I barely remembered to brush my own teeth in the morning. Being responsible for a child, especially in the mess that was my life? That kid wouldn't have a chance. It would end up getting eaten by wild coyotes or something.

One side of Aiden's lips tipped up. "What are you thinking?"

"What are *you* thinking?" My heart was pounding.

"I'm thinking . . . a lot of things, but if this is what the gods are feeling in you, we need to really think about what we're doing." He reached over, tugging on my bottoms. "I know this isn't happening at a good time."

I did laugh at that. "Yeah, that would be horrifically bad timing."

"But would it be so bad?" he asked.

The look on his face, the open honesty, and—*dear gods*—the hint of acceptance startled me. "You would be okay with this?"

Aiden lowered his gaze for a moment and then shifted so he was sitting in front of me. He took my hands in his, and I suddenly realized how serious this was. I was a little slow on the uptake. "This isn't the right time for us," he started, threading his fingers through mine. "Not with everything going on, but . . . but how could I not be okay?"

I was actually speechless. Someone needed to record this moment.

"I love you, Alex. That's never going to change, and although neither of us is ready for this, I can *get* ready for this. Both of us can, and we will face this together. I can't be that bad at being a father. I mean, I basically had to raise Deacon, and he's still alive." He laughed softly as a slight flush spread across his cheeks. "But if you are, we really have to think about what we're doing. I know neither of us can walk away from what we have to do—what *you* have to do—but we need to make some adjustments."

I couldn't even fathom what kind of adjustments we'd need to make. If I was pregnant, could I really go out there and fight? Could I transfer power from Seth? And good gods, what kind of kid would I be popping out? Part half, part pure, and part Apollyon?

This kid could destroy the world.

But Aiden . . . gods, I wanted to cry. I wished I could get those tears to fall, because I was so lucky to have him. So many guys would be in another state by now.

The tears didn't fall, but I could move. I scrambled onto my knees, and he knew what I wanted. His arms opened, and I crawled into his lap, wrapping my arms around his neck and clinging to him like an octopus.

"You're perfect," I said, my face buried in the crook between his neck and shoulder.

"I'm not perfect." His hand sifted through my hair, resting against the back of my skull. "I just can't be that upset over the fact that we might be having a baby."

I squeezed my eyes shut as a sharp pang of unbridled emotion shot through me. Among the hailstorm of fear and confusion, a fine, barely-there sliver of . . . of *happiness* filled me like a wisp of smoke. Halfs were products of pures and mortals and not allowed to procreate. Besides that, Sentinels didn't have kids—not even the pures who chose that kind of duty. They simply didn't live long enough to raise them. So I had never really even considered the idea of having a child, but this—if this was what this was—would be Aiden's child, and how could I not want that? Especially, even as unprepared both of us would be for something so major, Aiden would be right there with me. Not out of any sense of duty, but because he loved me and would love our child.

And *me*? On every day that ended with a Y, I'd probably be the most irresponsible parent known to exist, but I'd love it with every breath I took.

My gods, my brain felt whacked, because I never thought the day would come that I would even think that.

Aiden pressed a kiss against my temple. "We need to see one of the doctors here soon and find out so we're a hundred percent sure either way, and then . . . well, we'll handle this together."

Oh, wow. Making a quick trip to the infirmary for a pregnancy test? That was going to be so awkward. A thought occurred. "Marcus is going to kill you."

A deep, rich laugh rumbled up from his chest. "Good gods, you're right."

I started to smile, but then reality smacked me upside the head and that little wisp of happiness was extinguished. "I can't be pregnant, Aiden."

"Alex—"

"You don't understand." I pulled back and slid off his lap, scooting toward the head of the bed. I sighed as I tucked my knees close to my chest. "It's not like I'm denying the way that male and female bodies work, but we haven't done *that* since Ares came, and there's no way, if I was pregnant, a baby could've survived the fight."

The silver flare dulled a little. "I hadn't even thought of that. Oh gods," he said, rubbing his jaw. "How could I not have thought of that? It would be . . ." He shook his head, jaw locking down.

I didn't know what to say to that, because the chance that I was pregnant would be so insanely slim. An ache pierced my chest. When his eyes dulled, so did the brimming excitement that had been in them. I hated to take that from him.

Aiden moved so that he was stretched onto his side, then

patted the spot beside him. Biting my lip, I wiggled down so I was lying beside him. Neither of us said anything, because I don't think either of us knew what to say. At some point, Aiden turned off the light beside the bed and then settled back beside me.

Long after I'd believed Aiden had fallen asleep, I took a deep breath, closed my eyes, and did something that felt incredibly insane.

I placed my hands on my lower belly.

My heart jumped in my chest even though my stomach didn't feel any different. Could I be pregnant and it—no, not *it*. It was a baby. It was Aiden's baby. Could *our* baby have survived the fight with Ares? Crazier things had happened. And in my life, I could almost expect that the impossible could and would happen. So even though I shot it down, there was a chance. I recognized that. I just didn't know what to think or do.

In the darkness, Aiden placed his hand over where mine rested on my stomach, and it stayed that way through the night.

6

Aiden left in the morning to scrounge up some breakfast. I offered to go with him, but he insisted I stay in bed and get some more rest. Nightmares had plagued me most of the night. Daimons breaking through the walls. Ares finding a way in past the wards. Loved ones dying all around me. My constant tossing and turning had kept Aiden up most of the night, but it was more than that. In the back of my head, I knew why Aiden had wanted me to stay. There was still a part of him that believed I could be pregnant. Hell, there was a small part of *me* that wondered the same thing.

Every time I thought there might be a chance, my stomach dropped and my heart jumped. I couldn't focus on that today, but it was the only thing I really thought of as I took a quick shower and got changed.

I caught sight of my reflection in the foggy mirror and winced. Even wet, my hair hung in way too many lengths. I needed to do something about it. Heading into the small kitchen and living room area joining the two dorm rooms together, I found a pair of scissors. Immediately, I remembered holding them before, after Caleb had died.

You should cut your hair.

Romvi/Ares had said that to me, and in my despair over losing my best friend, I had tried to cut my hair. Weird reaction then, but now?

I stared at the scissors, feeling a lump grow in my throat. Seth had stopped me. He'd been there for me the whole time after

Caleb's death, and even when I'd taken all my hurt and anger out on him, he'd remained by my side. We'd been two sides of the same coin, and if it hadn't been for him, the depression and self-loathing would've dragged me down.

What happened to you, Seth? I asked, but there was no answer through our connection. Nothing but the soft hum of the cord, and it really didn't matter what had happened. Everything that he'd done overshadowed the good things. And he was on Team Ares, and after what Ares had done to me I couldn't forgive Seth for that choice.

Sighing heavily, I left my room and headed across the hall to knock on Olivia's door. "Hey," she said as she opened the door, but her smile faded a bit when she glanced down and saw the sharp instrument in my hand. She didn't take a step back, but the look on her face said she wanted to. "What's up?"

"I was hoping you could do something with my hair before the meeting today." I started to wave the scissors but decided I'd look pretty psychotic doing so. "I kind of don't want to look like a weed whacker got hold of my head before meeting a bunch of people."

Her smile returned, lighting up her brown eyes. "Sure! I can do something." She took the scissors with deft fingers. "I'm actually glad you came to me because I wanted to offer, but I figured that would be kind of rude."

"It wouldn't have been. I know my hair is jacked up." I followed her into her dorm. "Thank you, though."

"No biggie. Come into the bathroom." Olivia had me sit on the rim of the bathtub, feet inside. She draped a towel around my shoulders and then picked up a comb. We were silent as she combed the tangles out, and then she finally said, "Yesterday was crazy, wasn't it? I've never seen anything like those birds. And all of those daimons?"

"I know. You and Luke were awesome, though." I stared at a bottle of shampoo as Olivia made a couple more soothing strokes with the comb. "Artemis said they'd been led there by Ares."

"I cannot believe a god would stoop to using daimons. There is something so inherently wrong with that." She picked up the scissors. "Keep still, okay?"

Sitting still was not my forte, but I tried. "Seth and Lucian were doing the same thing."

Olivia's hand stilled over my head. "I remember you saying that. I . . . I just don't understand any of this. I get that Ares wants war. Duh, he's the god of war. He thrives on this stuff. And Lucian? Power-hungry pure-blood? Check. But Seth? I don't get it. I don't know what they could be offering him that would make him do this stuff."

"Everything. He thinks he's going to get everything."

Scissors snipped. "You?"

"I don't think it has anything to do with me, not like that." I wanted to move, but I also didn't want my hair to end up being more uneven. "I'm just a . . . means to an end."

Olivia was quiet for a few moments as she maneuvered the scissors above my shoulder blades. "You know him better than I do. Seth always freaked me out, but I just never thought we would end up here. I never could have imagined any of this."

I don't think any of us ever thought this would be where we'd be sitting with the entire world on the verge of collapse.

"Are you nervous about today?" she asked, running the comb through my hair again.

"Yeah, a little. I mean, I have no idea what to say. I'm not the rah-rah kind of leader, and I'm not . . . very motivational."

"Just tell the truth." The scissors were back, and I sighed. "If Ares gets control of the God Killer and goes after Olympus, the gods will destroy everything in their path to stop him, including every pure and half out there."

"And if he manages to enslave mankind, pures will be next on his list." I frowned. "The whole thing sucks."

Olivia laughed softly. "That would be the understatement of the year."

"True."

She finished up the impromptu haircut, and I took a deep breath before I stood and checked myself out. "Wow." I leaned back, surprised. "It actually looks good."

Olivia rolled her eyes. "Did you think I would do badly?"

I shrugged.

"And you still came to me?" She shook her head as she backed out of the bathroom. "You've must've been desperate. Luckily, the shortest lengths were in the front, so it kind of blends in with the cut. You'll be able to pull it back and whatnot."

While my hair used to reach the middle of my back, it now rested on my shoulders, and without all the weight it was wavier than before. I actually felt sort of normal again. I smiled tentatively as I left the bathroom. "You did a really great job. Thank you."

"You're welcome. I'm glad I could do something." She patted the spot beside her on the bed. "Chill with me."

I shuffled over to her, sitting down. I thought about how Caleb had asked me not to tell Olivia anything about him and his life in the Underworld. It wasn't fair, because I knew Olivia still cared for him deeply, but Caleb wanted her to move on. It made it difficult, though, not being honest with her.

Olivia reached over, running her fingers over the back of my knuckles. "Does it still hurt?" she asked, looking up.

I fought the urge to pull my hand away. "It doesn't really ache today."

She sucked her lower lip between her teeth and slowly pulled her hand away. "I'm sorry."

My brows shot up. "For what?"

"For what happened to you," she said, clasping her slim hands together. "I didn't see you. Not until Apollo brought you back, but the way Aiden and your uncle were afterward. They were so . . ." She cleared her throat. "Anyway, I'm sorry."

I didn't know what to say at first, but then the words sort of blurted out. "I look that bad, don't I?"

"What?" Her eyes widened as she twisted toward me. "I didn't mean it like that! Oh my gods, I'm such a douche. I didn't even think before I said that. You don't look bad, Alex. The scars are so faint and I'm sure—"

"It's okay, Olivia. Honestly, it's the last thing I should even be thinking about." Especially considering what Aiden and I discussed last night and what might lie ahead. The urge to tell her about what could be a possibility hit me hard, but I really didn't know how to branch out into that conversation. "And I hate thinking about it because it makes me feel so shallow. Like, not even the acceptable level of shallowness."

"It's not shallow." She nudged me with her knee. "You're a girl. We're going to worry about stupid stuff like this. And if anyone says you're shallow for worrying about it, let's cut up their face and see what they think afterward."

I coughed out a dry laugh. "Wow."

"I'm serious." She winked. "So—" A knock on the door cut her off. She jumped up. "If it's Deacon, I'm going to body-slam him. He woke me up in the middle of the night because he couldn't sleep and Luke was out on the wall." She stopped at the door, twisting to me. "He made me put his hair into braids. And I mean those little tiny braids, and then he made me take them out."

A laugh bubbled up my throat. "Deacon is so bizarre."

"No joke." She reached for the door. "I swear to the gods, I could—oh! *Not* the annoying brother."

I looked up, spying a confused-looking Aiden, and I grinned.

"I'm looking for Alex," he said, carrying a plastic bag. "But I'm curious to know what my brother did now."

"You don't even want to know." Olivia stepped aside. "She's here."

"I see." Aiden lingered at the door, a slight smile on his full lips. "Like the hair."

I picked up a few strands. "Olivia did a kick-ass job."

"She did." He turned that half-smile on Olivia, and her cheeks deepened with color. "I brought some breakfast."

Hopping up from the bed, I headed toward the door. "Food is calling." I stopped in front of Olivia. "Thank you again."

"No problem." She sprang forward and hugged me. At first, I sort of froze. It felt weird, but good. I hugged her back, and for some reason, that felt like a huge step to me.

Aiden shoved about half a pig's worth of bacon at me. I mean, I could eat someone out of house and town on a normal day, but he watched like a hawk until I finished it all off.

"I really do like the hair," he said, after I returned from washing the greasy goodness off my fingers. He tucked a strand back behind my ear. "But you could be bald and I'd still think you were hot."

I made a face. "My ears are huge. That would not be attractive."

Aiden chuckled and pressed a kiss to the corner of my mouth. "Mmm, you taste like bacon."

"That's hot."

His hands settled lightly on my hips, and I leaned forward, resting my cheek against his chest. "Do you want anything else to eat?"

"Oh gods, no. I'm stuffed."

"Sure?"

I turned into his chest, rubbing my cheek against him much like a cat might when it wants to be petted. "I'm sure." I closed my eyes, knowing why he was suddenly all about stuffing my face. "Aiden . . ."

"I know." He circled his arms around me, dropping his chin to the top of my head. "I know what you're going to say, and I know what we talked about last night, but I think, before we completely rule out anything, we should be careful. You need to get checked out."

Once more, the idea of skipping down to the infirmary and asking for a pregnancy test was tantamount to sunbathing nude in front of a pack of daimons, but Aiden was right. Lifting my head, I met his gaze. "I will. I promise."

"Good." He lowered his head, kissing me to the point where I almost forgot about what I had to do. "You ready? Marcus will be waiting for us at the Council."

I wasn't ready, but I said yes. I quickly changed into a Sentinel uniform. The thrill I normally got from donning the all-black uniform was gone.

Completely gone.

You're not a Sentinel anymore.

Had I ever really been a Sentinel? The first time I'd put the uniform on and left to face my mom, I'd felt like one. The badass rush had filled me when I'd donned one after I broke the connection to Seth and prepared to enter the Underworld with Aiden.

I shouldn't be wearing this uniform now. The inner-annoying-Alex voice agreed.

But I kept it on, because I needed to look the part even if I didn't feel it. Strapping the daggers onto my thighs, I slipped the Glock Aiden handed me into the side holster. He patted my rear as I walked past him and, well, that made me feel a little better about the uniform.

My uncle was with Diana, waiting in one of the side rooms. There was a decent crowd out there, and the bacon I'd eaten was doing funny things in my stomach. Standing in the wings of the raised dais reminded me of when Lucian and Seth had turned on the Council.

Marcus still looked rough, but like all pures, he healed quickly. The bruises were fainter, and the swelling had gone down. "How are you feeling, Alexandria?"

One of these days, he would consistently call me Alex, and people would also stop asking how I was. "Okay. You?"

He gave me a tight smile. "Better."

Solos entered, and Aiden immediately started questioning him about the walls. The gate was holding. There'd been no more attacks, and scouts had been sent out, like the party that had met us at the wall before we entered the University. Luke was among them.

Deacon had been chatting with Olivia, but he'd quieted at that and sat up straight on the bench. His gaze shifted from his brother to Solos, and I was grateful Deacon hadn't seen the two Sentinels who'd been down by the burnt-out wreckage. His eyes, the only feature he shared with Aiden, were a bright silver. Worry etched into his features.

I made my way over to him. "Luke will be okay. He's an awesome Sentinel."

His lips tipped up in an uneven smile. "I know. It's just . . ."

No one, no matter how good they were, was truly safe, especially not a Sentinel. I wished there was something more I could say, but if Deacon and Luke were serious about each other, he was going to have to get used to the dangers Luke faced. It was a harsh reality.

"He'll be okay," I reassured him, and Deacon nodded, exhaling softly.

Val entered from the main room, a hand on the hilt of his dagger. His blue eyes were extraordinarily bright against his swarthy complexion. "Everyone's ready if you are."

My uncle turned to me and nodded. Full of nervous energy, I stepped forward, relieved when he and Aiden followed.

Walking onto the Council dais was freaky. After all, Head Minister Telly, the leader of all the Councils, had once tried to place me under the Elixir and commit me to servitude during a Council session. So, yeah, I wasn't a big fan of walking before the twelve thrones. All I could think, as I stopped in the center, flanked by two pure-bloods, was that I wished I had prepared a speech or something.

A lot of people were staring at me—well over three hundred, if I had to hazard a guess. In the back were all the Guards and Sentinels not on patrol, and the numbers were disheartening— maybe a hundred to a hundred and fifty. And most of them had to be from the University, meaning most of the others didn't make it here . . . or they had sided with the other side.

So not good.

Council members who resided at the University were easy to pick out. They were in their ceremonial robes: red, blue, white and green, representing the different houses of power. Fire. Water. Air. Earth. Council members who had taken refuge here weren't dressed in their finery, but the cool disdain of seeing a half-blood standing where they belonged was written all over their faces, as well as on the faces of many students and staff members.

One would think in a time of war that prejudice wouldn't be strengthened, but it seemed to only fortify the age-old beliefs that halfs were less than pures.

A Council member in the front curled her lips as she leaned over to another member, whispering what was probably a very flattering observation.

And then, before I could even open my mouth and say a single, embarrassingly inept attempt of joining the masses, a Council member in red robes stood and the real fun began.

"She should not be standing before the thrones of *Ministers*," he said, his hands forming fists against his robes. "This is not what the Council chambers should be used for. And a traitorous pure-blood stands there, too! One who used compulsion on his own kind. It's a disgrace."

Aiden arched a brow, looking wholly unrepentant.

I sighed and folded my arms.

A low murmur started from the back of the room. A student

shot to her feet. She was a pure-blood, a beautiful redhead who reminded me of Dawn, Lea's sister. "People are dying outside these walls, mortals and pures and halfs alike, and the first thing you have to comment on is the fact that there's a half-blood standing on the Council stage?"

The Council member whipped around. "As a pure-blood, you should respect the laws of our society!"

"Laws of our society?" The girl's eyes widened as she laughed. "Are you insane? I heard that daimons almost broke through the walls yesterday, and that a god was controlling them. Who gives a shit about our laws right now?"

I kind of really liked this girl.

Marcus stepped forward, clearing his throat as he tipped his chin up. "You may not agree with the use of the Council chambers, Minister Castillo, but that is not the point of this meeting."

As the Minister clearly stated why he felt this was the perfect moment to discuss his opinions, my gaze met Laadan's. I immediately thought of what she'd told me about my father while we were in Illinois. I'd hoped I'd find him here, but deep down, I knew he wouldn't be. He'd most likely stayed in the Catskills with the other half servants, protecting and leading them. Head Minister Telly had enslaved him, placed him on the Elixir, and even cut out his tongue, but my father . . . he was a leader.

And I was his daughter.

"This is stupid," I said, loud enough that it shut up the over-talkative Council member. All eyes were on me. I took a step forward. "We're arguing over whether or not I belong on this stage—this *stupid* stage. That's all this is. And these thrones? They're just chairs. Who cares? They mean nothing to me or to the rest of the world. They only mean something to you because you made them so."

The minister turned the color of his robes. "How dare you?"

"Oh, I dare." Tapping into some of the anger that simmered

in my stomach like a poison, I pulled it to the surface. "Yes, I am a half-blood. I am one of *many* trained to give their lives so you can sit in your precious *chairs*. So how about you show the halfs a little bit of respect?"

"Alexandria," Marcus said in a low voice, stepping up beside me.

I was on a roll, and there was going to be no stopping me. "But I am also the Apollyon. If I wanted to, I could blast your asses into next week, or use compulsion to gain everyone's agreement here, but I don't believe in forcing people to do things they don't want to. You could learn from that."

Several heads turned to one another. Whispers grew. The Minister tipped his chin up defiantly. "I see what you're getting at, but that does not change the blatant rape of our laws!"

"Rape of our laws? Whoa. That isn't insulting or anything." I shook my head at all of those nodding. "You people are insane. You don't get it. When Ares gets through the wards, which he will, he will be sitting on one of your precious thrones. None of you will be. And he will do with you as he pleases."

"He is a god," another Minister argued, a women in her late forties. "We are their servants. If he—"

"Oh, yeah, you'll definitely be his *slaves*. Maybe we should stop right here and invite him in. Karma is a big, fat—"

"Alex," Aiden said, shaking his head slightly.

I rolled my eyes, but took a deep breath and forced my gaze away from the Minister before I made him start squawking like a chicken. Honestly, that would make just as much sense as the words he was saying. I scanned the crowd. "I watched Ares kill people without lifting a finger. I heard his plans. He doesn't care about any of you. He sees pures just as you see the halfs. He will enslave you along with the mortals. He believes the gods should rule over the mortal realm once more, and that's a dangerous desire. He will make war on the mortals, on you, and any god who stands in his way. There will be no Council to argue over. There will be new rules and new laws to follow, and all of us will still be on the same level. I can promise you that. And if he succeeds in turning the First into a God Killer, then the other gods will rip this world apart to stop him. They've already begun."

Some stared back in disbelief, others wore masks of fear. One of the Sentinels in the back spoke up. "Can we even stop Ares?"

No, whispered that voice. *No one can stop Ares.* Pressure clamped down on my chest. Swallowing hard, I struggled to ignore the now-familiar anxiety rising within me.

"He defeated you. That's what I heard," said a student. "And you're the Apollyon. If you can't defeat him, how can any of our Sentinels or Guards do anything?"

"Maybe we can reach some sort of agreement with him," suggested an older pure. "Fighting is not the only answer."

One of the Guards scoffed loudly. "Ares is the God of War, not the God of Treaties."

"He *is* the God of War," argued the pure. "How can we defeat him?"

"So we do nothing?" asked Val from the side of the dais. "We let the fear of falling in battle lead us into surrendering? Is that how a Sentinel or Guard behaves?"

There were several shouts of disagreement, and all were from the Sentinels and Guards—soldiers who would never leave their posts.

"I don't know," I said, and again, the mass quieted. "I don't know if we can stop Ares. And you're right, he did kick my ass every which way from Sunday, but I know that no one is safe if he succeeds. I also know that we're not alone. We have Apollo, and Artemis, and other gods behind us, and we . . . we have . . ."

A strange feeling unfurled within me, sending a series of shivers like icy fingers all over my skin. I shook my head, causing a sharp pain to crack down my neck. I suddenly found it hard to breathe. It was like waking up unexpectedly and realizing I was already late for something.

"Alex?" Aiden stepped up beside me, his brows knitting. His eyes searched over my face. He placed a hand on my arm. "What's wrong?"

I saw him and Marcus, but every fiber of being was focused on *someone* else, outside this building and so very close. The crowd shifted nervously. A tremor coursed through my body. Deep inside my core, the cord snapped alive, thrumming frantically. The marks of the Apollyon bled to the surface, swirling over my skin. My heart hammered as tiny hairs rose all over my body.

"He's here," I said to Aiden, my voice a thready whisper. "Seth's here."

7

There were no sirens, and I knew there'd be none. Seth was too cool for that.

"Alex, hold up." Aiden grabbed my arm, pulling me to a stop just outside the Council building. Marcus was behind him, as was Val. "What are you doing? You just left in the middle of your speech."

"He's here. I know he is. I can *feel* him." Seth wasn't talking to me, but I could feel him in every cell. The cord was buzzing along happily, in a way it only did when he was near. "Tell Val to make sure everyone is safe, but I have to go."

"Something is happening at the gate," Val said, placing his hand over an earpiece. "I can't get a definite response from them, but something's going on."

"You don't have to go." Aiden's eyes turned a thunderous shade of gray. "We need to take a minute—"

"And what? Give him more time? No."

"He's right." Marcus stood at our shoulders. "What is our plan? Go out there and shake Seth's hand?"

My eyes narrowed on my uncle. "Actually, my plan was more to stab him in the eyeball and then decide what to do."

Marcus's jaw locked down. "I think you're missing the point. If he transfers your power or gains control over you, it is all over. We must think about this."

"He can't get control over me." My eyes flicked to Aiden's, and I willed him to understand what I didn't even really understand myself. I didn't want to face Seth, but I *had* to see him. I had to know that my instincts were right, that he was here and I wasn't going crazy. "We are so beyond that phase."

Aiden shook his head. "There have been no sirens, and Val can't get the Guards at the gate to respond. Think about that. We could be walking into a trap. *You* could be walking into a trap."

Seth could keep dozens of Guards quiet with a compulsion. That fact didn't change anything. I pulled my arm free, done with this conversation. Spinning around, I cut through the campus, heading for the gates. I didn't even look to see if Val was doing anything. Each step made the cord tighten. My skin felt stretched to the point of ripping by the time I passed the courtyard and inhaled the sweet scent of peonies.

"I swear to the gods, Alex, I will pick you up and throw you over my shoulder. You cannot go out there. Think for a second." Aiden was right by my side, head down low and his voice a low warning. "Remember what we talked about last night. If you're—"

"I remember," I shot back, picking up my pace. "And *that* has nothing to do with this."

"*That* has everything to do with this!"

I blinked, sort of stunned that he would yell at me, but how could I be surprised? Aiden would do anything to keep me— and the baby, if there was one—safe, but if Seth was here, there was no hiding. Nothing was safe.

Marcus appeared on my other side. "What did you two talk about last night? And yes, I know this isn't the appropriate moment for this discussion, but you two really need to find separate beds so there aren't any 'late night' chats."

I almost laughed, because wow, if only he knew how late in the game that advice was. "This isn't the right time for that talk. Trust me."

"That I don't find reassuring." Marcus thrust a hand through his wind-tossed brown hair, his bright green eyes narrowed.

"Alexandria, please listen to us. This isn't safe or smart. We have to *think* about this."

Aiden stepped in front of me, forcing me to skid to a stop. His hands landed on my shoulders. "You're starting to scare me. Okay?" His cupped my cheeks gently, forcing my eyes to his. "You're not ready for this—ready for *him*."

Alex?

I sucked in a sharp breath as I pulled away. Aiden's fingers trailed off my cheeks. The cord coiled tightly, straining inside me, and then expanded, yearning for its other half at the sound of Seth's voice. He came right through the shields. Was it because he was so close? Or was I truly unprepared because this was the first time that we had been near each other since I'd Awakened?

My gaze shifted beyond Aiden to the walls in the distance. *Seth?*

There was a pause, and then the cord snapped inside me. *We need to talk.*

I don't know what it was about those four words that set me off, but rage poured into me, so potent and so quick that I almost screamed in fury. "We need to talk." That, after everything, was what he had to say? I wanted to drop-kick that question into his face.

I took off, my boots digging into the loose dirt. Aiden shouted, and I heard him coming after me, but I was fast when I wanted to be, faster than him. I flew past the last of the statues and almost ran into a pack of Guards crowding the entrance to the wall. They didn't move, didn't speak.

They were *enthralled*.

"Move," I shouted, shouldering the Guards aside. "Get out—" The words died on my lips. I came to a complete stand-still, but it felt like the ground was moving under my feet. "Oh my gods . . ."

He stood a foot away from the closed gates, separated from me by iron and titanium. His hair was longer than it had been when he'd come back from the Catskills, falling over his forehead in a mess of blond waves. He was dressed as a Sentinel; all the black was a contrast against his golden skin. His impossibly perfect features were devoid of the typical, ever-present smirk, but the inky black marks of the Apollyon glided across his skin, and his iridescent amber eyes were fixed on mine.

Seth was beautiful. It was like the gods themselves had pieced him together, and in a way, they had. There'd always been a lack of humanity in his beauty, the whole time I'd known him. As I stared at him now, seeing him for the first time in months, there was something brimming in his eyes and etched into his features that had never been there before.

It made me uneasy in my own skin.

Movement behind him drew my attention. Luke stepped forward as if in a daze. He didn't even blink as he unlocked the gate. Hinges groaned, and then the heavy gate swung open. It was just Luke with Seth, but I knew there were others. Every instinct in my body told me an *army* waited over the crest, just waiting for the signal to attack us.

Seth stepped forward, his eyes only leaving mine to take in my altered appearance. That emotion strengthened in his eyes and face, and I refused to believe what I was seeing. In that moment, I wanted to kill him *and* I wanted to touch him. Weird, but I figured it had something to do with what we were.

"Alex," he spoke out loud, shattering the trance.

The very thought of him made my skin crawl. I wanted to find a wool brush and scrub all the memories of him out of my head. I hated him for what he'd become, for what he'd allowed, and I hated him for the fact that a part of me still loved him, because he was a part of me—a part that had turned on me like a venomous pet snake.

Aiden skidded to a stop beside me, breathing raggedly. He was talking, but I wasn't hearing him or my uncle shouting at the immobile Guards.

My brain clicked off—never a good thing for me and definitely not a good thing for Seth. I shot forward, sidestepping Aiden who tried to get between us as I drew my Glock.

"Make one move I don't like, and I'll put a bullet right between your eyes." My hand didn't shake. Whatever fear lived inside me was vanquished by the growing, nearly out-of-control rage. "I know it won't kill you, but I sure as hell know it will hurt."

Emotion flashed in Seth's eyes. It wasn't surprise. More like a lick of pain or regret, but then again, I was probably giving the douchebag more credit than he deserved. He slowly lifted his hands.

"Release them from their compulsion," I ordered, my finger steady on the trigger. "Now."

His amber gaze shifted to where Luke stood motionless with the Guards. He didn't say anything, but I felt the ripple of power brush over my skin like a smooth caress.

"What the . . . ?" Luke stumbled back a step, placing his hands on the sides of his head. He looked up, saw who was standing there, and sucked in a breath. "Holy shit."

Seth's stare swung back to meet mine. The tension in the air increased as the others came out of their compulsion and, for the first time in their lives, saw two Apollyons together. "We need to talk," he said again.

My head cocked to the side. I hadn't forgotten the musical lilt of his voice, but hearing it in person was nothing like the voice that came through our whacked-out connection. The cord hummed along, but out of the corner of my eye, I saw Aiden moving around to Seth's back, leveling his own gun on the First. I knew that, if Seth took one step toward me, Aiden would pull the trigger.

And I also knew Seth could disarm us both before either of us blinked.

"There's nothing you could possibly say that I want to hear." I took a breath, forcing myself *not* to pull the trigger for the fun of seeing him go splat. "And if you think you're going to be able to convince me to side with you after what Ares did, you can go screw yourself."

"That's not why I'm here."

"Bullshit."

His head tilted to the side, a near mirror image of what I had done. Again, his stunning amber gaze traveled over my face. He shook his head, and then he dropped onto his knees and closed his eyes.

Okay. Sure wasn't expecting that.

I opened my mouth, but there were no words. Glancing at Aiden, I saw he looked as dumbfounded as I felt. A keen wariness kept me from lowering my gun. Seth could be a tricky little devil, but this? I didn't know.

Seth's arms fell to his sides. He didn't speak out loud. *You're right. This won't kill me, but I deserve it. So do it.*

So stunned by what he said, I spoke out loud. "What?"

Do it. A breath shuddered from his body. *If it wipes out the memory of what Ares did to you, then do it. Do it!*

Taken aback, I stared down at him. *You felt everything, right? Everything that he did to me?*

Seth's eyes fluttered open, and I didn't want to believe what I saw in them. Regret was too late for both of us. "Everything," he said out loud, voice hoarse.

"What's he talking about?" Aiden demanded.

I shook my head as my stomach plummeted. *You know how I felt? What I wanted?*

He squeezed his eyes shut. *Yes.*

And you want me to take those memories from you? You really think a bullet will do that? Fuck that. I lowered the gun, hand shaking. Violent anger rushed to the surface. *I can't get rid of those memories, so neither can you.* "Fuck you."

On guard, Aiden shifted behind Seth. "Come on, Alex, talk to me. What's going on?"

"I never meant for any of this to happen," Seth said before I could answer. His eyes were open again, and there was no denying the pain in them. And there were only two things that waited behind that kind of sharp-edged hurt: anger and the truth. "I would never be okay with what happened. I didn't know he was going to do that to you."

"Is he talking about Ares?" A misleading, deadly calmness entered Aiden's voice as he stepped forward, the muzzle of his gun coming awfully close to the back of Seth's head. "That he didn't know what Ares was going to do?"

Seth turned his head to the side, looking over his shoulder. "I know it doesn't change anything or make it right, but I didn't know, and I would never be okay with anyone hurting Alex."

"*You* hurt Alex, you son of a bitch." A dangerous glint filled his gray eyes.

The First bit down on his lower lip as his lashes lowered. "Well, you have a good point there, *Saint* Delphi, but I love her—"

"Don't shoot him!" I warned Aiden, catching how Aiden's finger spasmed on the trigger. "Whatever you do, don't shoot him."

A muscle popped in Aiden's jaw. "I can't make any promises."

A weak, barely-there smirk appeared on Seth's lips.

"Don't," I said, slipping my gun into its holster, unwilling to take my eyes off Seth. Shock rippled through me. "Other than trying to piss you off, he's not trying to trick us."

Aiden's eyes widened. "How can you be so sure?"

How could I be? It was something I just *knew*. "Seth wouldn't bow to anyone unless . . ." I couldn't even finish, because Seth turned back to me and our eyes met again.

I'm so sorry, he said, and although it wasn't out loud, the apology rocked me to my core. Seth never apologized. That wasn't his thing. *I'm so, so sorry.*

Blood drained from my face, and then quickly returned, spreading along my cheeks. "He's not trying to trick us."

Aiden stared. "Alex—"

"He's not. I . . . I just know." My hands suddenly felt weak. "Why are you here, Seth? You know we can't trust you. And you can't be near me." Even now, the cord stretched tight between us, drawing me to him like a moth to an Olympus-made bug zapper. Part of me yearned to get closer to him in spite of whatever common sense said, how I felt about him, and about a dozen other things.

"I know you won't take my word or hear me out. You don't have any reason to. That's why I brought you something."

My stomach roiled, because the last time he brought me a gift, it had been an obliterated Head Minister Telly. "You brought me something? You bring me some bat-shit crazy stuff, Seth."

"You're going to love this." A little bit of his dark humor crept into his glowing eyes, but it quickly dulled. "Can I stand since you're not going to shoot me?"

"Like I said, I'm not making any promises," Aiden replied, his lips tipping up grimly.

Seth's chest rose. "I wasn't asking you."

"And I'm the one with a gun still pointed at the back of your head."

"Well, then," Seth murmured.

I sighed. Even though I didn't believe Seth was trying to trick us, I didn't fully trust him. And when he said I would love something, I would rather spin-kick myself in the face than see what he had up his sleeve. "Stand very slowly."

Seth rose to his feet fluidly, keeping his hands raised at his sides. Daggers and a Glock hung from his waist and thighs. I caught Marcus' eye, and while I'd prefer someone else but him to get closer to Seth, he nodded. He moved forward quickly, removing the visible weapons, and it was clear Seth allowed him to. We couldn't do anything about his deadliest weapons—the control of the elements and akasha.

"What, Seth?" I asked.

He tilted his head back to the gate. "Give them a second."

"There's movement outside the gates—Sentinels." A Guard gripped the handle of his gun. He took a step forward, held tilting to the side. "There's a Minister with them."

"What?" My gaze darted back to Seth. "Who is it, Seth?"

His gaze locked with mine. "The one person you want to see dead more than me."

I held his stare. "Let them in, but be ready for a Trojan Horse."

Seth gave a little grin as he turned his gaze to the gate. Aiden kept his eyes trained on him, and I was sure if baby Apollo walked through that gate and shook his baby butt, he wouldn't look.

My heart pounded as the first Sentinel came through the gates, followed by another. They exchanged wary stares with the Sentinels on our side as they stepped aside, revealing who stood between them.

"Holy crap on a cracker," I whispered.

Between the two Sentinels stood a completely out-of-it Lucian—my stepfather and the pure-blood responsible for Seth turning on the Council. I *did* hate that man more than I hated Seth. He'd used Seth's need for a family, for acceptance, against him, twisting it into some kind of sick familial bond. Lucian had never been a fan of mine, not since he'd married my mother, and one of the few reasons he'd paid any attention to me was because I was the second Apollyon. As long as he controlled Seth, I could give him what he wanted—absolute power.

His long, dark hair looked oily and unkempt, and those obsidian-colored eyes were glazed. He was definitely under a compulsion, but that didn't explain why he was here. I took a step to the side, my fingers hovering over the handle on my gun. "What is this?"

"He knew," Seth said simply.

My head jerked toward him.

He knew, he repeated, taking our conversation private. *We were at the Catskills, and I knew . . . I knew that Ares had left, but I didn't know that he'd gone for you. He didn't tell me that. He promised that you would never be hurt in any of this and . . . so did Lucian. I believed them. I completely believed them.*

I started to feel like I was going to hurl. I didn't want to hear any of this, but I had to.

But then I connected to you, and I knew something was happening. You were in so much . . . . Seth trailed off, his eyes drifting shut. His face tensed. *I went to Lucian, and I told him what I'd felt on your end. I told him how bad it was and how I hadn't agreed to this and never would. That I couldn't be okay with what Ares had done, and Lucian, he knew. He knew why Ares had left. He knew what Ares would do if you didn't submit.*

My gaze shifted to my stepfather. He stared back at me blankly. I didn't know what to feel as Seth continued, or maybe I was feeling too much. This man may've loathed the ground I walked on, as I was a constant reminder of my mother's only true love, but to know what Ares planned to do and be okay with it? Had he not felt even a sliver of compassion for me? Nothing?

You need to be broken. Lucian had said that to me once before. Well, if he agreed with what Ares had done, he had succeeded. I had been broken.

Lucian laughed. Seth's voice twisted up my insides. *He laughed, and in that moment, I couldn't do this any longer. When Ares returned, I told him I was going to find you and transfer your power to me. That you'd be weak enough for it to work, and that I was bringing Lucian to talk to those who were here and sway them to our side. Ares believed me.* Seth laughed out loud, the sound as dry and shattered as broken twigs. "I'm a lot like him."

"Ares?" I whispered, aware that everyone who had cognitive control was staring at us.

He gave a curt nod. "I get my . . . *blinding* arrogance from him. He wouldn't dare think that I'd disobey him. Well, he will soon, very soon. I doubt he'll be happy."

"Wait," Marcus said, stepping forward. "You two need to stop with the covert conversations. What the hell is going on?"

Seth ignored him and took a step toward me. He didn't make it very far before Aiden's gun pressed against the back of his head. "One more step," Aiden warned, eyes flashing. "And we'll find out how an Apollyon survives a head wound."

"You have no idea how badly I want to find that out myself," Seth replied, one side of his lips curling up. "Did I tell you about the time I slept—"

"Seth," I snapped, drawing his attention back to me. "Can you take Lucian out of the compulsion, or did you fry his brain?"

"I didn't fry him." His eyes met mine again. "I figured I'd leave that to you."

I didn't need to ask Seth to release Lucian, because a second later, Lucian stumbled forward, dragging in air as if he'd been underwater. His dark eyes cleared as his gaze took in his surroundings.

"What is going on?" he demanded, pulling himself away from the two Sentinels. His hands pressed into his chest. "Seth?"

"How many Sentinels do you have with you?" I asked Seth, staring at my stepfather.

"Hundreds," he replied, his voice weary. "An army of them, all loyal to me."

Lucian's head swung toward Seth. "What? Yours? Seth, what are you doing?"

"And he laughed?" Tears filled my eyes, but they did not fall. The hurt inside me twisted into something ugly and violent.

"Yes," came Seth's reply.

There was always a chance Seth was playing me, but I had no doubt in my mind that what he had said about Lucian was true. My stepfather had known what Ares was going to do. And he had *laughed*. To me, there was nothing more evil than that. Seth wasn't a completely innocent bystander. He'd made his own decisions, but Lucian had aided that process. He'd led Seth down that road. Maybe he hadn't held his hand, but who knew where all of us would be if Lucian hadn't had *friends* in higher places and hadn't used Seth the way he did.

I didn't feel calm, but there was an acceptance that slipped into my bones, mixing with the coldness inside of me. The only thing that was warm as I stared at my stepfather was the cord connecting me to the First.

In my head there were two outcomes. Being the bigger person was one. Revenge was the other. Two options, and that cold voice inside me told me there really wasn't any choice between the two.

Aiden shifted warily. "Alex, what's going on?"

Moving lightning-fast, I drew the Glock and fired one round. Lucian didn't make a sound.

Falling over backward, he landed in a motionless heap—his black eyes fixed sightlessly on the cloudless sky and his dark hair spilling out around him like an inky puddle of blood—with one small, titanium-laced bullet hole in his forehead.

Grandma Piperi had said I'd kill the ones I love. She'd been right and wrong in this case. I did kill Lucian, but I'd never loved him. I would've, maybe at one point in my life, if he hadn't treated me like the antichrist or, later on, an object.

Aiden swore under his breath, but he kept his gun leveled on Seth.

"Gods." Marcus exhaled hard as he stared at the Minister. "Alexandria . . . ?"

I stepped back, legs shaking. "That takes care of one problem, doesn't it?"

My uncle shook his head slowly, and in those deep, forest-green eyes, there was fear. I couldn't bring myself to be that affected by it.

Seth stared at me, almost like he hadn't really believed I'd do what I did. I don't know what he thought I *would* do. Pat Lucian on the head? Smack him, and have that be all? But that tortured tautness to Seth's expression deepened until I felt stronger stirrings of unease.

"Alex," Seth whispered, and that single word was heavy and sad.

Had I done the wrong thing?

It was a little too late now to be questioning that, I supposed.

The gun was still hot in my hand as I slipped it back into the holster. I turned to Seth. "I still don't completely trust you."

"I didn't think you would." The glyphs seeped into his skin, disappearing. "So what do we do now?"

Aiden snapped forward, cracking the butt of the pistol off the back of Seth's head with enough force to kill a mortal. Seth slumped over. Apollyon or not, that was going to take him out for a couple of hours. Aiden met my wide eyes. "I'm not taking any chances, either."

8

Seth was taken to one of the cells under the main Council building. The bars were made of titanium and the Guards stationed to watch him were pure-bloods, but if Seth wanted to get out, he was going to get out. We didn't have Titan blood or Hephaestus to build an Apollyon-proof cell, so we were taking a huge risk by housing Seth. But we really had no other option. We also had hundreds of Sentinels loyal to Seth on the other side of the gate, and who knew how long they'd remain there if they didn't hear from him. Only good news was that he'd be out for a while, but when he came to, well. I'd deal with that when I had to stampede that bridge.

Right now, I needed to shower.

Sweat slicked my skin like leftover residue from the adrenaline that had coursed through my veins upon seeing Seth, but it was more than that. I felt grimy and grubby inside and out, like I hadn't bathed for days.

I felt *dirty*—like, morally corrupt.

My heart was pounding a little too fast as I scrubbed until my skin turned a bright pink. I squeezed my eyes shut and took several breaths.

Had I been wrong?

Had killing Lucian been the wrong thing to do? Morally speaking? Duh. It was wrong, but hadn't he deserved it? Hadn't he had it coming to him?

"As a Sentinel, I'll kill daimons. That's not the same as playing jury and executioner."

The spongy loofah fell from my suddenly limp fingers, landing with a wet thud against the shower floor. My stomach roiled as I bent at the waist, nauseated. Water beaded across my back, but I barely felt it.

When I had pulled that trigger, I hadn't felt a damn thing. There had been anger right before that, even a brief welling of sadness in response to Lucian's cruelty, but nothing when my finger squeezed. As if taking a life was an insignificant action.

There was something wrong with that—wrong with *me*.

It seemed like yesterday when Seth had wanted to kill Head Minister Telly and I'd told him it was wrong. That even as the Apollyons, we couldn't make those kind of decisions.

But I had.

I had killed Lucian.

In cold blood, whispered that nasty little voice. *You didn't even blink.*

True. I hadn't felt a damn thing as I'd pulled that trigger, nothing beyond anger, but even then that fury hadn't felt tangible. Gods knew I totally had an anger management problem, but I had never snapped like that. Throwing apples was one thing. Shooting people in the head was taking it to a whole new level.

What was wrong with me? Better yet, what was I turning into?

Forcing several deep breaths into my lungs, I straightened and let the suds rinse off my body. I turned off the shower and grabbed a fluffy towel, wrapping it around me.

The numbness was inside me, seeping through the pores, coating my skin. I felt like I needed to take another shower and keep taking them until it washed away whatever this was.

I didn't check myself out when I opened the door and stepped into the adjoining room.

Aiden sat on the edge of the bed, hands resting on his knees. The Glock was next to him, and the daggers were unhooked, placed in a neat line beside the gun. He lifted his head, his dark gray eyes slowly moving over me until centering on mine. My heart jumped in my chest, and I felt the muscles in my lower stomach tighten.

When I was around Aiden, I wasn't numb.

I could feel so much.

Crossing the distance between us, I stopped between his spread legs. Aiden sat up straighter, his gaze questioning. Air hitched in my throat as he lifted his arms. I moved forward, placing my knees on either side of his hips. He folded his arms around me, sealing my chest to his as I rested my cheek against his shoulder. Minutes ticked by in silence. His hand trailed up and down my back in a soothing gesture that beat away at the numbness, but I wanted to feel more. *Needed* to feel more.

I rocked back in his lap and placed my hand on his cheek. A jolt of awareness ran from my palm up my arm. Unseen to him, the marks of the Apollyon bled through my skin, swirling down my arm until they reached my hand.

His lashes lowered. "We need to talk about what happened, Alex."

Talking was the last thing I wanted, right next to thinking. Feeling was the only thing I was interested in at the moment. I leaned forward, pressing my forehead against his. Our mouths lined up perfectly, and Aiden's chest rose sharply.

His hand tightened into a fist against the small of my back. "This isn't talking."

"I don't want to talk." I brushed my lips across his. Nothing more than a quick sweep of our mouths, but Aiden's embrace tightened. "I want to feel you."

"Alex—"

I pulled back a little and dropped the towel, surprising even myself since I was definitely on the body-conscious side of things at the time.

Aiden held my gaze for a moment, and then it dipped, and I

felt his stare as if it were a heated touch. Warmth rose to my skin as he dragged his eyes back up. Knowing Aiden, he wanted to do the right thing. There was a lot we needed to talk about—the numbness I felt, the fact that I'd frozen in battle the day before, the meeting in the Council, Seth, the fact that I'd just shot my stepfather in the head, and the possibility of us becoming very unprepared parents. The Aiden I *knew* would want to hash all that out, because every single item was important, but the Aiden I *loved* wouldn't ever turn me down again.

He placed his hands on the sides of my face and guided my head to his. The moment our lips touched it was like waking up after a too-long sleep. Sensation raced through my system, pouring into my bloodstream and chasing away the coldness. The kiss deepened, and I knew that Aiden was right where I was. We would talk, but it would be later. Much later.

"What is this?" Aiden asked, his voice deep and husky.

"What?"

His fingers skimmed over my hip and lower back. He was touching the oddly shaped scar. I stiffened. Grabbing his hand, I moved it away. I kissed him deeper, harder, drawing his attention from it until I knew he wasn't thinking about it any longer. His hands slid across my shoulders and then down to my waist, leaving a shivery wake behind. He tugged me to his chest and, though he was still in his uniform, his skin seared mine. Kissing Aiden was like taking a deep breath of fresh air after not being able to breathe. His kisses chased away all the what-ifs and strange feelings that had twisted inside me.

Aiden's lips blazed a path down my throat, and my head tipped back. He wrapped an arm around my waist as his other hand drifted up my stomach and then further up, eliciting a sharp gasp from me. A deep, nerve-frying sound came from within his chest, and every muscle under my hands knotted in response. His lips neared the sensitive spot, and his breath rasped in my ear. There was a painstaking moment when neither of us moved and it was just our hearts pounding in our chests, thundering in our veins, and then in an instant, the exquisite feel of his lips against my pulse wasn't enough.

I pulled back to get my hands on that annoying shirt of his and opened my eyes.

All-white eyes stared back into mine. Lips were twisted into a cruel smirk. The face was frightening familiar—chillingly handsome and devoid of compassion. "You can never win."

Icy terror froze the scream building in my chest as I jerked back, breaking the hold around my waist. I thumped onto the floor. Ignoring the burst of dull pain across my backside, I rocked to my feet and lurched to the side, grabbing Aiden's pistol. It was only as my fingers closed around the handle when I realized how fruitless shooting Ares would be.

I swung the gun around anyway, because I figured it had to sting at least, but I froze because it wasn't Ares standing there.

It was Aiden, his eyes wide and the color of the sky before a violent summer storm. His hands were at his sides, and his chest rose and fell sharply. "Alex? What . . . what are you doing?"

I drew in a ragged breath, but it never reached my lungs. A boulder had landed on my chest, crushing me as I took a step back. I didn't understand what I was seeing. It had been Ares— it had been him! His face—his voice.

"*Agapi mou*, talk to me. Tell me what is going on," he said, his voice hoarse but his eyes still holding mine. "What's happening?"

"Aiden?" I whispered, my hand shaking.

He nodded slowly, and the one word he spoke was hoarse. "Yes."

The pressure turned into slicing fear and confusion as I stared at him. The logical part of me screamed that this was Aiden standing before me, that Ares couldn't get inside the University, but I couldn't let my guard down, because if it was him . . .

"It wasn't you," I whispered, my finger spasming danger-ously over the trigger. "It wasn't *you*."

Tension pulled at his lips. "What do you mean? Because it's me. I'm here with you, *agapi mou*. I'm right here."

A tremor coursed down my arm as uncertainty spread into my chest like a gulp of too-cold water. I knew I should probably lower the gun before I accidentally did shoot Aiden, because it had to be him standing before me, but I couldn't do it.

"Is it Seth?" he asked, his fingers curling into his palms. "Is he doing this?"

"Seth?" I blinked. "No. It wasn't you. It was . . . it was Ares."

An immediate pain flickered across his face, spreading sorrow into his brilliant silver gaze, and I didn't like the look because it was such a deep hurt. "I'm here with you. I've been here with you this whole time, *agapi mou*."

The next breath I took scalded my throat. "I think . . . I think I'm going crazy."

"Oh, Alex . . ."

Those two words broke my heart in a way nothing ever had before. The ache in them settled in my bones like lead. I shuddered.

"Look at me," he said in a low voice. "You know it's me."

Then Aiden stepped forward, and he was the bravest being in this world to do so with a gun pointed at his heart. Slowly, as if not to frighten me, he reached out and gently prised my fingers off the gun. My heart turned over heavily. Without taking his eyes off mine, he placed the gun back on the bed and picked up a quilt. He draped the soft material over my shoulders, pulling it closed in the front as he pressed a small, tender kiss against my forehead.

That tiny show of affection broke me.

"I'm sorry," I said as my body shook. I'd almost shot Aiden. I could've seriously hurt him, if not *killed* him. "Oh my gods, I'm so sorry, Aiden."

"Shh," he murmured, wrapping his arms around me and gathering me close. He sat down on the bed, and I pressed my cheek to his chest above his thundering heart. I squeezed my eyes shut. "It's going to be okay, Alex. Whatever is going on, we're in this together, remember? And it will be okay. I promise you."

A new terror flooded my senses as Aiden held me, one hand curled around the nape of my neck and the other smoothing up and down my back. He rocked slowly, murmuring something that I really wasn't hearing because all I could focus on was one thing.

It was quite possible that I'd taken a detour straight into Crazyville, which would explain a lot. Would anyone be surprised? People cracked under stress all the time, and half-bloods, even though we were trained to keep our heads together, weren't any different. But did it matter? Not really, because one thing was true.

Aiden wasn't safe around me.

Aiden and I didn't talk.

I think he was worried about pushing things too far for the time being since I was obviously rocking a first-class ticket to certifiable insanity. After all, a few hours ago I'd shot someone in the head, then I'd hallucinated Ares and pulled a gun on Aiden . . . while I was buck-ass naked.

Talk about an awkward mood killer.

Somehow, we ended up stretched out on the bed, and Aiden finally drifted off into a fitful sleep. It was late, but I couldn't sleep. My mind raced with everything. If I was crazy, which I had a good feeling I was, how could I lead the Army of Awesome against Ares? This had trouble written all over it.

And Seth was awake.

He wasn't trying to communicate with me, and the fact that I knew anyway was freaky on a whole new level, but his consciousness existed on the fringe of mine. He was up, and he was antsy.

And so was I.

As quietly as possible, I pulled myself away from Aiden and dressed in the dark. I figured if I ended up putting my shirt on backwards, I could blame it on my lunacy. Going crazy had to have some benefits, right? Maybe I'd just go fully crazy.

I crept from the room and closed the door behind me. I tried to tell myself I didn't know what I was doing, but I did. Every part of me knew where I was heading, especially the annoying cord inside me. It was buzzing around like an over-eager puppy that needed to be smacked on the nose with a rolled-up newspaper.

Actually, *I* needed to be smacked with one.

Moving through the shadows, it took no time at all to make it to the Council building. The entrance to the catacombs housing the cells was heavily guarded.

None of the Guards looked thrilled with the idea of stepping aside and allowing me access to the First. Not that I blamed them. Everyone knew what would happen if Seth transferred my power to him, but he was here, and that fact alone was risky.

Solos moved up the narrow stairwell, his eyes narrowing as he spied me standing before the Guards. "What's up, Alex?"

"I need to talk to Seth."

He positioned himself in front of me. "Do you think that's a good idea?"

"Do you have any other suggestions other than knocking him out every couple of hours?"

His lips quirked into a grin that lessened the severity of the jagged scar running from his right eye to his jaw. "I really don't see a problem with that."

I laughed, but it felt and sounded forced. "Neither do I, but I need to talk to him to figure out what the hell he's really doing here and if the Sentinels on the other side of the gate are going to be a problem."

"They're probably going to be a problem," Solos replied.

He was a fountain of reassuring comments. I shifted my

weight impatiently as I tucked the shorter strands of hair behind my ear. "I'm not here to connect with him," I said in a low voice. "He doesn't hold that kind of power over me anymore. And besides, I won't let him get close enough to even try."

Solos looked away, his jaw working overtime. "I don't like this. Don't get me wrong. I don't think you're going to turn Evil Alex on us, but it's the middle of the night and Aiden isn't with you."

My brows rose. "And what does that have to do with the Apollyon locked in our cell?"

"I just feel a hundred times more comfortable when Aiden is around, especially if you're chit-chatting with Seth," he admitted.

"Aiden's asleep, and he needs to rest. Besides, I don't need a babysitter." Of course I did, but I sure as hell wasn't admitting that. "Come on, Solos, don't make me *make* you do this."

He regarded me closely and then exhaled through his nose. "*Don't* make me regret this."

"What faith you have in me," I muttered as he stepped aside and I walked past.

"It has nothing to do with faith." Solos was right on my heels as I went down the steep stairway. A wave of cool air seeped through my jeans. Putting on the tactical pants of a Sentinel had felt wrong, all things considered. "And no offense, I don't trust anyone. I learned the hard way many years ago, and I see the reminder of that every time I look in the mirror."

I bent under the low archway and stepped into a wide chamber. Seth wasn't here. My gaze fell to the titanium door across from me, and then I glanced over my shoulder. "Your scar?"

Solos leaned against the wall and folded his arms. "I didn't get it shaving."

"I thought you got it fighting daimons."

He gave a slight shake of his head. "I got it when I was nineteen."

As wrong as it might be, I was morbidly curious. "How did it happen?"

There wasn't an immediate response, and the cord inside me tightened with impatience. "I was out one night patrolling, and toward the end of my shift, I met this woman. She was the most beautiful woman I'd ever seen. One thing led to another and, well, I *was* a nineteen-year-old guy. It was a one-night stand, no commitment or exchange of names, and all that was her idea, not mine. Sign me up for that."

"Of course," I said, figuring out where their meet-and-greet had ended up, but not how a hook-up had resulted in such a scar.

"But she wasn't an ordinary woman, Alex. She was a goddess."

My mouth dropped open.

"Aphrodite," he said, tipping his chin down. "Apparently, she was bored and decided to pay a visit to the mortal realm. Wrong place, wrong time kind of thing. Or right place, depending on how you look at it, and who was I to turn that down?" One side of his lips tipped up as I gaped at him. "As you can imagine, good old Hephaestus wasn't too happy about that."

"I would think not," I said slowly.

"He gave me this scar." He gestured at his right cheek. "And he would've killed me if Aphrodite hadn't intervened. I pretty much had to make myself nonexistent when Apollo brought him to build that cell for you, but I have to say a couple of hours with her was worth it."

A surprised laugh burst from me, and Solos' uneven grin spread. "But I learned to never really trust someone when they say things will be cool, you know? And I learned to never, ever trust a god—or anything they create. They're the snakes in the grass that you never see coming."

*   *   *

Solos remained in the circular chamber, and as I walked down the narrow hall lit by torches on the walls, I couldn't help but feel like *I* was a snake in the grass. So was Seth. We both were dangerous beings created by the gods, and we could and had turned on everything and everyone around us at one point or another.

Maybe our violent natures were the product of those who created us. No one else in this world was more off their rocker than an Olympian god.

I tucked away Solos' story as I rounded a corner and saw the cell several feet in front of me. The light from the flames flickered across the titanium bars. A darker shadow was pressed against the bars, and it took me a second to realize it was Seth, his back to the hall.

Stopping a few feet from where he sat, I ignored the near-intoxicating pull of the cord—of our connection.

"Are you coming to knock me out again?" he asked, his voice oddly absent of the lyrical lilt.

I crossed the remaining distance, stopping just out of his reach. "I haven't quite decided yet."

"You can save yourself the effort. I'm not plotting a daring escape, and I don't have any plans to rain down chaos and destruction."

"That's good to know."

"Is it?" He turned his head, and his profile came into view. His eyes were closed, and the long lashes, darker than his blond hair, rested against the tops of his cheekbones. "Does St. Delphi know you're down here, Alex?"

My eyes narrowed. "I'm not talking about him."

One side of his lips curled up in a quick grin and then vanished. "Good, because I really don't want to hear about how happily in love you two are. I rather you'd knock me out."

Considering I'd just pulled a gun on Aiden, I wouldn't say there was a "happily" in that equation right now, but his comment took me aback. I inched to the side and knelt down out of his reach. "Let's be real with one another. You never loved me like that. You know that, right?"

Seth didn't respond for a long moment, and then he tipped the side of head back against the bars and let out a weary sigh. "You're right, but I never had the chance."

Again, I was knocked off-guard by his candidness. Seth was like the king of vague and unhelpful responses, worse than a god most of the time. I stared at his profile for a long, tense minute; the words sort of just burst from my mouth like a dam breaking under pressure.

"I loved you. It's not the same way I feel about Aiden, but I *loved* you, and you betrayed me. You sided with Lucian and practically held me hostage so that I would be forced to connect with you! And I still had hope for you. I *still* defended you. And then you turned me into Evil Alex and started a war alongside Ares! People have died, Seth." My voice rose and cracked as my legs weakened. I sat down, my hands limp between my knees as I stared at him through the bars. "And not just recently. How far does all of this go back? To my mom? To the daimons that were at Deity Island and killed Caleb? To all of those who died at the Catskills? Were you and Lucian using daimons then? You were, weren't you?"

There was another pause, and then his eyes opened. The bright amber glow startled me. "I'm sorry."

My chest tightened with pressure. "People are dead. People I loved. People I've never met, and for what?"

"If I could go back and change it all, I would. I'd never take that post guarding Lucian," he said quietly. "I would've gone AWOL if I'd known this was how it was going to play out, Alex."

My mouth opened as I shook my head. This Seth—this regretful, apologetic creature—was not the Seth I knew. "Your personality disorder is starting to show."

His lips tipped up in a wry grin. "Look who's talking."

"You have no idea," I muttered, and then louder, "Where did all of this go wrong, Seth?"

"When I was born."

My shoulders tensed. "That's not true, Seth."

"Actually, it is. You were supposed to be the First, Alex. All the Apollyons came from Apollo. I was created for this—for what Ares wanted. It was the same with Solaris and the First. So, yes, it's true. Everything went wrong at that moment." He laughed, but it was like all my laughs after Ares. There was no warmth behind it. "Hell, things went wrong hundreds of years ago when Ares decided he wanted to rule the world."

"No," I said, swallowing. "You've always done what you wanted, Seth. And you didn't know about any of this when we met. You made these decisions. You went—"

"Have you ever tasted aether, Alex?" He flipped around so quickly that my heart thumped. Facing me, Seth gripped the bars until his knuckles bleached. "Not like how a daimon feeds, but to have so much aether in you that you could do *anything* you wanted and feel *everything* you never could before? Did you know that it feels like lightning in your blood? Have you experienced the taste of supreme and ultimate power? Have you?"

I shook my head slowly.

"Sure, Lucian promised me a lot of things, and so did Ares when I met him in the Catskills, but those promises were nothing in comparison to what it felt like once you had Awakened. It was like tapping into pure power." A feverish glint brightened his eyes as they latched onto mine. "After that, I didn't need their promises, because I knew—*I knew* I could get whatever I wanted, I had the power to do so. And that power . . ." He let go of the bars and rocked back. "There's nothing like it, Alex. I became addicted to it, and it blinded me to everything else. It was my weakness. It *is* my weakness."

I didn't say anything to that, because a part of me had always known the power wasn't his strength.

"You have no idea how hard it is to even be near you right now. The connection calls to me—your aether, everything." He shot forward, wrapping his fingers around the bars once more. "It's all I think about, and if I did manage to transfer your power to me, I don't think even Ares could control me. It would all be over."

I lowered my gaze. "You're better than that."

"I'm not, and you know that, so cut that shit out." He laughed that cold laugh again. "But you are."

"I'm not better than you."

"You are," he insisted quietly. He shifted, and I looked up. His forehead was resting against the bars. A haunted look crept into his face. "You are."

The back of my eyes burned. "In case you don't remember, I shot a man in the head earlier just because I wanted to."

"He deserved it."

I flinched. "I didn't feel a damn thing, Seth. Not an ounce of remorse or regret. Nothing. That's . . . that's not right."

"He deserved it, Alex. You have no idea what he was doing, what he abused with his power." Our gazes locked, and he took a deep breath. "But I never wanted to see you do something like that. Maybe I did before, but after what Ares did to you? After seeing what *I've* done to you? I don't want any of this. I want it to be over, and the only way we can finish this is if you take on the power of the First. You need to become the God Killer."

I gaped at him. There was no way he knew our plans.

"It's the only way to stop Ares, Alex." His throat worked as he swallowed heavily. "And I can't do it. If I take on that power, I can't promise what I'd do. It has to be you, and I know it can be done. You have to—"

"I know," I cut him off as I scooted forward. "I know how to do it, Seth, but . . ."

His lips parted. "But you can't do it until it's damn close to time—until we are face-to-face with that son of a bitch, because the longer the power is in you, the crazier you get. Trust me."

"I'm already crazy," I whispered.

"What?"

I repeated myself, and I don't know what made me admit what I said next. Maybe because, in a way, Seth and I were the same person whether I trusted him or not. "I'm not the right person to be doing any of this. There's *something* wrong with me. Ever since I fought Ares, I haven't been right. I don't feel things the way I used to. I don't feel anything half of the time. I froze in a fight, and I mean really froze. I thought I saw Ares earlier and pulled a gun on Aiden."

His brows rose. "What's wrong with the last part?"

My shoulders slumped.

"Hey, I'm kidding. And I'm also curious why you'd do that. The sun rises and sets out of Aiden's ass, according to you."

Nice imagery. "I thought . . . I thought he was Ares."

"Like you saw Ares in place of him?"

I nodded numbly. "I don't know if I can do any of this, and then there's also this chance I could be . . ." I trailed off before I said too much and totally let my guard down.

"You could be what?" he asked. When I didn't answer, he turned sideways and settled down next to the bars. *What, Alex?*

Having him switch to talking that way was always unnerving. *I don't know. I think . . . Aiden thinks I'm . . .* I shook my head. *It doesn't matter. It doesn't change anything.*

Seth stared at me so long I started to worry that he could read my thoughts. Then his eyes widened slightly. *Are you . . . ?* A strangled sound came from his throat. "I can't even think it. Are you pregnant?"

Unable to confirm or deny, I said nothing, and that must've been answer enough because Seth swore under his breath. Squeezing my eyes shut, I dropped my head into my hands. My fingers curled into my hair, and the thin, raised scars on my face felt rough against my palms.

Alex? His voice was a thready whisper, and then out loud, he said, "I'm sorry, Alex, for everything I had a part in."

I shook my head without lifting it or removing my hands. I was unsure of why he'd apologize after that. It wasn't like he had anything to do with my potential babymaking shenanigans with Aiden. That was all us.

We sat like that for a few minutes, neither of us speaking. I searched inside of me for . . . for something more than a twinge of sadness, an emotion beyond anger and confusion, anything more substantial than vast emptiness.

There was nothing.

Seth's sigh shuttled through my thoughts. "I saw your father, Alex."

9

I didn't think I heard Seth right at first.

Slowly, I lifted my head and locked my gaze with his. "What?"

"I saw your father when I was at the Catskills," he repeated quietly. "Not before you Awakened. I didn't see him when I was there at that time, but when we arrived about a month ago, he was there—is still there."

My mouth worked, but there was no sound. I scooted forward, coming closer to Seth than I probably should have. I drew in a breath, but it got stuck. "Did you . . . how is he?"

"I didn't talk with him, Alex, but he's there with the other servants. The Elixir isn't working, and he seems to be keeping them safe. He can't leave. None of them can with Ares there." He paused, and my heart dropped. "He appears to be okay, but Ares knows who he is, Alex."

I stared at him as those words sunk in. "But he's okay for now?"

For now. Seth reaffirmed silently.

Closing my eyes, I squirmed under the sudden pressure in my throat. *And Ares knows he's my father?*

"Yes."

"Does he have any plans to use him against me?" I asked, already knowing and fearing the answer.

"I would like to give you the answer that would make it better." There was a pause, and then I felt his fingers graze my arm. Electricity passed from his skin to mine, and my head jerked up. I backed out of his reach, watching the marks of the

Apollyon glide up his arm and onto his neck. Seth pulled his arm back through the bars. "He will use any means necessary, Alex. He can't get to you right now, but the moment he can, he will dangle your father in front of you."

I looked away, pressing my mouth closed until my jaw ached with the effort. I knew I wasn't feeling everything I should be considering how much danger my father was in. I let out a ragged breath. "It's not just me he's going to come at. It's you, too."

"I know." Seth laughed dryly, and my gaze fell back to him. "But what does he have to hold over my head other than you?"

And I got it then. Once Ares realized Seth was batting for the opposite side, he'd force Seth's hand by forcing mine, and he'd use my father and everyone I cared about to make that happen.

"Shit's bleak, isn't it?" Seth said.

I huffed. "You have no idea."

"Then why are we doing this? Seriously? We could leave."

I pinned him with a look.

He laughed again, and this time, he sounded more like himself. "You could bring St. Delphi along."

"I'm sure he'll appreciate the invite." Truth was, the idea of running away was tantalizing as hell. It wasn't like I hadn't considered it before, and we could hide for as long as we could, but it wasn't right. "There's enough of me left inside that knows I can't do that."

Seth cocked his head against the bars but said nothing.

"I especially can't after what Ares did, but it's more than that. There are so many innocent people who will end up enslaved by him or dead. I couldn't live with myself."

"I could."

One side of my lips tipped up. "Of course."

There was a stretch of silence, and then he said, "You're so different."

I didn't know what to say.

"It's not because you're crazy, but I know what you went through."

The muscles along my back tensed. "I wanted to die." There. I said it out loud, and it sounded just as horrible as when I thought it.

Seth lowered his gaze. "I know."

"Part of me wishes—"

"Don't say it." Seth stood quickly and backed away from the bars. A niggle of shame rose like a weed, and he looked away. "I know you're not going to let me out. It's probably better if you don't until we have a plan that we can act on immediately. It will make everyone else feel better."

"Would it make you feel better?" I pushed to my feet.

Seth backed farther into the shadows of his cell. "It should make *you* feel better."

I was pretty sure I belonged in a cell, too, like the one Seth was in.

"You don't," Seth said. I must've thought that at him. "You're not crazy, Angel."

"Don't call me that."

Seth didn't respond. The conversation was obviously over. I lingered for another moment, unsure if there was anything else to say at this point. I ended up not saying anything as I turned around and headed toward the titanium door I'd left cracked open.

One thing I knew for certain: Seth wasn't going to trick us. And if he came after me, it would be like a daimon going for aether and for no other reason. It didn't mean he was safe, but it was better than him working with Ares.

Opening the door, I spied a lithe form leaning against the wall. It wasn't Solos.

Crap.

I closed the door behind me, took a deep breath, and faced Aiden. Locks of dark hair fell over his forehead in uncontrollable waves. His hair was starting to curl like Deacon's, and I favored that wilder look. Right now the edges of that hair brushed equally dark eyebrows—eyebrows that were currently slammed down. His lips were in a taut, tight line, and his eyes were a gunmetal gray. He was not a happy camper.

"Hi?" I said lamely.

The muscles in his folded arms rippled under the black shirt he wore. He was so still he was almost a part of the wall. "You left in the middle of the night."

I shifted my weight from one foot to the other. "I did."

"Without saying a damn thing," he added in voice that was too calm. I knew him well enough to know how misleading that was. I was entering the danger zone. "Especially after what happened between us? Did you stop and consider what I would think when I woke up and found you gone?"

He had a point. "I'm sorry, but I'm okay."

"Obviously, you're *not* okay."

I opened my mouth, thinking he was referencing the whole gun thing, but then I realized something else. Knots formed in my stomach. "How much did you hear?"

Aiden unfolded his arms. "Enough."

My brain winced. Doesn't sound possible, but it was. "Aiden—"

"Hearing you say that you loved him was . . . well, there aren't many words for that."

Heat rushed my face. "I said not in the same way I feel for you."

"Wait." He held up his hand, silencing me. "For days I've been trying to get you to talk to me about everything. I figured you weren't ready, so I haven't pushed it, but then you leave me in the middle of the night to go talk to *him*."

Uh. Oh.

"And then you tell *him* what's going on in your head when you've barely told me anything?"

Backed into the corner, I reacted the only way I knew how—the only way the old Alex, the Alex before Ares, would've reacted. "Maybe you shouldn't have been eavesdropping." The moment those words left my mouth, I wanted to drop kick myself in the face, because Aiden had a right to be pissed. "It's rude," I finished weakly.

"Are you serious?" Aiden pushed off the wall, and his eyes flashed quicksilver. Double uh-ohs. "You *went* to him."

Whoa. Wait a second. "It's not like that. I didn't go, *go* to him."

"It's not like that?" Aiden stopped directly in front of me. He lowered his chin, and his eyes flashed with anger. "You told him how you were feeling—what you haven't been feeling—"

"I've told you that!" My hands clenched into fists as my own anger surfaced like an old friend. *Yes.* I grabbed onto that anger. At least it meant I was feeling something.

"You told him you wanted to die." His voice broke on the last word, and the quick burst of anger inside me vanished. Pain poured into his expression, paling his face. "And I know you were about to say that part of you still wishes you had died that day."

I took a step back, wanting to deny that, but words left me and the shame came again, stronger this time. I wrapped my arms around my waist, trying to stop it from spreading. Aiden was the last person I'd wanted to know how weak I'd been—how weak I still was.

"It kills me to know you think that." A muscle ticked in his jaw as his gaze locked with mine. "Why wouldn't you come to me with that?" He shook his head, his throat working. "Why would you go to him of all people? After everything he's done?"

"You don't understand." And he didn't. No matter what, Seth and I were the same person. That didn't mean he was all forgiven, but Seth knew what I'd been through without me telling him, and I never wanted to share that with Aiden. I knew I needed to tell him that, but the words wouldn't come out.

Aiden drew in a shallow breath. "You told him you thought you were pregnant." He looked like I had stabbed him in a chest with a Covenant dagger. "How could you even trust him with something like that? What if he's playing us? What if he takes that knowledge back to Ares?"

"He's not playing us."

His eyes widened as his stance shifted. "How can you be so sure, Alex? We all saw what Seth was like way before you did, and none of us had a connection with him. He has control over—"

"He doesn't have any control over me! I know he's not playing us. I *know*."

"Maybe you're right," he said, the heat dying in his eyes. "But that's not a risk I'm willing to take, and you didn't stop to take that into consideration. You . . ." He stopped and looked away, thrusting his hand through his hair. "You didn't take how I would feel into consideration."

"I . . . I'm sorry. It's just . . ." I shook my head helplessly.

He then did something I honestly couldn't remember him ever doing to me before.

Aiden walked away from me.

I went back to the room I was sharing with Aiden, but he wasn't there, and by the time I'd drifted off to sleep waiting for him, he hadn't returned. And when I woke up, there was no sign of him, but he had made an appearance at some point while I'd slept.

The quilt that had been pushed down to the edge of the bed had been spread over me.

I knew that wasn't a white flag, and Aiden had every reason to be upset with me. I wished I had explained why I told Seth what I had. Not that I really believed Aiden would've been a hundred percent understanding, but it would've been better than apologizing or saying nothing.

Or telling him not to eavesdrop.

I pulled myself out of bed and took a quick shower. My empty stomach growled as I pulled on a pair of jeans and a shirt that belonged to Aiden. It swallowed me, but it smelled like him. Before I left the room, I scrubbed my hands down my face.

I would find Aiden, and somehow I would make this up to him.

Going to Seth had been wrong when I had been with the one person who had always been and always would be there for me. My intentions hadn't been malicious or shady, but they still stung like a hundred bees. The only good thing to come from it was that I knew Seth wasn't playing us.

Convincing everyone else would require nothing short of a miracle.

The first place I checked for Aiden was the common area in the dorm. He wasn't there, but Luke was sitting at one of the tables along with Deacon and Olivia.

And there was a mammoth plate of bacon and sausage links in front of them.

Lured by the wonderful, greasy scent, I drifted over to their table, my mouth watering at the sight. Bacon made everything better.

"Want some?" Deacon offered, knocking a mess of blond curls out of his face. "Because you look like you're about to start eating our faces if we don't give you some."

Olivia's nose wrinkled. "Ew."

I sat beside Aiden's brother and helped myself to a heaping of the crispy goodness. "Thank you."

I was munching away on my fourth slice when I felt eyes on me. Glancing up, my gaze met Luke's. His cheeks were red, as if he'd been kissed by the sun. "What?" I asked around a mouthful of bacon.

"I don't know how he did it—Seth." He sat back in his chair, rubbing his hand along his jaw. "I remember being out by the cars and seeing a few Sentinels I didn't recognize, and then the next thing I know, I'm standing inside the gate and there you two were."

"Compulsion," Deacon said, turning to me. "I've been telling him that all morning."

"He has," Olivia threw in.

Luke frowned. "I know it was a compulsion, but damn, I never felt something like that before."

"I have." Olivia looked at me pointedly, and my appetite vanished at the reminder. "You weren't responsible, Luke." She speared a link with her fork. "And now we have another crazed Apollyon—no offense, Alex—locked in a cell."

"None taken," I muttered, and then sighed. "It really isn't your fault, Luke. Deacon could do a compulsion, but one from an Apollyon packs a punch."

Luke didn't look relieved by that, but he grabbed a handful of bacon, so I figured if he was eating like that, he wasn't too traumatized.

"So what are we doing with Seth?" Deacon asked after a few moments.

A shudder coursed through Olivia. The girl had never been a fan of Seth, and I remembered what Aiden had said last night. Everyone had seen what Seth was really like, but not me. Well, and not Caleb, because Caleb had been a major fanboy when it came to Seth.

Oddly, there was no slicing pain when I thought about Caleb.

"We aren't going to do anything right now," I said finally. Everyone at the table stared at me. My gaze lowered to the half-eaten plate of bacon. "Seth isn't working with Ares anymore. I'm not saying we should welcome him with open arms or invite him in for breakfast, but he's not our big enemy right now."

"What?" Olivia's voice was an octave higher. "How can anyone be sure of that?"

"That's a good question." Deacon slid me his unopened bottle of OJ. "Thirsty?"

I murmured my thanks again and took a drink. "Well, for starters, that cell is only holding him because he's not trying to escape. If he wants out, he'll get out faster than any of us could, including me. Secondly, he doesn't want to become the God Killer anymore."

Luke rocked back on his chair, eyes widening. "Come again?"

Olivia stopped with another sausage link halfway to her mouth and gaped at me. Shifting in my seat, I felt heat spread across my cheeks, but I wasn't sure why. "He doesn't want to be the God Killer. He wants me to transfer the power from him."

"How did he find out that was our plan?" Deacon asked. He was suddenly serious, which was a rarity for him.

"He didn't. He suggested it without me saying anything. Seth's got . . . well, like I said, he no longer wants anything to do with Ares and Lucian . . ." My brows pinched. "Lucian is no longer an issue."

"I'd say," Luke said under his breath and then louder, "Not to beat the dead-and-buried horse, but how can anyone, including you, trust anything that Seth says? I mean, if he changes his mind . . ."

We were all screwed.

I got that, but I couldn't really vocalize why I trusted Seth. His issues with his twisted addiction were his own business. No longer hungry or in the mood to convince them when I had Aiden and a whole slew of other people to talk to, I pushed up from the table. "I'll see you guys later."

I made it to the door before I realized Deacon was following me. He fell in step beside me as we walked out of the dorm. "You know they were just vocalizing their concerns, right?" he said, shoving his hands into his jeans. "They didn't mean to upset you."

"I know." I squinted against the bright glare of the sun. "And they didn't upset me."

"You sure about that?"

I was. Like always, I really wasn't feeling much of anything. We continued down the pathway in silence, passing a few pure-blood students. They stared.

"Aiden is in a mood. Like a 'if you breathe in my direction, I will nunchuck you into next week' mood," Deacon announced as we passed one of the training centers.

My stomach sank a little. "Nunchuck? I don't think he knows how to use them."

"My brother knows how to use every weapon known to man. Nunchucks are no exception."

A small grin tugged at my lips. "I'll take your word for it."

"So, are you gonna tell me what crawled up his ass, besides the fact a fleet of potentially crazy Sentinels is poised outside our gates and his arch-nemesis is chilling in a cell right under his nose?"

"Have you seen Aiden?" I asked instead.

He nodded. "He's in the dean's office with Marcus."

Veering toward the main Covenant building, I didn't look forward to going to the room where I'd last seen Ares.

"So, you're not going to talk to me about Aiden?"

"Are you going to follow me all the way to the dean's office?"

"Yep." Deacon shot me a quick grin.

"There's a lot of steps."

"I need my exercise."

I sighed. "Aiden's mad at me."

"I doubt that."

"Oh no, he's definitely mad at me." I tucked my hair back behind my ear and glanced at Deacon. He elbowed me gently in the arm, and the corner of my lips pulled up a little, but it quickly slipped away. "He's mad because I went to see Seth."

Deacon raised a brow. "He's mad over that?"

"Well, I left in the middle of the night, didn't tell him what I was doing, and there's other stuff, but . . ." I shook my head, not wanting to really get into it. "So he's a little perturbed at the moment."

He didn't respond as we stepped into the main building and passed the Guards, waiting until we reached the stairwell. The cord inside of me strained since we were near Seth.

"Well, considering all the crap with Seth, I can get why Aiden isn't happy."

"I know." I rounded the second floor. "I'm not mad at him. He has every right to be upset."

Deacon hopped up the stairs, chock-full of energy. I hated him. "He'll get over it. My bro loves you, like *really* loves you. Like, he's *in* love with you, Alex."

I cast him a smile. "I know. I just hate that he's mad."

He looked at me, his eyes a brilliant silver. "I think that's the first time I've seen you really smile in a while." He spun around, opening the door to the top floor. "You doing okay?"

"No." I stepped through the doorway. "But I will be."

Deacon dropped his arm over my shoulder as we headed down the long hall. There were no guards at the dean's door, because there was no dean to protect, not really. "We'll be okay," he said, squeezing me. "I'm all into positive thinking these days."

The door to the dean's office was cracked open, and without a second of hesitation, Deacon slid around me and opened the door, pulling me in behind him. "Hello!"

Marcus looked up from the desk, brows raised. Over his shoulder, Aiden straightened. His gaze went from me to Deacon, and then back to me. There was nothing to be gained from his expression, but the tips of my ears burned.

"What's going on?" Marcus asked.

Deacon dropped my arm and plopped into one of the leather chairs. "I have no idea. I just have nothing better to do."

Aiden folded his arms as he pinned his brother with a look.

Well aware that we probably weren't welcome at this moment for a multitude of reasons, I inched my way over to the other seat and sat.

Taking a quick inventory of the room, I was happy to see that, with the exception of the boarded-up window, everything had been repaired. The aquarium was gone and the desk had been replaced, as had the carpet. But I knew, if I pulled up the carpet, there'd be bloodstains underneath.

Some of them would be mine.

"Alex."

My chin jerked up at the sound of Aiden's voice, and our gazes collided for a brief second. I'd come to talk to him, but I'd lost my courage the moment those thundercloud-colored eyes had focused on mine. "I don't have anything better to do, either."

"So what are you two doing?" Deacon asked, batting impossibly long lashes.

Marcus leaned back in his chair, and his cool emerald gaze drifted over us. "We were discussing what to do with the Sentinels outside the gates. They haven't caused any problems yet. In fact, it appears they are now guarding the gates from outside."

My gaze flicked over to Aiden. He was staring at me in that intense, consuming way only he could pull off. It was the same way he used to watch me while I was in grappling class. I shifted in my chair. "Well, um, that's good news, right?"

"We hope." Marcus scratched his chin. "Aiden was telling me you talked to Seth last night?"

Oh.

Oh crap.

I squirmed some more. "Yeah, I did."

"And you believe him?" he asked. "He's turned over a new leaf?"

"I'm not sure I'd say he's completely turned over a new—" A quick fissure of energy rolled down my spine, and the marks of the Apollyon raced across my skin. Electricity filled the room, and my senses flared. I knew the feeling. A god was here. I shot to my feet and started to turn.

Apollo stood behind me. "Hi."

I jerked back, smacking my hand over my pounding heart. "Good gods . . ."

One side of his lips curved up. He looked completely unrepentant, but he was rocking those baby blue eyes instead of the creepy god ones.

"Why must you keep doing that?" Aiden shook his head. "Gods."

The god shrugged. "How else should I do it? Ring a bell first?"

"That's actually a great idea," Aiden replied dryly. Deacon was on his feet, eyes wide, and he immediately started to backpedal out of the room. "I think I need . . . to, um, go find something else to do. Yeah."

Momentarily distracted from Apollo's sudden appearance, I narrowed my eyes at Aiden's brother. "What is it between you two?"

Deacon froze near the door.

The lopsided smile on Apollo's face spread. "Well, I would never kiss and tell."

My mouth dropped open as Deacon's face turned blood red. Oh jeez. Suspicions confirmed. Wow.

"What. The. Hell." Aiden stepped around the desk, glaring at Apollo. "Have you—?"

"Wait." Apollo held up a hand, his voice brokering no argument. He stared at me for a second. "Come here, Alex."

"Uh . . ." I didn't move, and I sure as hell didn't want to get between Aiden and Apollo. "No thank you. Find another diversion tactic."

Apollo's head moved to the side. "Alex—"

I sensed Seth the second before I heard a shot outside, and then he barreled through the door, skidding to a halt a few feet behind Apollo. There were daggers in his hands.

Amber eyes dilated, Seth took a deep breath and let it out slowly as his gaze landed on Apollo. "Oh. It's you."

Well, now we knew Seth most definitely could get out of that cell when he wanted to. Out of the corner of my eye, I saw Aiden draw his gun. Deacon crept back to our side.

"Yeah, it's me." Apollo seemed to grow in height, which was a bit frightening considering he was already Godzilla-sized.

A handful of Guards appeared behind Seth, all of them out of breath and a bit banged up. Seth shrugged and turned, handing the pair of daggers back to an empty-handed Guard. Several of them began talking at once.

"He just got out. No warning," one Guard said. "We tried to stop him."

"Sorry," Seth said. "I thought it was another god, one more annoying than this one."

My eyes widened.

Apollo smiled tightly. "Oh, you're so cute."

Seth smirked. "I am fabulously sexy, the last time I checked, but I'll go back to my cell now. Breakfast would be nice, by the way. I'm starving."

"This isn't a hotel," Aiden said, his gun leveled on Seth.

The Apollyon eyed the gun in Aiden's hand and then arched a brow. "You really like pointing that thing at me."

"You have no idea how much joy it gives me."

Seth got that look on his face—the one that said he was tossing out bait and knew Aiden was about to bite. "Don't let me forget. I do owe you for the knock over the head yesterday."

"You want that again?" Aiden smirked. "Keep talking."

"Oh, for the love of gods everywhere, stop it," I said. "This is ridiculous." Everyone turned to me. "Obviously you don't think he's tricking us, Apollo, or you'd have blasted him with some god juice by now."

"Just because I haven't doesn't mean I won't."

Seth opened his mouth, but I jumped in before he could make the situation worse. "And it's rather pointless. He can get out if he wants to. So what's the point of making him go back into the cell?"

"I can knock him out again," Aiden suggested calmly. "He'll stay put for a while after that."

"You're really starting to annoy me." Seth turned to Aiden, his eyes glowing faintly. "You know what your problem is?"

I rolled my eyes.

"Do tell." A muscle spasmed in Aiden's jaw.

"One word." Seth took a small step forward, a grin playing across his lips. "Jealousy."

I threw my hands up. "I give up. Not like we don't have real problems to deal with, but let's continue the boy-fight."

"Actually, as entertaining and long overdue as this boy-fight is, Alex has a point for once. Surprising, huh?" Apollo earned a death glare for that. "Aiden, put your gun away. Marcus, there's no need for daggers." Then he eyed Seth. "If you have nothing to hide, you aren't going to run from me."

Seth's spine straightened. "I would never run."

I had no idea what was going on, but Seth held himself still as Apollo took two long strides and placed his hand on the center of the Apollyon's chest. Surprise flickered across Seth's face, and then Apollo stepped back.

"He's telling the truth. He's no longer working with Ares, but that doesn't mean he's not still a threat," Apollo announced, and I had a feeling I knew what the god was referencing. And then he turned to me. "We need him here anyway. He's not the problem. You are."

"What?" He was staring at me. "Why me? I'm, like, the voice of reason for once."

"It's not that." Apollo faced me completely. "Guards, leave the room and close the door behind you."

They didn't even hesitate. They scattered like cockroaches. Unease formed little knots in my belly as I glanced at Aiden. He hadn't put the gun away, and looked like he was going to aim it at Apollo next. Deacon had successfully pinned himself against the wall, out of everyone's path.

"Have you been marked?" Apollo asked, his nostrils flaring.

I shook my head, taking a step back. Sweat dotted my brow as I eyed the door. I wanted out of this room really badly. "I have no idea what you're talking about, but you're starting to freak me out."

Apollo's eyes flipped from blue to white—no pupils, no irises. Static crackled in the air. "Come here," he repeated.

I needed to get out of here. Blood pounded in my veins. Every ounce of my being screamed for me to leave. Apollo wasn't—

He shot forward—over the roaring in my head, I heard Aiden shout—and clamped his hand down on my shoulder. I staggered under the weight.

"Did he mark you?" Apollo demanded, his expression furious. "Did Ares mark you?"

Those all-white eyes became my whole world.

"What is going on?" Marcus asked, but he sounded far away.

Apollo reached around me and grabbed the hem of my shirt. By the time I realized what he was doing, it was too late. He yanked up the shirt, exposing my back. Aiden exploded, yelling at the god as I tried to twist away.

"There it is." Apollo's hand landed on the oddly-shaped scar, and my entire body jerked as if I'd been shocked. "Phobos! Deimos! Show yourselves!"

Seth cursed.

I started to think Apollo might've lost his damn mind, but then, without any warning, there was a deep wrenching inside me. I broke the god's hold and stumbled back a step. A tremor worked its way through my body, rippling through every muscle. The room tilted.

"Oh, gods," I whispered, doubling over and clutching my stomach.

"Alex?" shouted Aiden.

"Don't touch her!" Apollo got in between us, holding Aiden back with nothing more than a raised hand. It was like an invisible shield appeared between us. "Deimos! Phobos! Σε διατάζω να σου αφήσει αυτό το πλήθος!"

The skin ... oh gods ... the skin under my hands *moved*, pushing out against my shirt and my palms, and formed ... *fingers*. Pressure expanded my stomach, and I dropped to my knees. Something slithered through my chest, into my throat. I couldn't breathe. Aiden's voice sounded further and further away as a sensation like icy, sticky fingers crawled under my scalp. It slipped down to the base of my skull, joining the mass in my throat.

Tears streamed from the corners of my eyes as I threw my head back. I opened my mouth to scream, but thick, white smoke poured out of me, steaming to the ceiling. Through the haze of tears, I saw the smoke spread and then drop into two separate pillars. There was a final tugging motion deep in my chest, as if something was digging in and not wanting to let go, and then it broke. The last of the smoke slipped out of me.

I fell forward, catching myself with my hands. Breathing raggedly, and with trembling arms, I lifted my head.

"Holy crap," someone whispered.

The pillars of white smoke spun like mini-tornados, taking shape with each dizzying pass. Two sets of legs. Two sets of arms. An ear-piercing cry reverberated through the room. A burst of wind rattled the chairs and the desk, and then there was nothing.

Silence.

Two gods stood in the room, their forms translucent, but there was enough mass to them to make out their identical features. They weren't as tall as Apollo, but I had a feeling they weren't fully formed.

One of them drifted toward me, too quick for me to react.

Through his eerily handsome face, I could see Seth's legs coming forward. "You're prettier on the inside . . ." the god said, his voice slick like a snake.

"Than you are on the outside," the other said.

The first one gave a mocking smile. "Then again, you're not . . ."

"All there, are you? It's nothing but rot," the twin finished, chuckling. It sounded like ice falling.

"What a shame," the first spoke again.

The second floated closer, his wispy lower body dissipating. "And who's really to blame?"

"In the end?"

"When there's nothing left to defend?"

I shrank back, horrified. They were like the twisted oompa loompas of the Olympian world.

More and more, their forms faded out, but their words were clear. "You're all destined to die. Taste the fear . . ."

Strong arms encircled me from behind, pulling me back from the gods and against a hard chest. Aiden turned, using his body to shield mine, but it didn't stop me from hearing their final words.

"It will all be over by the end of this year . . ."

A loud sigh swept through the room as the smoke dispelled. The twins were gone.

"Well," Apollo drew the word out. "That made absolutely no sense."

Muscles weak, I slumped over and would've face-planted on the carpet if Aiden hadn't caught me. He gripped my arms, but my skin felt too sensitive, too raw as he gently lowered me to the carpet. I crawled away, dragging in deep breaths.

"What . . . what was that?" Deacon asked, his voice hoarse.

Shaking, I sat back and lifted my head. There was a balloon expanding in my stomach, moving up my chest.

Apollo stood in the middle of the room with his hands on his hips. "*That* was Phobos and Deimos. The gods of fear, dread, panic, and sheer terror. They are Ares' sons. When you fought him, he marked you, giving them access to your psyche. I knew something was off about you while you were in Olympus, as did Artemis when she was here, but I didn't see it until now."

I blinked slowly. "What?"

"Phobos and Deimos have been riding you, feeding off your emotions, and choosing and amplifying which ones you feel."

Seth paled as he took a step back. His eyes met mine. "I didn't know." He raised his hands. "I had no idea."

"That's what Artemis meant by something being inside of her?" Aiden was kneeling beside me. Horror whipped through his voice. "They were *inside* her?"

"Yes." The white light dimmed in Apollo's eyes and blue irises appeared.

"I thought . . . I thought I was going crazy. I thought I was pregnant. I didn't think . . ." I was too shocked, too *everything* to care about what I had just admitted to everyone in the room, to even acknowledge Aiden's sharp inhale or how broken it sounded, or the way Seth turned his back, like he couldn't bear to look at me. "They were inside me this whole time?"

"Since you fought Ares," Apollo confirmed. "I'm sorry. If I could've come sooner, I would've known."

Staring at the god, I had a hard time accepting what he said. I got it. I believed it, but to think another god—*gods*—were inside my head and my body, tinkering around, messing with me and being with me the whole time floored me. A floodgate broke, and the balloon in my chest burst. Rage flooded me, burning like lava through my veins. It tasted like blood and acid.

The room tinted amber.

Seth whirled around. "Uh, guys . . ."

The hair lifted off my shoulders and neck. Aiden called my name, but I was beyond hearing. I was beyond listening.

I lost my shit, right then and there.

10

I don't remember leaving the dean's office, but must have, and I assume no one tried to stop me. I needed to be alone. I needed space.

I made it to a room down the hall.

I stood inside, the door swinging shut behind me, my chest rising and falling rapidly. I was feeling too much—anger, hurt, loss, hate, love, and everything else that had been muted while Ares' sons had been camped out inside *my body*. All the emotions at once were a poison in my blood. The lid on the bottle inside me had been completely unscrewed. Emotions broke the surface in a rush, and it felt like I had been drowning this whole time.

A burst of power left me.

The heavy oak desk in the corner, as well as a line of chairs and small tables, lifted into the air. They rose to the ceiling. My fingers curled in, nails digging into my palms. Wood creaked and groaned, then splintered. The furniture shattered like dry, brittle bones.

A volcano erupted inside me.

I opened my mouth and screamed. I didn't recognize the sound. Windows cracked. Shards of glass fell, and stopped before they hit the floor.

It wasn't enough—the destruction wasn't enough. It could never be enough. Every cell inside me had been violated on a level I couldn't begin to comprehend.

The room shook and the building shuddered as I took a step forward. My feet lifted off the floor. Below me, the tile warped and peeled up, breaking apart in large, uneven sections that rose into the air. Another shockwave of akasha rolled out from me. Blue light pulsed, incinerating the flooring.

In a flash, I felt the rage and shame of being so broken by Ares.

I hadn't mourned all those who'd died at the hands of Ares until that moment.

I hadn't feel the loving embrace of my mother's arms or the loss of her all over again until that very second.

I felt the damage that'd been done to my body and head all over again.

I tasted the bite of fear and the tang of fury when I remembered the condition of Aiden's hands when I first saw him after waking up. I tasted them again when I remembered seeing Marcus' mangled face.

I felt the horror of pulling the trigger and killing Lucian.

I felt it all.

I felt *alive*, as if I was finally *awake*, and it was too much.

Another scream tore through me, and the walls trembled.

The door opened behind me, and I slowly turned around, breathing through my nose. Seth stood there. My feet touched the floor.

"You need to try to calm down," he said. "Or you're going to bring this whole building down."

Calm down? Oh, shit was about to get real up in here.

I flew toward him, my arm snaking back. My fist cracked off his jaw, snapping his head back. Seth stumbled a step and bent over, clutching his face. The burst of pain flaring across my knuckles felt damn good.

"*Gods*," he grunted.

Jerking my leg up, I slammed my knee into Seth's stomach. A harsh expletive exploded from his mouth as I grabbed fistfuls of his shirt and shoved him backward. He caught himself against the wall with one hand.

"Okay." He spat out a mouthful of blood. "I'll admit I deserved that."

The stupid cord in me didn't understand the violence, but it liked that I was touching him. For that reason alone, I dropped down low and spun. I took his legs out from underneath him. Seth folded like a paper sack, hitting the destroyed floor on his side.

I vaulted to my feet and then dropped into a crouch.

Seth was back up in record time, his golden brows slammed down. "Okay. You want to work out your aggression. I'm all for that, *Angel*."

"Don't." I dipped under his arm and sprang up behind him. "Call." I slammed my hands down on his shoulders and brought my knee up. "Me. That!"

Seth twisted away before I could say hello to his spine. He faced me, pushing the longer strands of hair out of his gleaming eyes. "Come on. Bring it, Angel."

The sound that came from me would've sent most people scurrying for the hills.

He lifted his hand and gave the universal "come get some" sign. "Work it out of your system. You can't kill me."

I wasn't sure if my anger was so much directed at him or if he just made for a very convenient punching bag, but I launched myself at him. I hit him in the midsection, knocking him backward. We crashed into what was left of the desk and toppled over it. In a rather impressive feat, Seth shifted and hit the floor under me, taking the brunt of the fall. I was on top of him, straddling him. My arms rose up and I brought them down on his chest, over and over. I hit him, and I *kept* hitting him. His face blurred through the sudden wetness in my eyes. What the hell? The dampness rose and spilled over. My hands ached, but I couldn't stop. Tears streamed down my face and the whole time . . . the whole time Seth let me hit him. He didn't raise a hand. He didn't stop me.

My body shook and my arms ached. The sobs came from deep within me, from that dark and rotted-out place that had cropped up when Ares shattered my bones. My fists landed against Seth's chest once more, weaker this time, and I couldn't lift them. I hunched over, my chin dropping to my chest, and I cried so many tears I was sure I was going to drown the whole world with them.

"Stop." Seth gripped my arms. "Come on, Angel, stop."

I wished I could, because crying on top of Seth wasn't my ideal way of licking my wounds in private. It was a whole lot of pathetic and awkward, but it was like the seal that kept me from crying had been broken. There was no turning back now.

Seth made a sound, and then he rolled. A second later I was lying on my side. For several long minutes, we were stretched out the floor like two idiots, his arms like a vise, restraining me from doing any more damage to him or the poor, unsuspecting room. It took more time than usual for the tears to finally ease off, and for me to calm down enough to speak.

"Why you?" I asked, my voice thick and gross-sounding.

Seth sat up slowly, pulling me into his lap, my back against his front. "And why not Aiden?"

I didn't answer because it was obvious.

"You would've killed anyone else who came in this room."

My head hung limply. "That wouldn't have stopped him."

"I had to tie him up and stash him in a closet." When I stiffened, he tightened his arms and laughed. "I'm just kidding. I didn't do anything other than use my deadliest weapon—logic. Apollo may've had to restrain him a bit, but he's right outside this room waiting."

"Logic?" I laughed, and although the sound and feel of it didn't hurt, it sounded strange to me. "You never used that before."

"I know." He was quiet for a long moment. "But I'm very familiar with this kind of rage, Alex, and I know what you felt.

And you haven't really dealt with everything until now. Aiden thinks he knows how you feel, and maybe he has an idea, but I *know* what you felt and I *know* what you went through."

I was still ashamed that anyone had been privy to those horrible, wretched moments when I'd prayed for death and wanted it more than I'd ever wanted anything. It was so weak, and I had been so broken, flayed open to the core.

Seth rested his head on mine and sighed. "I wasn't lying. I *never* wanted something like that to happen. Out of everything I have done and caused to happen . . . it's the one thing I can never ask forgiveness for."

And I wasn't sure I could ever truly forgive him. I knew he hadn't done this to me, but he'd played a significant part in all of it. But I was too tired and just . . . too done with everything to hold onto the anger anymore, because it was doing what Ares and his sons wanted. It was chipping away at me, killing me.

I relaxed and closed my eyes, concentrating on the steady rise and fall of Seth's chest. A little part of me still felt lost, and I wasn't sure when I'd feel whole again or if I really ever would, but I knew what was happening right now. It was that connection between us and the calming effect it had.

Seth had done this before. He'd used it to calm me down when I'd had nightmares, and he'd used it to connect and control me, but now, when I was at my most vulnerable, he didn't twist the connection back on me. He used it to help me.

Some time passed before I was in any condition to stand and face things. My legs and arms felt strangely weak. I glanced over my shoulder at Seth and cringed. A deep crimson stain was already spreading across his jaw. "Sorry about your . . . face."

Our eyes met, and an uneven grin appeared on his face. "No, you're not."

"You're right."

Seth stepped forward, and I eyed him wryly. "You know you can take a timeout, right? Take the rest of the day to just, I don't know, deal with it all. Get some rest."

I was exhausted in the way one felt only after going through an emotional upheaval. The idea of laying my little head down on a soft pillow was more appealing than eating cheese fries loaded with bacon. "I'm sure Apollo has a reason for showing up other than yanking those freaks out of me."

"He can wait." Concern flickered in Seth's eyes, and it was odd seeing that. As long as I'd known Seth, it was rare to genuinely see him care about someone other than himself. Then again, I wasn't giving him credit. I'd changed. He'd changed.

"No. I'm fine." I turned to the door. "We don't have time for me to take a nap."

"We have time." Seth followed me. "Not like tomorrow is going to be any different than today."

Who really knew if that was true? Denying the urge to agree and go find the nearest bed, I opened the door. It was slightly off its hinges, so it scraped the floor and opened only halfway. I sighed as I squeezed through. I wasn't surprised when I saw Aiden and Marcus leaning against the opposite wall. Both seemed to relax a little when they saw me standing and obviously not looking like I'd stuck my hand in an electric socket.

Though I did come to an abrupt halt when my gaze centered on Aiden again. It was like seeing him for the first time—the broad cheekbones, the full, expressive lips, his dark, unruly hair, and those brilliant smoky-gray eyes. A veil had lifted from my vision, and I couldn't—didn't want to look away. How much had Ares' sons affected? Everything, it seemed.

Marcus' gaze shifted over my shoulder, and his brows rose. A small grin tipped up the corner of Aiden's lips. No doubt he was happy to see that I was unscathed while, on the other hand, Seth looked like he'd run into a wall.

My uncle recovered first, stepping forward. "Are you okay, Alexandria?"

"Other than the fact I just spewed out two gods like a drunk college chick? I'm feeling *fabulous*."

Relief shuttled across his face. He clapped a hand on my shoulder. "There's my niece."

I cracked a grin at that while I kept an eye on the two guys. Aiden and Seth were eyeballing one another like they were about to start boy-fight, round two.

Marcus squeezed my shoulder and then dropped his hand. For him, that was a whole exercise in bonding, and I was okay with that. I turned, catching Seth's attention. My eyes narrowed and his rolled. Raising his hands in surrender, he pivoted around and headed into the dean's office. Marcus was right behind him. Before I entered the room, Aiden caught my arm and stopped me. We were alone in the hall.

"Alex," he said, his voice low and rough.

Turning to him, I looked up and met his gaze. My mouth opened, but a sudden knot clogged my throat. I threw myself forward, pressing my forehead against his chest and breathing him in. He shuddered, and then he wrapped his strong arms around me. He dropped his head, pressing his cheek to the top of my head as he held me in a tight, heart-melting embrace. I clung to him like a deranged baby monkey, soaking in his warmth and the absolute feel of him. There was *a lot* we needed to talk about, but this hug? Gods, I needed this hug.

I needed this hug from Aiden.

"Shit, Alex . . ."

Squeezing my eyes shut, I let out a choked laugh. "It's funny when you cuss."

"Only you would laugh at something like that," he said, and I heard the relieved amusement in his voice. Fingertips appeared under my chin, and Aiden lifted my gaze to his moonlight-colored one. "You're with me now?"

I blinked back tears. "Yes. Yes, I am."

"Good." His thumb smoothed over my jaw as his intense gaze searched my face. "I'm happy to have you back."

Turning my cheek into his palm, I swallowed hard. "I'm sorry."

"I'm the one who should be apologizing, especially for last night. I was jealous, and that was stupid, I know, but I'm—"

"No." I shook my head slightly. "No, you were right to be upset, but that's not what I'm talking about. That's not what I'm apologizing for."

His brows rose.

My chest ached. "I know . . . I know there was a part of you that was okay with the idea of us having a baby. I know there was a part of you that was excited in spite of everything else, and I'm sorry that's not what was going on. I'm sorry that it was *this* and not—"

"Stop." Aiden dropped his forehead to mine and slid his strong hands up to cup my cheeks. "You do not need to apologize. Ever. Do you understand me? None of this is your fault. And you haven't done anything wrong. What we thought? It doesn't matter."

"You have to be disappointed," I whispered, curling my fingers around his wrists.

"Never," he swore. "If anything, I'm upset this happened to you. I'm freaking pissed that it did, but, Alex, we have a lifetime ahead of us to have that conversation and feel that way again."

My breath caught. "You're perfect."

"And you know that's not true."

"It is."

A throat cleared behind us, and then Apollo said, "Seriously, you two? It's not like you're keeping a god waiting or anything."

Aiden drew back with a soft groan. "Sometimes I hate him."

My lips curved up. "Sometimes."

"I heard that," Apollo said. "And I'm pretty sure there's

someone else you hate more than me. I'll give you two clues. Starts with an S and ends with an H."

There was an audible huff from inside the office.

I started to grin.

"Well, you got that right." Aiden's eyes were fixed on me. "You want to do this right now?"

I nodded, and then Aiden lowered his head once more, kissing me in a way that truly felt like the very first time. When he lifted his head, his eyes shone with everything he was feeling in that moment. I knew what he'd said moments before was the truth. He believed we had a lifetime to feel that odd little burgeoning of hope again, and I latched onto that.

Together, we turned and headed past Apollo. He followed us in and took up stance in the middle of the room. "Well, the gang's all here. Almost. We are missing a few, but this will do."

We were missing Solos, Luke, and Olivia, and it didn't feel right that they weren't here. And it felt really weird that Seth was here. He was leaning against the wall where the daggers had once hung. He arched a brow at me.

"Your mark should be gone, which means the twins won't be able to get back into you," Apollo said, and I resisted the urge to yank my shirt up and check right then. Then he turned to Seth. "And don't think you and me are okay. It's great you're no longer Ares' little bitch-boy, but you're still a punk-ass."

Aiden snickered.

"And I hope your jaw really hurts," Apollo added.

Seth smirked. "Hey, if you want to go a few rounds again, Golden Boy, we can do it."

"This is an awesome start to our Army of Awesome meeting number two," Deacon murmured.

The air around Apollo crackled, and I let out a loud sigh and propped myself against a chair. "So, I'm assuming you had a reason for coming here besides helping me and arguing with Seth."

"That's right."

I waited, and when Apollo said nothing, I crossed my arms. "And that would be?"

"We need a plan," he replied.

"Wow." Seth folded his arms. "That's a unique concept."

"Seth," I hissed, shooting him a look.

"That's okay," Apollo replied, smiling at Seth in a wholly creepy "hide your kids" kind of way. "When you least expect it, I'm going to turn you into a pink flower that smells like cat pee."

I choked on my laugh. "Oh, my gods . . ."

Seth's eyes narrowed into thin, amber slits, but before he could volley back, a whole different conversation sprouted out of the depths of my very own personal hell.

"I'm sorry." Marcus was leaning against the desk, looking a bit green. "Am I the only one stuck on the fact that *these two* thought they might've been . . . that you could've been . . . that there might have been . . . ?"

"That we could've made you a great-uncle," I supplied since he'd obviously run out of words. His eyes narrowed, and heat spread across my cheeks. "Can we not talk about that right now?"

"I second that," Aiden muttered, shifting awkwardly.

"I disagree." Apollo's "hide your kids" smile was now spreading across his face. "This conversation is going to be epically entertaining."

"For you." Aiden cut him a dark look.

"Exactly," the god replied.

Marcus ignored that. "I don't know how many times I've told you two that you shouldn't be sharing a room." He turned to me. "I don't care how old you are or that you're an Apollyon, Alexandria. You're my niece; therefore, I am responsible for you. And you?" He spun on Aiden, whose eyes widened. "You know better."

"Oh my gods," I moaned. I rather have run naked through

the quad than had this conversation both with my uncle and with an audience. Especially with *this* audience.

"Don't 'oh my gods' me." The color had returned to Marcus' face. It was red. "Do I really need to have a conversation with you about responsible sexual activity?"

Seth looked like he wanted to shove a dagger in his eye.

"I think you do," Apollo suggested.

"Oh! You're one to talk!" I whirled on Apollo. "Seriously? If I was to Google 'irresponsible sexual activity,' it would be your picture staring back at me!"

Apollo made a face at me—actually *made a face* at me like he was ten years old or something.

Marcus was now staring at Aiden like he wanted to take his dagger and use it on Aiden in an area much lower than the eyeballs.

"Okay, can we move on to the important stuff?" I demanded, losing my patience. "If not, then this is wasting my time, and I'm going to bed. That just might include irresponsible sex, because I've had a really crappy day!"

Five sets of eyes settled on me. One set was particularly interested in what I had just said.

"What?" I rolled my eyes, scowling. "Get on with it."

Apollo sent Seth one more scathing look, which I was sure wouldn't be the last one directed at the First. "As I said, we need a plan, and although I have many talents . . ."

For some reason, I couldn't help but look at Deacon. He flushed.

"I am not a strategist, not like Ares."

The look on Seth's face said he was wondering why Apollo was here then, but before he could vocalize that opinion, another fissure of energy whipped through the air. The aether in my veins hummed, and the marks raced to the surface. Seth and I stiffened in anticipation.

A shimmery blue form appeared and then solidified beside

Apollo. A second before, there had been nothing but a glittery waterfall, and now there was a tall brunette woman dressed in a tailored business suit. Her hair was pulled up in a tight bun, which did nothing to lessen the ethereal beauty of her face. In her slim, almost delicate-looking hands, she held a rolled parchment.

Gods were like opossums. You could go your whole life without seeing one, but once you found one of them, you found the whole freaky family.

Every pure in the room bowed, leaving Seth and me standing straight like two douches. We apparently were a little slow on the show of respect. The goddess didn't seem to notice or care.

"Athena, please meet the, uh . . . Army of Awesome." Apollo arched a brow. "Or whatever they are calling themselves."

The goddess of wisdom, strategy, and a whole slew of other things inclined her head. "Nice title."

"Nice suit," I said, my gaze dipping to her pointy heels.

Her all-white eyes centered on me, and one side of her lips tipped up. "I picked it up at Saks along with this amazing leather satchel and these to-die-for shoes."

"Oh." I slid Aiden a glance. He studiously ignored me. "They're very nice, too."

She strode forward, placing the parchment on the desk. Marcus swallowed and stepped to the side, giving the goddess a wide berth. It was a map. A really crudely drawn map of trees, mountains that looked like upside-down Vs, and stick people. Apparently, drawing was not one of Athena's skills. "The plan, and I assume that has not changed," she paused, passing an arched look between Seth and me, "will require the God Killer to get close to Ares. Currently, he's camped out—"

"In the Catskills," Seth interrupted, and I thought of my father. He was *there*. Seth came forward, eyeing the map. "He's got around the same number of Sentinels that I have here with me, plus mortals. All of them are under compulsion."

"Ares' compulsion?" Marcus asked, and when Seth nodded, my uncle sighed. "There's no way to break a compulsion from a god, is there?"

"Not unless you take out the god, or so we assume," Apollo said. "Dionysus has confirmed that the mortal encampment is several miles out from the Catskills."

"We would have to get past them, and then get through the walls of the New York Covenant, which are guarded by Sentinels." Seth tapped his finger along what appeared to be an uneven brick wall, squinting. "But that's not all. Ares is heavily guarded."

"Guarded by what?" I asked.

"Daimons," Seth said, looking away. "And you know how he's controlling them."

My stomach roiled. I did. He was feeding them pures and probably halfs—dinner in exchange for loyalty. I remembered the days when the Council didn't believe daimons could reason. Now the daimons had most likely drained those Council members dry.

"And the automatons." Athena glanced at Apollo. "Hephaestus has completely lost control of them."

The god sighed. "Don't start."

Her eyes narrowed. "I warned all of you that using them was a bad idea. We had no idea what god was responsible for this, and using a creature designed for war without such knowledge was a poor plan."

It was. The half-machine, half-bull fire-breathing creatures had turned on us and were now under Ares' control.

"So not only will your . . ." Her nose wrinkled. "Your Army of Awesome have to get past the mortals, they will have to face Sentinels, daimons and automatons before even reaching Ares."

Aiden folded his arms. "That is, if he doesn't come after us the moment we set foot out of the University."

"He won't." Athena tapped her finger down on a square,

which I assumed was the Covenant building. "He knows how heavily entrenched he is, and moving an army would make him vulnerable to attack. Before the First left him, he would've risked it. But not now that he knows the God Killer is coming for him. He will remain where he is and wait for you to come to him. He knows you will suffer losses in the process."

The truth weighed heavily. We *would* suffer losses.

"Getting past the mortals will not be hard," she continued. "The loss of their lives will be unfortunate, but we have to sacrifice the few to save the many. Then there are the Sentinels, daimons and automatons, but it is fighting Ares that will take everything."

"We can't just zap him with a God Killer bolt and call it a day?" I asked.

Athena arched a brow. "It's not like he's going to stand still and allow you to do that, and we know what happened last time you faced off with him."

"Thanks for the reminder," I muttered.

"It is only to serve a much-needed point. None of you are trained to battle a god, let alone Ares. Even I couldn't prepare you, not effectively. He can and will outmaneuver and out-plan you, and he knows that." Athena waved a hand over the map, and it disappeared. Neat trick. I was jealous.

"So are you saying that we cannot defeat him, not even with the God Killer?" Marcus asked, and the crinkled skin around his eyes appeared more noticeable.

"No." She faced us and hopped up on the desk, demurely crossing her legs. "War is partially strength, partially skill, and partially psychological. We have the strength in the Apollyons and the Sentinels, but we do not have the skill, and we do not have anything that will put Ares at unease. Without the last two factors, we will not succeed."

I frowned. "Are you also the goddess of depressing facts?"

Apollo snorted.

"I am just being realistic," she stated coolly. "But I do have an idea."

Here we go. A bit of excitement thrummed through me. An idea was better than everything else she'd been spouting, because right now, I didn't need Phobos and Deimos inside my head to believe we were embarking on a suicide mission.

"It is a risky idea, but we really have no other choice. If the God Killer fails, it will be an all-out war, and we know what happened the last time the gods went to war," Athena said.

Aiden shifted his weight. "Thousands died."

"And it will be millions this time." Apollo studied the goddess. "What is your idea?"

A small smile appeared. "We use Perses."

Apollo stiffened, and I didn't understand the reaction. "The demigod? Are we going to go slay Medusa or something?"

"No. Not Perseus. *Perses*."

I stared at her. "Okay. I'll admit, I slept or doodled through most of my classes. I have no idea who you're talking about."

"That is a lovely discovery." Marcus pierced me with his Dean of Academics stare. I withered like a poor little flower left out in the sun without water.

"Perses is the god of destruction and war," Apollo explained, eyes wide. "He was nearly indestructible and nearly unstoppable."

I shook my head as I glanced at Aiden, relieved to see he looked just as clueless as me. "Okay. Is there another god of war that I'm unaware of?"

"You guys populate like rabbits," Seth added, grinning slightly. "It could be possible we haven't heard of him."

Deacon's lips twitched, but Athena's next words knocked the smile off his face and silenced the entire room.

"No," she said. "Perses is not an Olympian. He is the Titan god of destruction."

I I

I gaped at the goddess in what must have been the most unat-
tractive manner known to man. "A Titan?" I squeaked out. "A
mother-freaking Titan?"

Athena nodded. "A Titan."

"Whoa." Aiden ran his hand through his hair before clasping
the back of his neck. He turned sideways, shaking his head.
"Wasn't expecting that."

"I don't think anyone was expecting that." Apollo stepped
toward Athena. "Let's break down this idea step-by-step. How
would we be able to use Perses? The last time I checked, he was
in Tartarus."

"He is still there." Athena tipped her chin up. "And as you
know, he is not dead. He is only entombed."

"And how do you think we're going to release him?" Apollo
demanded, brows slashed. "Zeus would never agree to this."

"I *am* Zeus' favorite child." Her smile beamed.

Apollo's blue eyes rolled. "That's something to be proud of."

She tsked softly. "I can get him to agree to anything, and he's
desperate, Apollo. You know that's true. The last thing he wants
is a full-out war."

"The last thing he wants is to do anything. That lazy son
of—"

"True." Athena raised her hands. "But I will get his
backing."

"Okay. So if you get his backing, what about Hades? He will
never agree to releasing Perses," Apollo argued.

"He will if Zeus demands it."

Apollo laughed deeply, and the sound shook the chairs. "Hades controls the Underworld. He will deny it just *because* Father demands it."

"I'm sure you can get Hades to understand and agree. That will be up to you." She tapped her manicured fingers on her bent knee. "And you know how Hades likes to make a deal."

Last time I'd seen Hades, he'd wanted to kill me. This idea was going downhill fast.

"All right, let's say we get Hades to agree to release Perses. How in the world would we be able to control him?" Apollo asked.

"Perses is just one Titan. He is powerful and a bit . . . crazy, but Ares nearly died by his hands during the war, if you remember correctly. Perses can train the God Killer. He could train hundreds of our people to fight. We will have the skill, and we will have the psychological upper hand." She smiled again. "Besides, Perses will do anything to be free. Any of the Titans would. Put the fear of gods in him, or whatever it is the mortals say. Make him behave, and in return, Hades can give him better accommodations."

"Oh, this is rich." Apollo laughed.

"You're serious about releasing a Titan?" Seth blinked slowly, as if coming out of a daze. When Athena simply nodded, he turned to me. "Ares would never expect it."

There were honestly no words.

From what I remembered about the Titans, those who stood against Zeus had been imprisoned since they could not truly be killed. Titans were badass, like "they put the 'bad' in badass" kind of badass. The last time they were topside, it had been a bloodbath. No one, not even the Olympians, messed with the Titans. And now we were talking about unchaining one and working with it? And hoping for the best?

Oh, this had apocalypse written all over it.

And people thought I made bad decisions?

But Seth was right, and so was Athena. Ares would never expect something as crazy as this. Perses was the Titan god of war and destruction. If anyone could prepare us for coming face to face with Ares again, it would be him and no one else.

"Okay," I said, letting out a deep breath. "Let's unleash a Titan on the unsuspecting world."

The others agreed, and plans were made to meet with Hades. The atmosphere was much better, and that probably had to do with the absence of Phobos and Deimos and the fact that we had something, no matter how crazy, to work with. Still, I couldn't help but think we might be making the whole situation worse.

I knew Seth wasn't being housed in the cell anymore, but I also knew he wasn't in this dorm. There were others, and he'd wisely chosen one that didn't house a decent number of people who wanted to commit an act of homicide when they were around him.

And it had put some much-needed distance between us.

The stupid cord in me wasn't happy about the separation, but it had ceased its incessant buzzing and humming. I liked to think that I was gaining some control over the obsessive need to be near Seth, and if both of us survived this, it was something we both needed to work on.

We *would* survive this.

I couldn't allow myself to think anything else. When Deimos and Phobos had been inside me, it was all I could think about. We would fail. I would die. Those I loved would die. Now that their influence was gone, I felt like myself again. Things weren't all rainbows and puppy tails. I could still lose people, and after I discovered there was a good chance the Olympians would take out my rosey-red behind after fighting Ares, there had been moments when I wanted to find a corner to rock in.

But I was a born fighter, and I would fight. That's who I was at the core.

Alone in my room, I stripped out of my clothes and kidnapped another one of Aiden's shirts to sleep in. The soft, well-worn cotton slipped over my head and ended at the thigh. I wasn't sure if he was truly okay with me hijacking his clothes, but he wasn't there and I simply liked his shirts.

Dragging myself to the bed, I tucked my legs under the covers and rolled onto my side, facing the door. The last I'd seen of Aiden, he'd left with Marcus to go over the newest developments with Solos and the crew. As exhausted as I was, I had bowed out of the third meeting with the Army of Awesome. There was just too much going on in my head to face everyone.

Lying there, waiting for Aiden to return, I told myself again that we were actually planning to release a Titan. Crazy pants right there. Obviously, I'd never met a Titan, and a part of me was excited by the prospect of coming face-to-face with such a legendary being.

A freaking Titan.

I gave a sleepy snort.

My eyelids grew heavier as the minutes ticked by. I didn't want to fall asleep, because there was so much I needed to talk with Aiden about, but I was sinking through the bed. After Deimos and Phobos had been yanked out of me, the emotional storm that had followed had been a cleansing of sorts, but it had also tuckered me out.

I realized then that I hadn't thanked Seth.

That was the last thing I remembered thinking before I felt something warm and slightly rough graze my cheek. Stirring restlessly, I forced my eyes open.

"Aiden," I whispered.

A slight smile appeared on his full lips. His hand stilled on my cheek. "I didn't mean to wake you up."

"It's okay. I didn't mean to fall asleep. I was waiting for you."

"You need to sleep, but I . . ." His thumb smoothed on my cheek again. "I couldn't stop myself from touching you."

A wealth of warmth blossomed in my chest at those words, and then spread when I realized that Aiden was under the covers and he was shirtless. Maybe even pantsless. "I'm not complaining."

In the soft light from the nightstand, his eyes were a luminous silver. "How are you feeling?"

Wiggling closer, I bit back a sigh as his hand slid around the nape of my neck. "I feel . . . I feel good. I mean, hurling up those gods changed things. That was crazy, right?"

His lashes swept his cheeks and then lifted. The intensity in his gaze was consuming. "It isn't something you see every day."

My lips tipped up at the corners. "It's a relief to know that a lot of what I was feeling wasn't coming from me."

"I have to agree." His knee rose under the covers, and soft flannel brushed my bare legs. Damn. He did have pants on. "Want to talk?"

What I really wanted to do was cross the scant distance between our mouths, but I did need to talk to him. There had been so much I'd held back while the gods had been squatting in my head, and there was so much Aiden needed to know, so I told him everything from how I'd felt when I fought Ares to what it was like the moment all those violent emotions rose to the surface.

When I was done, he smoothed his hand over my cheek. His hand had stayed on me the whole time. "Do you feel that way now—the way you felt with Ares?"

I met his gaze as I placed my hand against his warm chest. "I think there will still be moments when it . . . well, when it sucks, but I don't want to die. I'm glad I didn't." I laughed, a little embarrassed. "I don't feel that way anymore."

"Good." Aiden inched his head over and kissed me so softly,

like he was being cautious, and then pulled back. He slipped his hand off my cheek, placing it over where mine rested against his chest. "It killed me, Alex, when I heard you admit that to Seth. All I wanted to do was go in there and hold you, figure out some way to make it better."

"I'm okay now." I turned my hand over and threaded my fingers through his. "But I'm still scared."

"That's normal."

"I know. And I know it's okay to be scared."

He squeezed my hand. "Damn. I should record that statement."

I laughed, and it was a real sound. It was good. "I never thanked Seth, and I need to, Aiden. He helped me calm down. He didn't try to manipulate me. If it hadn't been for him, I would've brought that building down."

His eyes latched onto mine. "About Seth . . ."

Swallowing heavily, I prepared myself. "I can't blame the gods for that. I knew what I was doing when I went to see Seth. I should've woken you and told you where I was going. That was my fault."

"He was right," he said, as if he hadn't heard me.

I blinked. "What?"

"The little bastard was right." He let out a heavy sigh. "I was jealous when I found you with him. I was jealous afterward. I am *still* jealous."

"I—"

"I heard what you said," he stated quietly, not looking away. "I heard you say that you loved him."

My eyes widened and my stomach dropped as a horrible feeling opened up in my chest. How had I forgotten that he'd overheard me saying that too? For a moment, I didn't know what to say. Awkward didn't even cover it. "I did say that, but it's not the same—"

"Same way you feel about me." His eyes shut briefly. "I know.

I honestly know it's not, but hearing that . . . ? I wanted to punch him. I still do for various reasons, but mostly because I know that there will always be a part of you that does love him. That you two will have this connection for the rest of our lives, and that's something I can never compete with."

An ache opened up in my chest, and I closed the distance between us, practically crawling onto him. "I'm sorry."

His brows rose as he rolled onto his back, wrapping an arm around my waist. "For what, Alex? *I* should say I'm sorry. I was a dick to you because of my stupid jealousy. You shouldn't have to apologize."

"But you shouldn't have to deal with a freaky Apollyon connection." I peered down at him. "What normal couples have to deal with that?"

"We deal with a lot of things normal couples don't deal with," he replied dryly.

"I know! That's why I'm sorry you have to deal with . . . with Seth and me on top of everything else. If it was me, and you were connected to someone, I'd probably stab her in the eyeball every time I saw her."

Aiden's lips quirked up lazily. "Really?"

"It's not funny." I smacked his chest lightly. "I would. I wouldn't be able to deal with it, so I totally get your jealousy. I just don't want you to feel that way, because I love you. I'm *in* love with you. Forever and ever, and all the corny things I can attach to that."

He chuckled deeply, and the sound brought a smile to my face. "I know you do. And I have to work on not hating him for this. I have to remember that there are other reasons to want to kill Seth."

I laughed, and he rewarded me with another tender kiss that curled my toes. It didn't go any further than that. He guided my head down to where his heart beat steadily in his chest. I wanted to take that kiss further, but the moment my cheek hit his skin, I found my head too heavy to lift.

Aiden told me how the rest of the group had taken the news about releasing Perses. He also had explained to them that Apollo had checked Seth out, and the First could be trusted . . . as far as anyone could really trust Seth. Then he explained to them about the evil god twins, and for that I was eternally grateful. That was the last thing I wanted to explain all over again.

It didn't take long for me to drift back off to sleep as Aiden talked, not with the rise and fall of his chest luring me off or with his hand playing in my hair. I wasn't sure how comfortable it was for Aiden, considering I was sprawled half on top of him, but when I woke in the morning, neither of us had moved. I was still on my side, one leg thrown over his and my cheek on his chest.

Pleasant pressure built inside me. I wanted a million mornings of waking up like this. I was going to have those mornings. I stayed there for a little while, feeling and listening to Aiden breathe. My mind started to wander over so many things—Seth, my father, my friends, the state of things for half-bloods, the future if we defeated Ares, and what would happen if we failed. By the time I got tired of where my mind had gone, half his body had to be numb. I started to push off.

Aiden's other arm swung around with startling quickness, and his hand landed just above my knee. "Where do you think you're going?" he asked, voice gruff from sleep and from . . . from something else.

A flutter started in my stomach as I raised my head to look down at him. His dark waves were going in every direction. His eyes were heavy-hooded, and his lashes were thick. The slight stubble on his jaw pushed over the edge into dangerous territory. Only Aiden could look so sexily sleep-ruffled. "Nowhere?"

"Sounds about right." One hand curled around the edges of my hair while the other crept up my thigh, causing me to shiver. "How long have you been awake?"

"Not long." My gaze dropped to his mouth. Those lips were perfect.

He made a deep sound in his chest, and that flutter picked up in my stomach. "What time is it?"

"No clue." I couldn't tear my gaze away from his lips. "But I think we might've slept in."

"Maybe." The hand slipped up to my neck, and he guided my mouth to his. There was a quick flash of concern over brushing my teeth and kicking morning breath, but that worry went out the window the moment our lips touched.

The kiss was slow, lazy, and never-ending. It felt like forever since he'd kissed me like that when, in reality, it had really only been a handful of hours, but I lost myself in that kiss, in Aiden. And kissing him now was nothing like it had been those hours before. I felt the pressure, the intense sweetness, and the love behind every stroke of his tongue and sweep of his lips, to my very soul. The hand in my hair tightened while the other traveled north, up my thigh, and then over the curve of my hip.

Aiden's hand stilled and then swept back down, causing me to suck in a sharp breath. He pulled his mouth away from mine and opened his eyes. They were a pure, heated silver. "You're not wearing anything under this shirt, are you? Like, at all?"

I giggled. "I think you know the answer to that." He had to, especially considering where his hand drifted to in that moment. I wasn't giggling anymore. I was barely breathing.

He made that sound again, that absolutely sexy male sound that rumbled through him and then me. "You're killing me, *agapi mou.*"

"I'm sure that's *not* what I'm doing to you."

Aiden moved lightning fast. He rolled me onto my back and was above me, on me, pressing his leg between mine. His lips found mine like they'd been born to do so. This kiss was different. Hungry. Starving. My hands slid up the hard sides of his stomach and then onto his back. Those sculptured muscles flexed under my hands as the kiss deepened until my senses were spinning.

There was probably a lot to do today.

Some would also say there were a lot more important things we could be doing at this very moment.

I would argue against that point voraciously, because there was nothing more important than this. Not when those wonderfully rough hands skimmed under the borrowed shirt. His hips rocked against mine, and a fire raced throughout my blood. I wrapped my fingers around the band of his pajama bottoms.

"*Agapi mou*, I've missed you." His lips moved across my jaw and trailed a heated, shivery path down my throat, and then back to my lips. "I need you."

My heart stuttered. "Yes."

Who knows what I was really saying yes to? Anything at that point. Karate chop a few daimons while I was naked? Sure. Do trig formulas for fun? Okay. As long as he kept kissing me, kept calling me *agapi mou*, and kept touching me, I'd say yes to a lot of things. Too bad we weren't doing this while I was still in school. I could've used his kisses as an amazing studying incentive.

His hand hooked around my hip, urging me to wrap my leg around his, and I stopped thinking. If only I got these damn pants off—

A sudden pop and crackle preceded the overwhelming and very unwelcome presence of a god. Aiden's lips stilled against mine. My eyes popped up, latching onto his quicksilver ones. No way. I refused to believe it. No freaking way.

"Hades will be here in twenty minutes," Apollo announced from somewhere way too close to the bed. "Either speed this up or pick it up later, kids."

"Oh my gods," I whispered, horrified.

"Oh, and I hope you two are being *responsible*," Apollo added. And then he was gone. There was a muffled, hoarse shout from a room nearby.

"Damn him," Aiden muttered, dropping his head onto my

shoulder. He shuddered. "Damn him to the Underworld and back again."

My cheeks burned. "A bell—the first chance we get, we are buying him *a bell*."

12

A god popping in and out of your bedroom was, unsurprisingly, a major mood killer.

After Apollo vanished, neither of us was willing to risk him coming back with a ten-minute warning. Aiden had offered to speed up the get-ready-together process by sharing a shower.

From the bed, I raised my brows. "I don't think that would be a quick shower."

"You're right." He backed toward the bathroom door, his pajama bottoms hanging too low on his hips to be legal. "Can't blame me for trying."

He disappeared, and I flopped onto my back, groaning. I was going to ninja-kick Apollo in the face when I saw him.

Today, I didn't put jeans on. I wore my Sentinel uniform.

My hair was still damp when we headed to the dean's office. I don't know why we had to keep meeting in there. It wasn't so much because of what Ares had done in that room but because there were a lot of stairs to climb.

A lot.

The whole crew waited inside the office, and I knew Apollo was in there with Hades. I ran my hand over my arm, watching the marks glide seamlessly across my skin.

"Itchy?" Aiden asked.

I shrugged a shoulder. "The marks always go crazy when there are gods nearby."

As we walked toward the dean's office, he reached over, trailing his fingers along my arms. "Do they still react when I touch you?"

Heat crawled through my veins, and I nodded. The marks had followed the path of his touch. "Yeah, they still like you."

One side of his lips curled up, and a look of male pride crossed his face. I shook my head. Boys.

We entered the office, and all the godly power in the room, plus Seth's presence, was a bit overwhelming at first. I clenched my hands into fists to keep myself from bouncing off the walls or monkey-climbing Seth.

The two gods stood a good head taller than everyone else. They were shoulder to shoulder, but they couldn't have been more opposite of one another. Where Apollo was all golden skin and sunlight, Hades was dark as night.

Aiden sent Seth a downright frightening glare as he strolled toward the people clustered around the two gods. At least he didn't punch Seth, so that was a start in the right direction. I guessed.

Seth lingered in the back, leaning against the wall as he eyed the two gods with an edge of distrust. I took a deep breath and approached him. A new wariness crept into his expression. "What's up?" he asked.

"I didn't say thank you."

One golden brow rose. "For what?"

"For helping me out yesterday," I explained, turning so we stood side by side. "I didn't say thank you, so thank you."

"You've said thank you three times now."

"Yeah." I leaned against the wall. "I can say it again, if you want."

Seth turned sideways, facing me. When he spoke, his voice was low and held a biting, hard edge to it. "I don't want you to say it at all."

I arched a brow, but before he could elaborate, Marcus cleared his throat, drawing my attention.

Two gods stared at us.

I swallowed. Eerie. At least Apollo had normal eyes. Hades,

on the other hand, looked like someone had forgotten to give him irises and pupils.

Seth pushed off and went to stand by the opposite wall, his back stiff and shoulders tensed. The gods tracked his movement like lions watching a gazelle. Then Hades turned to me.

The god's lips spread into a tight smile. "Nice to see you again, Love."

With the exception of wanting to kill me that one time, Hades was an exceptionally gorgeous man. And he had a British accent, which made him that much hotter. I had no idea why Hades had one, and I'd yet to hear another god with the same accent.

"No puppies this time?" I asked.

His eyes narrowed at the reminder. The last time we'd met, it had been in a convenience store in Middle of Nowhere, West Virginia, and I'd taken out a few of his prized three-headed hellhounds.

"No puppies. Yet." Dressed in a sleeveless tunic, Hades' biceps flexed as he folded his arms. "So, it's true?" He swept the rest of the room with an arch look. Olivia shrank back, her normally caramel-colored skin pale. Hades' grin spread. "You all have a favor to ask of me?"

Marcus glanced at the Apollo. "You haven't told him?"

"Oh, he has. I was hoping that someone in here had used their intelligence and changed their minds." Hades smirked. "Although, I see that is highly unlikely."

Luke elbowed Deacon, who kept his face perfectly blank.

"Does everyone in this room understand the danger of releasing Perses?" Hades asked, standing in the middle of our loose circle. His leather-clad legs were spread wide, thighs like tree trunks. The silver cuffs at his wrists glinted in the light. "I'm not talking about a slight risk of him killing someone we don't want dead. He will, mark my words. Perses is what you would call . . ."

"Unpredictable," Apollo threw out, grinning. "We are well aware of that, as is Zeus, and from what I hear, he has sanctioned Perses' release."

Athena *was* his favorite child.

"That means squat to me, and you know that. Zeus has no power over my realm. And before this conversation proceeds any further, I want everyone to fully grasp what they are agreeing to."

"We understand," Seth said, gaining the boss of the Underworld's attention.

"Do you?" Hades turned to him, head cocked to the side. "You've been around Ares. Let me ask you a question. What does Ares thrive on the most?"

"More than one thing—war and fear," Seth responded blithely, and I flinched. "But most of all, he loves winning."

"Correct, but Perses thrived on the bloodshed of battle. He used to bathe in the entrails of those he'd defeated."

Olivia turned green.

"Not only that, Perses fought to destroy—not to win. There's a big difference there." Hades paused, and it felt like cold wind had circled its way down my spine. "And what has happened since Ares decided to play in the mortal realm?"

Aiden shifted his weight, his jaw set in a tight, grim line. "There's been conflict—countries everywhere on the verge of war. His presence affects mortals. We know."

"And what do you think will happen if you add Perses to the mix?" Hades asked. "His influence is stronger than Ares'. Those countries on the verge may make war just because we've released him. Is that another risk you're willing to take?"

No one answered, because seriously, we could be exchanging one apocalyptic situation for another. "We have to take that risk," I said finally, meeting the all-white eyes of Hades. "And we'll make sure he behaves." Hopefully.

"You think he'll behave because I'll release him into Elysian

Fields afterward? Do you have any idea what crimes Perses was responsible for?"

I could only imagine.

Apparently Hades didn't want me to use my imagination. "He created the term 'rape and pillage.' He wiped out entire generations and civilizations for the *fun* of it. He killed our brethren just to hear them scream and plead for their lives. He took our children and ripped them apart because he *could*. That is what you are releasing into the mortal realm. That is what you're asking me to give paradise to."

My heart rate kicked up. I got what Hades was saying. It was like allowing Hitler into Heaven or something, but I wondered if Hades had ever heard of the whole throwing stones and glass houses thing. "And how is that any different than what you guys have been responsible for throughout history?"

Hades took a step toward me, and over his shoulder I saw Aiden and Seth stiffen, but I didn't need them. I held my ground and lifted my chin. The god stopped a few feet in front of me.

Akasha, the fifth and final element, simmered in the pit of my stomach. The marks on my skin tingled in warning, but I refused to look away from his unflinching stare. "What? It's the truth. How is a Titan truly any worse than an Olympian running amok? Any worse than what Ares is already doing?"

A slow, almost-reluctant smile graced Hades' lips. "You want to know the difference?"

"Yes." Did he know how creepy his eyes were? Probably.

Hades leaned down, coming so close that we shared the same breathing space. "A God Killer can kill an Olympian. Not a Titan. And a Titan can kill an Apollyon."

My brows shot up. "Oh." Well, then . . .

"Yeah, 'oh.'" Hades wheeled around, eyeing Aiden, who had made it halfway across the room before Apollo had intercepted and blocked him. "So does everyone still want to hold a welcoming party for a bloodthirsty Titan that no one can kill if he decides to not play along?"

Unrest filled the room. Luke and Solos shifted their gazes, no doubt having second thoughts. Deacon looked like he had no idea how he'd ended up in this room, and Olivia was slowly shaking her head. Only Aiden, Marcus and Seth looked resolute.

"You've stopped the Titans before," Aiden said, voice level and calm despite the rising tension. "And there were many more than one at that time."

"It took all of us to stop the Titans, one at a time. And if we manage to stop Ares, we will be down one," Hades responded. "So it wouldn't be easy."

Apollo squared his shoulders. "You offer him paradise. He will behave."

"You think?" Hades folded his arms again. "And I thought you weren't really down with this plan?"

"It's not the best thing, but it is all we have, and you know that's true, so stop posturing. What do you want in return for releasing Perses?"

Hades' jaw worked like he was crunching bone. "And for offering him paradise?"

The Sun god looked like he wanted to toss Hades *at* the sun. "Yes. And for that."

Here it comes, I thought. What could Hades possibly want that we could give him in return for his assistance? The souls of our firstborn children? A giggle rose, but I squelched it, because it seriously could be that.

Seconds turned into an eternity, and then Hades finally spoke. "You."

I blinked, at first having no idea who he was speaking to, but then I saw his attention fixed on Aiden. My heart thumped against my chest like a caged bird.

"What?" I demanded, my voice too thin.

Hades' lips curled into a smirk. "I want him."

A flash of bewilderment raced across Aiden's features. "You want me?"

I had no idea where this was going, but I did not like it.

"He doesn't swing that way," Apollo commented, his blue eyes alive with amusement. "And I didn't think you did, either."

Someone, I suspected Seth, choked on a laugh.

Hades shot the other god a scathing look. "I want his soul."

13

I was seconds away from discovering what would happen when an Apollyon hit a god with a bolt of anger-fueled akasha. Seth sensed my fury. Hell, he had to be drowning in it. He was edging along the wall, coming closer and closer to me.

Or the exit.

"No," I said, and then louder, "Hell to the no, you cannot have his soul."

Hades whipped toward me, and the tense pull to his lips told me he didn't like my tone. Well, he wasn't going to like my foot up his ass, either. "I would've asked for yours, but Apollo wouldn't have allowed that."

I so did not care. "You cannot have his soul. I don't care what we need you for."

Apollo heaved a heavy breath. "Alex."

"No!" I spun on the god. "No way."

Hades' smirk infuriated me. "But you haven't even heard the details."

I stormed up to the god, already tasting his blood. "You can take your details and shove them up your fake British—"

"Alex!"

Clamping my mouth shut, I tensed my shoulders as I turned to the one person in this world who could get me to shut up. Aiden stood to my right, and the moment our gazes locked, I saw it. He wanted to hear Hades out. Knots spiraled tightly in my stomach.

"No," I said again, my voice a pitiful whisper. "I don't want to even hear it."

He held my gaze for a second longer and then turned to Hades. "What are the details?"

The god oozed smugness. "I want your soul."

"I think we've covered that," I snapped.

Hades ignored me. "Your soul would belong to me once you've died to use however I see fit."

I took a breath, but it got stuck. However he saw fit? My hands itched to get around his thick neck.

"I could always use a guard with your boldness and skill," Hades continued.

Images of the guards of Hell, in leather and astride giant warhorses, flashed through my mind. I couldn't—wouldn't picture Aiden as one of them.

"And I wouldn't take your life," Hades went on while I started to picture myself lopping his head off with a giant sword. "When you die, not by my hand or through any trickery on my part, I will have your soul. I give my word."

I thought of what Solos had told me. Snakes. "And we're supposed to believe that?"

"He's not lying," Apollo said, eyes narrowed. "He gave his word. It's unbreakable."

I laughed, and the sound was coarse. Trust a god's word? Were they on meth? I twisted halfway and saw Deacon's expression as he stared at his brother. Stark. Accepting. Oh gods, he knew. I whirled on Aiden. "No! We'll find another way."

"There is no other way." Aiden crossed the short distance between us and gently placed his big hands on my cheeks. "You know that."

"No." I gripped his wrists. "There has to be something else."

"Is there? Minutes ago, Perses was our only option," Hades oh-so pleasantly reminded me.

Outrage caused the akasha in my veins to start begging to be used. Loudly. "It's your soul, Aiden. When you die, you will have to go to work for him or worse. You won't go to the Elysian

Fields. You . . ." I broke off, unable to say what was so selfish but true.

We wouldn't have eternity together.

When I died, barring I didn't kill Hades right now, I'd go to Elysia, and Aiden would not be there. He'd never be there, not until Hades allowed it. And he would never allow it.

Tears filled my eyes as Aiden lowered his forehead to mine. "I don't plan on dying for a long time, *agapi mou*. We have today, and we'll have many tomorrows, but only if we get Hades' help. We won't have any of that if we don't stop Ares."

"But—"

"This is bigger than both of us." His thumb caught a tear that had snuck out, wiping it away before anyone besides Seth noticed. And there was no hiding how I felt from the First. He was standing close to us, his expression devoid of its usual smirk. Aiden smiled, but it *hurt*. "We have to do anything and everything to stop this."

"I don't care," I whispered.

"Yes, you do."

I shook my head. "Not if it means this, I don't. I don't care."

It wasn't fair. It wasn't fair that we had to keep making sacrifices. We could possibly face losing a mortal life together, and now we wouldn't even have an afterlife? Sorrow rose in me swiftly. "You wouldn't want this for me."

"I wouldn't," he admitted, "but that's not the situation, and we need this."

"You do," Hades cajoled, and I wanted to claw his face into tiny, bloody pieces.

Seth shifted closer. I didn't see him, because I couldn't look away from Aiden, but I felt him. "Aiden is right," Seth said quietly, but it was still intrusive. "You know there's no other choice."

"I don't want you to have to make this choice," I insisted. Yes, I was being selfish, but it didn't just affect me. It also affected his brother and his family. If Hades didn't allow it, he'd never see his mother and father again. This was too much.

Aiden's striking face blurred through the haze of tears. "I know." His lips brushed the corner of my lips. "But we have to."

I opened my mouth to protest more, but he took advantage of that moment. He deepened the kiss and kissed me like we were the only two people in the room, in the world. Tingles shot up and down my spine in a wave of electricity. I leaned into him, kissing him back with everything I felt. Aiden tasted of salt, of mint, and of love.

Someone, maybe my uncle, cleared his throat.

Aiden slowly lifted his head, and the room came back into focus. My cheeks burned. "By doing this, we are giving ourselves a future together. Okay? We have to do this. I have to do this, and there's nothing that can be done to change that."

"Oh, this conversation is *so* not over," I promised, blinking back tears. "I'm going to spin-kick you in the head for this one later, but okay. Okay."

Aiden chuckled, but he wisely stepped back and turned to Hades. "Okay. You have my soul when I die."

"See?" Hades eyed me over Aiden's shoulder. "Was that so hard?"

"I hate you," I hissed.

"It's nothing personal, Love."

"Yeah, and the last time you said that to me you wanted to kill me." My hands curled into fists.

The god of the Underworld shrugged. "Okay."

"That's it?" Seth asked, the hollows of his cheeks more pronounced. "You're not going to even shake on it? He says 'you can have my soul' and you say okay?"

I shot Seth a glare.

Hades smiled again. "That's all I need."

Seth's amber eyes rolled. "That's anticlimactic."

The god was unbothered by that as he settled his attention on

Aiden and me. "You two will be responsible for Perses, meaning you will come with me and take him out of Tartarus."

My spine stiffened. "We have to go to Tartarus?"

Static crackled around Hades' eyes. "I think showing you two what could possibly lie in store for your pure-blood may incline both of you to work extra-hard to ensure that Perses sticks to the plan."

I gasped.

"Wait." Seth stepped forward. "I'm going with them."

Aiden opened his mouth, mostly like to passionately disagree, but Hades cut him off. "I think that is a great idea. Then the *three* of you will be responsible for Perses and what role Aiden takes on in the afterlife."

My stomach dropped, and I felt like I was falling. Before I could protest, Hades was already making plans. We would leave for Tartarus within the hour. He would take us straight there, no need for finding a gate or facing any of the guards. It was all happening too fast. Aiden was talking to Deacon in low, hushed tones, and Solos was with Marcus, surrounded by Olivia and Luke.

My unease about the deal settled in me like sour food. My heart pounded in my chest way too fast, and if I didn't know any better, I would've sworn Phobos and Deimos were back, but they weren't. Fear formed an icy knot under my breastbone.

Alex . . .

I didn't turn to Seth. *What if Perses doesn't do what we need him to? What if he runs off and slaughters an entire nation? Hades will put that on Aiden. He'll have his soul and—*

We'll make sure that won't happen. The confidence in Seth's words pushed through our bond. *St. Delphi won't end up in Tartarus, I promise you.*

The fact that Seth would promise something like that didn't go unnoticed. *Either way, he'll own Aiden. No matter what happens. Aiden will be like a half-blood, nothing more than . . .*

Air leaked out of my lungs. Aiden would be like a slave, like every half-blood was now and would be, even after we took care of Ares. Aiden's own words came back to me in that moment. *This is bigger than us.* Realization whirled, and an opportunity presented itself. Hell, the opportunity had always been there, but I'd been too self-absorbed to realize it, too caught up in my own problems to . . .

To use the power I held in my hands to change things.

"Wait!" I called out.

"Alex," Seth said in a quiet voice.

I shook my head, breathing deeply. Apollo turned to me, inclining his head. I readied myself. "Wait. There's something I want before we do this."

Hades chuckled deeply. "What position are you in to bargain, Love?"

If he called me "Love" one more time . . . I reeled in my temper and focused on Apollo. "You want us to go down into Tartarus and fetch Perses, watch over him while he helps us, and then you want me to become the God Killer and take out Ares, right?"

Apollo shifted his weight. "That sounds about right."

My heart turned over heavily. "I will only do this if you do something for me."

Hades scuffed. "Again, Love, what position are you in to bargain with us?"

I slid my gaze toward Mr. Tall, Dark, and About to be Missing an Eyeball. "Without me, you don't have a God Killer. You can't make me become it, and you can't make me fight Ares."

"We can be very persuasive," Hades growled.

"Yeah, and Ares tried to be persuasive, and I still didn't give in." I looked at Apollo. "I know you guys can't make Seth or me do it. We could leave you guys to this mess. You need us *willing*."

Apollo's lips twitched as if he wished to smile. "What do you want, Alex?"

"I want you to free the half-bloods. I want you to get rid of the laws requiring them to either become Sentinels, or Guards, or servants. I want you to give them the same rights as pure-bloods. I want the Breed Order revoked."

Silence.

It was so quiet that you could hear a fly run into a wall. Everyone was staring at me like I'd just pulled up my shirt and asked for some beads.

And then Seth chuckled deeply. "Clever, Angel."

I ignored the nickname. I also ignored the way Aiden's eyes went from the purest color of gray to silver in a nanosecond. "I know you can do it, Apollo. I know you can make the other gods agree. You do this for me, and I'll be all about taking a tour of Tartarus."

Apollo stared at me as he slowly shook his head. "There was so much more you could've asked for, Alex."

My brows knitted. "Like what? What could be more important than that?"

His gaze held mine, and suddenly I knew what he meant. I could've asked for his protection, because once I took care of Ares, it would be open season on my arse. I knew Apollo would already do what he could to ensure that I walked away, but it seemed useless to waste this opportunity on something that Apollo might not be able to stop.

The god nodded curtly. "Okay. Once everything has settled, we will change the laws and the Elixir will be no more. You have my word, no matter the outcome."

No matter the outcome. Meaning if Ares kicks our asses into the next generation. I wanted Apollo to do it now, because I had the patience of a hyena, but I could understand why he couldn't. The last thing we needed was more half-bloods, thousands of them, coming off the effects of the Elixir in the middle of this mess.

My gaze traveled across the room, skipping over the shocked

expressions of Luke and Olivia. I think, in that moment, they realized the same thing Solos must have by the look in his wide eyes. After all this was said and done, they would have something they'd never had before.

Complete and utter control of their future.

14

Olivia hugged me so hard I thought my lungs would deflate. She held on, her lithe form trembling. It was a good hug, reminding me of the ones my mother used to give me. "The whole evil-twin god thing is so messed up. I'm sorry, but I'm glad they're out," she said, and then in a lower, hoarser voice, she added, "Thank you."

I knew why she was thanking me—for the deal. I squeezed her back and then leaned away. I kept my voice low. "So what are you going to do?"

"After this craziness with Ares?" When I nodded, a far-off look crept into her pretty eyes. She dropped her arms, shaking her heard. "You know, I don't know. I never thought about it, but now I do have something to think about, and it's . . ."

"Amazing," Luke said, dropping a quick kiss on my cheek. "I think I'm going to enroll in college."

Both Olivia and I stared at him.

"What?" A flush spread across his cheeks. "I actually like school."

"Freak," I muttered.

Hades was growing impatient. *Surly bastard.* I said goodbye, giving my uncle a stiff and somewhat awkward hug. Tension and elation warred in the room. The agreement made with Apollo, who was actually going to remain here instead of popping back to Olympus, was obviously a big deal, but what the three of us were about to embark on could quickly become dangerous.

Perses could kill us all and make a run for it.

Continuing that line of thought wasn't what I wanted to be focus on as I made my way over to where Hades stood between Aiden and Seth. My eyes bounced between the two guys. Then again, I wasn't so sure that Perses was going to be the problem.

Aiden and Seth were sizing each other up like they were ready for a caged death match.

Sidling up to Aiden, I elbowed him in the side.

He glanced down at me, eyes the color of the ocean during a storm. "I'm proud of you."

Oh, the swelling in my chest could've lifted me right up to the ceiling. I smiled up at him, smiled so widely my cheeks ached.

"I would've used that favor more intelligently, Love." Hades smirked. "There was so much you could've asked for."

And Hades burst my bubble with a quickness I should have expected. "Thanks for your input," I muttered.

"You're welcome," he replied. "Is everyone ready for our little field trip?"

With Apollo's seal of approval, Seth was given his toys back, so all of us, even Seth, were decked out in our Covenant daggers and Glocks. Our eyes locked for a moment. There was something in his amber gaze that unsettled me.

Aiden reached down, threading his fingers through mine. "We're ready."

Without any warning, the floor dropped out from under us.

"Holy daimon babies!" I gasped, stumbling back as the world righted itself once more. "Good gods . . ."

Aiden patted his hands over his chest as if checking to make sure he was all there. Seth looked a little out of it. None of us had been prepared for that method of traveling.

The god of the Underworld watched us. Amusement bled into the air around him. "It's easier that way, don't you think?"

I smoothed my hand over my hair, relieved to find it still

attached to my head. When the floor had moved under us, it had felt like we'd fallen a million feet. "Did you just . . . just *teleport* us?"

"Something like that." Hades turned, putting his hands on his hips. Tipping his head back, he let out a loud, ear-piercing whistle, causing me to jump.

"So this is the Underworld?" Seth turned, taking in his surroundings.

Forcing myself to get over the fact that I wasn't exactly sure how Hades had managed to teleport us, and the whole science behind that concept, I looked around. I recognized where we were.

"Thank the gods it's not the Vale of Mourning, huh?" Aiden said.

I nodded. That vast, depressing stretch of the Underworld was not a place I wanted to visit again. We were just outside the Vale, several feet from the congested road that led to the Plain of Judgment.

Seth watched the recently departed making slow progress with a troubled look. A lot of the deceased were Sentinels, their black uniforms in various stages of distress. Seeing them . . . well, I had to think it was a painful reminder of what he'd been a part of.

The sound of pounding hooves drew my attention from the First, and I turned. "Holy gods . . ."

I jerked back, bouncing off of Aiden's chest. An arm circled my waist, steadying me. Good gods in Olympia, the horses were the size of elephants. Four of them. Their coats were as dark and shiny as midnight oil, their manes glossy and groomed. They looked like extremely large horses with the exception of the all-white pupils behind their black-leather eye shields. "I don't remember them being this big."

"Me, neither."

Seth neared one, head cocked to the side. The horse whinnied. "They're like the Hummer of the horse world."

I almost laughed, but then I noticed the saddles on each of them. I glanced at Hades as he ran a large hand down one of the horses' manes. "These *are* bigger than what you saw last time. They are from my personal stable." He grabbed the saddle and swung himself up with astonishing ease. "It is not a quick journey to Tartarus. We will ride them there."

Glancing at one of the horses near me, I hesitated. "Why didn't you just pop us into Tartarus?"

"Tartarus is an ever-changing landscape, adapting to its . . . newest arrivals." He shrugged. "I would hate to pop my newest acquisition into a lake of fire."

My eyes narrowed.

Hades smirked at me as he wrapped a meaty hand around the reins. "We don't have all day. There's a mean game of Mario Kart waiting for me when I get back."

Resisting the urge to run up to Hades and knock him out of the saddle, I wheeled around. Seth had already found his horse and was in the saddle, looking very proud of himself. Then Aiden was on his, swinging a leg over the horse, which left me staring at the last one, the one that reminded me of a T-Rex.

It sniffed at me.

"You might want to get used to these magnificent creatures." Hades' smile was cold and pleased as he looked at Aiden.

An ache hit me in my chest at the reminder of Aiden's deal. I turned, ready to lay into him for agreeing, but drew up short. I was face-to-face with a massive horse head.

Walking up, I awkwardly patted its nose. "Nice horsey."

Its lip curled up, revealing oddly sharp teeth. Did horses have sharp teeth? Or just Underworld horses? My gaze traveled over the massive chest and leather saddle. How in the hell was I supposed to get on this thing? The stirrup was so far off the ground I was going to need a stepladder to access it.

"You put your foot in the stirrup," Seth said, tipping his chin down.

"I know," I snapped. But I didn't move any closer. The horse turned its elegant head back away from me and snorted. "I've never ridden a horse before."

Hades sighed.

Heat crept into my cheeks. Honestly, I was sort of afraid of horses. Normal ones could break your bones. These could eat you.

Aiden guided his horse toward where I stood, smiling slightly as he looked down. "Come on."

I stared at him.

The slight smile spread, revealing a dimple in his right cheek. "There's room for both of us up here. Ride with me."

Okay. I was scared of horses, and that made me a wuss, but I thought about all those romance novels my mom used to read with the hero astride a horse, and then there was Aiden, larger than life astride a horse, and that was . . . well, that was hot.

"I really don't care if you ride alone or with Loverboy here, but can we move this along?" Hades tightened his hand on the reins, turning the horses. "I am not known for my patience."

I shot him a scathing look, which was ignored. Crossing the distance between Aiden and me, I reached up, putting my hand in his. With astonishing ease, he hauled me up into the saddle in front of him. After a few seconds of awkward fumbling, I was seated on the horse, clenching the edge of the saddle.

Well aware that both Hades and Seth were staring at us, I remained stiff as Aiden snaked an arm around my waist and tugged me back between his thighs. His heat immediately seeped into my tense muscles.

"How cute," Seth drawled.

"Shut up," Aiden said, and then much lower, directly in my ear, "This is the greatest idea I've ever had."

I shivered.

We started off then, galloping along the crowded road. It took a little while to get used to the jarring motion of the horse and even longer to get familiar with the stagnant, sweet-scented air blowing in my face. About a half an hour in, four guards suddenly flanked us, their faces pale and somber. I tried desperately not to picture Aiden becoming one of Hades' henchmen, but I couldn't help but wonder why Hades had even asked for Aiden. It wasn't like there was any shortage of people who had some kind of penance to pay, and wasn't that what these guards were doing? Working off their sins in the afterlife? Or was it something else?

I knew it was punishment. Hades knew we'd snuck into the Underworld to see Solaris, and he obviously wasn't happy about that. In a twist of irony, our journey had been rather pointless now. Seth wanted me to become the God Killer, and he knew how to make the transfer. We'd ended up not needing Solaris.

The barren landscape turned lush as we neared the crossroads. The bare, brown ground gave way to thick, bright-green grass. The congestion of those recently deceased grew as the spired tips of Hades' stone palace finally came into view.

And so did Tartarus.

The eerie red glow off in the distance was hard to ignore. So was the very faint, almost untraceable scent of sulfur. I couldn't believe we were actually going there willingly.

My unease grew with every passing moment. I was waiting for it to happen, and when it finally did, Seth swore loudly.

A loud pop thundered through the air, following by a whoosh as the ground trembled under the hooves of our horses. The sky lit up, bleeding red and orange as a ball of flames shot up, spreading first into fiery wings, and then the jaws of the dragon opened, emitting the horrifying scream that stuck with us. The fiery dragon swooped back down, its tail flaming as the ground shook once more.

"Holy shit," Seth said, eyes wide. "What in the hell was that?"

"Tartarus' welcoming party," Hades replied. "Get used to it.

I have a feeling you'll see it up close and personal more than once."

Seth snorted, as if the very real possibility of him ending up in Tartarus wasn't a big deal, but my stomach roiled at the thought. I looked at him as we rode on, remembering quite clearly where the Solaris' First was currently located.

Did Seth deserve eternal damnation for his actions?

He glanced over at me, his expression unreadable. Our gazes locked. His perfectly pieced face was emotionless, but something churned in his eyes. *Seth?*

There was no answer. Instead, those amber eyes, so much like my own, flicked back to Aiden. "Hey, Saint Delphi."

Oh, Lord.

Aiden stiffened behind me. "Yes?"

Seth guided his horse beside us, and I wondered where both of them had mastered horseback riding. "If you find yourself needing some extra space on that horse, I have more than enough room on mine." Seth's tight smile grew as I stared at him. "We could . . . share."

Heat roared off of Aiden. He hadn't missed the innuendo. "Not going to happen."

One shoulder rose in response. "It was just an offer."

"Can you not talk?" Aiden retorted.

"Hey, all I'm saying is, for a while there, we really did share—"

"Seth!" I hissed, my cheeks burning.

"What?" he replied innocently, and if I wasn't so afraid of being stomped to death, I would've jumped off this horse and beaten him senseless.

Our little quarrel hadn't drawn the attention of Hades or his guards, and I sure hoped it stayed that way. Besides being annoying, this was as embarrassing as the time I nearly broke someone's neck doing a take-down incorrectly in class. Mainly because I had messed up then, and I also had messed up when it came to Seth and Aiden.

Aiden's voice was deceptively calm when he spoke. "You never had her, Seth. We weren't sharing anything."

"Hmm. That's not how it seemed to me. You know, there's a reason why I call her Angel."

"Oh, for the love of the gods," I muttered, glaring at Seth. I was damn sure he'd been calling me that long before any parts of our bodies had touched. "Knock it off. Both of you."

Seth winked.

He finally quieted down, but Aiden was stewing. I could feel the tension in him as we rode on, but there was nothing I could do, because I had a feeling anything I said to calm him down would only instigate the butthead beside us. Besides, my mind went elsewhere.

A huge part of me had hoped to see Caleb, but as we galloped past the Plain of Judgment, heading straight for the eerie red glow of Tartarus, I knew I wouldn't get to see him this time. As if sensing my thoughts, Aiden dipped his head and kissed my cheek. Squeezing my eyes shut, I allowed myself to fully relax into him since it didn't appear like the mammoth beast underneath us was about to eat us.

Tracking time in the Underworld was difficult. What felt like an hour here could be only a half-second above ground, and it seemed like we'd been on the damn horses for longer than an hour. But the scent of sulfur grew, and the sky darkened into an ominous mixture of orange and deep blue, like the sky before a violent storm at dusk.

As we traveled on, the grass was replaced by a fine trail of fire that smoldered along the ground, following the road to Tartarus. The group of people traveling along the road was heavily guarded, and I wondered if that was why Hades' guards had appeared.

Those on this road wore ragged, torn clothing. Their chins were tipped down, and their progress was slow as they shuffled along, chained at the ankles and wrists.

The dragon made another appearance, and this time I could feel the heat of the morphing fire.

A heaviness permeated the air as we passed under a crudely-built stone archway, and I shuddered. Bare trees stood, their branches thin like bones, stretching toward the sky. Up ahead, a rocky hill rose sharply, and beyond the crest, the glow of orange was stronger. Aiden's arm tightened around me as the horses slowed, whinnying softly. The atmosphere shifted dramatically, and it was more than the fact that night had descended like a heavy, suffocating blanket. The only light was from the thin rows of fire and the glowing torches posted every so many feet. A sour tang of bitterness coated the inside of my mouth, and a fierce bite of hatred choked my heart.

Seth was staring at something to our left, and my gaze followed his. The river Styx had reappeared, its murky waters flowing swiftly, but it wasn't the river he was staring at.

Dozens of women in bloodied white gowns were near the bank of the river. Some were bending, reaching into the dark waters. Others carried jars away. The jars were leaking. By the time they were a few feet from the road, the jars were empty.

The women silently turned back to the river.

"Who are they?" I whispered.

"They are the daughters of Danaus," Aiden said. His hand rested over my stomach, and his thumb moved in absent, smoothing circles.

"They murdered their husbands on their wedding nights, at their father's request. This is their punishment."

I wanted to look away from them, because I couldn't comprehend an eternity of fruitless labor, but I couldn't tear my gaze away as our horse rode on. I craned my neck, watching the women turn back to the Styx, slowly, sadly, their jars empty. Their appearance was significant.

We had entered Tartarus.

15

Tartarus wasn't very scenic.

Imagine the worst section of any town, and then imagine that neighborhood on fire and throw in some random torture scenes between the run-down shacks. That was Tartarus.

Fire was everywhere. Bushes on fire. Trees burning. The Styx at some point had turned into a river of flames as it slithered between stone buildings. Some were standing and, of course, on fire. Others were halfway destroyed, large sections crumbling to the ground.

It was like the apocalypse happened and then stayed around.

The stench of sulfur and blood was almost unbearable, but the heat . . . oh, dear gods, I was seconds away from pulling my shirt off. Sweat beaded on me, rolling between my breasts.

"This would make a lovely vacation spot," Seth muttered.

I started to respond, but my eyes latched onto a flaming . . . a flaming wheel? "What the hell?"

Hades glanced over his shoulder at me, those freaky eyes doing the static thing. "That's Ixion."

As we grew closer to the tragedy, I could see that there was a man in the center of the large wheel. "Oh, my gods." I clamped my hand over my mouth.

"Don't make a pass at Hera," Hades remarked, moving along. "Zeus doesn't take kindly to another man making a move on his wife."

That was absolutely ridiculous if you took into consideration the fact Zeus couldn't keep it in his pants.

"Stop staring," Aiden murmured in my ear, and when I still didn't look away, he reached around and turned my cheek. "I thought Ixion was located in the lowest part of Tartarus?"

I made a face. Only he would know who Ixion was. Aiden had to have been such a goody two-shoes in school—the kind of kid who'd raised his hand with the answer to every question. *Dork*. I loved him.

"We took a shortcut, so we're several levels down." Hades stopped his horse and swung down. We'd hit a dead end consisting of dark, slick-looking boulders. "There is another portion of Tartarus that isn't spoken of in myths."

Seth dismounted with the grace of a feline. "And that's where we're heading?"

"Yes. We're going into the Tombs of Tartarus."

"The Tombs of Tartarus?" Aiden repeated, sliding his arm off my waist.

Ha! Something he didn't know. I cast him a look over my shoulder and then slid off the horse. I stumbled a step when my feet landed. The ground was oddly . . . *soft* and buoyant.

Hades snorted. "It amazes me that you're an Apollyon with all your agility."

My mouth opened to fire back, but I squinted. Something was up with the ground. I took a step and my feet sank about an inch in. Aware that Aiden had landed behind me, I bent down and ran my hand over the pale pink ground. It felt like . . .

I jerked my hand back and looked up, horrified. "The ground feels like skin!"

A slow smile crept onto Hades' face. "Zeus got bored with the whole rock and eagle bit."

Rock and eagle bit . . . ? Then it hit me. "Prometheus?"

"You're standing on him," Hades remarked.

My stomach turned. "Oh gods, I think I'm going to vomit."

"Perfect," the god said.

Seth's brows rose, but he remained quiet. I forced myself to walk forward, desperately ignoring my gag reflex with each cushiony step. Behind us, several guards dismounted as Hades strolled toward his right. He stopped in front of a smoothed section of the rock and placed his palm to it.

Beside me, Aiden cocked his head to the side. His dark hair was damp and curled around the temples. The wall before us trembled quietly, and then the slab of stone glided open, beckoning us into the darkness.

One of the guards stepped forward, a torch in hand. He handed it to the god and then moved back, hands on his daggers—big, wicked-looking daggers.

"We keep the Titans in the tombs," Hades explained as he stepped forward. "They're separated from the rest and have to be handled delicately. Their damnation comes in the form of eternal sleep."

Cool air washed over my sticky skin as I followed Seth and Hades, and even though it was freaky to be walking into tombs, I welcomed the colder temps. My eyes adjusted quickly. The stone walls were covered in glyphs, much like the ones that appeared on Seth's and my skin.

"Sleep doesn't sound like damnation," I said.

"We couldn't handle them if they all were awake." Hades continued down the narrow hall. "Their powers are weakened in the Underworld, but if all of them were up and moving about, it would be a problem."

"So it works the same way as it does for the Olympians?" Aiden asked, staying close behind me. "They feed off each other's power."

"Yes." Hades came to a split in the hall and hung a left. The temp dropped another couple of degrees as we headed down roughly carved steps. "Once Perses gets topside, he's going to get some of his power back. He won't be at a full charge, but he'll be as powerful as any lesser god."

"Any lesser god" meant Perses was going to be powerful.

Maybe not at the same level as Hades or Ares, but he wasn't going to be any weakling. The next hall was wider, opening up into a circular chamber. In the center was a small pool that smelled faintly of jasmine, which made me think of the pool Aiden and I had gone swimming in the last time we were in the Underworld.

I caught Aiden's stare and knew he was thinking the same thing I was. The corner of his lips tipped up, and I flushed.

"Seriously? Could you guys go longer than five minutes without making googly faces at one another?" Seth walked between us, scowling. "It's distracting."

Aiden smirked, and then opened his mouth. I cut him off before we got into another battle of wits that ended with me wanting to crawl under Prometheus' skin. "How many of the Titans do you have down here?"

"All of the ones who want to cause problems." Hades disappeared into another corridor, and I sighed, hurrying to catch up to him. "Very few are in Elysian Fields. Cronus and his cronies are all here."

Cronus was the father of Zeus, Hades, and who knew how many other gods. A shudder snaked down my spine. Hades kept his own father imprisoned in a hell-tomb. The hallway was a tight fit. Luckily, we weren't in it for very long. We entered another chamber, but this one was different.

We were in the tombs.

Twelve tombs, to be exact. I thought it was odd—the number. Twelve Olympians. Twelve entombed Titans. They were in some kind of capsule-like containers, embedded deep into the stone wall. A thick layer of reddish ice covered them, revealing only a humanoid shape beyond the barrier. But from the looks of it, Titans were tall.

Like gargantuan-size.

"Do you know that I'm actually older than Zeus?" Hades asked as he placed the torch into a sconce in the wall. "As are

Poseidon, Demeter, Hera, and so on? But because Cronus was a dick—and he was a *huge* dick—and our momma only saved Zeus, the world thinks Baby Brother was the first to be born."

"Didn't Cronus eat you guys?" Seth asked.

I made a face.

Hades laughed. "The whole 'swallowing us' crap was symbolic for hiding us. He held us in captivity until our baby brother set us free." He walked along the iced-over tombs, and his eyes narrowed as he stopped in front of the tomb in the center. "Screw you, Dad."

I passed a look at Aiden, who slowly shook his head, but then Hades stepped to the left and let out a heavy sigh. "There was a time when Perses wasn't so bad, and maybe the years have changed him, but I'm not holding my breath." He turned to me. "Are you sure you want to do this, Love?"

My gaze crawled to the tomb in front of him, and my pulse picked up. "Like I've said, we really don't have any other choices."

Hades stared at me for a long moment and then turned back to the tomb. "You don't." He placed his hand on the center of the tomb. I wanted to step back, but I forced myself to stand where I was. I was pretty sure running through the tombs would only end up with me being lost, and then Seth would make fun of me for the rest of my life.

The ice shuddered, and a spiderweb of cracks formed underneath Hades' palm, rapidly spreading across the front of the tomb. Seth and Aiden flanked me, and for once, both boys were quiet and not picking at each other.

Ice slipped away, shedding from the tomb, and hit the floor, making tiny sounds like a distant wind chime. Within seconds, the Titan was revealed.

Perses *was* tall—almost seven and a half feet, maybe more. And he was unnaturally still inside his tomb. Thick lashes fanned cheeks the color of supple brown leather. His skull was smooth, free of hair, and his features were angular and exotic—full lips, sharp cheekbones, and a well-defined brow. He was beautiful in the way all the godly creatures were: inhumanly perfect.

As still as the Titan was, he looked dead. Not even his chest moved, but an air of danger surrounded him nonetheless. I couldn't imagine what it would be like once he was released.

Leather pants and a tunic stretched over broad, thick muscles. There were cuffs on his wrists, adorned with odd symbols I didn't recognize.

"What is it with gods and leather?" I muttered.

Hades slid me a long look. "We make it look good."

They did. Couldn't argue that, but the gods' hotness didn't compensate for their overall creepiness and deranged thought processes.

"Last chance," Hades said, looking over his shoulder at us.

There was a pause, and then Aiden said, "Do it."

With a slight shake of his head, Hades turned back to the Titan and placed his hand on the center of its chest. A red glow radiated from the god's palm and then washed over Perses. No words were spoken or rituals completed. It appeared that Hades alone had the special touch.

Hades stepped back and folded his arms. We didn't have to wait long.

The Titan shuddered once and then opened his eyes. I tried to squelch the gasp but couldn't. Unlike the Olympians, his eyes were pitch black. The whole eye—the exact opposite of the Olympians. And if I'd thought the gods' eyes were messed up, it was nothing compared to the Titan's.

Perses' gaze landed on Hades and his lip curled up. "You've got to be kidding me."

My brows shot up at the sound of the deep voice. So wasn't expecting that to be the first thing for the Titan to say when he came out of the deep freeze.

Hades tilted his head to the side as a slow, lazy smile spread across his lips. "Hello, Perses, how was your nap?"

"It was great, asshole."

Oh. Dear.

The spine of the god stiffened. "I can see your attitude is the same as it was when we chained you into this tomb."

"*Barely* chained me," he sneered. The Titan raked our little group with a passing look and then swung his head back toward us. The violent curl of his lips slipped away as his eyes narrowed. "I'm awakened to find an asshole, a child of a demigod, and two Apollyons before me? I must admit, I am curious."

I was surprised by how well Hades was handling the insults being flung his way.

"We need your help," I forced myself to say. "That's why you've been awakened."

One dark eyebrow rose into a perfect arch. "You need *my* help?" The Titan tipped his head back and laughed so deeply I thought I felt the ground under my feet tremble. Laughing was good, though. At least he wasn't trying to kill us. "My help? I cannot imagine what ludicrous situation you've all have gotten yourself in if the Olympians are coming to a Titan for help."

"Well, you see . . ." I cleared my throat and gave him the quick and dirty version of events. The whole time he stared at me until I felt like my insides were spread across my clothing. "We know you can prepare us and you can——"

"Cause Ares to lose some of his confidence? Make him uneasy?" Perses' chuckle echoed throughout the cavern. "You need me as the psychological ace up your sleeve."

"Basically," Aiden replied evenly.

The Titan didn't even look at him. "Ares must really be making a mess of things if Zeus has given permission to release me."

"It is bad. He has the mortals on the brink of an all-out war. The gods have practically torn the world apart. Innocent people are dying . . ." I trailed off as a look of boredom crept into his expression. "You don't care about any of that. Okay. That's cool. We don't need you to care."

"That's a good thing, child, because I don't care."

I took a deep breath. What if Perses refused? Would he really willingly go back to being an oddly-colored ice cube? "We need you to help us defeat Ares. You know, the god of war."

Perses huffed. "He is not the true god of war. I am."

"That's not what he's saying," Seth added, picking up where I was heading with this.

"He says no one, past or present, can defeat him," Aiden threw in. "Maybe that's the truth."

I forced a casual shrug. "If you don't want to fight him or—"

"If you say I'm afraid, you obviously do not value your life, Apollyon." Perses took a step forward, and ice slipped down my spine. "It has nothing to do with fear."

"I don't think it does." My gaze bounced to Hades, who was being oh-so helpful through all of this. "But don't you want the chance to go toe-to-toe with Ares again?"

A muscle popped in his jaw. "The only reason any of us were enslaved was because I was tricked." He growled low in his throat as he spared a brief glance at the quiet god. "Ares is no match against me. He never was and never will be."

"Then you could prove it. You don't have to care about any of us to prove it," I said, close to begging. "If you help us, Hades will not put you back here. He'll release you into Elysian Fields."

Perses stared at me for a long moment and then turned to Hades. "Is that true?"

"I don't like it. Frankly, I think you should be in Prometheus' place."

The Titan's eyes narrowed. "That is not an answer."

Hades folded thick arms across his chest. "If you do as you

are told and don't cause any problems, you will be released into Elysian Fields. If not, we will chain your ass to a rock and strip your skin from your body, one tiny section at a time."

"Is that so?" He raised a brow. "Seems like to me you'll have your hands full with Ares and won't have time to spend an eternity torturing me."

Hades stepped up, unfolding his arms. "You forget Ares has no power in my realm unless I grant it, and he cannot enter without my permission. Ares can rip the mortal world apart, but if you betray us, we will take the time to track you down, and I will spend eternity getting my jollies off on your suffering."

"Poor Persephone." Perses stared down his nose at the god. "It must be hard on her if that's what gets you off."

I wrinkled my nose.

"If her name drips from your forked tongue one more time, I will rip it out," Hades promised, his voice deadly low.

Was his tongue really forked?

Perses' lips curled up on one side. "What? You don't like me talking about your wife?" He looked over at us. "Is abduction as a means of marriage still all the rage these days?"

"Uh . . . no," I said, shaking my head. "It's really frowned upon."

Hades' cheeks deepened in color. "You're really pushing me."

"I haven't even begun to push."

Aiden sighed and said under his breath, "Well, this conversation has really digressed."

"Yeah," I muttered, crossing my arms as I watched the two try to out-snark each other.

This is going smoothly. Seth's voice filtered through my thoughts.

I kept my eyes on the Titan. *He's not that . . . bad. I mean, all things considered, right?*

His answering chuckle tugged at my lips. *I sort of like him.*

Of course.

"So, let me make sure I understand this clearly." Perses was apparently done antagonizing Hades. "I help you prepare for war and lead the charge against Ares, and I will be returned to Elysian Fields in one piece? I must clarify that. You Olympians can be oh so tricky."

"Yes," I said, shifting my weight when his heavy gaze landed on me. "In one piece, happy and whole." I frowned. He didn't look like the happy type. "Or in whatever mood you prefer."

Perses moved forward so fast I hadn't even seen him move. One second he was in front of Hades, and the next he was towering over me. Neither Aiden or Seth had a chance to react. "Swear it," the Titan said. "And you will have my word."

"We promise." The words tasted like ash on my tongue. "We swear it."

"I agree—"

Hope swelled in my chest. Well, this wasn't *too* hard.

Perses smiled. "On one condition."

Oh. I tried not to show my distrust. "What is your condition?"

His smile returned, and it was hungry. I wished he'd take a step back. "I need something strong to drink, and I need a woman. Maybe two."

16

Jennifer L. Armentrout

Vegas.

I was in Vegas with a Titan who needed to get drunk and get laid.

What in the holy Hades? Like, at what point in my pretty short time on Earth had my life veered off so that I would end up here?

If someone said this was going to happen a few hours ago, I would've told them to get off the drugs, but Hades had poofed us just outside the Palms Place, a colossal shimmery hotel near a million glittery casinos. It felt like my stomach was still in the Underworld as I gazed at the Sky Tube connecting the Palms to a casino.

I'd never been to Vegas. I remembered not too long ago, before I'd Awakened and the world went to hell, Aiden and I had made plans to get assigned to a place like Vegas. There was a huge—or used to be huge—community of pures out here, and that meant there'd be daimons to stab and all that jazz. But I wasn't sure if the community still existed here or if they'd fled to one of the Covenants.

"Vegas," Perses' deep voice rumbled. "It's like an Olympian playground?"

A wry grin pulled at Aiden's lips as he twisted toward us and ran a hand through his hair. "Vegas is basically a playground for adults."

The Titan smiled. "Then it is my kind of place."

"We need to get a place for the night." Seth looked up at the lighted hotel. "This should work."

Hades had given us explicit orders to meet him back here at noon the following day, which hopefully was enough time for Perses to do, uh, his thing. As the four of us headed toward the front entrance of the Palms, we passed several mortal tourists. The world had gone to hell in a hand basket, but by the teeming streets and crowded sidewalks, nothing had really changed here.

Mortals had a wonderful ability of sticking their heads in the sand, even as the entire world came down on top of them.

I envied that.

Perses strode past two laughing college guys. They immediately quieted when the spied the near eight-foot-tall man in leather. Although I'm sure there were stranger things to see in Vegas, he was sure going to draw a lot of attention.

We'd made it about a foot when a string of curses exploded behind us. I whipped around, as did Aiden. The two college guys were pushing each other, dangerously close to the curb. Under the glowing street lamps, their faces were red with anger.

Perses chuckled.

A shiver ran down my spine. "It's you, isn't it? Already, you're affecting mortals."

He shrugged and kept walking.

I glanced at Aiden, and we shared the same thought. *This is not going to go well.*

The lobby of the Palms was opulent and wildly calming compared to the glitz of outside. I lingered back as Seth strode to the registration desk. I knew he was using compulsion, and I couldn't bring myself to feel bad about it. I looked up, awed by the size of the dazzling crystal chandelier.

Aiden smoothed his thumb over my cheek. At the same time, he was keeping an eye on Perses, who was keeping an eye on a cluster of young women dressed in short, sexy dresses—the kind of dress I'd wear if given a chance.

Then again, I'd seen the scars on my legs. I doubted the world wanted to witness that hot mess.

So here we were, standing in Vegas in our Sentinel uniforms next to a giant Titan, looking like damn fools among all the fancy-dressed patrons of the hotel and casino.

Correction.

The guys could have been wearing used garbage bags, and they would still have looked hot. Every female around us openly gawked at the trinity of hotness. I, on the other hand, looked like I belonged in a paint-ball arena.

Aiden's hand slipped to my shoulder as Seth returned, several key cards in his hand. He grinned. "I got us Penthouse A."

"Penthouse A?" I took the card, curious.

We left the lobby and headed for the elevator just as I thought I heard a fleshy smack, like one of the women had just slapped another across the face. We were on the top floor—almost half of the top floor.

Penthouse A had three bedrooms and a game room. The place was completely decked out. It was the kind of room that catered to the filthy rich—lush furniture, stocked bar and fridge, Jacuzzi tub, TVs in the bathroom mirrors, and a breathtaking view of Vegas from the all-glass wall.

Perses and Seth each picked out rooms, and the Titan immediately disappeared into one of the bathrooms. I couldn't imagine what he thought of modern technology, but he seemed to figure it out, because as I neared the open door, I heard the shower running.

Glancing over my shoulder, I saw Aiden disappear into the last bedroom. I tucked my hair back and walked forward, hesitating just inside the door. Seth was sprawled across on one of the plush white couches, glass in hand. Man, he'd found the liquor quick enough. He arched a brow when he spotted me, and the cord tightened within me.

"Want a drink?" he offered. "It's scotch. Found it in the bar."

Getting liquored up was probably the only way I was going to make it through this night, but I shook my head. "What are we going to do with him?" I nodded back toward the hall that led to the bathroom.

"Let him get what he needs for the night." Seth laughed to himself as he swished the golden liquid around in his glass. "Ladies and liquor—the fundamental L's of life."

"We can't just let him roam Vegas by himself. He walked past two guys and they nearly had a wrestling match."

"I wasn't suggesting that." Seth finished off his drink and stood. "I'll watch him."

Yeah, I wasn't so keen on that. "Do you think that's a good idea?"

"Better than staying here with you two." He strolled up to me. "There's only a thin wall separating our rooms. I think I'd rather spend my night frolicking in high-priced strip clubs."

I rolled my eyes. "Nice."

"Just being honest."

"You don't have any money," I felt the need to point out.

He chuckled. "Do you really think *I'll* need money?"

If any guy could get attention in a strip club without money, it would be Seth, but that was beside the point. "Aiden could go with him," I argued.

Seth cocked his head to the side. "Aw, Angel, are you trying to spend time with me?"

Hearing the shower turn off, I winced. I so did not want to be in here if Perses decided to walk out with no clothes on. I doubted he cared about privacy. "Look, I'm just making—"

"You don't trust me." Seth leaned against the wall in front of me. Close. Very close. "I wouldn't if I were you."

I frowned. "Well, that's a reassuring statement, Seth."

He shrugged one shoulder as he stared down at me.

Growing frustrated, I looked behind me when I heard a door close somewhere in the suite.

"You know he's right inside your room, waiting. And he's probably doing push-ups or something to keep him from coming in here and stopping me . . ." He bent his head, so that his mouth was inches from mine. "From getting this close."

I sucked in a breath as the cord in my belly jumped.

His lips formed a half-smile. "So, why don't you help out the Saint and go back to him before we make another scene."

Taking a step back, I met his gaze. "Don't be a douche."

"Don't be a pain in my ass." He reclaimed the distance, crowding me, and for a second, unease gave way to a spark of fear. "It's better if I go out with Perses."

I didn't understand the sudden shift in mood with him. While he'd been in the cell, and after the evil god twins had been yanked out of me, Seth had been understanding and repentant. Now he was back to the Seth I wanted to shank with a rusty spork.

What's up with you? I tried the whole mental path thing, hoping it would help. The last thing anyone needed was the two of us going at each other's throats.

His eyes flared. "Nothing is up."

Bull. You're incredibly moody.

"Incredibly moody?" Seth tipped his head back and laughed. *You have no idea.*

"Then tell me."

Seth blinked and then he leaned in again, speaking loud enough for everyone and their mother to hear. "I'm really not interested in talking with you. Other things? Maybe. You know, for old times' sake."

"You were wrong," Aiden announced from behind me, appearing in the doorway like a damn ghost. "I wasn't doing push-ups to stop myself. I was just visually entertaining myself with all the different ways I could break your jaw. So back the hell off."

Seth snickered as he pushed off the wall, raising his hands.

"Look, all I was doing was telling her I would pull babysitting duties. She wanted me to stay and you to go. Don't hate on me."

My nails dug into my palms. *I'm on to you, jerk-face. You're trying to piss me off on purpose.*

Seth winked, but then the door behind him swung open and Perses swaggered out, dressed in a white suit.

Momentarily distracted, I moved so I could see around Seth. "Where did you get the suit? Wait. I don't even want to know."

Perses laughed as he checked himself out in a gilded mirror. He wasn't wearing a shirt under his jacket, and when he turned, the cut of his broad chest really drew the eyes. Speaking of eyes, they looked mortal now. "So the male Apollyon is *babysitting* me." He walked up, clapping a large hand on Seth's shoulder. "That will work."

Remarkably, Seth had no reaction to the Titan getting all hands-on. "We'll have fun."

There was something in Seth's voice that said he wouldn't be having that much fun. I folded my arms, feeling like a mother who knew her child was about to go out and raise all kinds of holy hell but couldn't prove it. It wasn't that I thought Seth was going to try to take out Perses and run back to Ares. I believed with every cell in my body that he hated Ares as much as I did, but there was something going on.

"What happened to your face?" Perses asked, startling me as he twisted back to the mirror and straightened his jacket.

Aiden stopped whatever he was doing behind me, which probably involved giving Seth "I'm going to kill you while you sleep" looks, and placed a hand on my lower back. "That's none of your business," he snarled.

The Titan simply laughed deeply. "The pure-blood is touchy, isn't he?"

Seth snorted as he headed for the door. Apparently he was

going to wear his Sentinel uniform for his night of hell-raising. The daggers and gun were no longer visible, but I knew he still had them on him. "You have no idea," he replied.

"You know . . ." Perses faced us once more, and his brand spanking-new irises shone like polished obsidian. "I could end you in half of a second."

I shifted so I was standing in front of Aiden. The knot of unease between my breasts grew and then doubled when Aiden somehow ended up in front of me.

"I know you can end me with a snap of your fingers," Aiden said, his body tense. "But it is still none of your business."

The smile on Perses' face widened.

I forced my muscles to relax as I stepped to stand side by side with Aiden. "Ares did it."

Perses cocked his head to the side as his gaze moved from me to Aiden and back. "I assume those are not your only scars?"

I shook my head.

At the door, Seth had paled visibly. He looked like he wanted to bolt. I couldn't blame him. So did I.

"How bad was it?" Perses asked.

While I had no desire to discuss this with anyone, let alone Perses, we needed to keep the Titan somewhat happy. And if that meant strolling down Awkward Lane, then so be it. "It was really bad. He kicked my ass."

The Titan was unaffected by the statement, but he tipped his chin toward Seth. "Where were you when this was happening? Aren't Apollyons bonded if there are two at the same time?"

Seth didn't answer immediately. "I wasn't there for her," he said, and those words were like a cold wind.

"Interesting." Perses shrugged his broad shoulders, stretching the material of his suit jacket. "It's a shame."

I frowned, not following where he was going with that statement. "What is?"

"What was done to you," Perses replied. "I bet you were beautiful at one time."

Sitting on the most comfortable couch known to man, I picked at the dinner Aiden had ordered from room service after Perses and Seth left to go do things it was best not to think about. Aiden sat beside me, the TV was on, and we were trying to be normal, but my mind was elsewhere. I felt edgy, restless.

Aiden laughed softly, drawing my attention. A small smile pulled at my lips. "What?"

"You haven't heard a word of what I've been saying, have you?"

My cheeks flushed as I shook my head. "Sorry. I'm just distracted. What were you saying?"

"It honestly wasn't anything important." He put his empty plate on the glass coffee table and twisted toward me. Taking the plate from my hands, he also set that aside, and then faced me. "Are you okay?"

With anyone else I'd get annoyed with that question, but coming from Aiden, it made me love him more. "I'm fine. Really, I'm not lying."

"Something is on your mind." He reached out, gently clasping my cheek and causing a delicate shiver to skate over my skin. "You're still beautiful. You know that, right?"

A wider smile pulled at my lips.

"What Perses said isn't true." He bent his head, brushing his lips over mine. The touch was barely there, but I felt it in every part of my being. "You are still as beautiful as you were the night I saw you standing in that warehouse in Atlanta."

I placed my hand on his chest, kissing him back as his heart jumped under my palm. "Thank you, but it's not what Perses said that's bothering me." I pulled back, running my teeth over my tingling lower lip. "I mean, yeah, I'm as shallow as the next girl, and hearing that kind of sucked, but it's not like I haven't accepted that I'm not going to be entering beauty pageants any time soon."

"What's going on in there, then?" Aiden tapped his forefinger off my temple.

At first, I wanted to say nothing and just enjoy this quiet time with Aiden, because I doubted we would have many more moments like this for a long time, but there was no reason to keep things to myself. No matter how small it was, I owed that to Aiden.

"It just seems bizarre to be sitting here while everything is going on." I shook my head, frustrated for a hundred different reasons. Unable to sit still, I stood, and the floor was cool under my bare feet as I padded over to the window. Vegas at night was like seeing the stars on the ground. "It's not like we have endless time on our hands. Ares is doing gods-know-what right now. Our friends are back at the University, where we're not."

"Apollo is with them. He'll keep them safe."

"I know." I pressed my forehead against the window and blew out a breath. "And who knows what Seth and Perses are getting themselves into. You saw it outside, right? He walked past two guys and they started fighting. That and Seth's charming personality is a winning combination."

"You're worried about what kind of trouble they're getting into?" he asked, and I heard him stand.

"Yes. No." I sighed and turned toward him, leaning back against the glass. "It's just ridiculous that we're doing this. Perses *is* going to cause trouble. And Seth? I doubt he's really going to try to stop him."

Aiden stopped a few feet in front of me. "You want to go see if we can find them? Maybe tail them?"

Tipping my head back, I closed my eyes. That seemed like a reasonable idea, but ... "No. Seth will feel me the moment we get near him, and it's not ..." I stifled a groan. "There's something going on with him."

Even though he didn't say anything at first, I felt his sudden shift in interest. Tension poured into the air, and the cord tightened deep inside me. "Do you think he's up to something?"

"Seth is always up to something." I let my arms fall to my side and squeezed my eyes shut until I saw little white dots. "I know it's not anything to do with Ares. It's something else. I can feel . . ." I trailed off as it hit me. I did groan out loud then. "Dammit."

"What?" Aiden's voice was closer.

"I feel frustrated, restless, and pissy, but I didn't know why. It's not me. I'm picking up on Seth through our bond. And I know that's weird and you probably didn't ever need to know that, because it's worse than having PMS—"

Without warning, I felt Aiden's lips touch the center of my throat, and I gasped. Opening my eyes, my gaze locked with his. "Gods, you're as quiet as a ninja."

One side of his lips tipped up, and his hands settled on my hips. "So, you're telling me that Seth's not in a good mood, therefore you're feeling the effects of it?"

"Yeah." My mouth was suddenly dry. Trapped between his body and the glass window, I felt my pulse kick up. "It's been awhile since we've been around each other. I forgot that it does that."

Truth was, I knew that was part of the reason why I was feeling antsy, but I also knew there was something else going on with Seth. I couldn't put my finger on it, though, and I didn't want Aiden to worry needlessly.

His hands slid up my hips and settled on my waist. "So how do we fix this?"

"Fix it?"

Aiden dropped his forehead to mine. "Seth can be in whatever mood he wants to be in, but there's no reason for you to have to feel it if there's something we could do."

I was about to tell him that it really wasn't that big of a deal, but then he tugged me forward, watching me as he did so, and I didn't say a word.

"Maybe you need a distraction," he murmured, lashes dipping but not quick enough to shield eyes that were now a heated silver.

What I needed to do was to stop whining and enjoy the downtime. Maybe we could go out and sightsee. I almost laughed, because seriously, that would be so inappropriate given everything, but I honestly didn't want to be anywhere that required me to share Aiden's attention.

Because the kind of attention Aiden was giving me right now was the stuff dreams were built of.

Forcing myself to let out a long breath, I shook it all off—Seth, Perses, and Ares. I pushed away the fact that Aiden would be employed in the afterlife, and thoughts of the battles that lay ahead, and the uncertainty of our futures no matter what happened. I wanted to be *here* with Aiden, because he was *here* with me. I focused on those pink, bedazzled walls in my head, hopefully cutting off Seth's access to what I was feeling. So didn't need a peeping Seth for this.

"A distraction would be nice," I agreed in what I hoped was a serious voice.

His fingers curled around my side, tightening. He pulled me into the warmth of his body, and I tipped my head back. "Any ideas?"

My mind produced some really naughty ideas like rapid fire. So many, so quick, I was actually worried for myself. "Maybe you could kiss me? That seems to always distract me."

"Hmm, I could do that." He lowered his lips to mine, and electricity zinged through my veins. It was that spark—the spark I only had with Aiden. When he lifted his mouth from mine, I almost whimpered. The kiss wasn't nearly long enough. "I'm not sure that worked at distracting you."

I shook my head, my heart racing. I placed my hands on his chest, fisting his black shirt. "Try again?"

"I can do that." He moved his hands to my back, and then his lips were pressing against mine, coaxing them open. The kiss was deep, shattering in the way it completely took me over. I clung to him as one hand flattened against the small of my back and the other caught the ends of my hair. "Did that distract you?" he asked, his voice thick.

I was barely breathing or standing on my own. "A little."

"A little?" he said, and his chuckle caused me to shudder. "I'll have to try harder."

Aiden's hand drifted down my lower back and around the curve of my waist. His long fingers slipped under the hem of my shirt, and I jerked when they touched my skin.

"Still trying," he said, using the hand in my hair to guide my head back and expose my throat. He pressed tiny, hot kisses against my throat as his hand slipped up, curving over my breast. I moaned his name, and he made this deep sound in his throat.

"Keep trying," I said, letting my eyes fall closed as his lips pressed against my pulse.

Aiden murmured something and shifted his body against mine, wringing another breathy moan from me. In this moment, everything was about us and only us, and I welcomed it. A second later, my shirt landed somewhere on the floor, and the glass against my back was cool. He snaked an arm around my waist and lifted me up. I wrapped my legs around his hips as he brought my mouth back to his.

There was something raw and feral in the way he kissed me then. It was a possession, a welcome one that staked a claim on my heart and soul. He turned, and in one powerful surge he trapped my back against a nearby wall and pressed the entire length of his body against mine. I wanted to feel his skin against mine, but with the way he was sealed to me, that wasn't happening.

Our mouths collided, hungry and demanding as I threaded my fingers through his hair. His lower body rocked against mine, sending sharp pulses through me. The marks of the Apollyon raced to the surface, causing my already sensitive skin to tingle. We kissed like we were drowning in one another, and each time he rolled his hips, I felt like I'd shatter apart.

"Gods, Alex," he said between kisses. "You'll never know what you do to me, how you make me feel."

I had a pretty good idea. I brought his mouth back to mine, and I don't know how he could obliterate my senses with his kisses and still manage to walk, but he did. He stalked toward the bedroom, his hands tight on my hips. My back parted the gossamer canopy over the bed, and then he laid me down, his mouth trailing off my lips and gliding down my heated skin, followed by his hands.

Sitting up, I tugged his shirt off, and he laughed when I tossed it outside of the bed, outside of our little world. The sound brought a smile to my lips, and he froze over me, his knees planted into the bed on either side of my thighs.

"I love seeing you smile," he said, cupping my cheek. "And I miss it when it's gone."

A knot formed in my throat as my fingers traced the hard lines and rises of his chiseled stomach.

"I missed this."

He smiled as he lowered himself, putting most of his weight on the elbow next to my head. When he kissed me again, it was much slower but no less intense or soulful than the ones before. He kissed me until my body burned under his, and then he moved south, slipping the straps of my bra down my shoulder and then getting rid of it completely. Those lips sought out every scar, and there are many, and I never felt more beautiful than I did in that moment.

Or when he flicked open the button on my pants, and then hooked his fingers under the band, slipping them plus another very important article of clothing down my legs. The air was cool, but not for long. Aiden returned to me, and I got the top button of his pants undone before he starting moving down.

It wasn't like the first time, when Aiden had stopped to ask permission. He didn't hesitate. He dropped a sweet kiss against the inside of my thigh, and then there was lightning in my body. Even tapping into akasha couldn't compare to the feeling. I broke apart into a million, dazzling pieces.

When he lifted away from me and leaned out of the canopy, I whimpered.

"Condoms," he said, reaching into the drawer of the night-stand. I heard clothing hit the floor, and I rose halfway up. "Found them earlier."

I laughed, relieved that we were playing this safe since it was doubtful the shot was still working. "Nice how they keep those stocked."

"You should've seen the rest of the stuff in here." He came back to me, and my breath caught as my gaze dropped. He was absolutely beautiful. "Maybe later I'll show you."

My curiosity was piqued, but then Aiden kissed me again, and I wasn't thinking about what could be in that drawer. He nipped at my lip, and I opened to him. His tongue slipped inside, curling my toes as he settled between my legs. His mouth left mine, traveling down my throat and between my breasts. He hovered there, my body arching against his until he traveled back to my mouth.

"*Agapi mou*," he murmured, capturing my lips in a searing kiss as he thrust his hips.

There were no more words, not with our bodies moving together, our tongues twisting and our hearts pounding. I rolled him onto his back. His muscles tensed and rippled under my hands.

The sweetest fire burned through me as I leaned down, whispering against his lips. "I love you."

Aiden shifted me so I was on my back once more, his body shaking as he moved over me, *inside* me. A powerful tension curled inside me, and I coiled my body around his. My chest swelled so much, warring with the other intense feelings inside of me so that when I cried out, it was almost too much.

Sometime later, our breathing still rapid and heavy, Aiden pressed kisses to the lids of my eyes, to my cheeks, and then to my parted lips. He threaded his fingers through mine, holding them down beside my head, kissing me softly. "I love you."

And then he started all over again.

17

Something crashing to the floor jarred me awake. I shot up in bed, clutching for the sheet as my eyes adapted to the darkness. The canopy was still, but my heart was racing and I felt . . . I felt ridiculously happy. Like everything in the world was right.

What Aiden and I had done into the late hours of the night had been earth-shattering, but this was different.

Aiden stirred, rising halfway up on his elbows. "What is it?"

Before I could utter a word, what sounded like a heavy body hitting the floor broke the silence.

"What the hell?" Aiden swung his legs off the bed.

I stood, finding his shirt in the darkness. It fell to my knees when I slipped it on. I grabbed the dagger off the nightstand, and by the time I made it to the bedroom door, Aiden already had his pants on and gun in hand.

But the pants were unbuttoned and hung low, and well, with his sleep-tousled hair and his cut abs all on display, I got a teeny tiny bit distracted for a second.

Aiden caught my stare and his lips tipped up. I forced my gaze away before I said screw it and jumped him.

Outside the bedroom, we headed for the door to the living room. He unlocked it and entered first, which was stupid considering I was the Apollyon, but he was a guy.

Flipping on the light, he drew to an abrupt halt and laughed—laughed deeply and loudly. Tension eased out of my muscles. Whatever was going on couldn't be bad if he was laughing.

I peeked around him and my mouth dropped open.

Perses was sprawled on the floor, missing his jacket. There were red marks on his white slacks, some a dark crimson. Others were a deep red and more like smudges along the zipper.

A basket of meatballs was on his chest—half were in the carton, and half had rolled down his twenty-pack abs.

The Titan reached down, picked up a meatball from somewhere near his belly button, and popped it into his mouth. "These things are so damn good."

There were no words.

Seth leaned against the couch. No shoes. No shirt. His amber eyes were glassy and unfocused. Now the half-stupid happiness I felt upon waking made sense.

"You two are completely trashed," I said, eyes wide.

Seth raised a hand, busted knuckles bruised and raw. "We are . . . not drunk."

"Really," Aiden drew out the word.

Fighting the smile on my face, I loosened my grip on the blade. "What happened to your hands?"

"Nooothing," Seth replied, chuckling.

Perses chewed loudly on another meatball.

I glanced at Aiden. "Is that blood on your pants, Perses?"

"Among other bloodily fluids," he replied, and then he snorted.

"Gross."

Aiden shoved the gun in the back of his pants and folded his arms. "I'm assuming it's not your blood?"

The Titan laughed.

Okay. I was starting to get a little worried. "It's not a mortal's blood, is it?"

Seth pushed to his feet and swayed to the side. He sat—er, fell back—onto the couch. "No. We ran into some daimons."

I stared at him. "And you decided to get into a hand-to-hand bitch fight with them? You could've just used one of the elements or akasha."

"Your buddy has a lot of pent-up aggression," Perses said, picking up a meatball. He sat halfway up and tossed the meatball. "I like him."

Even drunk, Seth had ninja reflexes. He caught the meatball with a laugh. I had no idea what to say.

"All right, as entertaining as this is, make sure you two are sober enough by noon." Aiden turned, catching my free hand. "Have fun."

At the door to our room, I glanced over my shoulder. Seth was leaning way to the side, eyes drifting shut, expression slack. It was then when I noticed that, like Aiden, his pants were unbuttoned. Between him and Perses, I wondered how they'd even made it back to the hotel room.

Back inside the bedroom with the door locked, Aiden pulled the gun out and placed it on the nightstand.

"Wow," I said, grinning.

He laughed. "Wasn't expecting that."

"Me neither."

After relieving me of the dagger, he stepped back and eyed me. Even in the darkness, I could feel his intense stare. "I know I've said this before, but I like seeing you in my clothes."

Warmth spread over my cheeks, and heat flooded my veins. "Good. I like wearing them."

"But you know what I like better?"

I didn't get a chance to say anything before he hooked his fingers under the hem of the borrowed shirt and tugged it over my head. The material fluttered to the floor as he clasped my hips, lifting me up.

Aiden's lips brushed mine as he spoke, eliciting a series of shivers. "I like taking them off."

Hades appeared exactly at noon, not a second early or late, and didn't ask any questions. He popped us back to the middle of the University, and while I was a little woozy on my feet from the method of travel, Seth looked like he was going to hurl up everything he'd drunk the night before. That explained the way my stomach was churning. Bastard.

Which was confirmed a second later when Seth said, "I think I'm going to vomit."

Aiden cast him an amused look. "Lightweight."

"Shut up," Seth moaned, clutching his stomach.

The air in front of us shimmered, and then Apollo appeared in front of us, startling me enough that I took a step back. My eyes narrowed on him. Couldn't any of the gods just walk somewhere?

Okay. If I could pop in and out and avoid stairs, I'd do it, too.

And I'd probably get the same amount of sick pleasure Apollo got out of doing it.

Hades stepped forward, eyeing Perses before he turned to Apollo. "I hope you're right and this idea works." He tossed a sneer at the Titan, who scoffed loudly. "The son of a bitch doesn't deserve a chance, and you know it."

The sun seemed to soak through Apollo's skin as he leveled a stare on the other god. "As I recall, you had no other suggestions."

Hades smirked. "I did. Shut down the Underworld and let you guys battle it out." He shrugged. "You didn't like that idea." With that, the god disappeared.

"I have never been a fan of Hades. Over-pompous asshole," Apollo muttered.

I arched a brow. That was something coming from him.

The Titan's lips curled up. "You're still a glowing bundle of fun, Apollo."

Apollo narrowed a gaze on Perses. "Do not start with me. You know what has to be done. And I promise you, if you cause us any problems, you'll end up on Prometheus' rock, except it won't be an eagle pecking away at you."

"What would it be, then?" Curiosity marked Seth's tone.

Apollo's smile was chilling. "I'll do it. Personally. Strip by strip with a dull blade dipped in cobra venom. And then, when I'm done at the end of the day, I will sew you back together to just start all over the following day."

"Wow," I murmured. "Inventive."

Perses didn't look impressed. "I've heard worse threats."

My eyes widened. Beside me, Aiden hid his smile while scrubbing at his chin with his palm. Seth had a far-off look on his face, as if picturing what Apollo had said. Didn't think it was possible, but he turned even more pasty.

"Are you okay?" I asked.

Seth waved one hand. "Yeah, perfect."

"So where is the army I'm to train?" Impatience filled Perses' tone. "All I see are buildings and a few children of demigods peeking around corners. I hope they aren't your warriors."

I snorted. "No, they're not. They're students. Our army is trained. They're—"

"Trained as Guards and hunters, right?" Perses chuckled mockingly, and I sort of wanted to see Apollo break out the dull blade. "They may be skilled when it comes to hunting daimons, but are they skilled enough to fight?"

"They won't be fighting Ares," Aiden explained, earning an interested look from the Titan. "Ares is heavily guarded by mortal soldiers, daimons, and automatons."

Perses' brows knitted. "Your army should be able to defend themselves against two of them. The automatons would be a problem, but they'll just have to be quicker. I do not see what you need me for."

"As Sentinel and Guards, we've never tried to work together in groups larger than three or four. We were never trained on war tactics. And *I* need you," I said, hating myself for having to say that. "I need you to prepare me for facing Ares. You have already seen how that went the first time."

Seth's eyes tightened. "You also have to prepare me to fight Ares."

The likelihood of me letting Seth near Ares was right up there with me actually cooking myself a dinner that was edible. I opened my mouth, but Aiden jumped in.

"And I need to be trained on how to fight him as well."

"Guys, the last time I checked, I was becoming the God Killer, which would make me pretty badass as it is. And with Perses' training, I'm going to also be kickass."

"That doesn't mean you don't need backup," Seth retorted.

I wished he'd just go puke somewhere. I swallowed hard against the sick feeling leaking through the bond.

"And you're not facing Ares alone," Aiden added.

And I wished Aiden would go hold his hair for him.

Apollo rolled his eyes. "Children, really, Alexandria is a big girl and doesn't need two boys rushing to defend her."

I smiled broadly. "Exactly."

Neither Aiden or Seth looked like they agreed, and the look Aiden sent me promised that we'd talk about this later. Oh, we would. He wouldn't like the outcome. There was no way in holy Hades Aiden was getting within a city block of Ares.

Perses exhaled roughly. "I can spend the mornings training your army and the afternoons working with one or three of you. I really don't care how many, but I can tell you this. Ares would've sensed my presence the moment I stepped into the mortal realm. He knows I'm here. He will be unnerved by it, but the longer we take, the more time he will have to rebuild his confidence or bring in more reinforcements. We attack immediately, within the week, or we lose our advantage. Because if you have spies, so does he."

I glanced at Apollo. Perses had a point. We couldn't string this out. We would need to move fast, but would we be ready? Would *I* be ready?

Apollo's jaw tensed, and then he nodded curtly. "A week

from now, on Monday, we move on the Catskills. We take on Ares."

Training with Perses was like running into a brick wall, getting back up, and face-planting into it again just for the fun of it.

We'd started immediately with our training. Of course, Aiden and Seth took part. It was a waste of breath to try to convince them otherwise.

Just like when Seth and I used to train, we drew an audience of Sentinels, students, and staff. Word got out quickly that there was a Titan on campus, something that most people never thought they'd see. I couldn't blame them for gawking. Among those crowded around the largest training room in the athletics building were my friends.

Which was great, because there was nothing like having friends and strangers around to watch you get your ass kicked.

And we were getting our asses kicked.

I'd hit the padded floor more times than I could count, taking turns with Seth and Aiden, who were doing no better than me.

It was Seth's turn, and I eased myself down, biting my lip when my tailbone hit the mat. "I think I broke my butt," I moaned.

Sitting beside me, Aiden reached over, rubbing his hand along my lower back. The touch ached at first, but the steady burn started to ease my muscles. "Yeah, that was a pretty nasty landing you took."

It had started out so perfect. I'd gotten behind Perses, who, by the way, was weaponless, and had sprung up and spun out, about to land a beauteous spin kick when he whipped around and caught my leg, throwing me down like a rag doll.

My butt had broken my fall.

Seth was currently backed into a corner by Perses, dodging the Titan's vicious strikes. In theory, we had a week to train before leaving for the Catskills. It was a twenty-three hour drive, and Marcus was currently rounding up a billion vehicles for the trip.

The army mostly needed standard tactical training, but us? We had to actually knock Perses down and gain the upper hand before our training would be complete. Sounded easy until I realized that Perses was like Ares on steroids. Either way, by Monday morning, we were leaving, prepared or not.

I glanced over toward the door. Deacon spotted my gaze and winked. I grinned at him, and my gaze moved on. Several pures were staring at Aiden and me. Apparently, a pure-blood touching my back was more shocking than a Titan kicking an Apollyon's ass.

I rolled my eyes and turned back to the match in front of us.

Dipping under Perses' outstretched arm, Seth came up behind the Titan, and just like I had, he prepared to deliver a vicious kick. Perses turned and dipped, catching Seth's foot. Unable to keep his balance, Seth hit the mat on his side.

Perses tipped his head back and laughed. "Next."

When one of us went down, it was the next one's turn. Aiden dropped his hand and pushed himself up. Passing Seth on the mats, the two idiots exchanged smirks.

Seth dropped down beside me. I glanced at him. "I don't know why you two are giving each other that 'I'm superior' look. Both of you are getting your asses kicked."

He shrugged one shoulder. "Doesn't mean we have to hug it out."

Turning my attention back to Aiden, I watched him beautifully execute an uppercut that did absolutely nothing to detour Perses' brutal punch to the stomach. "You know this is pointless, right? Neither of you needs to be subjecting yourself to this. I'm going to become the God Killer. You won't be fighting—"

"We will be fighting with you," Seth argued, his voice low. He too watched Aiden and Perses. "Just because you're the God Killer doesn't mean you can go in there alone."

"I won't be." I winced as Perses' kick caught Aiden in the thigh. "I'll be with Perses."

"And that's not really backup. Who knows what he'll do in the end? You need someone there with you." Seth leaned back, stretching out his legs. "And you and I both know Aiden would be a distraction."

I clenched my jaw. "Aiden will not be with me."

He snorted. "Does he know that?"

"He will." I looked at him. "Seth, we need to talk about when we'll transfer power."

"That's not what we're talking about now. There's no way I'm letting you go face-to-face with Ares with just Perses. It's not going to happen, and I'm not going to argue with you. You'll need me there to run interference, if anything," he said, returning my stare. "Besides, we shouldn't make the transfer until we're in the Catskills."

I opened my mouth, but Aiden hit the floor on his back and Perses yelled out, "Girl! Your turn!"

Sending Seth a quick glance, I pushed to my feet. "We'll talk about this later."

He arched a brow.

While passing Aiden on the mats, he reached over, tugged on the hem of my shirt, and then kept going. I stopped in front of the Titan, muscles locking up. Over at the door, Deacon whistled and shouted, "Show him what a girl is capable of!"

I took my eyes off Perses for a second to smile at Deacon, and that was all it took. Out of the corner of my eye, I saw Perses' hand zooming for my face. At the last moment, I dropped down. The speed in which Perses' fist shot past my head, stirring wisps of my hair—*gods*. If that had connected with my head, he would've probably knocked me out cold.

"Never take your eyes off the opponent," Perses said, chuckling.

How many times had Ares said that when we knew him as

Instructor Romvi? Nothing flipped my kill-and-maim switch like hearing those words.

I rolled forward and popped to my feet behind Perses. Spinning around, I dodged his second punch and dipped under his arm. I knew I was fast—faster than Aiden, who was like a freaking ninja, and faster than all other half-bloods. But Perses was like Ares. Fighting was bred into their blood. There was no one in this realm better than them. I could only hope to be their equal.

But I wasn't Perses' equal at the moment.

The second I shot up in front of him, he anticipated the move and kicked out, his booted foot connecting with my midsection. Pain exploded along my stomach, and I doubled over. His hand slammed into my shoulder, and I lost my balance. Toppling backward, I hit the mats on my back, hard.

Perses was suddenly in my face, looming over me. A smirk graced his lips. "God Killer or not, girl, he will own you if you fight like this. And as you know, he can't kill you, but he can make you beg for death. Is that something you want to experience again?"

Anger burned through my veins like poison. "My name is not 'girl,' and no, that's not something I want to experience again."

The smirk slipped off his face. "Then get back up, *girl*."

Meeting his stare, I rolled into a sitting position. Ignoring the slice of pain, I got back up.

18

By Wednesday, I was sure my entire back was an array of violets and blues. I was, literally, one giant walking-and-talking bruise. Aiden and Seth hadn't fared any better. Last night, when Aiden and I had gone to bed, we'd been too sore and too tired to take off our pants.

Needless to say, Marcus had given up on the separate bedroom thing. Not that there was any point now. Neither of us could do anything even if our body parts touched.

The Army of Awesome was faring a lot better than us. Numbering near a thousand, they were learning basic tactical maneuvers. It was like the videos of boot camp I remembered seeing on TV. If anything, I think Perses was just trying to harden them instead of teaching them any real skills. He was worse than any Covenant Instructor I'd ever seen.

The Titan was a cesspool of insults.

Later that night, after a long soak in some kind of herbal mixture Laadan had provided, I sat on the bed, too tired to make my way back to the common area for food.

Thankfully, Aiden was possibly the most wonderful man in the whole universe. He brought a plate full of chicken tenders and fries to the room.

"Nice shirt," he commented, nudging the door shut with his toe.

I glanced down at myself, grinning. "Sorry."

He laughed as he eased down beside me, placing the tray

between us. "As I've said a hundred times before, I like seeing you in my clothes."

A flush covered my cheeks. "I was too tired to put pants on."

Peering up through his lashes, he grinned. "And I'm not going to complain about that." He picked up a can of soda, popped the tab, and handed it to me. "I lost the battle of wills with Deacon."

"Uh-oh."

Deacon wanted to travel with us to New York. He felt, since he'd christened the name of our army, he was some kind of official mascot or something. Of course, Aiden wasn't happy with that, and I couldn't blame him. Deacon was safer here. Who knew what we'd meet on the road, and what we'd find in New York once we got there?

"I've told him about a million times that I'd feel better with him staying here." He picked the breading off his tenders, causing me to smile. "But I'm not winning this battle."

"He'll probably just sneak out with us, anyway." I bit half of my tender off, breaded skin and all. "And he's worried, you know. Not just about you, but Luke, too."

"I get that." He tossed the breading onto the plate. "Doesn't mean I have to like it."

I watched him meticulously remove more breading and then took a deep breath. "Speaking of not wanting people to get hurt and the whole keeping them safe thing? We need to talk about that."

He peeked up, his fingers stilling. "Details?"

Finishing off my tender, I took a drink before I continued. "I'm not asking you to stay behind here, because I want you to go with me. And I know you wouldn't do that anyway."

Aiden lowered the chicken piece, his head tilting to the side. "Damn straight."

"But I need you to know that I can't face Ares with you by my side." I rushed on, so that the words that were forming on his tongue couldn't get out. "I know why you want to be there, and I respect that. Hell, I love you for that. But Ares is going to go after you to just get to me."

He dropped the tender. "Alex, you're asking the impossible."

"No, I'm not." I met his thundercloud-gray stare. "I love you, Aiden. I love you more than anything. And the fact that you want to be there for me is amazing. But I can't have you there. Ares knows how much you mean to me, and you'll be a distraction. I hate to say that, but it's the truth."

A muscle began to throb in his jaw. "I'm not sure if I'm supposed to feel insulted by that."

"You're not!" I resisted the urge to throw a piece of chicken in his face. "Look, I get that the idea of me going in there without you—"

"Makes me freaking sick to my stomach?"

"Well, yeah, that, but you have to understand that, because I love you, I don't want to have to worry about Ares getting hold of you."

The muscle was really ticking now. "And because I love you, that's why asking me to let you do this by yourself is insane."

Striving for patience, I shoved a handful of fries in my mouth before continuing. "I'm not going to be by myself. Seth will be there."

"Oh, and that's supposed to make me feel better?"

"Not like I haven't tried to get him to change his mind too." My eyes narrowed. "But he's an Apollyon."

"And I'm a trained Sentinel who can handle myself," he shot back. "And besides, you think I'll be safer with the army?"

"If I could have my way, you wouldn't be there at all, but I'm not asking you to do that. I'll feel better knowing that you're not near Ares." Wiping my hands off, I folded my arms. "And I know, deep down, you understand that."

Silent, he picked up the tray and stood, placing it on the small desk. He turned to me and scrubbed both of his hands down his face. A wince creased his features as he lowered his arms. "Alex . . ."

"It's the same reason why you don't want Deacon with us, but I'm hoping—I'm praying—you'll listen to me." I tucked my legs under me and pulled down the hem of the shirt. "And seriously? You owe me."

"I do?" He moved toward the bed.

I nodded. "Yeah. The whole soul and Hades thing? I don't need you possibly dying next week and ending up as Hades' henchman for eternity."

"I'm not going to die, but you do realize being with the army isn't exactly safe."

Hope sparked in my chest. "But I know you will get through that. I know you will." I couldn't believe anything else. Truth was, being a part of that army was dangerous, but being there against Ares was suicidal.

Aiden eased down on the bed beside me. "I don't like this."

"You don't have to like it. Just like I didn't like the idea of you giving up your soul to Hades. All you have to do is understand it."

The moment those words left my mouth, I internally patted myself on the shoulder. There were moments when my maturity surprised me.

He shifted onto his back, resting his hands on his flat stomach. His eyes were closed, and thick lashes brushed the tops of his cheeks. The muscle in his jaw thrummed along like a hummingbird, but as I watched him, it slowed down. Aiden took a deep breath, the ticking stopped, and he finally opened his eyes.

They were the softest shade of gray as they locked with mine. "I don't agree with this. I *hate* it, Alex, but I get it. If it were the other way around, I wouldn't want you near him. Hell, I *don't* want you near him, but you have to. So, yeah, I'll stay with the army."

Relief eased the tense muscles in my shoulders and neck. I leaned over him, kissing his cheek. "Thank you. I know it wasn't easy for you, so thank you."

He rolled into his side, resting his head on his curved elbow. Reaching over, he skimmed his hand up my leg, swerving to miss a nasty bruise. "When are you and Seth going to do the whole transfer of power thing?"

"Good question." Now that I'd worked this one thing out, it was time to figure out the next problem. "He wants to wait until we're in the Catskills."

His dark brows knitted. "Why?"

I shrugged a shoulder. "I really don't know. He said something earlier about the power being hard to handle, so maybe he thinks I'll crack and, I don't know, start zapping everyone in sight."

Aiden laughed. "That's ridiculous."

"Yeah, I don't know, though. My only other option is to hold him down and do it, and I don't see that going well."

He arched a brow. "I have no problem with that idea. I'll gladly hold him down."

A grin pulled at my lips. "You're terrible."

"Just being helpful."

I kissed his cheek again and then sat back. "I'm going to try to talk to him again. I think we need to do it soon, before we leave for New York."

"I agree." His fingers toyed with the hem of the borrowed shirt.

In the quiet moments that followed, I leaned over again and kissed him for a third time. "For good luck," I whispered. "We're going to war."

His lashes fluttered closed. "We are."

"Did you ever think you'd be in this position?" I placed my hand on his smooth cheek, and he pressed into it. "I never did. Not in a million years," I admitted.

"Me, neither." He pressed his hand over mine, holding it there. "I don't think any of us would have predicted this."

I bit down on my lip. In that flash of a second, I felt incredibly . . . young. I wanted Aiden's reassurance. "And you think it will get better afterward? Go back to normal?"

"I do." He kissed my palm again. "Let's talk about less depressing things. Do you still think there's something up with Seth?"

I laughed. "Is that really a better conversation for you?"

"Maybe." He grinned a little, and my heart toppled in my chest. "So?"

I started to respond, but there was a knock on the door. By the time I tugged the quilt over my legs, the door swung open and Deacon popped in, not even waiting for an invite.

The mop of blond curls bounced as he jumped to the foot of the bed. "Hi, guys!"

Aiden sat up slowly. "Hi, Deacon. Are you aware that it's customary to wait until someone answers the door or says 'come in?'"

"Not like I was interrupting anything. Both of you still have your clothes on."

I laughed. "He has a point."

Aiden shot me a "you're not being helpful" look. "So, what's up, Deacon?"

"Marcus is looking for you. He's in the common room, so I figured it would be better if I was the one who checked in on you two, just in case you were naked." He winked, and I smothered another giggle. "You're welcome."

Groaning, Aiden sat up. "Okay. You do have a point."

"Thought so." As his brother stood, Deacon dive-bombed the bed, causing me to bounce. He flicked my hand lightly. "Marcus wants to talk about the Council or some boring shit like that. His ladylove wants to talk plans about re-building. Then again, I sort of zoned out for half of the conversation."

My brows rose. There was an open seat on the Council that had belonged to Aiden's father. Since Aiden had never taken the seat, it was left open, something that had ticked away at Aiden. He knew that his father would've wanted him to follow in his footsteps rather than become a Sentinel.

Aiden ran a hand through his hair. "All right. Well, this should be interesting."

His brother snorted. "I'll stay here and keep Alex company."

"You do that." Aiden moved around the edge of the bed, swooped down, and kissed my cheek. "I'll be back in a few."

I waved him goodbye and watched him leave. Then I glanced at Deacon. My brows rose as his fingers flew over his cell phone. "Whatcha doing?" I asked.

"Just wait." No more than a few seconds later, the door opened again and Luke and Olivia poked their hands in. Deacon tipped his head back, grinning up at me. "Slumber party?"

I laughed as I waved them in. "Sounds like a great idea."

Olivia scooted in next to me, while Luke stretched out across the head of the bed. She reached over, grabbing the remote control. "We may be leaving for a few days to fight in a war, but that doesn't mean we're too old for a slumber party."

"So very true." I took the pillow Luke handed me and snuggled down.

The four of us watched a bad movie well into the night. It was one of the most relaxing moments I'd had in a long time. When they got up to leave, I sat up, holding the pillow to my chest.

"Let's make a promise," I said.

Three sets of eyes settled on me. "What?" Olivia asked.

I felt kind of corny about what I was about to say, but oh, what the hell. "After all of this is done and over with, let's promise to do this at least once a week. No matter what we're doing or where we are."

A wide smile spread across Olivia's face. "That's a promise I'll love to make."

"Same here," agreed Luke, dropping his arm over Deacon's shoulders.

Feeling good about making plans to do something normal, I dozed off and didn't wake up until I felt Aiden sliding into bed behind me. I tipped my head back toward him as he slipped an arm around my waist. "How was everything with Marcus?"

"Okay." He kissed my cheek and tugged me back against him. "He wants me to take my Council seat once everything is . . . settled."

I'd figured as much. "What do you think?"

Aiden was silent for a long time. "There are things that I could do on the Council, things that I could help make right, especially when the Elixir stops working for the rest of the half-bloods. It's just . . ."

He didn't finish. The Council seat was a lot of things to Aiden—more than just responsibility. I turned so I was facing him and cuddled up close, wiggling so that my head was under his. "You don't have to make a decision now. You have time."

"You're right." His hand slid up my spine and settled there. "We have time."

After another grueling training session on Friday, I found myself limping into the dean's office. Our AOA was leaving in the late morning on the following day. There was a lot to be discussed, and I had scored an invite. So did Seth. The only other times we'd been called to the dean's office in the past was because I'd done something I was about to get in trouble for, and those meetings usually ended in insults being slung back and forth.

Like when I'd threatened to cut Seth with one of Marcus' daggers.

I had to smile at that memory.

Easing down into an empty chair, I glanced around the room. Marcus was behind the desk, because where else would he be, with Diana alongside him. Aiden and Solos hovered by the desk like two hawks, both wearing intense expressions that told me this was going to be a serious conversation. Even Apollo was there. He'd been hanging around a lot, watching over the training. Right now, he was holding a Newton's Cradle like he'd never seen one before, his hand hovering over one of the small, silver balls. I looked around again, frowning.

Looking for Perses? Seth glanced at me from where he was leaning against the wall. *Last I saw him, he was heading into an empty room with two pure girls.*

"What?" I screeched out loud before I could stop myself.

Several sets of eyes landed on me, and Seth smirked. Aiden's gaze narrowed between the two, and I began to suspect that we were about to have a repeat performance of threatening Seth.

Apollo let go of the silver ball and it swung sideways, knocking into the next ball and creating a chain reaction. A wide smile broke out across his face.

"Did no one ever tell you two that it is not nice to communicate telepathically with one another while others are present?" Marcus said, folding his hands on the desk.

I pursed my lips. "No, actually, no one has said that."

He smiled tightly. "Well, I am."

Busted, Seth said.

Gripping the edges of the chair, I stared straight ahead. *I hate you.* "So, what's up?"

Other than the fact Perses is getting some instead of being here?

Apollo picked up a silver ball from the other side and let that one go.

Oh my gods . . .

Marcus' look turned suspicious as his gaze bounced between Seth and me. "Solos was talking battle strategy with Perses. We figured, since you two play an intricate role in this, it would be smart to bring you in on these meetings."

Seth strolled forward and dropped down in the seat beside me. "What's to discuss? From what I understand, it's fairly simple. The army will attack the front gate while Alex and I sneak in with Perses."

Perses had discussed his plan with us the previous day between rounds of kicking our butts. Aiden was still taking part in the additional trainings even though he'd agreed to remain with the larger group once we launched our attack against Ares.

Propping his hip against the desk, Solos pointed down at a map of the New York Covenant, a much better map than the one Athena had created. "It's really not that simple. We have to find a way to sneak you in. I'm sure you remember how well-guarded the Catskills is. Getting past the preliminary fences will be no problem. The wall is another story."

An insolent smile twisted Seth's lips. "There was a breach in the east wall. I've already told Perses. It's not a huge hole, but it is large enough for a person to slip through. Unless Ares is interested in masonry work, I doubt it has been repaired."

"It's unlikely that Ares would leave the breach unguarded," Aiden said, his eyes a steely gray. "You won't just walk in there."

That smirk on Seth's face grew. "I wasn't planning to just walk in there."

"Okay," I sighed, interrupting before a battle of wills erupted. "So we will have to scout the wall first. We can—*Apollo*!"

The god looked up. In his hands, the Newton balls knocked off of each other once more. "What?" he asked.

"*What*?" I shot him annoyed look. "Seriously. Have you never seen a Newton's Cradle before? Every time you move the first ball, it's going to move the rest of the balls."

"No." His gaze dipped to the cradle. "Gravity is cool."

"Oh my gods," I moaned, slumping in my seat. "My brain hurts."

Apollo let go of the silver ball once more and then placed the cradle on the edge of Marcus' desk. "I imagine you're leaving with the army on Saturday?" he said to Solos. When the half-blood nodded, he glanced at Aiden. "And you will travel with Alex?"

"Do you need to even ask that question?" Aiden replied, placing his hands on the desk and leaning in.

Apollo shrugged.

"I will leave with the army, as well," Marcus announced, sitting back in the chair.

Diana cleared her throat delicately. "If I may make a suggestion?" My uncle nodded, and she smiled. "I think you are needed here more, Marcus."

His eyes immediately sharpened into green crystals. "I'm needed in the Catskills."

"I know you feel that way," she started again, patiently and understandingly. "You are a Sentinel at heart, Marcus, but there is so much we have to do. More than just fighting."

"She's correct," Apollo said, apparently ready to contribute to the conversation. "Rebuilding is just as important as war, and that process starts long before the war is over."

Marcus' jaw tightened. "You are here, Diana, plus other surviving members of the Council."

"The Council is in ruins, Marcus. We need you here, and we need you alive to help rebuild after all this is said and done," Diana argued, and I couldn't but wonder if something deeper drove her conviction. If so, I didn't blame her. I would cut off my left arm to convince Aiden to remain behind. "We need you here."

Several agreed, and Marcus stiffened in his chair. "I'm a trained Sentinel. I have assets that will be of—"

"We know that." It was Aiden who spoke. "But I have to agree with Diana. We have this covered."

"We do," Solos confirmed. "Defeating Ares means nothing if we can't deal with the chaos afterward. And there will be chaos. We have Covenants that are destroyed or heavily damaged, and entire Councils have been wiped out. And we will have half-bloods coming off the Elixir and out of servitude. We will need leadership—strong leadership."

A proud grin crossed my lips. Marcus would make a great leader. He already was. And I could easily see him taking the role of Head Minister. Marcus might act like he had a stick shoved in a very unmentionable place half the time, but he'd be righteous and fair. Strict, but he would always do the right thing by pures and halfs.

Our eyes met, and I don't know what he saw in my expression, or if my smile had anything to do with what he did next, but I like to think it did.

Marcus rubbed a hand across his brow, sighing heavily. "I want to be there, but . . . you're right. I need to stay here."

"Well, now that's settled, I think I'm going to find something soft to lie on." Seth popped up from his chair, his movements not nearly as fluid as normal. He glanced at me, and a mischievous glint filled his amber eyes. "Want to join me?"

I rolled my eyes.

Annoyance flashed into Aiden's eyes, turning their hue into a stormy gray as he pushed off the desk and straightened. "Very amusing."

Seth winked as he backed away. "Hey, just being gentlemanly."

"Go somewhere else, then," Aiden replied.

Chuckling, Seth dipped out the door as I shook my head. While Seth and I had been more than friends at one point and our feelings for one another did run deep, I was a hundred percent certain that Seth was just trying to cause Aiden to stroke out.

Once Seth exited, the conversation moved back to the Council, and my interest also exited. Pushing up for the chair, I limped out of the office after telling them I was heading back to my room. I foresaw another herbal bath in my future. I had two more training sessions with Perses, and while each of us was getting better, none of us had taken him down.

Yet.

One of us had to take him down before we left for the Catskills.

I'd made it halfway down the stairs before Apollo poofed in front of me, startling me. I jerked to the side and lost my balance. Teetering on the edge of the step, visions of bones crunching rang in my head. He caught my arm, stopping my fall.

"Gods," I gasped, grasping the handrail with my free hand. "Is it necessary to do that?"

"You're okay." He dropped my arm. "We need to talk."

I leaned against the railing, eyeing him wryly. "What? You got bored with the Newton's Cradle?"

His lips tipped up at the corners. "Why haven't you transferred the power from Seth yet?"

"He wants to wait until we get to the Catskills." I paused as his eyes narrowed. "Look, I'm going to try to get him to do it before we leave, but—"

"Seth doesn't want to do it, and I bet it's because he's not sure he can let you do it." Apollo cursed, and unease blossomed deep in my belly. "This could be a potential problem."

The unease gave way to irritation. It pricked at my skin and poked holes in my insides. "You know, I love how you just pop in and out whenever you want to and offer little to no answers. Nothing really helpful either, but boy oh boy, there may be a problem!"

Apollo's expression slipped into a scowl, but I was on a roll. No stopping me now. "You know, all of this is bullshit. I said it before, and I'll say it again, Ares is *your* problem. He's the gods' problem." His mouth opened, but I kept on going. "And don't you dare say it's Seth's problem! Ares created this mess ages ago when he started this crap with Solaris and the First. But you guys didn't really do anything then, did you? You sent the Order in to kill them instead of getting to the bottom of what was happening."

"Alex—"

"And now it's happening again. We are going to war for you—for the gods. People will die. My friends and the people I love could die! I could die!" My voice cracked, and I took a step down. My throat felt like it was on fire. "I haven't forgotten that, Apollo. I know I could die in the end."

He clapped a heavy hand on my shoulder and squeezed. "I promise you, Alex, that no matter what happens, I'll take care of you. I told you that, and I *always* keep my promises."

A knot in my throat made it difficult to speak. The probability of my inevitable death at the hands of those who needed my help wasn't something I'd forgotten about. In reality, it was just something I couldn't fixate on. Since the hellboy twins had been exorcised from me, I had refused to dwell on it, and the reason why descended in startling clarity in that moment. In the end, no matter what Apollo wanted, he would not disobey the other Olympians. Doing so would further split them, and it could become disastrous.

Blinking back tears, I looked away, working my throat until I was sure that, when I opened my mouth, it wasn't a sob. "I don't want to die."

"I know," Apollo said, and his voice was surprisingly gentle. "I will do everything in my power to make sure that doesn't happen. I haven't let you down yet, have I?"

My gaze crawled over the gray cement walls, finally settling on his. Had he? He'd skirted the truth and divulged information only when he felt like it, but had he let me down? I didn't answer the question. "The gods should be fighting. You know that, Apollo. They should be a part of this."

Seconds passed. "You're right."

Wow. I was stunned into silence. Next thing I'd knew, Aiden and Seth would start to make out and profess their undying love for one another. "I'm right?"

"You are. They do need to be involved. They need to fight."

It took me a couple of moments to remember how to use my tongue. Hope kindled in my chest like a fledging, delicate fire. If the gods would fight, then the losses on our side would be less. "And you can make this happen?"

Apollo lowered his chin. "I will do everything I can to get them involved."

"You should. This is their fight."

"This is everyone's fight," he corrected. "Because it's everyone's future."

19

Saturday had been a day full of pain.

While we were getting better at fighting Perses, we still were getting our butts handed to us. Seth had come close to taking Perses down with a kick. The Titan had stumbled, but he hadn't fallen. He'd come back at Seth, and within seconds the First was on his back.

But Sunday got worse.

"Mats are for the weak," Perses announced as I bounced across the blue butt-saver, and that comment took the happy right out of my step. He raised a hand, and the mats flipped up on their own, starting to fold like accordions. "Warriors do not need mats."

Jumping back, I missed being smashed and folded by less than a second. Under the mats was nothing but cold, hard floor. I sighed, knowing this was going to sting, and as usual, we had a crowd watching. Three pures had mixed among my friends. Solos was already cringing.

Perses motioned me forward. "Come on, girl."

I took a deep, calming breath before I stalked toward him. Attacking in anger seemed like a good idea. The gods knew I was known to do so from time to time, but I made mistakes in the heat of it, and making mistakes with Perses or Ares wouldn't end well for me.

He immediately launched at me, swinging a meaty hand at my head. Easy. I dipped down, avoiding the attack. Springing up, I twisted to the left as he kicked out with a booted foot. I blocked him at the knee, and then struck out for his throat. Perses countered, sneaking a punch that caught my arm and spun me. I tried to twist out of it into the fall, but as I turned, he threw his arm out, hitting me across the chest. Air exploded out of my lungs. Stumbling back, I was unprepared when he kicked out, sweeping his legs out from underneath me. I hit the hard floor on my back, knocking the oxygen out of my cells this time.

"Ow," I moaned, bending my knees. I blinked the ceiling back into focus, clearing the white flecks of light from my vision.

Aiden's curse rang loudly.

Hovering over me, Perses' laugh grated on my nerves. "I hope, when you become the God Killer, Ares stands still for you."

I flipped him off.

The Titan tipped his head back and laughed. "Charming."

Rolling to my feet, I limped over to the side, passing our little audience. Olivia caught my eye and smiled sympathetically. *Almost,* she mouthed.

Almost didn't really count. I joined the guys by the wall. "Well, that was a fail."

"It wasn't." Aiden tucked a stray piece of my hair back behind my ear. "You did well."

"She looked like a pancake when she hit the floor," Seth remarked, earning a pissy look from both of us. He laughed as he jogged off toward Perses.

Sitting down, I took the bottle of water Aiden handed me and gulped it down. As Seth squared off against Perses, I readied myself for another round. When Seth ate floor, Aiden took his place. Half of my bones felt brittle, as if they were about to break, and I couldn't fathom why Aiden was subjecting himself to this when he didn't have to. Not that Perses was complaining. The more butts he was kicking, the happier he was. I stretched my legs out, easing the sore muscles. Every time I went up against Perses, I wanted to tap into akasha and just give a good old, aether-fueled bitch-slap in the—

"Holy daimon butts," I whispered.

Seth glanced down at me, frowning. "Uh, what?"

Popping up to my feet, a smile split my lips. "I got it."

He shook his head as he studied me. "Got what? Milk?"

"No." Excited, I couldn't wait until Aiden went down. Not that I really wanted that, but I wanted at Perses. "I know how to take him down."

Seth snorted.

I ignored his lack of faith in my ability. Never once during our training had Perses told Seth and me that we couldn't use our Apollyon abilities. We'd just assumed that we couldn't. After all, we were treating these training sessions like we were back in class, fighting instructors. But we weren't. We also weren't normal students.

Aiden caught a kick in the middle of the back, taking him to his knees.

"We're so stupid," I said to Seth, grinning.

His brows rose. "Speak for yourself, Angel."

As Aiden started back toward us, I passed him halfway, brushing my fingers down his arm. "I got this," I told him.

He smiled down at me, and as I continued forward, I saw the pures gathered at the doors exchange looks of disgust and disbelief. I flipped them off.

Perses yawned. "Back so soon, girl?"

"I can't wait to see your face when you hit the floor." I shook my arms out, letting the rush of power in my veins make it to my skin.

His gaze flickered over me, and I knew that he, like the gods, could see the marks of the Apollyon. A smooth brow rose. "Well, let's do this."

Backing off, we circled one another, eyeing each other for that fine, slim moment of weakness. Springing forward, he twisted in midair, kicking out, but I spun to the side. He landed in a crouch, shooting up. Summoning akasha, I welcomed the rush of power as I threw my hand out. Shock flickered across his face. A pulse of light arced across the short distance between us, smacking into his chest. It wouldn't kill him, but it definitely did the trick.

Perses stumbled back, his body bending at the waist. There were only a few seconds to complete this. Spinning around, I aimed my knee for his stomach. He tried to avoid the kick, but he wasn't fast enough. I caught him in the midsection. He went down on one knee as I straightened. Bringing my arm down, I slammed my elbow into his back, between his shoulder blades. He planted his hands on the floor to catch himself. Moving lightning-quick and putting every muscle into the motion, I brought my leg up. The toe of my sneaker connected with his solar plexus. Perses flipped.

He hit the floor on his back, his eyes wide.

Silence.

It was like the sound had been sucked out of the room. And then I heard Aiden yell, and then Luke, and then Olivia. I'd done it.

I'd taken down a mother-freaking Titan.

Ares could suck it.

Standing over Perses, a ridiculously large smile crossed my face. "I don't think you'll be calling me 'girl' anymore."

He grunted.

"What the hell?" Seth stalked up to us. "You used an element—akasha. How was that fair?"

Rocking back on my heels, I resisted the urge to start jumping around and clapping. "He never said we couldn't use our abilities. We just assumed we couldn't."

Seth stared at me.

Perses shifted to his feet. "She's right. It's only taken a week for you idiots to figure that out. Even that one," he said, gesturing to where Aiden waited. "He could've used fire, but he never did. To defeat Ares or any god, you will have to use every weapon you have. That was the lesson."

I almost giggled with glee—actual *glee*.

Seth's mouth dropped opened. "If that's the case, I've couldn't taken you down the first day."

"But you didn't." Perses smiled as he tapped a long finger against his head. "You need to start using this as well as your muscles."

Okay. I felt like clapping.

Seth rolled his eyes, but he turned to me. *Nice work, Angel.*

My smile spread, and I let my pride consume me for a moment. Perses ended the session shortly after that, and Seth disappeared out the door, parting the crowd like he was our version of Moses. I watched him go, knowing I needed to track him down. We had to do the transfer tonight.

Aiden hugged me when I joined him, resting his chin atop my head. "Brilliant."

I laughed as I squeezed him. "Not really. Think about how long it took me to figure out that we should've been using our abilities the whole time."

"Seth and I didn't figure it out at all, so you're one step ahead of us." He stepped back, sliding his hands off me. A shiver coursed through me, something that didn't go unnoticed. His eyes switched from gray to sliver. "What are you doing now?"

A flutter started in my stomach. "I'd love to do what you're thinking."

"But?"

"I need to talk with Seth." Stretching up, I kissed his cheek. Part of me might have done it because the gaping pures were still at the door even though our friends had disappeared. The other part did it because I liked kissing Aiden. "See you in a bit?"

Aiden nodded, but the tense line of his jaw said he wasn't happy. "You want me to go with you?"

I laughed under my breath. "No. That's not going to help."

He grumbled something and then said louder, "You did well today, you know that?"

A wide smile crossed my face. "Yes, I do."

Aiden chuckled. "Modesty?"

"Bah!" I started to turn, but stopped. "Hey, can we, like, chill tonight? Watch a movie with Olivia and the guys? Deacon and Luke?"

He nodded. "If that's what you want."

It was what I wanted. Tomorrow, when we left for New York, things would get, well, they would get *real*. And I wanted the night before to not be stressful.

With the exception of trying to convince Seth to transfer power, and hopefully, I wouldn't turn into the Terminator Apollyon afterward.

That would ruin our movie plans.

"Alex?"

I spun back to Aiden. "Yeah?"

"Be careful," he said, swiping up his water bottle.

"Always."

He smiled, but it didn't reach his eyes. I knew he was worried about what I was about to do, and I knew he wanted to be with me, but having Aiden and Seth in the same room wasn't going to help.

Walking toward the door, I raised an eyebrow at the remaining pures. They shifted to the sides, allowing me to pass.

I stopped in the hallway, facing them. "Hi."

The three pures exchanged surprised glances, but none of them spoke.

"Ah, you have nothing to say." I popped my hands on my hips and rocked back on my heels. "I know it's shocking to see a pure and a half together. And yes, we're together in the biblical sense."

Their eyes widened.

I smirked. "And seriously? That's not a big deal. So, why don't you three douche canoes go find something else to gawk at? Or, I don't know ... get a hobby. Or better yet, there's this huge war that's about to start. You guys could go figure how you could help instead of standing around like a bunch of bigoted ass-hats. Okay? Buh-bye."

Spinning around, I left them staring at me for a much better reason than age-old prejudices.

Back in the day, if I were looking for Seth, I'd probably have found him in the girls' dorms or somewhere where a lot of single females were mingling, but now? I wasn't so sure. With the exception of his wild and crazy night in Vegas, I hadn't seen him pay attention to anyone, really.

Troubled, I sighed.

All of us had changed so much in the last year. Sometimes I didn't recognize myself when I looked in the mirror, and not in the physical sense. It had to be the same for Seth—probably even more so for him.

Using the freaky connection between us, I headed down the marble pathway leading beyond the high-rising dorms. The cord began to tighten as I rounded the last dorm and the cemetery came into view.

A shudder snaked down my spine.

Seth was in the cemetery.

Yeah.

Picking up my pace, I reached the titanium-encased gates quickly. Among the mausoleums and a statue of Thanatos, the red and purple hyacinths swayed softly in the breeze. They caught my attention for a few moments as I walked to the center of the cemetery. Under the peaceful gaze of the stone Thanatos, I scanned the tombs.

There he was.

Sitting on a stone bench, Seth's back was to the path. He sat straight, his gaze focused on the olive trees. It was so weird seeing them here in South Dakota, but like the gardens, the cemeteries had a godly green thumb. But what was even weirder was seeing Seth out here. Hanging out in places where tombs were built to remember the dead wasn't his thing.

"Are you following me?" His voice carried on the wind.

I made my way over to him and sat beside him. "Maybe."

One side of his lips tipped up. "Did you come to gloat about taking out Perses?"

"No." A tiny grin fought to make a way onto my lips. I lost. "Maybe a little."

He chuckled. "Figured."

"I did damn good."

Casting me a sidelong glance, he arched a brow. "You did. I almost had him."

"So did Aiden," I reminded him. "'Almost' being the key word."

"Whatever." He turned back to staring at the trees. I wondered what was so interesting about the clusters of leaves.

"What are you doing out here?"

"It's weird, right? To be hanging out here?" He bent forward, resting his arms on his thighs. "I don't know. It's quiet. I like to come out here and think."

It was quiet, too quiet. Granted, we were sitting in a middle of cemetery. Not a very happening place. "What are you thinking about?"

He chuckled again, but the sound was weak and strangely hollow. "Like you really care."

I blinked and opened my mouth. His tone was light, but there was a coating of frost to his words. "If I didn't care, I wouldn't ask. You of all people know that."

Moments passed, and then a breath shuddered from him. "Do you know what I think about when it's quiet, Alex? I think about all the bad things I've done."

My breath caught in my chest like someone had punched me.

I didn't know what to say at first. What I had seen Seth do and what I knew he'd been a part of was enough to earn him a trip to Tartarus. Then there were the things I didn't know about and really didn't want to find out.

Shifting on the bench, I rubbed my hands over my sweats as a chill danced along my skin. It was cooler in this part of the campus, unnaturally so for the time of year. It seemed like forever passed before I spoke. "We've all done bad things."

"Ah," he said, scrubbing his hands down his face. A smile peeked through every few seconds, but when he finally dropped his hands, it was gone. "Have you ever killed an innocent person?"

Dropping my gaze, I shook my head. "No."

"That's the level of bad things I've done. Maybe you've kissed a boy you shouldn't have. Maybe you acted out when you should've thought more clearly about something," he replied. "Maybe you hurt someone's feelings or did the wrong thing, but nothing you've done will ever touch what I'm responsible for."

"I don't know what to say," I admitted quietly. "I can't tell you that any of that is okay. You'd know I was lying. But Seth? You weren't completely responsible for everything."

"When an addict kills someone to get money for drugs, are they not responsible? Or is it the drug dealer's fault?" When I didn't answer, he laughed dryly. "Anyway, obviously I'm not thinking about those things right this second. You're here. And I know there's a reason for you being here other than stalking me."

Now I felt kind of bad for why I had come looking for him. In spite of everything that Seth had done to others and to me, a part of me still cared for him and considered him a friend—and something more that could never quite be labeled. He needed someone to talk to. He needed someone to help him make things better. He needed someone who cared for him—cared for him more than I did.

Swallowing, I turned my gaze to the trees. I felt like an über-bitch for my next words. "I want to do the transfer of power now. That's why I came here." He was silent, but I could feel his eyes drilling holes through the side of my head. "I don't want to wait until we get to the Catskills. We should do it now. Get it over with so we—"

"No." Steel poured into that one word. "We wait until we're about to face Ares. Not a moment sooner."

I turned my head toward his. "Why not? And don't you say 'because I said so'."

His lips twisted wryly. "Damn, there goes my only explanation."

My eyes narrowed.

"We wait," he said, his eyes narrowing too. "It's not up for discussion."

"How can you say it's not up for discussion? You're not the only person who has a say in this."

"I'm the only person whose say matters," he replied.

Pushing off the bench, I stood in front of him. "Oh, now you're just pissing me off."

Seth smiled. "So?"

"This isn't funny, Seth. Why in the hell are you so adamant on waiting? I'm ready. You should be ready, too. This isn't just about you, buddy."

The infuriating smile remained fixed. "Like I said before, you have no idea what it's like to be the First, how hard it is. So you can't even imagine what it will be like when you become the God Killer."

Anger flooded my system. "Oh, come off it, Seth! All you do is whine about how 'terrible the need' is and—"

In a nanosecond, Seth was in my face. He moved that fast, causing my heart to jump. I jerked back. Apollyon or not, he *was* the First, and when he moved like that, it didn't create a happy feeling. "All I do is whine?" Anger flushed his cheeks, and his amber eyes glowed. "You have no idea, Alex. You're just the Apollyon. That's all you have to deal with."

I stepped back, trying to rein in my own anger. "I have to deal with our connection and the stupid cord inside me spazzing out all the time."

"Oh, you poor, little thing." He took a step forward, and the marks seeped into his skin. He was not happy. Perhaps I didn't know when to keep my mouth shut. "You have a cord to deal with while I have to deal with the fact that, every time I'm around you, all I can even *think* about is transferring the power."

The anger coursing through my veins immediately switched to the acidic burn of unease. I sidestepped him and the bench, thinking space might be good about right now.

Seth advanced, following me back up the path. "Every fucking time, Alex. I'm the First. It's what I'm supposed to do. It's what I was built to do. So resisting that is bad enough, but after having had a taste of that power? Oh, you have no idea."

My eyes widened. When Seth had pulled on my power to take out the Council and kill the furie, he'd tapped into just the tiniest bit of power that existed in the God Killer, and that tiny taste had been enough.

I swallowed hard as I stopped under the wing of a marble Thanatos. *Seth?*

"Don't," he spat, drawing in a deep breath. "I fight the need every single second of the day. I'm trying here, so I'm sorry that it comes across as whining."

Widening my stance, I prepared myself just in case Seth went completely crazy. "I'm sorry. I didn't mean it that way. It's just that—"

"It doesn't matter!"

His eyes flashed an intense shade of amber a second before sparks erupted from his bare arms. A bolt of intense light— akasha—flew out from him, smacking into the center of the statue.

Marble cracked like a whip of thunder. Stone splintered as I turned, sending chunks into the air. Throwing my arms up, I shielded my face as shards blasted through the air and dust thickened around me. Tiny chunks pelted my back and arms.

When it settled, I slowly lowered my arms. My heart pounded insanely fast as my gaze locked with his.

"Shit," Seth muttered, his chest rising and falling rapidly. "Just stay . . . stay away from me."

I didn't have a chance to respond. He spun on his heel, leaving me standing there among the remains of the ruined statue. There was no way we could stay away from each other. Right now, we needed each other, especially to transfer the power, but it was more than that.

But I didn't chase after him. I let him go. He won. We would wait, but we couldn't wait forever.

20

The skies were gray and overcast. Clouds were thick. A fine drizzle coated the ground and our vehicles. The slight chill in the air warned that autumn was well on its way. Perses had wanted to travel with the rest of the army, but none of us trusted him enough to let that happen. Gods only knew what he'd get himself into between here and the Catskills.

Luke and Olivia also were traveling with us, mainly because Deacon and I demanded that they did.

"Do you think Deacon will talk the entire trip?" Olivia asked, hoisting a small bag of weapons and tucking several small coins into a pocket on her leg. It was a depressing necessity after what had happened to Lea, and we all carried them now. Just in case. "I'm betting at least fifty bucks that he does until he passes out."

I laughed. "I'm not betting against that. On the way here, I thought Marcus was going to strangle him."

"I would've if he hadn't fallen asleep," Marcus said, coming out from behind us. "Or at the very least, I would've knocked him out."

Olivia giggled. "Want me to get that?" She gestured at my own bag of things made to stab and dismember.

"Nah," I said. "I got it."

Smiling at Marcus, she headed toward where Luke and Deacon stood behind a black Expedition. Deacon spun around and pulled Olivia into a dance you'd see in a ballroom while Luke took the bag of weapons from her. A laugh escaped my lips as I watched him dip Olivia over his arm.

"He's something else, isn't he?" Marcus folded his arms. "In spite of everything, he's ..." He trailed off, shaking his head. "He's just Deacon."

"That's what I love about him."

Marcus glanced at me, his expression unreadable. Several seconds passed. "Are you ready for this, Alexandria?"

"As ready as I'll ever be," I admitted, wiping the fine sheen of rain off my forehead. Seth appeared with Perses. They headed toward another vehicle. My stomach tipped over. I hadn't seen Seth since he'd left me in the cemetery last night.

Seth glanced over to where Marcus and I stood. Our eyes met for a second and then he looked away, saying something to Perses.

"You haven't transferred the power yet," Marcus said.

My lips pursed. "No. We're going to do it when we get to New York." *I hope*, but I didn't add that last part. Taking a deep breath, I forced my gaze away from Seth and turned to my uncle.

The lines around his eyes appeared deeper than they had been yesterday. Gray hairs liberally sprinkled his chestnut-colored hair. I hadn't noticed them before, but they had to have been there. His eyes were sharp with keen intelligence and clear with foresight, as usual.

In a second, I saw him as he'd been the first day I'd returned to the Covenant. He'd sat behind that shiny desk of his, full of stiff, unyielding authority, and his displeased stare had made me dislike him immediately. A lot had changed since the day he'd almost kicked me out of the Covenant. He'd changed. So had I. Somewhere in the last year, he'd gone from being the Dean to becoming my uncle. And I never would've believed that last year. I honestly hadn't believed that he cared one bit about me, but I knew now he always had. He may've had a hard time showing it, and I'd just made it even harder for him to do so. I'd been such a brat.

His lips tipped up at the corners. When he spoke, it was as if he knew what I was thinking. "I'm not sure I've ever told you this, Alexandria, but I am proud of you."

My eyes misted over, but I blamed the rain. "You never thought you'd say that, huh?"

"No, I always knew that one day I would say that," he replied, his slight smile softening his features. "I'd just hoped it would've been when you graduated from the Covenant."

"Same here," I sighed.

"You make sure you come back here." His voice thickened. "After all, you haven't technically graduated yet, and there are a few courses you need to finish up before you can."

I laughed, but the sound caught in my throat. "Okay. Deal."

Marcus nodded and unfolded his arms. He started to turn, but he stopped. An emotion I couldn't quite pick out flickered across his face, and a second later he hugged me. My uncle gave the most awkward hugs in history. But in a way, they were the best.

Closing my eyes, I inhaled the faint scent of his cologne and hugged him back.

"I know you will look for your father when you get there," he said, his voice low. "I know how much finding him means to you, but you need to be careful. There will be time afterward to find him."

"Okay," I said, even though I wasn't sure I meant it. As much as I wanted to believe that Apollo would hold to his promise, I couldn't be a hundred percent sure that there would be an afterward for me.

Marcus pulled back, and I swore his eyes were shiny. He muttered something about helping Luke and stalked off. After saying my goodbyes to Laadan and Diana, I waited off to the side while Aiden spoke to my uncle. No doubt he was getting some over-protective warning, because when Aiden joined me, he was a shade or two paler.

My brows rose. "You okay?"

His gray eyes shifted to mine. "Marcus can be really scary when he wants to be."

I grinned. "Yeah, he can."

He took my bag from me, placing it in the back as Deacon shimmied across the seat and situated himself between Luke and Olivia.

"You haven't seen Apollo, have you?" I asked, chewing on my lower lip.

Shutting the door, Aiden shook his head. I'd told him about Apollo's promise to bring in the rest of the gods and I'd also told him that, obviously, I hadn't transferred the power from Seth, but I'd left out the blowing up the statue part. "I wouldn't hold my breath, Alex. While I think Apollo wants to help and get involved, I don't think the others will."

"That's such crap." Familiar anger simmered in my stomach. "It's taking the absentee landlord theory to a whole new level."

"I know." He dug the keys out of his tactical pants. "But throughout history, they've all really only gotten involved once before, and that was with the Titans. Any other time, most of them don't get involved."

"This is different," I grumbled, beating the horse dead and then bringing it back to life to beat again. "This is one of their own—their problem."

"Maybe Apollo will surprise us." He bent down, brushing his lips over my forehead. "Either way, we have this."

Car keys dangling from his fingertips, Seth passed by us. "If you two can stop making doe-eyes at each for a few minutes, we're all ready to go." Behind him, Perses inspected the vehicle with a distrustful scowl. One of the other SUVs in our little section of the convoy revved an engine, and the Titan transferred his scowl to the other vehicle.

Aiden straightened, his gaze narrowing on Seth's back. "Jealous is an ugly thing."

"So is blind ignorance," Seth shot back, rounding the front of a Hummer.

Tension rolled off Aiden as he turned to me. "I really do dislike him most of the time."

"Yeah, well . . ." What could I say? The two of them would never be friends. "Ready?"

"We are!" Deacon shouted from inside the Expedition. "I've already got the first road game picked out, so freaking hurry!"

Shaking his head, Aiden smiled. "This is going to be the longest twenty-three hours of our lives."

Turned out, the next twenty-three hours of our lives weren't the longest, even when they turned into closer to twenty-six hours after our caravan hit a traffic snarl outside of Chicago. I switched places with Aiden and then Luke, giving all of us time to rest up.

As expected, while awake, Deacon kept us somewhere between entertained and five seconds away from pulling the SUV over and duct-taping his mouth shut.

When we entered New York, we followed Seth's vehicle, keeping to the back of the massive group of Sentinels and Guards. Solos checked in periodically with Aiden from where he rode in one of the lead vehicles. They hadn't run into any problems, but there was no way Ares didn't know we were coming. Any number of people we passed on the way here could've been spies, mortal or not, even though we were traveling in small clusters of SUVs and cars so as not to stand out. Not to mention that Ares was a god, so it wouldn't be hard for him to figure out what we were up to.

But the fact that we reached the Catskills without incident had me squirming in my seat, restless and unnerved. When we'd traveled to South Dakota in the first place, we'd been intercepted by Ares' Sentinels, and that had basically been out in the middle of nowhere. How could it be this easy?

Upon entering the mountainous back roads, my unease

tripled to paranoid levels when the vehicle in front of us rolled to a stop. I exchanged a nervous look with Aiden. Ahead, Perses' arm appeared out the window, waving us forward.

"Why don't they use a cell?" Luke asked, peering over my seat.

"Does Perses even know how to use a cell phone?" Olivia asked.

I snorted while the knot of anxiety worked at giving me an ulcer in record time. "He seems like a quick learner."

Aiden slipped the Expedition into park and glanced back at his brother. "Stay in the car."

Deacon rolled his eyes. "Yes, Dad, because I couldn't possibly be of any help."

That statement was ignored as Aiden and I stepped out of the SUV and made our way over to Perses' side. Three Sentinels from the other vehicles joined us—I recognized them as halfs I'd seen in South Dakota, but I didn't know any of their names.

"What's going on?" Aiden asked.

Perses stepped out of the vehicle, his all-black eyes fixed on the thick tree line ahead. "Something's not right."

"Other than the fact we're stopped?" I asked, folding my arms. The air was chilly in the mountains, especially where the sun didn't break through the trees, and my black shirt didn't offer a lot of warmth.

His lips curled up at the corner in a sardonic twist. "I sense something abnormal among us."

I peered in through the car at Seth. He just shrugged. "Details?"

"There's violence in the air; the smell of battle that has yet to begin," Perses said, stretching his arms above his head. Bones cracked. The twist of his lips spread into a real smile. "Bloodshed is pending."

My brows rose as I glanced at Aiden. "Well, that's not freaky or anything."

"Yeah," he said, his gaze darting over the tree line and the empty, narrow south lane.

Seth shut the Hummer down and climbed out. "I don't feel anything, but then again, I'm not a Titan."

Perses chuckled deeply as he walked toward the front of the vehicle. "I am never wrong about these things."

Doors opened and closed behind us. "What's going on?" Luke called, joined by Olivia. Both had daggers in their hands. Sentinels from the other cars were close behind them. "Are we just taking a potty break or something?"

Aiden turned toward them, his mouth opening to respond just as the ground beneath our feet trembled. He looked down, brows furrowing. "What the . . . ?"

The vibration continued, growing in intensity, shaking the vehicles and rattling the trees that crowded the road. Asphalt cracked like an ear-piercing gunshot. A fissure spread along the side of the road, spreading toward the guardrail. I whipped around, following the progress of the crevice as it widened along the land, splitting open. Loose soil pebbled and rolled as giant elms shook until thick roots poked up from the ground.

"Deacon!" Aiden shouted, spinning. His brother was already out of the car, his eyes wide. "Stay near Luke!"

"Earthquake?" Olivia asked, one hand braced on the hood of the Expedition.

I shook my head. "I have a really bad feeling about this."

"Ditto," Seth said, joining us.

The trembling eased off and the earth seemed to settle, along with my stomach. The reprieve lasted seconds. From the wide crack in the ground, rich, dark soil spewed into the air like from a volcano. The earthy scent was overpowering as the dirt arced up and shot back down, landing in twenty or so different piles.

"Yeah," Luke drawled the word out. "That crap ain't normal."

The piles of dirt swirled along the ground in circles, then rose up, rapidly taking form. Legs appeared, thick and well-muscled, followed by torsos, broad chests and shoulders, and finally heads.

I blinked once and then twice. "What in the hell?"

The things resembled human males—human males who could've easily been pro wrestlers in another life. Soil traveled down their arms, taking shaping over the hands. Axes appeared in their hands, blades sharpened into deadly edges. Like, axes bigger than what I imagined Vikings used to carry once upon a screwed-up time.

These things . . . they were made of dirt, but the axes were very, very real.

"The *Spartoi*!" shouted Perses. "Warriors born of soil—sons of Ares!"

"Oh, shit," Aiden said, eyes flaring with recognition.

I had no idea what the Spartoi were, but seeing that full-grown men made of dirt had just popped out the earth heavily armed, and seeing that were sons of Ares, I was going to assume this was a very bad situation.

Their mouths opened in unison, letting out a heart-stopping battle roar that was matched only by the sound that came out of Perses' mouth. He launched himself forward, over the crack in the road, and met the first Dirt Man head-to-head.

"Yeah, screw this," Seth said, lifting his hand. The marks on his skin brightened and akasha blasted from his palm, striking one of the manifestations in the chest.

Dirt Man Two exploded outward, but all the tiny, million particles froze and then snapped back, reforming. The thing laughed, spewing tiny pebbles from its open mouth.

"Oh crap," I said, my mouth dropping open.

"The heads," Perses grunted, engaging his sickle blade. "You must remove their heads!"

I unhooked my sickle blade as Dirt Man Two threw his axe. It whipped through the air, narrowly avoiding Aiden, and smacked into a tree across the road, embedding deep. A second later, a red film covered the majestic elm tree, completely and utterly swallowing it whole. When the red haze disappeared, nothing of the tree remained.

"Holy crap," Luke said.

Another axe appeared in Dirt Man Two's hands.

Perses whirled, cleaving the head off of his Dirt Man's body. The creature collapsed into itself, the axe disappearing along with it. The Titan's laugh was disturbingly joyful.

Dirt Man Two charged forward, and I used the air element to fling him back against the trees. The thing shattered and came back together within seconds. Seth shot forward, avoiding the broad sweep of the axe as he brought the sickle around sharply, catching it under the chin.

"Two down," Aiden said, springing to the side as another axe flew by our heads.

Luke grunted as he shoved Deacon back toward the rear of the Expedition. "Stay back, pretty boy."

Deacon responded, but it was lost in the invasion of the Spartoi. One was heading straight toward me, a trail of soil chasing after it. I dipped down, engaging the sickle part of the weapon with a shake of my wrist. I sprung up behind the Dirt Man. The thing twisted as it swung the axe down. Heat flew off the weapon, causing me to jump back.

Dirt Man Three lurched at me. Darting to the side, I reached up and caught his arm. It fell apart under my hand, crumbling in a sheet of dry dirt. Ignoring the grossness of that, I swung it down and twisted hard, causing the creature to lose its grip on the axe. As it fell to the ground, I brought the sickle blade against the back of its neck.

"Three down!" I shouted, feeling a familiar adrenaline rushing inside me.

Olivia spun gracefully, relieving another of its head. "Four!"

Was it twisted that we were counting? I guessed not, because within a few minutes, we were down to ten. Even Perses was calling out numbers, but he seemed to be having a hell of a lot more fun than we were. A wide smile was on his face as he stalked a Dirt Man, easily avoiding the axes lobbed at him. It was like Christmas morning for the freak.

Turning at the waist, I found myself nearly losing my own head when one of them swung an axe. I had two of them, coming from both sides. I started to summon the air element again, but Aiden appeared in front of me.

In a graceful move, he spun and lopped off the head of one of the Spartoi. I wanted to take a moment to recognize the beauty of the way he moved, but another was running straight for me. Rushing forward, I met it with the sharp side of the sickle.

Drop! Seth's voice shouted in my head.

Without thinking twice, I hit the ground half a second before Seth's blade cut through where I'd been standing, taking out a Dirt Man that had been really close to putting the hurting on me. None of these things could kill Seth or me, or at least that was what I was banking on, but they could put us down long enough for Ares to swoop in.

Rising, I nodded at Seth. "Thanks."

He said nothing as he joined Luke in cornering two more of the creatures. Looking around, I saw that Deacon was safe and Aiden was now a few yards in front of him. Nothing would get past him.

I started toward another Dirt Man when a ball of flames landed about two feet from me. Fire licked over the ground. Startled, I spun, and my stomach dropped. Cresting the hill above us was one of the worst possible things we could've seen at this moment.

Horns, dark matted hair, and long, flat snouts that sloped into mouths full of strong teeth came into view. Their thick thighs and large hoofs made of titanium were next.

Automatons.

Perses shouted another battle roar, and the rush of adrenaline coiled tight around my heart. I spun and darted out, reaching the Dirt Man closest to me. The thing dove forward, but I ducked under its arm. Swinging around, I swung the blade down, dispatching another one of the freaky creations.

Something inside me clicked off as I ran toward the cars, dodging the axes and fireballs. We had to get rid of the Spartoi first. There were only a few left, so that was completely doable, and Perses was charging toward the bulls to keep them at bay for a while.

Hearing pounding footsteps behind me, I whirled and jerked to the side, narrowly avoiding another axe. Springing into the air, I spun and delivered a nasty kick that would've been so damn good if my foot hadn't sunk through the thing's chest.

We went down in a burst of dirt and rocks. Dust flew into my mouth and nose. I gagged, trying not think about the fact that I just swallowed some of the Dirt Man as I rolled away from him. He swung his axe through the air and brushed my thigh. A slice of pain shot down my leg as a thin slit formed in the pant leg. The Dirt Man roared to its feet, heaving the axe like a Viking straight from Valhalla.

Summoning air, I blew the S.O.B. back, slamming it into the Hummer. I popped to my feet and raced after it, taking it out. Through the smoke and clouds of dirt, I saw Aiden engaging an automaton. Like the Spartoi, the heads had to be removed.

One of the automatons lit up from the inside, like a blue X-ray, before exploding in a shower of sparks.

Or Seth could use akasha. That would work, too.

With the automatons coming closer and closer, our group was scattered. Perses was making short work of the monsters, but the falling flames were making it difficult to pay attention to any one thing.

A burst of flames shot from where Aiden and Deacon were,

smacking into the nearest automaton. Flames spread across the ground, and I darted around the blaze. Springing up, I caught a Dirt Man before it launched its axe at Luke.

Perses slammed the pointed end of the weapon into the chin of an automaton. Silvery blood sprayed the Titan in the face and chest. He didn't even blink as he yanked the blade to the side. He turned, and his smile was gory with blood.

In that moment, I understood the Olympians' distaste of Perses. To enjoy battle and war was one thing. Twisted, yes, but there were a lot of aggressive people out there. Perses didn't just enjoy it, though. The Titan got off on the violence and bloodshed.

For a moment, the Titan transfixed me. The way he dispatched the enemy with that level of glee would make serial killers across the nation happy.

A little sickened, I joined Seth and tapped into primitive, raw energy. Power rushed through me, and my skin tingled with the appearance of the marks. Using akasha, intense blue light erupted from me. Arcing through the air, it struck its target, reducing it to nothing but a pile of shimmery dust.

Out of the corner of my eye, I saw Olivia dart to the side to avoid an incoming fireball. My heart kicked in my chest as a Dirt Man let loose his axe. I shouted at her—I thought I did as I pushed off the ground, rushing toward her. In my head, I was screaming, but I wasn't sure any sound was making it past my lips. A horrible, terrifying feeling of déjà vu settled in my stomach. In a split second, I saw Lea in my head, but this wasn't Lea. No—no no no. This couldn't be happening again.

A flicker of recognition shot across Olivia's face a second before the Dirt Man's axe struck her in the chest. She hadn't even tried to move. I think, in that tiny second, she knew it was already too late.

"No!" I screamed, and then I screamed again.

Olivia stumbled back a step. The red film spread out from her chest, quickly slipping over her. In a heartbeat, she was gone.

Another hoarse scream tore through me, scratching my throat and darkening a part of my soul. Olivia was gone. She was gone. Just like that. Nothing in this world left of her.

Luke shouted as he spun on his Dirt Man, dispatching it, and then whirled back to where Olivia had been. He kept the saying the same word over and over again—the same word that was repeating itself in my head.

No. No. No. No.

Deacon rushed forward, but Aiden caught him around the waist. Tears streamed down the younger St. Delphi's face as he struggled against Aiden's hold. He was saying her name—screaming it, really.

My heart split open as my gaze returned to the spot. This wasn't fair. Oh gods, it *hurt*. How could someone be there one second and be gone the next? It didn't matter how many times people had died. I still couldn't fathom the quick and unforgiving end of existence.

And there was nothing left of her. Not a speck of flesh or clothing. Not even a weapon remained. No body to bury or mourn.

I hit the scorched earth on my knees, slowly shaking my head back and forth. All around us, the fight raged on with Seth and Perses taking on the remaining automatons. Flames burst a few feet from me, but I didn't flinch, and I didn't move.

Olivia was gone.

21

Things were a blur after that. Seth and Perses destroyed the automatons, and when they returned, the Titan hadn't given a damn that we'd lost someone.

That we had lost Olivia.

"We don't have time for this. We must move on."

I looked at him, searching for a fleck of sorrow, or compassion, or anything, but there was nothing. He stalked forward, walking right through the spot where Olivia had last stood.

Luke started toward the Titan, his hands curling into fists, but Aiden grabbed his arm, shaking his head as he all but dragged the half-blood to the Expedition.

"Get inside," Aiden ordered.

His eyes were still trained on Perses, and he wasn't budging.

"Luke," Aiden warned.

It was Deacon who got through to him. "Come on. Get in with me. Please?"

Luke blinked, and anger, hurt, and dozens of other violent emotions still infused his cheeks, but he climbed into the back seat with Deacon.

Alex?

I didn't respond as Seth passed me. I turned, opening the passenger door.

I'm sorry, he said.

My breath caught as I hauled myself into the seat. *I know.*

No one spoke as the vehicles ground into gear, easing around the fissure in the road, with the exception of Aiden checking in with Solos. He shared what'd happened in a low voice. I sat unnaturally still, with my cheek pressed against the window, watching the trees as we continued up the mountain. My heart was heavy, and my eyes burned. Pain lanced my jaw from how tight I was clenching my teeth. I was barely holding it together, but I knew we had to forge on. We had to, but it didn't seem right. I wanted to yell "STOP," and I wanted to make everyone, included the Titan, acknowledge that we had lost someone important to us, someone who was too young to die.

A tear streaked down my cheek, and I squeezed my eyes shut as I pressed my hand against the pocket that held several small coins—the ones I'd brought in case . . . in case we had to bury someone. We couldn't even bury Olivia, but she had the coins with her. She'd have them in the Underworld.

Olivia would get to be with Caleb now. He would find her, and she would be okay. Olivia was with Caleb now. I kept repeating that, because it helped to know that they would be reunited. They would be back together for eternity, and that was something to be happy about, because Olivia had never truly gotten over Caleb's death. Knowing that still didn't make this any easier to accept. At some point, Aiden reached over and found my hand. He squeezed.

I squeezed back.

We reached the heavily forested outskirts of the Catskills just before dusk. We parked the dusty Hummer in front of a sprawling house at the base of the mountains; Solos had directed us to the address, so we assumed it was full of allies. I stretched my tight muscles, then opened the door.

Behind us, Seth and Perses had already sprung free from their vehicle and were rounding ours. Up ahead, I could see a mass of Sentinels in front of the house, and there were several lights on inside. It seemed like more than what we'd left with, and sweet relief coursed through me. They had somehow made it around the automatons. Maybe they'd just been waiting for the Apollyon-Titan carpool.

"Ares has to know about this," I said, hopping down and walking toward the stone fence separating the gravel road from the yard.

Seth fell in step beside me, folding his arms. "I'm sure he does, but this kind of warfare reminds him of his glory days."

"He's right." Aiden hefted the bag of weapons onto his shoulder. "There's no way two enemies would be stationed this close together in modern warfare, but this . . ." He waved his arm in the direction of the waiting Sentinels and Guards. "This is like trench warfare."

In high school, before I'd returned to the Deity Island Covenant, I had read *All Quiet on the Western Front*. That was about all I knew about trench warfare, and that was enough for me to want to sneak into the Covenant and act like a nuclear missile.

I couldn't bear to lose anyone else.

Perses strode ahead of us, tall and silent, and I watched him for a moment. He'd relished the skirmish that had cost Olivia her life. The Titan thrived on the bloodshed and death. I didn't want to hate him, because it was what he was, but there was still no trace of remorse or sorrow for the lives lost.

Deacon stumbled past us, rubbing his red-rimmed eyes wearily. "I don't want to see the inside of a car again for as long as I live."

"I'll remind you of that the next time you have to walk any real distance and start whining," Luke replied, the words light but the look on his face grave.

He had been so close to Olivia, closer than me. An ache pierced my chest as I stepped through the narrow opening in the stone wall. The only thing I could console myself with was that I knew—*I knew*—she was with Caleb. She was with the boy she had loved so fiercely, had never stopped loving.

I was still holding onto that thought like it was a life jacket.

Solos jogged across the clearing, slowing down as he passed Perses. He cast the Titan a look before continuing toward us. He stopped in front of Luke, placing his hand on the half-blood's shoulder.

"I'm sorry," he said, and those two words carried so much weight.

Luke nodded and said something in a low voice before he walked past. Deacon's hand went to his lower back, and a small smile tugged at my lips when Luke moved closer to him as they followed Perses.

Aiden clasped Solos' hand as we met him. "How are things here?"

"Better than what you had to face," Solos replied. "I should've—"

"There's nothing you could've done," I interrupted, shifting my weight. I wanted a pillow—STAT. "It seems like there are more Sentinels here than there were with us."

"There are." His eyes gleamed with excitement. "Come on. I'm sure you guys could use something to eat. I'll explain on the way."

My stomach rumbled in response, and Aiden sent me a quick grin. I was too tired to be embarrassed. "So what's going on?"

"Our advance scouts met up with a group of about fifty Sentinels outside of the city. They're from the New York Covenant and were out scouting beyond the line of the automatons. They showed us a way around. We had a minor run-in with a few automatons, but we didn't lose any numbers."

They were lives, not numbers.

He knows that. Seth's voice startled me. I hadn't realized I'd projected those thoughts anywhere. *But looking at them that way helps keep the mind clear.*

I guess, I responded without much conviction.

"They brought us back here. There's at least a hundred more.

They've been here since Ares took over. They made it out after he did." Purpose filled his voice. "They know the set-up inside, where Ares has been holing up, how many he has beyond the walls, and so on."

All of that was valuable knowledge, necessary knowledge, and that was what Aiden was telling Solos, and then they were talking about more important stuff. But all I could think was that, if there were Sentinels here that had gotten out after Ares took over, was my father among them? Solos wouldn't know if he was, but Seth and Laadan had said that my father had stayed behind with the servants.

"Are there servants here?" I asked, interrupting them.

Solos glanced back at me. "Yes. There are quite a few. Most of them aren't under the effects of the Elixir anymore."

My heart tripped up in my chest, and my wide eyes met Aiden's. There was a reluctant hope in his gaze. I knew he wanted my father to be somewhere among those up ahead or in the house, but he was wary of that fragile dream and the crushing disappointment that was sure to come if he wasn't.

He was behind the walls when I was last here. Seth's words were as heavy as Solos' apology. *He could've made it out since then, but . . .*

But Ares knew that my father was there. I sighed. *It was stupid to hope, wasn't it?*

"Never," Seth said out loud.

Aiden glanced back, brows furrowed, but then he turned back to Solos.

Stones sat in my stomach. Man, that disappointment wasn't far behind. I tried to shake it off, because we had such huge things to accomplish. We would have to move on Ares quickly, probably by the following nightfall, but I wanted to see my dad. I needed him to know that I knew who he was.

If things went south fast, I wanted to see him before I . . .

I didn't allow myself to finish that thought. I had to trust that

Apollo would find a way to stop the Olympians from snuffing me out once I became the God Killer. He'd said he would take care of me. He'd sworn, and supposedly gods kept their promises.

Except in Solos' case, and just about every other story I could think of.

Sigh.

As we crossed the lawn, the Sentinels that had been gawking at Perses did the same as Seth and I neared. Several muttered curses when they laid eyes on the First, their gazes cold and unfriendly.

"Friends of yours?" I asked, watching one of them rest his hand on his gun.

Seth gave a lopsided shrug. "I'm sure we may have exchanged a few words before . . ."

"Before you pulled your head out of your ass?"

A laugh burst from him. "Exactly."

"You should sleep well tonight."

He stepped around a bag full of what looked like rifles. "I doubt any of us will really be sleeping."

I recognized some of the faces from the University, but there were a lot of strangers in the crowd, and many of them were my age. Young. I didn't feel young, not anymore, but I guessed technically I still was, and so were they.

Solos introduced us to the Sentinels who were in charge of the group from inside the Covenant. They looked battered but hopeful as they saw with their own eyes what Solos must've been telling them.

The Apollyons were unified, and we'd brought a Titan with us.

It sounded kind of badass, but then again, we *were* going up against Ares.

We headed into the house, which was really a mansion. Someone said it'd once belonged to a mortal in the government, but they had abandoned it when Ares brought in the mortal troops. Food was given to us, and I tried to eat quietly while Aiden conversed with the different Sentinels. I didn't see where Luke and Deacon had roamed off to, but I hoped, wherever they were, Luke was doing okay.

I picked at my sandwich, my stomach too full of knots to be hungry. Part of me worried that I was throwing way too many vibes at Seth, but I suspected he was blocking me. After all, he was a hell of a lot better at it than me.

Giving up on the food, I set the plate aside, left the large sitting room, and investigated the house. I lost count of how many rooms were downstairs after I walked through what looked like the third sitting room. Who needed this many rooms? And why were there so many short halls? It was like a maze.

Sighing, I pushed the shorter strands of hair that had escaped my ponytail out of my face. I knew I should be back in that room with Aiden and Solos. They had been talking about plans for tomorrow. I should've been leading those conversations—or at least paying attention. Or pretending to listen by being in the same room as them.

"You shouldn't feel guilty."

I jumped at the sound of Seth's voice, surprised that he was able to sneak up on me. Turning toward him, I found him under the archway. Well, there went the idea that he was blocking my feelings.

"Are you following me?" I asked instead of acknowledging his statement.

"Yes."

"Shouldn't you be following Perses?"

"Why?" He tipped his head down, and a lock of blond hair fell across his forehead. "He's behaving. Right now, he's outside with the Sentinels, getting them all wound up."

I sat on the edge of an antique couch that had the hardest, most uncomfortable cushions ever. "Do you think that's a good idea?"

"I think so. He'll get them ready to battle. We're going to need everything we have to get past the army Ares has and inside those walls."

I nodded slowly. "You think we can do it?"

"Most definitely." One side of his lips quirked up.

"And you think we can take out Ares?"

"I do." Seth strode over the couch and sat beside me. My initial reaction was to get up, especially since he was having so many problems ignoring the allure of the power that rested inside of me, but I stayed put. "Perses will make sure we get to him, and then he will weaken Ares, giving us time to make the transfer. You remember how to do it?"

"Yes." I clapped my hands together in my lap and peeked at him. The amber hue of his eyes was deeper. I decided to take a stab at the argument again. "Waiting until the very last minute is risky."

"You doing it now is risky, Alex. You don't know what it's like. I know—"

"I believe you," I said, and I really did. The power had corrupted Seth, and he was only the First. Becoming the God Killer was apparently going to turn me into an aether-crazed Terminator. Besides, yelling at him hadn't worked last time. "If I can't handle it after I take out Ares, you've got to get away from me. Quickly."

His frown did nothing to lessen his beauty. "I don't think I've said this to you right."

My brows rose.

His frown deepened. "You *can* handle it."

Now I was confused. "That's not what you said before."

"Like I said, I'm saying it wrong." Seth twisted toward me. "And I'm not being honest."

The knots in my stomach tightened, and I resisted the urge to hit him before he spoke, because I figured whatever he was about to say would deserve a five-finger hello to the face. "*Seth.*"

"Alex—"

"What in the hell could you possibly not be honest about now?" I demanded as a rush of anger rose inside me. "That you're waiting until the thirtieth hour to divulge?"

Seth looked away, his chin jutting out stubbornly. "You could lay off the attitude."

I flipped him off.

A reluctant-sounding chuckle parted his lips. "Okay. Do I think you're going to go a little power-crazy? Probably. You're already a little crazy."

My eyes narrowed.

"But you'll handle it. You always handle everything, and I . . ." He trailed off, shaking his head. "We have to wait until the last minute because I'm not sure I won't try to stop you. I'm not sure I won't try to take the power myself."

I stared at him, the scowl slipping off my face as his words sank in. Holy babies in a manger, this was a big deal. Apollo had been right. I had wanted to believe Seth that night at the University, but Apollo had been right.

Two pink spots appeared in his cheeks. "You're looking at me like . . . like I said the worst thing possible."

"Well, that is pretty . . . um, well, it's something." I shook my head. "Seth, if you think you're going to stop me and try to do it yourself, how in the hell is waiting to the last minute to do it a good idea?"

He didn't answer. Instead, he looked away, focusing on a really creepy deer head hanging from the wall.

Seth?

Lowering his chin, he rubbed the palm of his hand over his cheek. *I'll let you do it then. I know I will.*

How? What if you don't? What if—?

"I will," he snapped, lifting his head. His eyes were glowing. "I know I will then."

"Excuse me if I'm not reassured by that!" I started to stand, but he grabbed my arm. The tiny hairs on my body rose.

"I know I will, because too much will be riding on me to let you do it."

Was he saying that he'd perform better under the pressure? That somehow having our heads on the line would ensure he wouldn't suck me dry? What the hell was that? I tried to pull my arm back, but he held on. "I think we should do it now."

He closed his eyes.

"I'm serious. We could do it now." My heart was trying to come out of my chest. "I'll get Aiden, and then we'll do it. Afterward, he'll make sure we're separated and—"

"I'm not going to fail you or anyone. Not again. We'll do it then, as planned."

"Seth . . ."

The marks of the Apollyon went crazy, spinning and twirling across my skin, reaching his. His face contorted, and I felt the cord jump inside me. My pulse kicked into overdrive as every warning sensor went off. The last time, he'd said—

Suddenly, the tip of a Covenant dagger was under Seth's chin, pushing into the delicate skin of his throat. My gaze dropped to where Seth's hand was wrapped around my forearm and then back to the tip of the dagger. Definitely a silent way of saying "let go." Seth released my arm, finger by finger.

I looked up, and my gaze locked with eyes the color of warm chocolate.

Air halted in my throat, and my voice cracked on one word. "Dad?"

22

The huge, potential problem of Seth taking the God Killer power from me at the last and possibly worst moment known to mankind was suddenly insignificant.

I was staring at my dad.

My father.

He looked just like I remembered—a classically handsome face lined by the weather and his life, but his brown eyes were lively with intelligence and awareness. He was thinner, gaunter than before.

And he was wearing a Sentinel uniform.

Something in my chest came unhinged, like a door had been thrown open too fast and too hard. Tears poured into my eyes.

He was in a *Sentinel* uniform.

My father also held a dagger against Seth's throat.

"It's okay," I said, my voice hoarse. I glanced at Seth, who looked as surprised as I felt. "Seth?"

Standing slowly, Seth raised his hands. His amber gaze was locked on my father. "I'm not going to hurt her."

My father didn't look convinced. His lips curled in a sneer as he kept the blade against Seth's throat, but he let Seth back away. The First headed for the door, stopping once to look at us, and then he disappeared through the archway.

I stared up at my dad, too afraid to look away because I feared he might actually vanish, too scared to stand because I knew my legs wouldn't hold me. My throat clogged with emotion, and his face blurred. This whole time, from the moment I first received

Laadan's letter, I had hoped that I would see him again, but I never really thought that I would.

And here he was, on the night before battle, standing before me.

"Dad?" I croaked. It was all I could say. It was like I'd lost my ability to speak in comprehensible sentences.

He expertly sheathed the Covenant dagger the way we'd been taught in training. For a whole minute, he didn't move or look away. His gaze crawled over my face, and the lines around his eyes deepened, as did the furrow between his brows. I knew it was the scars, and even though he had never been in my life— couldn't have been—they had to affect him deeply.

Letting out a breath that he seemed to have been holding for years, he sat beside me on the couch. I didn't know what to say. There was so much pressure in my chest and my throat.

He reached out with one hand and cupped my cheek. His hand was cool, but I didn't care. I squeezed my eyes shut to stop the tears. The pressure increased, pushing at the seams. My dad didn't say anything, because he couldn't, but his touch . . . it was better than any words that could be spoken.

I struggled to pull myself together, waiting until I was more sure I wouldn't start sobbing all over him before I spoke. And of course, I said the stupidest thing possible. "It's really you?"

He nodded, a slight smile appearing.

Taking in a shuddering breath, I blinked a few times. "Did you . . . did you get my letter?"

Another nod.

"Okay. Okay." I took another breath. "How long have you've been here?"

He held up a finger, and then leaned back. Reaching into the side pocket of his tactical pants, he pulled out a small notebook and pen. He wrote something quickly and handed it to me. His handwriting was neat and small, so unlike mine.

"Two days?" I read out loud and then waited while he

scribbled something. "You heard that a group of Sentinels had arrived." My heart tripped up as I glanced at him. "You left the Covenant to see if I was among them?"

He nodded.

"How?"

My dad wrote: I knocked out the guard he had watching over me. He thinks I don't know that he knows who I am.

I laughed, and his lips twitched into another small smile. "Gods," I said, smoothing my hands over my thighs. I wanted to hug him, but I wasn't sure what he'd do. "When I was at the Covenant before, I didn't know it was you. If I had, I would've done something. I swear I would have."

His pen flew across his little notepad. Two sentences. I know. Not your problem.

"But you're my dad. It *is* my problem."

He shook his head no, and then wrote quickly. You look so much like your mother.

I smiled widely, blinking back another rush of tears. "Thank you."

There was a pause as he stared at me, and then he started scribbling away, faster than before. Your mother and I wouldn't have wanted this kind of life for you.

"I—"

He held up a finger and finished his note. Laadan kept me updated on you, telling me what she could. I would've wanted anything but this for you, but I am so very proud of you.

I sucked in a sharp breath as the tears welled up again. He was proud of me. How many times had I wondered if he was? There had been so many stupid things I'd done in my past, things that had gotten me in a world of trouble, and the gods knew I had a lot of stupid left in me, but my father was proud of me, and that was all that mattered after everything was said and done. The pressure expanded until it was too much.

Springing forward, I wrapped my arms around him and held

on like he might disappear in front of me. He dropped the pen and notepad, enfolding me in a powerful hug. The kind of hug I'd been missing my entire life. A hug that hadn't come too late, but just in time.

The tears came. There was no stopping them, but they were happy tears.

I stayed with my dad for hours, me talking and asking questions and him answering with a shake of his head or with his notepad. On and off, I cried. I kept thinking this was a dream, but the longer he remained by my side, the more I began to realize this was real.

Maybe an hour into our reunion, something else amazing happened. Something that I had never thought would.

Dad met the other most important man in my life.

He met Aiden, who'd come looking for me, and then I got to see what it was truly like to have a father in my life. He regarded Aiden coolly; he looked like he was thinking about using the dagger the same way he had with Seth.

Aiden was polite as ever, and he started to make a quick escape to give us privacy, but I captured his hand. Our eyes met and he nodded. I wanted him there, to share this with me, because none of us knew how much time we really had left and there was no point to missing an opportunity like this. Aiden sat on the floor by my feet, his hand and thumb smoothing over the back of my calf.

I would've loved to have met my dad under better circumstances. Maybe where the three of us could go out to dinner like normal people, but this . . . this was perfect in its own way.

Honored that he would leave those who were still behind the walls to see if I was among the Sentinels that had arrived, I fought the pain and the panic when he showed me the message I'd been dreading.

I have to go back to them. They have no one else.

My heart turned over heavily. "But Ares knows you're my father."

I won't be strolling in the front door, he wrote. I know my way around in there, and I stay out of Ares' way. If Ares was going to use me, he would've done so by now.

"How can you be so sure?"

Aiden continued the soothing gesture. "He may be right. Maybe Ares has some sort of code he operates by."

I doubted that. My chest seized at the thought of him falling into Ares' hands.

My father tipped his chin down as he scribbled on the pad. I don't want you doing what you're planning.

I opened my mouth, but he wrote on.

But I know you have to. Like I have to.

He was right. Damn my father for actually being the logical parent. My wildness came from my mom, but apparently I got my stubbornness from my dad.

When the morning was only a few hours away, my father hugged me goodbye, and I knew he was heading back to the Covenant. I didn't want to let go of him, and I didn't for several minutes. I held onto him, squeezing him as tightly as I could, and when we broke apart, there was a stinging pain deep in my chest. Seeing him go was one of the most painful things I'd ever experienced.

In a small room with a pile of blankets as a bed, I stared out the window over the camp.

"You should get some rest. We'll have to start out in the afternoon."

My head wasn't on the battle ahead. "What if I never see him again?"

Aiden came up behind me, slipping his arms around my waist and tugging me into the warmth of his body. "You will see him again."

Clinging to that, I tipped my head back against his chest and closed my eyes. "When this is all over, I want the three of us to go out to dinner."

He kissed my forehead. "Pick a place."

"Anywhere normal. Somewhere like Applebee's."

Aiden chuckled. "I think we can make that work."

Turning in his embrace, I rested my cheek against his chest. He held me as I rambled on about my dad, and then we moved on to less happy subjects. While I didn't want to tell him about Seth, I needed to.

"I don't like the sound of this," he said, resting his hands on either side of my head. "If he doesn't allow you to transfer the power or pulls any crap like he has before, you'll be a sitting duck for Ares."

The upcoming face-off with Ares was a constant, low-level hum of adrenaline that was like a pebble in my shoe. Annoying but tolerable. But adding in the possibility of Seth going rogue at the last minute turned that pebble into a shark's tooth.

"I'm going to try again, but I don't think it's going to work. Once Seth has his mind set on something, there's no changing it."

"But that's not acceptable." Aiden dropped his hands and turned, stalking toward the blanket. "It's too risky. If—"

"We don't have any other choice." I followed him. "And I think . . . I think he needs to do it that way, when the risk is the highest. Like a . . ."

"Like how an addict stops doing drugs because they're sitting in jail?"

I wrinkled my nose. "Uh, sure?"

"Inmates can still get drugs," he grumbled, reaching down and tugging his shirt off his head. Thick bands of muscle stretched and pulled taut.

"I'm not following this conversation." *For several reasons,* but I kept that last part to myself.

Aiden faced me. "I know the plan is for you and Seth to go with Perses to find Ares, but—"

"But we're not changing the plan, no matter how cray-cray Seth is." My heart acted like a spazz at the thought of Aiden being with us. "You cannot be there when we face off with Ares. He'll use you—"

"He can only use me if I'm incapable of defending myself, Alex." His brows lowered as his eyes flashed silver. Uh-oh. "I'm not your weakness."

"You're not. You're the opposite of that, Aiden, but I know Ares will go straight for you. He knows I'll be distracted because you're there. And it's what I'd do if I were him."

Aiden looked away as he shoved a hand through his hair. Several seconds stretched out, and then he released a ragged breath. "I know you have to do this, Alex, but it goes against everything in me not to be with you."

Biting my lip, I nodded. I knew it was going to take a near act of the gods to get Aiden to not follow us tomorrow. "If it were you asking me to not be with you, I wouldn't want to listen to you."

He let out a dry laugh. "You *wouldn't* listen to me, Alex. You'd go against me, and you'd find a way to be there with me."

"I would." I cracked a grin. "I would do it even knowing that you'd be distracted by me, because I'm selfish like that. You're not."

"I can be incredibly selfish." His gaze settled on me once more, and he placed the tips of his fingers on either side of my cheeks. "I've been nothing but selfish with you."

Confused, I frowned. "How?"

"I was selfish in wanting you, knowing what it could mean for you. I was selfish the first time I kissed you, touched you." The shiver his words brought forth didn't go unnoticed by him. A dimple appeared. "I was selfish the night I came to your bed when you were at my parents' house, and I've been selfish every day since then. The only time I hadn't been selfish was when I pushed you away, and that's the day I regret most."

My stomach fluttered like there was a jackrabbit inside it. "Aiden . . ."

"You're going to be separated from me tomorrow, and it's going to take everything in me to let you face Ares without me standing by your side, so I'm going to be very selfish right now." His finger trailed over my cheek and across my parted lips. "Because it's the only way I can be unselfish tomorrow."

Aiden's lips replaced his fingers then, and the kiss wasn't slow or gentle. It was fierce, consuming, and tasted of soul-burning yearning and desperation. Our clothing came off with a quickness that was rather impressive, and our bodies melded together on the thick blankets. Behind every touch and every kiss there was the knowledge that neither of us wanted to put forth into words. So we used our mouths, our hands, and our bodies to say what both of us were too terrified to speak.

This could be our last time together.

23

A cool, calm breeze lessened the effect of the strong afternoon sun beating down on us as we stood at the edge of the forest surrounding the Covenant. The sky was a bright, vibrant blue with only a few pillow-like clouds floating in the sky.

It was a beautiful day for a war.

Covenant daggers were strapped to my hips, and a Glock loaded with titanium bullets was holstered on my thigh. With my hair pulled back in a tight bun and my skin tingling with the marks of the Apollyon, I felt pretty badass.

Standing on either side of me were the silent forms of Aiden and Seth. Behind us, Perses and our AOA were ready. Deacon was staying behind, and after what'd happened with Olivia, I wished he'd remained at the University.

I hadn't seen my father among the faces, and I don't even know why I was looking for him. I knew he'd gone back. I *hoped* he'd made it back, but I still looked.

"Warriors know no fear, show no fear." Perses' deep voice boomed, upping the adrenaline in my system. "Many of you will fall today."

My brows rose. That's a motivational statement.

"But you will fall as warriors—the only true, honorable death."

He continued on, and I zoned him out. Motivational war speeches about dying honorably in battle weren't my thing. How about a speech where we were all awesomely alive at the end? I could get behind that. Besides, we had a helluva hike ahead of us, and I was using that time to clear my thoughts of everything that'd happened in the last couple of weeks. There was so much clogging up my head—Olivia, my dad, Aiden, and Seth, and where in the hell was Apollo, and so much more. I needed to be focused.

All these moments were leading up to the here and now, and by the time the sun rose the next day, blood would cover the ground like a crimson river. Blood of our own. Blood of our enemies. And blood of those who'd been manipulated onto the wrong side.

Twigs crunched and snapped under our boots as we crested the second hill. There was one more, and then we would be staring down at the walls. We had the high ground, but they would see us the moment we came down.

"Remember the plan," Perses said, stalking up behind me.

I nodded, because my vocal cords had frozen. The plan had been set into motion before we even left South Dakota, and I had had plenty of time to come to terms with it, but I hadn't.

At the last hill, Perses, Seth, and I would split from our group, leaving Aiden, Solos, and Luke behind with the army. Cannon fodder. No one said that. Instead, Perses had said they would be the distraction needed for us to get inside, but I knew that was what they were. The walls were protected by the automatons, and they would be picking off our guys in bulk. And then, when they made it through the entry gate, there was the mortal army . . . and gods knew what else.

And where the hell was Apollo?

The Sentinels who'd been inside the Covenant had given us the way in that we needed. The back eastern wall was exposed, a way in and out. There'd be guards, but nothing like what would be seen at the front. I knew in my heart of hearts that Aiden and Luke and Solos would make it. They had to. But the sharp tang of fear was in the back of my mouth.

Alex?

Seth's voice inside my head almost caused me to stumble. *What? You're having a lot of feelings right now.*

My gaze narrowed on his back as he moved ahead of Aiden and me. *And you're not?*

You're afraid, was his simple, two-word response. I contemplated pushing him down the rocky slope but figured I didn't need him bruised already.

There was a pause. *Being afraid isn't the problem, Angel.*

Stop calling me that.

He ignored me. *Use that fear.* Glancing over his shoulder at me, he winked. Aiden cursed under his breath, and Seth smirked. *Use anger. Don't let either of them consume you.*

Yes, sensei.

Seth snorted.

"I hate when you two do that," Aiden muttered.

"Sorry?"

He sent me a long look, but there was no anger in his steely gray eyes. Both of us hadn't been smart about last night. We might have gotten a few hours of sleep, spending those precious hours before and after committing each other to memory . . . and in ways that brought a blush to my cheeks in spite of the cool wind caressing them.

Neither of us wanted to admit that we both feared last night would be the final time we were together. I couldn't let myself focus on that, but it was a reality that couldn't be ignored.

We passed the nondescript outer fence and then quickly reached the last hill at dusk. I glanced over my shoulder, my gaze roaming over the assembled throng. All of them were ready. It was time to do this, to end this. Everything came down to this battle, and not just for us, but for the unknowing mortals, too. If we failed, the mortal realm would fall to Ares, and then Olympus would be next on his to-conquer list. The Sentinels and Guards behind us knew this, too. This whole situation was bigger than each and every one of us.

"It is time," Perses said. Excitement practically rolled off the Titan.

Seth nodded and turned to me. Part of me wanted to delay this moment, but this was one of those times when I had to pull on my big-girl pants. What I wanted to do and what I needed to do were two very different things.

I swore in that moment this would be the last time I'd ever have to make a choice between want and need. I spun around and hugged Luke and then Solos. "Be safe," I told them both. "Promise me. If not, I'll find you two in the Underworld and kick your asses. I swear."

Luke chuckled. "You'd actually do that, too. I promise."

"As do I," Solos added, bending his head and pressing his lips to my cheek. "And you do the same."

I nodded and turned away before I got all choked up, coming face-to-face with Aiden. Clenching Aiden by the shirt with one hand, I pulled his head down to mine and kissed him. And it was no chaste kiss. Or tender. Our lips bruised together, our bodies melding into the touch. I drank him up in that kiss, as he did me.

A few low cat-whistles brought me back to reality. I let go, rocking back on the heels of my boots, but he still held on. Aiden's eyes were liquid silver.

"I love you," I said. "I love you so much."

Aiden's lips moved over mine. "*Agapi mou*, I will be with you in no time."

Nodding slowly, I let out a long breath and slipped from his hold. Turning to walk to where Seth and Perses waited, I couldn't look back. Not even when the three of us started our hike to the east because if I did, I would run back to Aiden, and we couldn't delay this any longer.

We'd traveled about half a mile when Perses raised his hand, motioning us to stop. He tilted his chin up, expression sharp. Then he smiled wolfishly. A second later, a powerful roar whirled through the tall elms and firs, sending birds flying frantically into the air. It was the sound of rage and determination—a sound of war. I twisted toward the west. The dusky sky brightened in hues of orange and red, intensifying every couple of seconds.

"It has begun." Perses smile spread as if he'd been presented with a feast of his favorite foods. "We must hurry."

Heart racing, I dug in deep, latching on to the sense of duty and holding onto it with dear life. Along with Perses and Seth, I ran down the hill even though my heart was back at the gates with my friends and Aiden.

Sliding around outcroppings of large boulders and kicking up loose rocks and dirt, we stormed down the rocky slope. The twenty-foot white marble wall came into view and the sounds of battle from the front gate grew.

Perses darted further to the east, cutting across the sloping hill and heading for the east side of the protective wall. Several fireballs shot into the air, slamming back down to earth by the gate, and I winced with the impact, knowing that, when those flames had landed, lives had been lost.

We reached the bottom of the hill and the corner of the east wall just as that wicked sense all half-bloods had kicked in. Tiny hairs rose on my body, and shivers shot across the back of my neck.

"Daimons," I said, skidding to the halt as I pulled out my daggers and hit the button in the middle. On each side, blades shot out.

Seth did the same, but Perses looked like he wanted to use his hands and get bloody and messy. We rounded the corner, running smack dab into a cluster of daimons. Their mouths dropped open, letting out eerie, aether-starved howls. Their eyes, black and bottomless, stood out in stark contrast against their pale skin. Among them were daimon halfs, the most deadly of their kind.

It sickened me to see them here, knowing that Lucian, Ares, and even Seth at one point had controlled the daimons by feeding them innocent pures. Anger rose like a violent storm inside me, and I tapped into it.

I threw myself into the fray, taking out the first daimon with a brutal swipe of the sickle blade, cleaving its head clear off its body. Seth slammed a half in the chest with a booted foot, knocking it to the ground before he brought the pointed end of his weapon down into its chest. As I'd suspected, Perses was hands-on, snapping necks and ripping out important body parts.

A female daimon dove for me and I spun, catching the ugly thing in the stomach with my kick. She met the sharp end of my blade before she hit the ground. Dipping down, I sprang back up, whipping the sickle around in a clean sweep. Another came at me, and I jumped. Landing in a crouch, I flipped the sickle blade over and punched up, catching the daimon in the stomach.

I rose quickly, shaking the blood and gore off my blade as I twisted. Bodies of half-blood daimons littered the ground, but there were still more daimons, at least a dozen. Moving around them, I slammed the dagger end of my blade into the back of a daimon stalking Seth. Unlike the halfs, it exploded into a burst of shimmery dust—right in my face.

Yuck.

Perses kicked a daimon half-down and then grabbed it by its legs, lifting it up in the air. The thing screamed its fury, but Perses swung it like a baseball bat against the marble wall. I looked away before I could see that level of splat. There were some things you could never un-see, and that would've definitely been one of them.

Alex!

The sound of Seth's voice in my head spun me around. "Gods."

Rushing toward me, a daimon half howled hungrily and was joined by another and another. All the aether in the three of us had to be driving them crazy. They were teaming up, making it more difficult to fight as we had been trained.

A fierce wind blew from Seth, sending his trio of nastiness away from him.

Yeah, screw this.

Hooking the sickle blade to my hip, I threw my hand out, summoning the element of fire. Heat zinged through my veins, warming my skin. Sparks emanated from my palm, followed by an eruption of fire. It hit the center daimon and spread outward to the ones on each side, consuming them.

Three daimons hit the ground, screaming as they rolled and twisted. The smell of burnt clothes and flesh mingled with the metallic scent of blood.

When all the daimons were down or dust, we wasted no time. Rushing along the side of the east wall, we found the breach—a burnt-out, three-foot-wide section of wall. Wiggling through it for me was easy, but it took Perses and Seth a little finagling to get through the tight fit.

A few steps in and we were met with a set of charging automatons.

We so didn't have time for this.

Seth shot past me and raised his hand. The marks of the Apollyon whipped across his skin. Energy seeped into the air around us. In a burst of light, akasha spun from him and smacked into the first automaton, lighting it up. Joining in, I summoned the fifth and most powerful element, hitting my target.

The automatons were no more.

"That does come in handy." Perses stalked back to us, blood dripping from his face. Not his. I wanted to ask if he needed a hanky. "You two should use that more often. It would make this easier."

My eyes narrowed. "You have a god bolt. Why don't you use that?"

"I prefer my hands in battle. It means more."

That didn't even deserve a response. Shaking my head, I sent Seth a look. *This guy is nuts.*

But he's good.

Racing across the now-overgrown lawn of the Covenant, we passed destroyed and shattered statues of the gods. The only ones standing were those of Ares. The guy did nothing to hide his arrogance.

Suddenly, Seth reached out, grabbing my hand and forcing me to make a sharp turn to the left. I looked down, almost mistaking what I saw for dried-out branches.

But the brownish-white sticks weren't sticks at all. Nor was the tattered material clinging to it leaves.

"Oh, my gods . . ."

The remains of once beautifully crafted statues weren't the only things that lay seemingly forgotten on the ground. Every so many feet, there were . . . bodies in the grass. Some were old and nearly completely decomposed. Others were fresher, their skin a horrible array of purples and browns, their bodies bloated.

Be careful of where you step, he said.

When Seth let go of my hand, I looked up to see that Perses hadn't even stopped as he plowed through the remains of someone. Bile rose up the back of my throat, and it took everything I had to push it down. Perses was a necessary evil, but sometimes I really hated the bastard.

The sounds of battle at the gate raged on as we drew near the main Covenant building. Screams of pain mixed with shouts of victory and the sound of weapons fire. The fight had spilled forward, reaching the destroyed row of the Olympian Twelve statues, which was now the Olympian One. I could see many Sentinels and soldiers on both sides, clashing together in hand-to-hand combat. It appeared the automatons were down, but we were close enough to the fight that we now were drawing attention.

Several soldiers shouted, and a large group broke apart, racing toward us.

"The servants' entrance." Seth pointed at the side of the building, where the doors and windows were busted out. "We don't have time for this out here. We have to get to where he's been and—"

A soft, tinkling laugh halted the three of us, and my heart jumped in my chest. I *knew* that sound. The air shimmered in front of us, taking form, and forcing even Perses to take a step back.

The soft-as-wind-chimes laugh came again.

"You've got to be kidding me," I moaned. "Seriously?"

Two furies floated before us, their translucent wings moving soundlessly through the air. Blonde and delicately pale, they were frighteningly beautiful in a way that was deceiving. These creatures were ugly in their true forms. And vicious. Very vicious.

One moved closer, her hair drifting around her slim body. "We're not here for you."

"This time," the other finished.

The closest furie's smile was edged with unimaginable cruelty. "The gods have heard Apollo's pleas and have responded."

Well, color me surprised and call me shocked.

Static crackled through the air, and a low-level hum teased my ears. Turning around, my eyes widened.

"Shit," Perses exclaimed. "I don't believe it."

Across the lawn, about halfway between the group of soldiers and us, a mist gathered, blanketing the overgrown grass. Out of the wispy fog, nine forms took hold. Within seconds, nine Olympian gods stood there.

Artemis yanked the bow off her back and glanced over her shoulder, spotting us. She winked, and then turned, letting loose a silver arrow.

The furies rose into the air, shedding their pearly luminous appearances. Their skin and wings turned gray and scaly. Snapping snakes replaced their hair. They flew above the gods, and I saw one swoop down, catching a man in her talons. A spray of blood spurted into the air and something—oh gods— red and ropey spilled onto the ground, steaming.

The soldier had been torn in half.

Tipping her head back, the furie's laugh tinkled on the wind, prickling the skin on the back of my neck.

Perses' brows rose. "They are as bloodthirsty as I remembered."

I looked at him. "And creepy."

He smiled. "I think they're magnificent."

Of course he did. One of them had a mortal's head in its hands and looked like it was about to play volleyball with it. *Perses and the furie should hook up*, I thought bitterly.

"Come on," Seth called, motioning to us. He was by the shattered doors. "They got this."

That they did. One last look over my shoulder confirmed it. Apollo had obliterated the soldiers, and the gods were now joining the mess of fighting bodies around front. Hurrying after Seth and Perses, we were inside the Covenant, possibly steps away from Ares.

Stopping in front of us, Perses cocked his head to the side then glanced back at Seth and me, wiping the spray of blood off his cheek. A slow, calculated smile pulled across his face.

He disappeared.

Poof.

Gone.

Vanished.

Seth's mouth dropped open. "Shit!"

24

We stood just inside the servant's entrance, the hall splitting into two directions. Gray stains smudged the walls, as if there'd been a small fire.

I couldn't move or speak for several seconds. "I can't believe it!" I exclaimed. "That son of a—"

Soldiers poured into the entrance. Their camouflage uniforms were so noticeably mortal, but the armbands with Ares' symbol were anything but mortal. Their guns were raised, and they were ready to fire.

Crap.

Throwing out my hands, I tapped into the element of air. Wind gusted in behind the soldiers. Their boots skidded over the tile floor. The guns shook in their hands. Seth got in on the game. A few soldiers went down. Guns misfired, and one by one, the weapons flew from their hands, sliding across the floors. The soldiers scrambled to their feet as the winds died down.

Can we let them go? I asked.

Seth shook his head and started forward, withdrawing his daggers. *They're under compulsion.*

I wanted to argue, but the soldier closest to Seth engaged, swinging his arm out. There was a wicked-looking knife in his hand, the kind I imagined serial killers would covet. Anyone in their right mind would've run from us, but those under compulsion would fight to the death.

There was nothing we could do.

Seth dipped under the attacker's arm and sprang up,

slamming the hilt of one dagger into the back of a soldier while catching another in the chest. Vaulting over the body of the fallen soldier, I dipped down low and spun, taking the feet out from underneath another man. He sat up, impaling himself on the waiting dagger.

I pulled it free, the fleshy suction sound echoing in my head. Wincing, I ignored the stirrings of guilt and threw myself into the fray.

These soldiers were highly trained, no doubt strategically kept inside the Covenant to be the last line of defense if anyone made it inside. Rolling into a kick, I welcomed the sharp slice of pain, then sprang up, arcing the dagger to catch the soldier under the chin. Whipping around, I saw Seth grab one by the head and twist. The crack was lost in the punch thrown at me. I ducked, catching the attacker in the stomach.

Without any warning, my legs were taken out from under me with a brutal swipe, and my training kicked in. Allowing myself to fall, I twisted at the last second and rolled, bringing the soldier around so he was under me.

I saw his face for the briefest second. He was young—too young. Barely out of high school and with his whole life ahead him. A deeper pain, more intense than any kick or punch, sliced at my heart as I brought the dagger down on his chest, ending his life in seconds. Wet warmth hit my face.

Springing up, I breathed heavily as I wiped the back of my hand under my chin once and then twice. I didn't want any of the boy's blood on me. I turned as Seth caught the last soldier by the neck, slamming him into the floor with enough force to crack the tile, and the man's spine. His last breath gurgled out a moment later.

Seth looked up, his eyes meeting mine. Standing slowly, he hooked his daggers to his thighs and then motioned me forward.

Keeping my eyes off the floor, I followed Seth into the hallway on the right. This close, the aether in us acted like a silent guide, pulling us to where Ares was located. We crept down the wide corridor, silent and watchful for any more surprise attacks. It was the same hall that Seth and I had run down once before, except this time it wasn't littered with bodies. It was disturbingly empty, but there were scuff marks on the once-pristine floors and walls and patches of rust-colored stains every so many feet.

Seth saw me looking at the stains. "It was bad here, when Ares first occupied the Covenant. A lot of people put up a fight."

I raised my gaze, wondering how Seth slept at night.

He seemed to read the question from my thoughts because he looked away, a muscle thrumming along his jaw. "I don't sleep, Alex. Not very well or very long."

Part of me wanted to say something reassuring to him, but what could I say? Who knew how many innocent people Seth had ended? And for what? I had no idea how he could atone for that. Or, if he ever found forgiveness in other people, would he ever find it in himself? Drawing in a shallow breath, I moved in front of him.

We'd taken a few steps when words echoed down the hall. Familiar ones.

I heard Perses' deep voice taunting Ares, and I almost fell to my knees and started praising every god there was, maybe even a few random celebrities and fictional characters. The relief was that palpable.

He didn't abandon us.

Seth gave a curt nod. *I never thought he did.*

I rolled my eyes. *There was a moment when you did. Admit it.*

Whatever.

Creeping closer, I stuck to the wall. They were in the ball-room, the very same one where I'd faced off against the furies and killed the pureblood.

How fitting, Seth remarked.

I shot him a death glare, and he grinned—that cocky, insufferably arrogant grin that had been absent for weeks. My lips twitched in response, but I focused. I was happy that Seth had found his mojo or whatever, but I really didn't have time to pat him on the head.

Five doors, all open, lined the hall before the entry to the ballroom. Fingertips tingling, I peeked inside the first room. Nothing. I inched forward, resisting the urge to bum-rush down the hall.

"You can't beat me, Olympian." Perses' voice stopped me for a second.

Ares laughed, but it sounded off. Rattled. "Need I remind you that it was I who wrapped the chains around your wrists?"

"Only with the help of your brethren," Perses responded. "The very ones outside this wall, raging a war on your army. I doubt they will help you this time." He paused. "You're a fool, Ares. An arrogant fool. Make war for the pure bliss of it, but never make war in order to take control."

What the what?

I glanced back at Seth, who shrugged. Why Perses had run off just to lecture Ares was beyond me. Apparently he wanted to get the last word in or something. With gods, it was anyone's guess.

Now two doors away from the ballroom, I was a second from checking the room, when a Sentinel unexpectedly stepped out, startling me.

He opened his mouth, about to give away our location. I didn't stop to think. Springing forward, I grabbed the dagger off my leg with one hand and placed my other over his mouth. Our eyes locked for a brief moment. His blue eyes were unfocused, hazy—a sign of a compulsion. Remorse pricked at my chest, but I slammed the dagger into his chest, above the heart, to the hilt.

Seth caught the body, easing it onto the floor as I sheathed the dagger. He quickly surveyed the room and motioned me to continue. I stepped carefully around the body, inhaling deeply.

It had to be done, Seth said.

I know.

He glanced over his shoulder, eyebrow arched as if he didn't believe me, and he was right. Killing a Sentinel under compulsion sucked as bad as killing the mortals who were under Ares' control.

All right, I'll tear myself apart about it later, but for right now, I'm fine.

That's my girl.

I frowned. *That's twisted.*

Letting Seth check the next room, I slid around him. My heart pumped fast. The ballroom was next. Somewhere, the imaginary clock stopped ticking.

Seth caught my hand, spinning me around and into an empty, dark room. He pressed me back against the wall, his breath warm against my forehead. Raising my free hand, I was about to punch him in the face when his voice in my head stopped me.

Do it. Transfer the power now.

I'd be lying if I said I hadn't worried about this moment from the time Seth had suggested it. Even before it, when Apollo had said it was the only way, I'd worried. Seeing how Seth struggled with the allure, with the need that existed between us, I was prepared to knock Seth out and then transfer the power, if necessary.

He bent his head quickly, kissing my forehead. *Do it, Alex.*

Full of surprise, I hesitated as I stared into eyes that were identical to mine. *I'm not going to fail you,* he had said, and he hadn't been lying.

Now, he said again, closing his eyes as he let go of me.

My hand trembled as I reached between us, gripping his right hand. "Θάρρος." Courage.

A shock rippled across my hand and shot up my arm, followed by a wealth of warmth. Seth jerked, but remained there, his eyes closed. The tingling ended at my shoulder, and I felt it then, the collapse of fear in my chest replaced by fiery determination. This was right. I would not be stopped.

I cupped my hand around his right hand, squeezing it. "Δύναμη."

Strength.

A tremble rocked Seth, and another jolt skittered up my right arm, faster than the one before. The warmth turned to heat, and it spread across my shoulder blades. My body hummed. A thousand little pulses hit my muscles, tearing them down and rebuilding them. I felt like I imagined Aiden did—he was the healthiest person I knew, since he lived off of granola, chicken, and working out.

I pulled up his shirt and placed his hand over the mark on his flat, hard stomach and whispered, "απόλυτη εξουσία." Absolute power.

Seth gasped, and his eyes flew open. Their amber hue glowed vibrantly, locked onto mine like laser beams. The rush of pure power almost knocked me back against the wall. Every cell in my body fired up, and the marks on my skin burned.

"One more," Seth said in a low, hoarse voice.

My entire body trembled as I reached up, cupping the back of his neck. "αήττητο." Invincibility.

The air expelled from my lungs at the same moment it did from Seth's, and then it happened. Static charged the room as the amber cord appeared around Seth's upper arm. It spiraled down, entwining over his skin, reaching mine. The blue cord crackled, brighter and more intense than his. The two cords spun, overlapping, buzzing and spitting licks of blue and amber into the air. My hand fell from his neck, but otherwise I couldn't move. Neither could he.

Inside of me, at the base of the cord, something shifted and pulsed. Behind my eyes, a blinding light burst into an array of vibrant colors, receding quickly.

Under my feet, the floor moved. My lungs seized as Seth's

head kicked back, the veins in his throat protruding. A fire lit me up from the inside, rushing through my veins at dizzying speeds. It burned sweetly, cool and hot at the same time. Power poured into my chest, causing my heart to sputter and then speed up.

Shadows danced over the walls as the cords flared, twisting and becoming one, turning into a brilliant, intense white. My other hand slipped away from him, and my arms rose at my sides as the marks on my skin seeped away and reappeared. The now-white cord pulsed once more and then snapped back toward me. Seth lowered his chin, his amber eyes shiny as he met my gaze, and then his gaze dropped.

My feet weren't on the floor.

Nope.

I was floating again.

There was at least four feet between my shoes and the floor, and well, I felt damn good.

"Wow," I said, grinning.

Seth's throat worked. "Wow, indeed."

Moving my hands in front of me, I watched the glyphs slide over my skin. The color seemed sharper.

You gonna come down from there? He reached up, catching my hand.

Strangely, the cord inside me didn't jump. I willed myself down. *How do you feel?*

He cocked his head to the side. *Okay. I don't feel different, really.*

Which meant he was probably still craving akasha, but at least he wasn't hurt. For a moment there, it hadn't looked fun for him.

How about you?

It was hard to describe—the *power*. I wanted to run straight into a wall because I was pretty sure I could take it on, but I didn't feel uncontrollable since I wasn't running into that wall. *I feel . . . great. I feel . . .*

There was no fear in my heart, at least not the paralyzing kind. The strength made my muscles twitchy, and I felt ready in a way I hadn't before. Hours ago, I'd known I had to take on the God Killer power. I'd known I had to face Ares and destroy him, but had I really been ready? No. It had been something I knew I had to do—a duty.

Now I was truly ready.

I smiled up at Seth, my fingers curling into fists. "Let's do this."

25

Each step I took was filled with purpose and steely determination. My hands itched for a fight, but my blood sang for the release of the akasha brimming in my veins.

Ares was *so* about to get knocked down a peg or five.

In the back of my mind, I realized this was how Seth must've felt most of the time—the cockiness, the knowledge that nothing in this realm was more powerful than the First.

Until now.

I stopped in front of the closed ballroom doors and raised my hands, summoning akasha. Releasing it took nothing. Energy pulsed out from me. I blew the titanium doors right off their hinges, throwing them clear across the ballroom.

"Gods," Seth muttered.

Ares and Perses whipped around. Several feet separated them. The Titan's eyes widened. One of the doors hit the floor and slid, tearing up the marble. The other slammed into Ares, throwing him back against the wall.

My lips curled into a wide smile as I stepped into the room. "Whoops. Didn't see you standing there."

Perses chuckled as he tipped his head back. "And here is the God Killer."

With a battle roar, Ares threw the door off him. It winged through the air, catching Perses in the back and smashing him into the opposite wall. The marble cracked, and half of the wall came down, burying the Titan.

I wasn't worried. Perses was a big boy. He'd get back up. Eventually.

Ares wiped his hand over his mouth and scowled, but I could sense the unease in him in that fraction of a second. Perses' presence had done what we needed—knocking him off his game. "Well, look. The girl is the God Killer." His all-white eyes spit electricity. "I always knew you were whipped, Seth."

Seth flipped him off.

The god laughed as he moved his head to the side, cracking the bone. "Oh, I'm going to enjoy killing you, pretty boy."

"The feeling is mutual." Seth stepped forward so that he stood side by side with me.

"You look lovely," Ares remarked, turning back to me. "All juiced up, but oh, your face and body look like a road map. Sexy."

Seth stiffened beside me, but I laughed. "Sticks and stones, Ares. I thought you were more mature than that. And more clever. It's kind of disappointing."

"Disappointing?" Ares gave me a wide smile, but it wasn't as confident as it had been that day in the dean's office. "Oh, little girl, God Killer or not, you can't defeat me. This world will be mine."

"Really?" I took a step forward, skin tingling. "Is there anything else you want to say? Because I know how you like to give long, boring, and clichéd evil-villain speeches. Can we skip it this time and just get to killing you?"

He snarled and threw out his hand. White light pulsed from his palm, arcing straight for me. I spun, moving quicker than I ever had, avoiding the god bolt. He sent another at Seth, but he too was quick on his feet.

So over the smack talk, my muscles tensed and I charged the god. He averted my attack at the last minute, but Seth was on him, too. He deflected Seth's blow, pushing him back as I sprang up behind the god, shoving my foot into the center of his back with all my strength. That kind of kick would've taken out a demigod or a mortal, but with Ares, he merely stumbled forward and turned.

The look on his face said *bitch, please*.

He swung out and I dipped, but I was an instant too late. His fist caught my jaw, snapping my head to the side. Fiery pain shot across my face. Damn. He could hit. I hadn't forgotten that, but still.

"Ouch," I said. "Hitting girls isn't nice."

"But Ares wouldn't know that, would he?" Seth spun, catching Ares in the leg with a brutal kick. The god stumbled. "After all, I'm pretty sure he's only gotten lucky with Aphrodite, and *everyone* gets lucky with her."

Ares threw his arms out. He didn't touch either of us, but I was suddenly off my feet and flying backwards. I caught sight of Seth's shocked expression a second before I slammed into the wall.

I hit the floor on my knees, the air knocked out of my lungs. Before I could recover, Ares' knee collided with my chin, knocking me flat on my back. My head spun as I rolled onto my side.

"Not so badass now, are you? Why don't—?" He stopped, intercepting Seth's attack.

Lightning erupted from Ares' palm, and my heart spasmed with the first bite of fear since becoming the God Killer. Ares could kill Seth, just like Apollo could kill me. A cry froze in my throat as Seth drew up short, recognition flaring in his amber eyes. He darted to the side at the last second, and the bolt hit him in the shoulder, flinging him backward.

My relief was short-lived. Ares grabbed hold of the front of my shirt and hauled me off the ground. He snarled in my face, his features contorting inhumanly. "I will have Olympus and I will rule this realm. There is—"

Ares dropped me with a grunt and I hit the floor on my butt, too stunned at first to realize what had happened. Then, I saw it.

Perses had recovered and tackled the god like a linebacker. They slid along the floor, tearing up chunks of marble like it was paper. The Titan's fists rained down, catching Ares over and over again. His punches were faster than the eye could track.

Rock 'em, sock 'em Titan.

As I staggered to my feet, Ares slammed his palms into the center of the Titan's chest and yelled. The air snapped with power, and a moment later Perses was several feet away, lying in a bloody, twitching heap.

While he was down, I started toward Ares, knowing I needed one clean shot—one blast of pure akasha when he was at his weakest to end this. I was halfway toward him when my senses fired up.

Seth shouted as he struggled to his feet.

Out of nowhere, a freaking daimon came out at me, ragged teeth exposed and veins like tiny black snakes. I so did not have time for this. Engaging the sickle blade, I arced my arm up, catching the daimon at the neck.

That was all she wrote.

Seth rushed forward, hitting Ares at the waist as he fired off a god bolt at me. Knocked off-balance, his aim wasn't spectacular. The bolt caught me in the leg, and pain exploded in a rush of wet warmth.

Holy Hades, *that* hurt . . .

I staggered back and then fell as the pain ricocheted down my leg. He threw Seth off him like a Frisbee and sprang up fluidly.

On his feet, Ares was a hundred percent focused on me as he stalked forward. I kept my gaze trained on him as I picked myself up, spitting out a mouthful of blood. Red streaked his bare chest, and I felt a surge of satisfaction.

"All I need is you," he taunted. "And you *will* submit to my will."

And all I needed was for him to keep his creepy god eyes on

me, so he could keep talking his smack all he wanted. "Is that so? I think we know where I stand on the whole submission thing."

"We also know how the last time ended when you refused." Ares spared a quick glance at Perses' still-prone body. He laughed. "This time I know how to get what I want from you."

"Do tell." I took a measured step back, drawing on akasha once more. It whipped through my veins like white lightning, boiling my blood and burning my body from the inside. The urge to unleash it was almost too hard to deny, but it wasn't time.

Ares' lips curled into a sneer. "You will do anything to protect those you care for. I could go for that pure-blood of yours. Or how about your father? Both of them are outside, right?"

My fingers straightened. Behind him, Seth was on his feet, a Covenant dagger clutched in his right hand. "If you were going to use them, you'd have pulled that card by now, which tells me you don't quite know where my father is. And you haven't gotten to Aiden."

"I will," he promised. "And it's only a matter of time before they make their way in here. Both will come to your aid, and I know, oh yes, I know you'll do anything to keep them safe," Ares said. "And I will kill one of them, and you'll have to choose. I just need to bide my time."

Seth was almost on him.

I allowed myself a smile. "That's the funny thing about time. You never have as much as you think."

Ares opened his mouth, but his words were cut off by Seth's dagger. Shoved deep into Ares' back. The god reared and screamed. "I'm going to kill you!"

"It's a little too late for that," Seth said, yanking the blade out of Ares' back.

I snapped forward at the same moment Ares threw his arm out, sending Seth flying into the air. Seth hit a pillar with a sickening crunch I couldn't allow to distract me. Akasha rushed through me, and my vision tinged with white.

Ares whirled on me, swaying to the side as I unleashed the purest power in and out of the mortal realm. Throwing my arm out, akasha flared from my shoulder, just like the cord that had connected me to Seth. Spiraling down my arm, it erupted in a burst. Ares tried to move, but he wasn't fast enough.

The bolt of akasha hit him in the center of the chest, and I kept the stream of energy up, throwing everything into the attack. Light crackled and spit into the air. Wisps of fine smoke radiated above the cord.

Stalking forward, I kept on him, not giving him a chance to slip away. I could feel the energy in me waning with each passing second, but I gritted my teeth. This was it. There would be no second chances. When the akasha sputtered out, which it would, I would be down for the count.

But Ares . . . he was backing away, still able to walk, and I was weakening fast. I had no idea how much more I had in me or what it would take to truly kill an Olympian. But the stream of akasha pulsed, and then the light weakened. My breath expelled from my lungs harshly as an ache started behind my eyes.

Then Seth was beside me, grasping my free hand, and he squeezed. The cord between us reappeared, wrapping around our joined hands. Suddenly, it made sense to me. I drew in a breath, and Seth jerked as if a puppet master had pulled on his strings. The light from the akasha flared intensely, growing until it was too bright to look upon. Pulling from us both, the blast of energy became a white fire.

Ares' fury-filled roar developed into a terror-filled scream. A loud popping sound, like a hundred guns going off at the same time, followed. The akasha faded out, not snapping back to me, but simply fizzling like fireworks vanishing into the sky.

I still held onto Seth's hand, my body shaking as Ares came into view.

The god's eyes were wide, his arms stretched out at his sides. He tipped his chin down and his mouth opened, but no sound came out. A ball of crackling white light was embedded deep in his chest. The light spread out, following the intricate network of veins until his chest lit up.

I took a breath, but it got stuck.

Ares lifted his head as the white lines reached across his shocked face, covering his head within a second.

He disappeared under the white light.

The sound of deafening thunder cracked through the room. The air distorted and rippled, and I saw it coming a second too late. The sonic wave rolled across the room at frightening speed, slamming into Seth and me. It broke my hold on him, splitting us apart, and we flew backward, hit the floor, and slid. An explosion rocked the room, and fine, white dust poured into the air like snow. Starbursts flooded my vision like a thousand bombs going off.

And then there was silence.

Hands and arms shaking, I rolled onto my side and lifted myself halfway up. The wall across from me was gone. A hole had been blown straight through it, exposing beams and crumbling brick and sunlight.

I looked over my shoulder and let out a ragged breath.

The spot where Ares had stood was empty. On the floor, the blackened tile formed a perfect circle, like a brand. I knew in my bones that Ares was gone. The blast was a release of his essence, returning it to wherever it came from.

Shifting onto my butt, I winced at the ache that consumed my body as I scanned the room for Seth. The white dust had settled like a fine blanket of snow. Near the entrance of the ballroom, Seth lay face-down.

I stared at him for a moment, my brain slowly catching up to my surroundings, and when it did, my heart nearly exploded in my chest.

Seth wasn't moving.

Oh gods . . .

I staggered to my feet and rushed toward him, ignoring the weakness in my limbs. "No. No. No."

Dropping down beside him, I grabbed his shoulders and rolled him onto his back. "Seth," I whispered, shaking him. "Seth, come on."

His eyes were shut. Golden lashes fanned cheeks that didn't move. There was a wrenching feeling deep inside me, a splintering and tearing in my chest that felt so very real.

He *wasn't* moving.

I grasped his cheeks. The marks of the Apollyon—the beautiful blue marks flared under my fingers. No. No. No. I tried our bond to reach him. *Seth?* But there was no answer, nothing but a low hum. Panicked, I shook him again, and when he didn't respond, a broken sob racked its way through my body as I dropped my head onto his chest.

Grief tore through me—the kind I hadn't known would be possible to feel again, because I had felt this when I'd held Caleb as he died. No matter what Seth had done, the terrible things he'd started, he'd made it right in the end. And even if he hadn't, if it had been my hand in the end that brought him down, the pain would've still been there. Seth was a part of me—my other half. And I was losing that part. Forever.

I can't breathe.

"Neither can I. You're squashing me."

Jerking back, I let out a startled shriek. Seth stared back at me, his amber eyes slightly unfocused, but he was breathing. He was alive.

I smacked him. Hard.

"Ow!" Seth rolled onto his side, out of my grasp. "What the hell was that for?"

"Don't ever do that again, you jerk!" I smacked him again, hitting him on the hip. "I thought you were dead!"

Seth chuckled hoarsely as he rose onto his knees. "I was knocked out, Angel. Please don't do that again."

I stared at him, caught between wanting to hit him and hug him. "I hate you."

"I'm going to have to call bullshit on that." Lifting his chin, he squinted as he looked around. "You did it, didn't you? Ares is gone."

Sitting back, I followed his gaze. Pillars cracked. Walls destroyed. I nodded slowly. "*We* did it."

Our gazes locked, and a silly grin appeared on Seth's face as he extended his hand. I took it, and we stood together.

Then I remembered a very important, currently MIA Titan. Dropping Seth's hand, I turned around and scanned the room. Nothing. And Perses was kind of hard to miss, which meant he was gone. The gods weren't going to be happy about that.

"Crap," I muttered. "He bounced."

"There's nothing we can do about that now." Seth pressed a hand against his ribs. A grimace shot across his face. "He's their problem."

Not true. "He's our—"

The air thickened around us, filling with static.

"It's not going to be their first problem," I said, letting out a ragged breath as my heart jumped in my chest.

In front of the massive hole in the wall, shimmery forms appeared like rays of sunshine, one after another after another. I counted the glowing figures once, then twice. "Oh, crap."

Seth wrapped an arm around my waist. "I'm going to admit this. My eyes are kind of blurry, but there are eleven shiny things surrounding us, right?"

I practically plastered myself to him, nodding. There were eleven *shiny things* forming a wide circle around us. The Olympian Twelve—er, Eleven. Would've been twelve if Ares hadn't been obliterated. My breath caught.

Two floated forward, becoming more solid. Lifting my arm, I

shielded my eyes. Their light was so bright, so beautiful. For a moment, all I could do was be awe-struck by what I was seeing.

"You should have waited before you hit me. I think you broke me," whispered Seth.

"Uh, you'll be okay," I said, and Seth's muscles tensed around me.

"So, you think they're here to congratulate us?"

I lowered my arm, watching as the lights took on human forms. A male and female stood before us, their features not so distinguishable yet, but I knew they weren't Apollo or Artemis.

"I don't think so," I whispered.

"Maybe they're mad because you've been sleeping with a pure," Seth joked, but his voice was laced with unease.

I looked over my shoulder at him. "Really? That's the reason? It couldn't be that you took out an entire Council of pures?"

A wry smile formed on Seth's lips. "You're splitting hairs, Alex."

"Gods, you're so annoying."

He stepped forward, blocking me from the two closest gods. Rolling my eyes, I moved so that we were shoulder to shoulder.

Seth looked down at me. "If I tell you to run, you run."

"No." I grabbed his hand and held on. I didn't have the heart to tell him that they weren't here for him. "We face this together."

The shimmery light faded, revealing the gods around us, but I didn't see past the one in front of us. A million years could've gone by and I never, ever thought I would lay eyes upon *him*.

Zeus was not as I imagined.

I'd always pictured this older guy with a potbelly and bushy, gray beard, but that was not what Zeus looked like. Not in the slightest.

Dressed in some kind of white, linen pants, his chest and stomach were bare. And ripped—ripped like you could cut your fingers on those abs. The curve of his strong jaw was also bare of hair. He was sublimely handsome, his lips wide and eyes tilted exotically. His features were sharp, breathtakingly angular.

I could see a bit of a Titan in him.

The only thing my imagination had gotten right was his hair. It was shockingly white.

"You did well," he spoke, his voice as deep and commanding as Perses'. There was no anger in his tone. I knew in that moment, before Zeus even spoke again, that Apollo hadn't come through. My knees suddenly felt weak, and if I hadn't been holding Seth's hand, I would've sunk to the floor. "You will be rewarded greatly."

A shudder rocked through me, but Seth . . . he didn't understand—he didn't get what Zeus hadn't tacked on at the end. "Well, that's surprising," he murmured.

My gaze darted to the gods, finding Apollo standing next to a somber Artemis. Apollo shook his head no, and my heart sank all the way. I took a jerky step back, my skin turning icy.

"Don't," Zeus said, his voice level and calm. "This is the only way."

Seth's grip on my hand tightened. "What's the only way?"

Zeus ignored him. "You know this must be done. We cannot allow a God Killer to exist. The threat is too great, even greater than what Ares posed."

In that moment, I briefly considered trying to take out Zeus, but it had drained everything in me and Seth to kill Ares. It wouldn't work. Maybe I would lay some bruises on Zeus, but in the end, I couldn't defeat another Olympian. All I had was Apollo in my corner. He could walk away from this, refuse Zeus' bidding, because he was the only one who could kill me—besides a Titan, and our Titan had vanished.

But Apollo didn't look like he was going to disobey his father.

Oh, my gods . . .

Another shiver rocked my body as it really seeped in. This was it. I wanted to run. I wanted to fight, but as I stared back at the gods, I saw that it would all be so very pointless. If I fought, Seth would get hurt in the process. Badly. And who's to say that Zeus wouldn't turn to finding Aiden and my father to make this easier? I couldn't risk them. I couldn't risk anyone else like I'd done with Caleb, Lea, Olivia, and so many more.

It . . . it was now my turn.

Seth's head snapped back as if he'd been slapped. "No. You can't do this. We helped you! She did everything you wanted her to do!" He dropped my hand, forming his into fists. "You can't do this to her!"

Having not seen Seth this upset in a long time, I sucked in a sharp breath. My heart was trying to come out of my chest again. "Seth . . ."

"No!" He took a step toward Zeus, but I shot forward, grabbing his arm. His wide eyes met mine. "Alex, you can't—"

"There's nothing either of you can do," Zeus said, taking a step back to stand next to Hera.

She inclined her head to the side, and several strands of russet-colored hair slipped from her elegant coif. "It is for the best of everyone."

An angry flush flooded Seth's cheeks. "Are you serious?"

"Seth!" I tugged on his arm.

"What?" he snapped, turning on me. He gripped my shoulders. "You can't be okay with this. And you're not giving up!"

Was I giving up? I glanced back at Apollo and read the sadness in his expression. "I'm not giving up, Seth, but they won't allow the God Killer to live."

Seth didn't respond immediately, but when he did, he cursed harshly and blanched. "You knew! You knew that this would happen."

I shook my head and whispered, "Could happen. I knew this *could* happen."

"Could versus would? Are you shitting me? You knew this *could* happen, and you let me allow you to put yourself in this situation?" He shook me as more blood drained from his face. "How could you, Alex?"

Blinking back tears, I shook my head again. How could I say that he couldn't have handled the power of the God Killer and not make him feel worse?

"This is sweet," Hera said, stepping back so she joined the other Olympians. "He cares for her so deeply, and yet she loves another. Tragic."

Really? My gaze slid to her, but then Apollo stepped forward, breaking ranks. Each step was slow, purposeful. A lump formed in my throat. There wasn't enough time. I realized that then. The same crack I'd thrown in Ares' face had now turned back on me.

Karma was a bitch and a half.

And so was Fate, because this was Fate, wasn't it? Either way, I wanted to see Marcus one more time and share an awkward hug with him. I wanted to see my father once more, maybe have dinner with him. I wanted to watch Deacon and Luke laugh, and see Solos' smile.

And, oh gods, I wanted to kiss Aiden, just once more.

But there was no time. This was happening. All those moments, from the second my mother had taken me out of the Covenant, had been leading up to this. She had tried to prevent this—even as a daimon, she had tried to prevent *this*.

Grandma Piperi had said I'd kill the ones I love.

She had forgotten to tell me that I would also die in the end.

Gods, she sucked at the whole foretelling thing. But Solaris had known, hadn't she? She had sounded like she'd been seeing me again soon, and she would be.

This was so not fair.

"Alexandria," Apollo said gently. "It is time."

I turned to Seth, my heart racing. "Please—"

"No!" he yelled, still fighting the inevitable. "This isn't right. They can't do this. You don't deserve this. I do. They—"

"They're not going to take you," I said, tears welling in my eyes. "Listen to me, Seth. They're not. They can't kill you. Ares is gone, and I'm the God Killer. There's nothing we can do."

The full horror of the situation dawned in Seth's expressive face, and he placed his hands on my cheeks. He pressed his forehead to mine. "Oh gods, Alex, I don't want this to happen. Alex . . ."

I gripped his arms, forcing myself to breathe. "Please take care of Aiden. I know you two don't get along, but *please*. He's going to need someone. So please watch out for him. Promise me, Seth. *Promise* me."

There was a long pause, and I thought I felt his tears mix with mine. "I promise."

Those two words, well, they helped a little, but God Killer or not, I was scared and I didn't want to be alone. "Don't let go," I whispered, closing my eyes.

"I won't," he swore, his lips brushing my cheek. "I will never let go."

I started to shake. I didn't want to be scared. Where was that strength and courage I'd felt earlier? I wanted to be the one who faced Fate with her head high, but I *was* scared. I knew there was no coming back from this. I would never see my father, my friends, or Aiden again. My breath caught again, and each time I took a breath, I feared it would be the last one. "Don't leave me. Please? I don't want to be by myself."

"You're not." Seth slipped his arms around me, holding me close. "You're not alone." His tears *were* mingled with mine. "You're not alone. You'll never be alone, Angel. I promise you. You'll never—"

I took a breath and never heard his next words. There was a harsh expletive from Seth, and then the world ended for me on the heels of a burst of beautiful bright sunlight.

26

Dying the second time was nothing like the first time. When I opened my eyes, I knew I was in the Underworld, and I knew I was dead. Not like when I was stabbed by Linard. Nope. I was as dead as everyone else around me.

I also didn't end up on the banks of Styx waiting for Charon with all the other dead folks; there would've been a lot of them there after all the fighting.

My death was just all kinds of special.

When I opened my eyes, I was standing in the middle of Hades' palace. There had been no pain, no feeling of suffocation—a blink of an eye and my life was over and I was staring at the translucent, shimmery dress of Persephone.

The first things I saw upon dying were Persephone's breasts and nipples. Or at least one nipple, but there was definitely *a* nipple.

Something seemed wrong about that being the first thing I saw in the afterlife.

I was too dumbstruck by the whole dying thing to do or say much of anything. Hades was already back, and when Persephone dropped her arm over my shoulders, I was too out of it to be freaked out about her being so close to me.

"Where's Apollo?" I asked, because I wanted to see him, needed to see him.

The arrogance that was typically present on Hades' face was gone as he shook his head. "He will come when he can."

I didn't like that answer. Apollo should be here, not Hades.

Apollo had promised to take care of me, but I had ended up dead in Hades' palace, staring at Persephone's nipples. This was not what I'd expected when he'd sworn to make sure I was okay.

Hades strolled up to me and clasped my cheeks. I flinched out of habit. "You did an amazing thing today. We will forever be in your debt."

I jumped on that. "Then bring me back to life."

He shook his head and smiled sadly. "I cannot grant such things."

So I jumped on it again. "Then release Aiden from his promise."

And he shook his head once more. "I cannot grant that either, Love."

"You can't do anything?" I demanded. "You're a god and you're—"

"It all is done, Alexandria. It is over." Looking at his wife, he nodded. "Take her to her final resting place."

Her final resting place?

I shuddered.

Yep, that sounded just as disturbing as one would think.

Persephone ushered me out the back of the palace, and at first I was absolutely stunned by what I saw. It wasn't like any part of the Underworld I'd seen before.

"It's beautiful, isn't it?" Persephone asked. "This is the beginning of Elysian Fields, and it goes as far as the eyes can see. Like Tartarus, it is ever-changing, fitting to each person's version of paradise."

Elysian Fields was . . . it was striking, and it looked so real, so normal, that my heart ached at the sight. The sky was beautiful—cloudless blue and bright. The air was warm, and the light scent of jasmine reminded me of . . .

I didn't let myself finish that thought.

"Your paradise will be what you decide, Alexandria, and you can share it with others," Persephone explained as I stared over the lush rolling hills and, beyond, the rooftops of many homes. In the valley below, the tips of exotic-looking trees swayed, playing peekaboo with crystal clear waters below them. "It will be your choice."

My choice?

My choice had been not to die.

Persephone took my hand, and the ground seemed to swallow us up. A second later, we were standing in an empty field cluttered with white and yellow daisies.

"This will be your paradise," she said, and vanished.

And that was . . . that. She'd left me in an empty field.

I stood there for an ungodly amount of time, until the sky overhead started to darken and tiny, brilliant stars appeared to blanket the deep blue of night. I learned a couple of things about being dead during that time.

My lungs worked like they had when I was alive, because I kept feeling the air catch in my throat. I could still cry, because quiet tears tracked my cheeks. I'd always thought the sobbing, body-shaking tears were the worst, but I was wrong. Quiet tears fell in a way that scarred my soul and seemed to never end.

I'd also learned that, in death, I could still feel lonely.

But finally, after what already felt like an eternity, I found my paradise. I closed my eyes, willing the tears to stop, and for some reason, I thought about Deity Island, of the rolling waves and the clean, warm sand. In my head, I heard the seagulls and felt the wet spray of the ocean against my cheeks. And I thought of the small but perfect cottage that had sat at the edge of the marsh.

Opening my eyes, I let out a little yelp of surprise.

I was back in North Carolina. I had to be, because the ocean rolled calmly before me, its waves a deep, dark blue in the night, and sand was under my feet. I could smell the marsh and feel the dampness on my cheeks. I spun around and cried out when I saw the cottage—a light was on in the window, glowing a soft yellow. I took off, slipping over the sand at breakneck speed. The door was unlocked, and the wood was warm and real, so *real*, in my hand. I threw the door open and realized that, even dead, my heart beat in my chest like I'd downed a gallon of energy drinks.

Upon seeing the living room, I pressed a hand to my chest. It was exactly how I remembered: a small, efficient kitchen to the right, a large couch and TV, and very minimal design. In a daze, I walked back the short, narrow hall, passing a bathroom and then entering into the spacious bedroom.

The bed was *his*—the black sheets, the pillows, and the scent of the sea and something earthy, of burning leaves and man.

But *he* wasn't here.

Because *he* was alive and I, well, I was dead.

I spent hours in that bedroom, soaking up his scent, before I pulled myself away. I opened the back door at the end of the hall and saw the garden—an exact replica of the one on Deity Island, the very one where I had met Grandma Piperi.

Ripe blossoms and rich soils, trees I couldn't begin to even name, and enough flowers to start a botanical garden. There was even an old stone bench.

I turned back around, staring at the cottage.

Once I'd found my paradise and the sun came back up the following day, the others around me had become visible— houses and apartment buildings of all different sizes, farms, and sprawling cities. And sunny palm trees and snow-capped mountaintops. It was a smorgasbord of every place in the world.

But that wasn't all.

Paradise was simplistic, centering around needs but not wants. Over the course of time that seemed longer than normal days and nights, I learned how paradise operated.

What you needed, you got. It was as simple as that.

If I needed to be hungry, I would be hungry. And if I needed a juicy steak, it would simply appear after closing my eyes. If I didn't need to eat, there were no stomach pains. If I needed to wear jeans or a dress, all I had to do was open the closet, and there they would be.

There was more.

Apparently when you died and you were scarred up like I was, you got an afterlife makeover.

My hair was long again; it was the length it had been before Ares had given me the beauty-school-dropout haircut. Reaching the middle of my back, the ends were neat, and the strands were shiny and soft. At first, I'd been obsessed with my hair—touching it to make sure it was still there, picking it up and waving it across my face.

When you're dead, it's not like you have much else to do.

Up until that very moment, I was still surprised by what I saw. Leaning in until my eyes almost crossed, I studied my reflection in the mirror. The fine network of faint pink scars was gone. They were also gone from my body. I'd been restored, but the afterlife makeover had gone further than that. The daimon tags I'd received when I was in Gatlinburg, those patches of pale white skin on my neck and arms, were healed completely. And if I pulled up my tank top, the jagged scar left behind from Linard's blade and the first time I'd died was gone too.

Underworld was like a scar-be-gone.

I rocked back on my heels of my bare feet, sighing.

Strangely, what took the most for me to get used to were my eyes. They were different. The irises were brown, like they had been before I'd Awakened, but there was a thin line of amber around the pupils. I didn't know what that meant or why they were like that.

He . . . he would've been so happy to see my eyes brown again.

The inside of my throat thickened immediately, and I squeezed my eyes shut. *I will not cry. I will not cry.* Crying was bad in the Underworld, I'd discovered. Once you started, it was hard to stop and could become a one-way ticket to the Vale of Mourning. And that didn't sound like fun.

Tears pricked at my eyes nonetheless.

I knew I shouldn't cry, but it was hard because I missed my uncle and my dad. I missed Luke, Deacon, and Solos. I missed Seth and how easy it was for him to infuriate me. But I yearned for Aiden something fierce. With each passing second, it only got stronger, more intense. It didn't fade, my longing for him, and I didn't think it ever would.

"Alex?"

Looking away from the mirror, I turned to the boy lying on my bed. His shoulder-length blond hair was pulled back into a ponytail, but shorter strands had escaped, falling across his tanned cheeks.

Every day since the first day after I'd died, Caleb had been here for me. I'd spent time with my mom, with Olivia, and even with Lea, but I'd seen Caleb the most. I felt bad for sucking up so much of his time, because I was sure he and Olivia were trying to discover if you could make a baby in the Underworld every free moment they had, but I don't know what I would do without him.

"Come here," he said, patting the spot next to him.

I shuffled over and sat beside him. "Olivia's going to cut me if you keep hanging out in my bed."

Caleb laughed, and each time he did, I had to smile. I'd missed that laugh as much as I now missed life. "She's not going to cut you."

"I'm sucking up all your time."

"No, you're not." He reached over, tugging on the hem of my jeans. "And she understands. Dying isn't easy, Alex. Not for anyone, and definitely not for you."

I arched a brow.

Caleb tugged on the hem again. "Why don't you come with me tonight? Me. You. Olivia. There's this club I found a few weeks ago, near the palms. I think it belongs to some pure whose idea of a 'happily ever after' is a nonstop party."

Elysian Fields was as close to living as you could get, and there were a lot of things to do, people to meet, and whatnot. Lea had already hooked up with some half-blood *and* one of Hades' guards.

I shrugged a shoulder.

"I think it would be good for you, Alex. I mean it."

"I know." And I also knew where this conversation was heading.

Caleb didn't disappoint. "You need to get out and be happy. I know it's hard, but I'm worried about you. I'm scared. You could end up in the Vale, and there's no coming back from that."

"I don't want you to be scared," I said, staring at my finger-nails. They'd never been this smooth and buffed in life. "But Apollo lied to me. He said he would take care of me."

Caleb didn't say anything because this wasn't the first time I'd said it to him. I'd been saying it every day.

"And where has he been?" I asked, lifting my gaze. Sympathy crossed Caleb's boyishly handsome face. "Not once has he visited me. I feel like he used me, which was stupid, because he's a god and that's all they do, but I . . ." I trailed off, shaking my head. "I'm sorry. It's the Alex twenty-four hour whine channel."

"It's okay. Don't apologize." He patted the spot again. "Lie down with me?"

Stretching out beside him, I stared at the ceiling. "This reminds me of our . . ."

"Last time together topside?" he supplied, and then laughed when I cringed. "At least you don't smell this time around."

I laughed as I shot him a glare. "You jerk. I didn't smell then."

"Hell you didn't. You hadn't showered in days." He rolled onto his side, grinning. His blue eyes literally glimmered. "You were stinky."

"That's so wrong."

"Love you," he replied.

My smile spread, and honestly, if I could spend eternity with Caleb, I might be okay. I might not go into the Vale, but that wasn't fair to put that on him. He had made a life for himself . . . in the afterlife, but I snuggled closer to Caleb, into his open arms, and closed my eyes.

"It'll get easier," he promised, resting his forehead against mine. "It does."

I wanted to believe him, but I wanted Aiden and I wanted life, and paradise simply could not provide those two things.

27

I wasn't big on the Covenant garden when I was alive, but I kept finding myself in this one now. There was something calming and peaceful among the roses and peonies. I kept coming back to the old stone bench, especially in the mornings. Maybe I thought Grandma Piperi would magically appear and give me another messed-up prophecy for old time's sake. That would be fun.

Or not.

Making my way down the marble pathway, my gaze skipped over the intricate designs in the sidewalk. Somehow I hadn't noticed this before, but the carvings were the marks of the Apollyon. Interesting.

I rounded the thick nightshade bush and lifted my gaze. I drew up short, my eyes widening.

The bench wasn't empty today.

Apollo sat there, hands clasped between his knees. "It's about time," he said. "I've been waiting for about an hour."

I stared at him, my mouth hanging open. "I . . . I slept in."

He cocked his head to the side. "I hear you've been sleeping a lot."

I snapped out of it. "Where have you been?"

"I've been busy." He stood, towering over me. "I came as soon as I could."

"As soon as you could?" I repeated dumbly. "It's been more than a week!"

Apollo folded his massive arms. "Time moves differently

here, Alexandria. An hour or two here is a second in the mortal realm. It hasn't been that long."

"Since I died?" I crossed my arms, mimicking his stance. "I thought you were supposed to take care of me."

"I did."

My eyes narrowed. "I'm dead. I'm not quite sure how that's taking care of me."

Apollo unfolded his arms and strolled up to me. "You need to get over that tiny fact." Then he patted me on the head. Actually patted me on the freaking head. "Come on. We have something we need to do."

I turned, half-tempted to spin-kick him in the head, and while I was sure I could break out some of the moves, I didn't have any leftover, supercool Apollyon powers. Spin-kicking him probably wouldn't end well.

Apollo glanced over his shoulder, exasperated. "Are you coming? Time is ticking."

"Oh, I think I have, like, an eternity worth of time." I wanted to stay where I was, because I was feeling pretty damn childish, but I groaned and then followed him. "Where are we going?"

"You'll see."

I made a face at him as I struggled to keep up with his long-legged gait. Pissed as I was at him, I remained sullenly quiet as we walked. We made it to the edge of the garden before I couldn't hold back my questions.

"How is everyone?"

He looked at me sideways. "How do you think?"

My palms tingled, and anger heated my cheeks. "A part of me knew that this would be the outcome, but I hoped it would be different. I hoped because of what *you* said and what I was being asked to do. You let me down, Apollo. So the least you could do is give me a straight answer."

His blue eyes deepened, turning the color of the sky before a storm. I knew I'd struck a chord, but I didn't care. What could he do? Kill me? A quiet voice whispered in the back of my head that he could drop my unhappy ass in Tartarus, but I doubted he'd ever do that, no matter how much I ticked him off.

Apollo sighed. "They're not happy. Your uncle holed himself up in a room and drank himself into a stupor. Your friends? Inconsolable. I think you know how Seth feels. Maybe you don't—not to the full extent, anyway. And Aiden?" He paused, and the back of my eyes burned. "I have never seen a man break the way he did. And he broke. Set half the damn Covenant on fire. If his brother hadn't showed up when he had, I'm *positive* that he would've stayed in the burning building. Is that what you wanted to know? Did it make you feel better, Alexandria?"

"No," I whispered, my chest aching as if someone had split me wide open. Tears welled up and spilled down my cheeks. I wiped at them hastily. "That didn't make me feel better at all."

"I didn't think it would, but you insisted." He headed around the front of the cottage—the cottage I wasn't sure I could even look at now. "People loved you—still love you. Mourning is never easy. But they will heal, and they will continue to live."

And I wanted that—I wanted them to move on. Even as badly as I wanted to see them again, I didn't want them here. They deserved to live.

"The Elixir is no more," Apollo said. "I thought you'd like to know that."

I looked up at Apollo as we crossed the beach, the sand warm under my bare feet. Since I'd died, I'd boycotted shoes. "Thank you."

"Some of the servants will have lasting effects from being on the Elixir for so long, but many are functioning well. Many are presented with options they've never had before." He stopped, several feet from the edge of the lapping waves. "After Ares' defeat, an emergency Council meeting was called. Solos was given a spot on the Council."

My mouth dropped open. "Are you serious? A half-blood on the Council? Oh my gods, that's . . . wow, that's awesome. How did it happen?"

A small grin appeared on his lips. "Only a few days have passed, but a lot has happened. Aiden took his spot on the Council as well."

I sucked in a shallow breath as pride swelled through me. "He did? His parents . . ."

"He did. With his vote, among others, they officially revoked the Breed Order and gave those rights I promised you back to the halfs."

Oh, my gods galore, I felt like I needed to sit down. This was major.

"He also gave up his seat afterward. He gave his seat to Solos."

My eyes widened. "He did what? I mean, that's great about Solos, but why would he do that?" Then fear poured into my chest like ice. "Oh gods, he's going to be okay, right? He's not going to do anything stupid—"

"He's not going to do anything stupid. He will be okay," Apollo responded. "Change is coming for our society, Alexandria. It will take some time, but it will happen. Just like you will come to accept your new path."

Thrown off by that last statement, I took a step back, away from Apollo. "My new path?"

"Yes, it's time that you start to move on."

I gaped at him. "I just died!"

"And apparently enough time has passed for you to get ticked off about me not coming to visit you immediately." Apollo smiled widely at my death glare. "Remember what you did with Caleb to honor your mother and those who died last summer?"

"What?" The change of subject left me spinning.

"You used spirit boats as a way of moving on, didn't you?"

I frowned. "Were you peeping on me then, Apollo?"

He ignored that. "I think you need to do the same thing for yourself."

"What the what?" I stared at him, stunned into stupidity. "You want me to set a spirit boat into the ocean that's meant for me?"

Apollo nodded once more. "I think it's the perfect idea. It will be symbolic and hopefully a new start for yourself."

Several seconds passed while I waited for him to yell "just kidding" and slap me on the shoulder, but he didn't. "You're serious."

"Do I look like I'm joking?"

Actually, he looked like he wanted to hit me. "But that is so . . . weird."

"It is not weird." His gaze dropped over me. "But you should be dressed nicer than this, like you were when you did it before."

My mouth opened, but before I could utter a word, Apollo snapped his fingers, and my clothes changed. They changed while on my body. Jeans and tank top, my choice of afterlife attire, turned into the black tube dress I'd worn the day Caleb and I had set the little spirit boats free.

Smoothing my hands over the soft material, I lifted my gaze. "That's . . . that's creepy, because there had to be a split second when I was naked, so don't do that again."

He shrugged and then held out his once-empty palm. Not so empty now. A spirit boat rested in his hand, candle and all.

I hesitated. "You're really going to make me do this."

"Yes."

Fighting the urge to roll my eyes, I recognized that Apollo wasn't going to be swayed on this matter. And it was strange. Ever since Apollo had killed me, I'd imagined letting loose on him hundreds of times, but now that he was here, holding a damn spirit boat in hands, I didn't have it in me.

Maybe because I had agreed to become the God Killer, knowing how it would probably end.

Shaking my head, I took it from Apollo. The moment my fingers wrapped around it, a tiny flame encased the wick of the white candle. I held the fragile spirit boat in my hands. "You know this is twisted and morbid, right?"

"You need to let go of your old life, Alexandria."

"My only life," I muttered.

Apollo didn't respond to that.

Exhaling harshly, I turned toward the ocean. Sun glinted off the waves, and I knew the water would be warm and foamy, because that was how I liked it. But walking out to those waves with a spirit boat meant for myself wasn't as easy as anyone would think.

I stood there for several moments, so many thoughts racing through my head as a soft breeze rolled off the ocean and stirred my hair. Could I really do this without laughing or crying? Because I wasn't sure if it was funny or just really sad. And was I ready for this? Contrary to Apollo's annoying opinion, I did just die. Was I ready to move on? Did I want to?

That was a tough question.

The pain, the longing, and the yearning had become familiar to me. Letting go seemed like I was giving up, but that wasn't right. Even in my darkest moments, I knew that wasn't true. The truth was, I didn't want to be like this forever. I didn't want to be like this for another week. And I sure as hell didn't want to end up in the Vale.

I wasn't sure that a spirit boat would be the answer, but it wouldn't hurt to try. And who cared if I felt a little stupid for doing it? I was dead. Not like anyone was going to judge me here.

Taking a deep breath, I forced my legs forward. The sand gave way under my feet, and water tickled my toes. I kept going until the water foamed just below my knees. I stopped, staring down at my boat. I'd done this before. Hadn't I said that Mom was in a better place? She was—I saw her yesterday. We pulled weeds in the garden together. So wasn't I in a better place now? No more looming threats of death or dismemberment. No more messed-up Fate or duty. No more loss.

There was just the loss I'd already suffered.

But maybe that too would fade one day. And I'd see my friends and family again. I knew that. And maybe when it was time for Aiden, Hades would take pity on us. After all, the rotten S.O.B. owed us. He most definitely owed me.

Letting out a sigh, I bent down and placed the spirit boat in the ocean. My fingers lingered for a second, and I said the only thing I could think of saying. "Goodbye."

And so I let the boat go.

Straightening, I watched the waves carry it off, further and further out until I couldn't see the boat anymore. I wasn't sure I felt any better, but I thought it was a step in the right direction. It was something, which according to my own personal motto was better than nothing.

I turned around, about to yell back at Apollo and ask him if he was happy now, but as my gaze flickered over the god, something else caught my attention.

My heart stopped.

Dead or not, it *was* possible.

Air froze in my lungs. I couldn't blink, because I was *terrified* that if I did, what I was seeing would vanish, because it couldn't be real.

He couldn't be real.

Aiden stood at the shoreline, the water curling around his ankles, dampening the hems of the jeans he wore. The breeze caught the edges of his white shirt, lifting them slightly, and played with his locks of dark, wavy hair. Rays of sun kissed his broad cheeks, and from that distance, I could see that his eyes were a breathtaking, fierce silver. He was smiling.

He was smiling at *me*.

"Hey," he said, and oh my gods, it was his voice. A voice I'd thought I wouldn't hear again for a very long time—or maybe never again.

I placed my hand against my chest as my throat worked. "Is this . . . is this real?"

His smile spread, revealing those deep dimples in his cheeks. "This is real, *agapi mou*."

I couldn't move.

"Alex," he called, laughing softly.

"How are you here? Oh my gods . . ." My gaze darted to Apollo. "Is he dead? You said he would be okay! That he wouldn't do anything—"

"I'm not dead," Aiden interrupted, stepping forward. Waves lapped up his calves. "Come out of the water and we'll explain. Come on, *agapi mou*."

I was held immobile for another second or two, and then it seemed to sink in. *Aiden* was here. A cry parted my lips as I sprang into action. Holding my hair back from my face, I half-stumbled and half-ran toward the beach. He came forward, meeting me halfway.

Throwing myself at him, I nearly knocked him down, but he regained his footing, wrapping his arms around my waist as he pulled me against his chest. The feel of him, warm and real, against my chest was wonderful and sent a thrill through me. His scent, the mixture of sea and soap, filled me.

It also ripped me right open.

Tears fell from my eyes as I burrowed against his chest, squeezing him so tightly I was surprised I wasn't hurting him. Though he held me the same way, whispering in my ear words I couldn't understand above my sobs. And I was speaking, but the words didn't make much sense.

But finally, his hand slid up to my cheek, leaving a trail of fire in its wake, and he made this deep sound in his chest a second before his lips brushed across mine. Another cry came from the depths of my soul, and the kiss deepened. The kiss reached into me, wrapped its way around my heart, and jump-started it in a way that it never had when I was alive. And I kissed him back, tasting the salt of my tears and of the sea on his lips.

Apollo cleared his throat.

Slowly, as if we had all the time in the world and didn't have an audience, Aiden slowed the kiss down at his own pace, nipping at my lower lip as he lifted my head. I was breathless as I opened my eyes.

He kissed my forehead and then eased me down onto my feet. Keeping an arm around my waist and tucking me close to his body, he turned us toward Apollo and we waded back to the sand.

The god was smiling. Not the creepy smile that he usually graced the world with, but a real one.

"How?" I asked, clutching the front of Aiden's shirt as if I planned to hold him there. "How is this possible? Is he visiting me? Is he—?"

Aiden chuckled as he smoothed his free hand under my chin. "I'm not visiting."

My heart almost imploded at that, but I didn't understand.

Apollo took pity on me. "Remember when I told you that I would take care of you? It was a promise I wasn't going to break, but this—this is not all me."

"It's not?" I still held onto Aiden's shirt.

"I knew that this could be the outcome long before you agreed to it," he explained. "A lot of things in life aren't fair, and there are lessons to be learned from that, but there was no lesson to be gained in your death. So when I took you to Olympus after your first fight with Ares, I made sure that, no matter what happened, you would be rewarded."

"By giving me Aiden?" I asked, and well, while I really appreciated that, it didn't seem fair to Aiden. Elysian Fields was nice and all, but it *was* the Underworld.

"No," Apollo said. "I gave your mother a drink to give you. Remember? I told her it would help you heal?"

I remembered that. "It tasted good, but . . . strange."

That smile was back, tipping his lips up at the corner. "It wasn't a normal drink. It was ambrosia."

My lips slowly parted as I stared at him. Ambrosia? The nectar of the gods? Those who were gifted with ambrosia became immortal. "I don't understand. I'm dead. That couldn't—"

"You had a mortal death, Alexandria, but you are not truly dead, not like those around you. By setting the spirit boat free, you set the next stage of your existence into play. You are immortal. To get technical, you are now a demigod."

My jaw was on the sand. There were no words. None at all.

"But for every gift, there has to be an exchange," Apollo continued. "You did have a mortal death, and my brethren were not aware of what I'd done. They say it will upset the strands of Fate if there is not an exchange. Follow me?"

Uh, *no*, but I nodded.

"You will have to spend six months in the Underworld—six months Underworld time—and then you will be allowed to spend six months—six months mortal time—in the mortal realm."

"Like Persephone?" I shook my head when he nodded. "Holy gods, I don't know what to say. Thank you and—wait!" My heart jumped as I looked up at Aiden. "If I'm immortal, then what about Aiden? He can't stay in the Underworld for six months. I don't understand." Not that I was ungrateful. If I could see him and my dad and friends just for six months topside, I'd take that, but I was thoroughly confused. Aiden had said he wasn't visiting, and I knew I was missing something. "Someone help me out here."

"That's the other half," Aiden said, dropping his chin and kissing the top of my head.

"And that had nothing to do with me," Apollo said. "I would've made sure that Aiden could visit you when he could and for however long he could be here, but this ... this is all because of Seth."

I blinked. "Seth?"

"If you're surprised, just imagine how I felt." Aiden's arm tightened. "Seth made a deal with Apollo and Hades before I even knew what was going down."

"What deal?" I looked at Apollo. "What deal did Seth make?"

"First, you must understand that Seth never should've been, Alexandria. You were always meant to be the Apollyon, and Seth knew that. To him, for you to be the one who died, he couldn't live with that," Apollo explained, and my skin chilled. "When he came to me, I told him that you would be fine. I told him that you'd been given ambrosia, and I explained the exchange to him. I even told him that you would see Aiden again, and that in the end, you were being taken care of and you would be happy, but that wasn't enough for him.

"He knew that, when Aiden died, his soul would go to Hades, and who knows what mood Hades would be in when that day came. And in the end, you would out-live Aiden. You would have to watch him grow old and die while you stayed the same during those years he aged. Seth didn't want that for you."

Aiden's hand smoothed over my hip as he spoke next. "Seth offered an exchange. He offered his servitude to the gods, which is needed, since no one can find Perses and none of the Olympians can kill Seth."

"We need him on our side, so we were willing to deal," Apollo confirmed. "He offered his servitude and obedience in exchange for ambrosia for Aiden. And then he offered to Hades to take Aiden's place once he died. And as you would guess, Hades was over the moon with the prospect. We accepted."

My eyes widened. I didn't know what to say. Seth ... oh my gods, that little punk ... that wonderful little punk. "He gave up his life to the gods, basically? You'll be able to call on him whenever." And knowing Seth, that would drive him absolutely crazy. "And when he dies?" I shook my head, beyond words.

What Seth had done was unbelievable. He'd sacrificed so much. My heart was pumping fast. I wanted to cry again. I probably would. And I wanted to laugh, and I wanted to find Seth and shake him because he hadn't needed to do this. He shouldn't have. My future with Aiden wasn't more important than his future, no matter how badly I wanted that.

I was blown away.

"Seth didn't want you to know he did this, and while I have honored most of his requests, I felt you needed to know what he has done for you. He gave you this, Alexandria. He gave Aiden this. And I know it is hard for you to accept. And it was hard for Aiden to fully accept, surprisingly," Apollo added dryly. "But it was Seth's decision, and it cannot be undone. And when you go topside in six months, you should find him and thank him."

I was actually going to hug and squeeze and love the dude. Then smack him. And then hug and squeeze and love him again.

"We are not sure what it does with your connection. You are no longer the God Killer, as you did die a mortal death, but this has never been done before." Apollo shrugged. "You may still be connected once you're in the mortal realm. You may not be. We don't know."

There was so much I wanted to say. My head was spinning. I hadn't expected any of this, especially not what Seth had done. He had given us everything. I couldn't imagine how I could repay him, but I would find a way one day.

Apollo's smile was soft then, the most human thing I'd ever seen from the god. "His journey is not over, Alexandria. And neither is yours. Or Aiden's. Remember that."

Choked up in a ridiculous way, I nodded and then, without any warning, Apollo faded out. I stared at the spot where he'd stood for a long moment, then turned into Aiden's embrace.

One side of his lips curved up, and a dimple appeared in one cheek. "We owe Seth a lot."

"Everything," I agreed, my fingers still digging into the front of his shirt. "We owe him everything."

Aiden lowered his head, brushing his lips over mine. My mouth immediately opened to his. I sank into him, ready—

"Oh. I almost forgot."

I jumped a good four inches off the ground at the sound of Apollo's voice, which was right in *my* ear. "Oh, my gods, will you ever stop doing that?"

"No. Make sure you give Hades some hell while you're down here." He winked, and then he disappeared again.

Aiden looked from where Apollo had been, then to me, and then laughed. "Do they have bells in Elysian Fields?"

A laugh bubbled up in my throat. "Yeah, I'm sure they do. You kind of need something, and it appears. Like, if you want to eat some coconut shrimp, you get coconut shrimp."

"Really?" He laughed again, looping his arm around my waist. "What about Big Macs?"

"Yep. Even Big Macs."

"Wow. This must really be paradise for you then."

The knot of emotion was back in my throat again. "It . . . really isn't. I've missed you terribly. I . . ." I stopped myself.

He pressed his lips together as he smoothed his thumb along his jaw. Then he glanced over his shoulder. "Is that what I think it is?"

I bit down on my lip, hoping this didn't make me come across like a total creeper. "It made me happy, and it felt . . . it felt like you, so it turned out to be a part of my paradise."

Aiden's hand slipped down my arm, and he threaded his fingers through mine. When he spoke, his voice was rough with emotion. "Show me?"

I led him into the cottage, and as he looked around, seeing the familiar living room and kitchen, his hand tightened around mine. I felt my cheeks flush. "It has a bedroom and a bath, like yours, but there's a garden in the back. I know it's not—"

"It's perfect. You're perfect." His silvery gaze landed on me. "I'm sorry I couldn't get here sooner. I know—"

"Don't," I said, placing my fingers over his lips. "You have nothing to apologize for. Apollo told me about the Council and the Breed Order. What you were a part of was amazing. Solos on the Council, and how the Breed Order was revoked, and—"

Aiden swooped down, silencing me with a lingering kiss that left me breathless when he lifted his head. "Nothing that I did was truly amazing, Alex. It was just what needed to be done. I only wish it hadn't taken so long from your perspective."

He told me then that Seth had made his deals before the Council meeting, within hours of my death, but that he had taken care of the Council seat and spoken with his brother before he'd left with Apollo.

"Deacon," I gasped. "Oh gods, you won't see him for six months. And it will be even longer for him with the time-moves-differently thing."

"It's okay."

I shook my head. "But he's your family, and I know he means the world to you."

"He does mean the world to me, and I'm going to miss him, but he'd try to kick my ass if I didn't come to you." Aiden grinned. "He knows how I feel about you. He saw how I was . . . afterwards. He understands, and he's happy. Besides, we'll see him again."

Then it struck me. Excited, I almost started bouncing. "Oh, Aiden! You'll get to see your parents. I haven't seen them, but they're here. Somewhere."

"I know, but as terrible as this sounds—and gods, it probably is—right now, I don't care." Using my hand, he turned me around and hauled me against his chest. "That's not what I want right now, *or* what I need."

Grandma Piperi's prophetic words came back to me. There is want and there is need . . . To her, those two things had been very differently entities, but right now, they were one and the same.

He placed the tips of his fingers on my cheeks, the hold heartbreakingly tender as his gaze moved on my face. "Look at you," he said. "Your eyes . . ."

I stood still, letting his fingers trail an unseen path across my face. "I look a lot better half-dead or whatever, huh?"

"You've always looked beautiful to me, Alex." He trailed his fingers over the line of my jaw and down my neck. His hands trembled as he slid them down my shoulders. "Gods, Alex, I'd thought after what happened with Linard, I'd never face losing you again. Even when you were connected with Seth, you were still alive. And even if you didn't want to be with me, you were living, and in the end, that was all that mattered."

Aiden took a deep breath. "But when I came into that room and saw Seth and Apollo, but didn't see you, my heart stopped. It broke me," he admitted with quiet honesty. "Because all I wanted was a future with you, and it had been taken from me again."

I closed my eyes against the rush of tears.

"But here we are," he murmured.

"Here we are." I blinked open my eyes, my chest swelling with the emotion I read in his gaze. We'd been given that future because of Apollo and Seth. And there was no way I was going to dishonor that gift by not living every second of that future. "I love you."

"*Agapi mou*, you are my everything."

Aiden kissed me. Words weren't necessary at that point. He'd experienced every moment of loss that I had, every second of desperation, and it was reflected in every touch, every sweep of the lips, and every soft moan. We were greedy with one another, finding ourselves in the bedroom. In no time, our limbs were tangled together, and when our bodies joined, everything slowed down. Our want for one another was all-consuming, but for the first time since we'd locked eyes in Georgia, we had all the time in the world to enjoy our love. And we did.

Long after our breathing returned to normal, Aiden hovered above me, his hand slowing tracing the line of my jaw. I smiled as something occurred to me. "We're demigods now." I laughed as a wealth of emotion built in my chest. "We're actually *demigods*."

His lips responded, curving upward and spreading until deep dimples appeared, and my heart melted in the way only he could make it. "Yeah, we are," he said.

"You know what that means?" I stared into those silver eyes. I had an infinite number of moments like this ahead of me to share with Aiden.

"They're going to tell stories about us."

Aiden lowered his head, kissing me softly, deeply, and so lovingly that tears pricked my eyes. "They already are."

ACKNOWLEDGEMENTS

Acknowledgements are never easy to write. There's always this stress when it comes to writing them, because you fear you'll forget someone. But the acknowledgements for this book are pretty damn important to me. It's the end for Alex and there has been so many people who've been with her from day one, all the way back in late 2007 and early 2008, and helped shape her into the Alex we've all come to love . . . or hate.

The Covenant Series has had a lot of beta readers during its time that lent their insightful advice and knowledge. Chu-Won Martin was literally the first person to ever read *Half-Blood*. She holds the first reader's card and because she didn't laugh in my face after reading it, we're here where we are today. A big thank you to Lesa Rodrigues for always being eager to delve back into the Covenant world and reading early manuscripts that were nothing more than chicken scratch. Thank you to Carissa Thomas, Julie Fedderson, and Cindy Thomas for reading these books before they ever reached the hands of a reader. Thank you to the peeps over at Query Tracker for helping shape up the query letter that landed the contract back in 2010. A big thanks to Molly McAdams, who has probably read the last couple of books in the Covenant Series months and months ahead of release and always makes me feel good about the story. A huge thank you to Stacey Morgan for critiquing *Sentinel* and many other books one chapter at a time and suffering through all the changes I end up going back and making and not telling her about.

Of course, a big thank you to Kate Kaynak for taking a chance on *Half-Blood* and to the team at Spencer Hill Press for whipping it into shape, to Kevan Lyon for always being the über-amazing agent that she is, to Rebecca Mancini for introducing the Covenant Series into the foreign markets, and to Brandy Rivers for well, being awesome in general.

Now here comes the hard part, because there will inevitably be people I forget to mention, but I do want to name all those that I can remember off the top of my head. These are the readers and the bloggers who've done AMAZING things for the Covenant Series and were there since the very beginning. Thank you to Vee (and yes, I'm going to spell your name the way I say it. Or Vi. Or Vivian.), Valerie from Stuck in Books, Momo from Books Over Boys, the entire crews over at Books Complete Me, Mundie Moms, Good Choice Reading, all the sisters at YA Sisterhood, Kayleigh from K-Books, all the peeps who take part in the Covenant Read Along, the Greer family—especially Papa Greer—Reading Angel, Amanda from Canada, and oh goodness, my brain has not run out of names because *Ghost Adventures* is on the TV and I'm drawn in by the douche-tastic-ness of it all.

Of course, none of this would be possible without my family and friends, who put up with the fact I spend more time writing than speaking to any of them in real life.

And finally, to all the readers, I can never thank you enough. I'm so honored to have taken this journey with you. This may be it for Alex, but you know . . . stories never really, truly end.

Loved this book? Discover more fiction
by Jennifer L. Armentrout . . .

Rediscover the bestselling series.
Go back to the very beginning of . . .

Covenant

By Jennifer L. Armentrout

The Hematoi descend from the unions of gods and
mortals, and the children of two Hematoi – pure-
bloods – have godlike powers. Children of Hematoi
and mortals – well, not so much. Half-bloods only
have two options: become trained Sentinels who hunt
and kill daimons or become servants in the homes of
the pures.

Seventeen-year-old Alexandria would rather risk her
life fighting than waste it scrubbing toilets, but she
may end up slumming it anyway. There are several
rules that students at the Covenant must follow. Alex
has problems with them all, but especially rule #1:

Relationships between pures and halfs are forbidden.

In the *Covenant* series:

Half-Blood

Pure

Deity

Apollyon

Sentinel

Daimon: the prequel to *Half-Blood*

Elixir: a *Covenant* novella

Available now in eBook and paperback

Enjoyed this book?
Want more?

Head over to

CHAPteR 5

for extra author content,
exclusives, competitions – and lots
and lots of book talk!

Our motto is
'Proud to be bookish',

because, well, we are ☺

See you there...